Praise for the novels of

SUSAN WIGGS

"A lovely, moving novel with an engaging heroine… Wiggs's talent is reflected in her thoroughly believable characters as well as the way she recognizes the importance of family by blood or other ties."
—*Library Journal* on *Just Breathe* [starred review]

"Wiggs is one of our best observers of stories of the heart. Maybe that is because she knows how to capture emotion on virtually every page of every book."
—*Salem Statesman-Journal*

"Delightful and wise, Wiggs's latest shines."
—*Publishers Weekly* on *Dockside*

"The perfect beach read."
—Debbie Macomber on *Summer by the Sea*

"With the ease of a master, Wiggs introduces complicated, flesh-and-blood characters…sets in motion a refreshingly honest romance…and even finds room for a little mystery."
—*Publishers Weekly* on *The Winter Lodge*
[starred review] One of *PW*'s Best Books of 2007

"Wiggs explores many aspects of grief, from guilt to anger to regret, imbuing her book with the classic would've/could've/should've emotions, and presenting realistic and sympathetic characters…another excellent title [in] her already outstanding body of work."
—*Booklist* on *Table for Five* [starred review]

"A human and multilayered story exploring duty to both country and family."
—Nora Roberts on *The Ocean Between Us*

Also by

SUSAN WIGGS

Contemporary Romances

LAKESIDE COTTAGE
TABLE FOR FIVE
SUMMER BY THE SEA
THE OCEAN BETWEEN US
HOME BEFORE DARK
PASSING THROUGH PARADISE

Lakeshore Chronicles

FIRESIDE
SNOWFALL AT WILLOW LAKE
DOCKSIDE
THE WINTER LODGE
SUMMER AT WILLOW LAKE

Historical Romances

THE DRIFTER
THE LIGHTKEEPER

Chicago Fire Trilogy

THE FIREBRAND
THE MISTRESS
THE HOSTAGE

Calhoun Chronicles

A SUMMER AFFAIR
ENCHANTED AFTERNOON
HALFWAY TO HEAVEN
THE HORSEMASTER'S DAUGHTER
THE CHARM SCHOOL

And coming later this year...

AT THE KING'S COMMAND—August 2009
THE MAIDEN'S HAND—September 2009
AT THE QUEEN'S SUMMONS—October 2009

SUSAN WIGGS

Just Breathe

Recycling programs for this product may not exist in your area.

ISBN-13: 978-0-7783-2656-4
ISBN-10: 0-7783-2656-X

JUST BREATHE

www.MIRABooks.com

Printed in U.S.A.

In memory of Alice O'Brien Borchardt—
gifted writer, cherished friend.
You live in the hearts of those who loved you.

ACKNOWLEDGMENTS

It took a special effort to bring this book to publication. I gratefully acknowledge my fellow writers for their gifts of friendship, humor and patience in reading my early drafts: Anjali Banerjee, Kate Breslin, Carol Cassella, Lois Faye Dyer, P.J. Jough-Haan, Rose Marie Harris, Susan Plunkett, Sheila Rabe, Krysteen Seelen, Suzanne Selfors and Elsa Watson.

Heartfelt thanks to Greg Evans, creator of the comic strip Luann; to former fire captain Tom McCabe of the Kern County Fire Department—a real-life hero; and to Glenn Mounger, international man of mystery.

And, as always, thanks to the team of experts who make books happen—my agent, Meg Ruley, and Annelise Robey of the Jane Rotrosen Agency; my editor, Margaret O'Neill Marbury, and Adam Wilson of MIRA Books; and to Donna Hayes, Dianne Moggy, Loriana Sacilotto and so many others for making this business a guilty pleasure.

Part One

JUST BREATHE

One

After a solid year of visits to the clinic, Sarah was starting to find the decor annoying. Maybe the experts here believed earth tones had a soothing effect on anxious, aspiring parents. Or perhaps that the cheery burble of a wall fountain might cause an infertile woman to spontaneously drop an egg like an overly productive laying hen. Or even that the soft shimmer of brass chimes could induce a wandering sperm to find its way home like a heat-seeking missile.

The post-procedure period, lying flat on her back with her hips elevated, was starting to feel like forever. It was no longer standard practice to wait after insemination but many women, Sarah included, were superstitious. They needed all the help they could get, even from gravity itself.

There was a quiet tap on the door, then she heard it swish open.

"How are we doing?" asked Frank, the nurse-practitioner. Frank had a shaved head, a soul patch and a single earring, and he wore surgical scrubs with little bunnies on them. Mr. Clean showing his nurturing side.

"Hoping it is a 'we' this time," she said, propping her hands behind her head.

His smile made Sarah want to cry. "Any cramps?"

"No more than usual." She lay quietly on the cushioned, sterile-draped exam table while he checked her temperature and recorded the time.

She turned her head to the side. From this perspective, she could see her belongings neatly lined up on the shelf in the adjacent dressing room: her cinnamon-colored handbag from Smythson of Bond Street, designer clothes, butter-soft boots set carefully against the wall. Her mobile phone, programmed to dial her husband with one touch, or even a voice command.

Looking at all this abundance, she saw the trappings of a woman who was cared for. Provided for. Perhaps—no, definitely—spoiled. Yet instead of feeling pampered and special, she simply felt…old. Like middle-aged, instead of still in her twenties, the youngest client at Fertility Solutions. Most women her age were still living with their boyfriends in garrets furnished with milk crates and unpainted planks. She shouldn't envy them, but sometimes she couldn't help herself.

For no good reason, Sarah felt defensive and vaguely guilty for going through the expensive therapies. "It's not me," she wanted to explain to perfect strangers. "There's not a thing wrong with my fertility."

When she and Jack decided to seek help getting pregnant, she went on Clomid just to give Mother Nature a hand. At first it seemed crazy to treat her perfectly healthy body as if there were something wrong with it, but by now she was used to the meds, the cramps, the transvaginal ultrasounds, the blood tests…and the crushing disappointment each time the results came up negative.

"Yo, snap out of it," Frank told her. "Going into a funk is bad karma. In my totally scientific opinion."

"I'm not in a funk." She sat up and offered him a smile. "I'm fine, really. It's just that this is the first time Jack couldn't make the appointment. So if this works, I'll have to explain to my child one day that his daddy wasn't present at his conception. What do I tell him, that Uncle Frank did the honors?"

"Yeah, that'd be good."

Sarah told herself Jack's absence wasn't his fault. It wasn't anyone's fault. By the time the ultrasound revealed a maturing ovarian follicle and she'd given herself the HCG injection, they had thirty-six hours for the intra-uterine insemination. Unfortunately, Jack had already scheduled a late-afternoon meeting at the work site. He couldn't get out of it. The client was coming from out of town, he said.

"So are you still trying the old-fashioned way?" Frank asked.

She flushed. Jack's erections were few and far between, and lately, he'd all but given up. "That's not going so hot."

"Bring him tomorrow," Frank said. "I've got you down for 8:00 a.m." There would be a second IUI while the window of fertility was still open. He handed her a reminder card and left her alone to put herself back together.

Her yearning for a child had turned into a hunger that was painfully physical, one that intensified as the fruitless months marched past. This was her twelfth visit. A year ago, she never thought she'd reach this milestone, let alone face it by herself. The whole business had become depressingly routine—the self-injections, the invasion of the speculum, the twinge and burn of the inseminating catheter. After all this time, Jack's absence should be no big deal, she reminded herself as she got dressed. Still, for Sarah it was easy to remember that at the center of all the science and technology was something very human and elemental—the desire for a baby. Lately, she had a hard time even looking at mothers with babies. The sight of them turned yearning to a physical ache.

Having Jack here to hold her hand and endure the New Age Muzak with her made the appointments easier. She appreciated his humor and support, but this morning, she'd told him not to feel guilty about missing the appointment.

"It's all right," she had said with an ironic smile at breakfast. "Women get pregnant without their husbands every day."

He barely glanced up from checking messages on his BlackBerry. "Nice, Sarah."

She had touched her foot to his under the table. "We're supposed to keep trying to get pregnant the conventional way."

He looked up and, for an instant, she saw a dark flash in his gaze. "Sure," he said, pushing back from the table and organizing his briefcase. "Why else would we have sex?"

This resentful attitude had started several months ago. Duty sex, for the sake of procreation, was no turn-on for either of them, and she couldn't wait for his libido to return.

There had been a time when he'd looked at her in a way that made her feel like a goddess, but that was before he'd gotten sick. It was hard to be interested in sex, Jack often said these days, after getting your gonads irradiated. Not to mention the surgical removal of one of the guys. Jack and Sarah had made a pact. If he survived, they would go back to the dream they'd had before the cancer—trying to have a baby. Lots of babies. They had joked about his single testicle, they'd given it a name—the Uni-ball—and lavished it with attention. Once his chemo was finished, the doctors said he had a good chance of regaining fertility. Unfortunately, fertility had not been restored. Or sexual function, for that matter. Not on a predictable level, anyway.

They had decided, then, to pursue artificial insemination using the sperm he'd preserved as a precaution before starting aggressive treatment. Thus began the cycle of Clomid, obsessive monitoring, frequent visits to North Shore Fertility Solutions and bills so enormous that Sarah had stopped opening them.

Fortunately, Jack's medical bills were covered, because cancer wasn't supposed to happen to newlyweds trying to start a family.

The nightmare had come to light at 11:27 on a Tuesday morning. Sarah clearly remembered staring at the time on the screen of her computer, trying to remember to breathe. The expression on Jack's face had her in tears even before he said the words that would change the course of their lives: "It's cancer."

After the tears, she had vowed to get her husband through this illness. For his sake, she had perfected The Smile, the one she summoned when chemo landed him in a puking, quivering heap on the floor. The you-can-do-it-champ, I'm-behind-you-all-the-way smile.

This morning, feeling contrite after their exchange, she had tried to be sociable as she flipped through the brochure for Shamrock Downs, his current project, a luxury development in the suburbs. The brochure touted, "Equestrian center designed by Mimi Lightfoot, EVD."

"Mimi Lightfoot?" Sarah had asked, studying the soft-focus photographs of pastures and ponds.

"Big name to horse people," he assured her. "What Robert Trent Jones is to designing golf courses, she is to arenas."

Sarah wondered how challenging it was to design an oval-shaped arena. "What's she like?"

Jack had shrugged. "You know, the horsy type. Dry skin and no makeup, hair in a ponytail." He made a whinnying sound.

"You're so bad." She walked him to the door to say goodbye. "But you smell delicious." She inhaled the fragrance by Karl Lagerfeld, which she'd given him last June. She'd secretly bought it, along with a box of chocolate cigars, for Fathers Day, thinking there might be something to celebrate. When it turned out there wasn't, she had given him the Lagerfeld anyway, just to be nice. She'd eaten the chocolate herself.

She noticed, too, that he was wearing perfectly creased trousers, one of his fitted shirts from the Custom Shop, and an Hermès tie. "Important clients?" she asked.

"What?" He frowned. "Yeah. We're meeting about the marketing plans for the development."

"Well," she said. "Have a good day, then. And wish me luck."

"What?" he said again, shrugging into his Burberry coat.

She shook her head, kissed his cheek. "I've got a hot date with your army of seventeen million motile sperm," she said.

"Ah, shit. I really can't change this meeting."

"I'll be all right." Kissing him goodbye one more time, she suppressed a twinge of resentment at his testy, distracted air.

After the procedure, she followed the exit signs to the elevator and descended to the parking garage. Freakishly, the clinic had valet parking, but Sarah couldn't bring herself to use it. She was already indulged enough. She put on her cashmere-lined gloves, flexing her fingers into the smooth deerskin, then eased onto the heated leather seat of her silver Lexus SUV, which came with a built-in car seat. All right, so Jack had jumped the gun a little, buying this thing. But maybe, just maybe, nine months from now, it would be perfect. The ideal car for a soccer-mom-to-be.

She adjusted the rearview mirror for a peek at the backseat. At present, it was a jumble of drafting paper, a bag from Dick Blick Art Materials and, of all things, a fax machine, which was practically a dinosaur in this day and age. Jack thought she should let it die a natural death. She preferred to take it to a repair shop. It had been the first piece of equipment she'd bought with her earnings as an artist, and she wanted to keep it, even though no one ever faxed her anymore. She did have a career, after all. Not a very successful one, not yet, anyway. Now that Jack was cancer-free, she intended to focus on the comic strip, expanding her syndication. People thought it was simple, drawing a comic strip six days a week. Some believed she could draw a whole month's worth in one day, and then slack off the rest of the time. They had no idea how difficult and consuming self-syndication was, particularly at the beginning of a career.

When her car emerged from the parking lot, the very worst of Chicago's weather flayed the windshield. The city had its own peculiar brand of slush that seemed to fling itself off Lake Michigan, sullying vehicles, slapping at pedestrians and sending them scurrying for cover. Sarah would never get used to this weather, no matter how long she lived here. When she had first arrived in the city, a wide-eyed freshman from a tiny beach village in Northern California, she thought she'd encountered the storm of the century. She had no idea that this was normal for Chicago.

"Illinois," her mother had said when Sarah had received an offer of admission the spring of her senior year of high school. "Why?"

"The University of Chicago is there," Sarah explained.

"We have the best schools in the country right here in our backyard," her mother had said. "Cal, Stanford, Pomona, Cal Poly…"

Sarah had stood firm. She wanted to go to the University of Chicago. She didn't care about the distance or the god-awful weather or the flat landscape. Nicole Hollander, her favorite cartoon artist, had gone there. It was the place Sarah felt she belonged, at least for four years.

She'd never imagined living the rest of her life here, though. She kept waiting for it to grow on her. The city was tough and blustery, unpretentious and dangerous in some places, expansive and generous in others. Great food everywhere you turned. It had been overwhelming. Even the innate friendliness of Chicagoans had been confusing. How could you tell which ones were truly your friends?

She had always planned to leave the moment she graduated. She hadn't pictured raising a family here. But that was life for you. Filled with surprises.

Jack Daly had been a surprise as well—his dazzling smile and irresistible charm, the swiftness with which Sarah had fallen for him. He was a Chicago native, a general contractor in the family business. His entire world was right here—his family, friends and work. There was no question of where Sarah and Jack would live after they married.

The city itself was part of Jack's blood and bone. While most people believed life was a movable feast, Jack could not conceive of living anywhere but the Windy City. Long ago, in the dead of a brutal winter, when she hadn't seen the sun or felt a temperature above freezing for weeks, she had suggested moving somewhere a bit more temperate. He'd thought she was kidding, and they had never spoken of it again.

"I'll build you your dream house," Jack had promised her when they got engaged. "You'll learn to love the city, you'll see."

She loved him. The jury was still out on Chicago.

His cancer—that had been a surprise, too. They had made it through, she reminded herself every single day. But the disease had changed them both.

Chicago itself was a city of change. It had burned to the ground back in 1871. Families had been separated by the wind-driven firestorm that left nothing but charred timber and ash in its wake. People torn from their loved ones posted desperate letters and notices everywhere, determined to find their way back to each other.

Sarah pictured herself and Jack stepping gingerly through the smoldering ruins as they tried to make their way back to each other. They were refugees of another kind of disaster. Survivors of cancer.

Her front tire sank into a pothole. The jolt sent an eruption of mud-colored slush across the windshield, and she heard an ominous thud from the backseat. A glance in the mirror revealed that the fax machine had done a swan dive to the floor. "Lovely," she muttered. "Just swell." She pressed the wiper fluid wand, but the ducts sputtered out only an impotent trickle. The warning light blinked *Empty.*

Traffic crawled in a miserable stream northward. Stuck

at a stoplight for the third cycle, Sarah thumped the steering wheel with the heel of her hand. "I don't have to sit in traffic," she said. "I'm self-employed. I might even be pregnant."

She wondered what Shirl would do in this situation. Shirl was her alter ego in Sarah's comic strip, *Just Breathe*. A sharper, more confident, thinner version of her creator, Shirl was audacious; she had a screw-you attitude and an impulsive nature.

"What would Shirl do?" Sarah asked aloud. The answer came to her in an instant: Get pizza.

The very thought brought on such a craving that she laughed. A craving. Maybe she was already showing signs of pregnancy.

She veered down a side street and punched in "pizza" on her GPS. A mere six blocks away was a place called Luigi's. Sounded promising. And it looked promising, she saw when she pulled up in front of the place a few minutes later. There was a red neon sign that read, Open Till Midnight and another sign that promised Chicago's Finest Deep Dish Pizza Since 1968.

As she pulled up the hood of her coat and made a dash for the entrance, Sarah had a brilliant idea. She would take the pizza to share with Jack. His meeting was probably over by now and he'd be starved.

She beamed at the young man behind the counter. The name Donnie was stitched on the pocket of his shirt. He looked like a nice kid. Polite, a little shy, well-groomed. "Pretty nasty out there," Donnie commented.

"You said it," she agreed. "Traffic was a nightmare, which is why I took a detour and ended up here."

"What can I get you?"

"A thin-crust pizza to go," she said. "Large. And a Coke

with extra ice and…" She paused, thinking how good a nice cold, syrupy Coke would taste. Or a beer or margarita, for that matter. She resisted temptation, though. According to all the fertility advice books she'd read, she was supposed to keep her body a temple free of caffeine and alcohol. For many women, alcohol was often a key factor in conception, not a forbidden substance. Getting pregnant was a whole lot more fun for people who didn't read advice books.

"Ma'am?" the kid prompted.

The "ma'am" made her feel old. "Just the one Coke," she said. Right this very minute, a zygote might be forming itself into a clump of cells inside her. Giving it a shot of caffeine was a bad idea.

"Toppings?" the kid asked.

"Italian sausage," she said automatically, "and peppers." She glanced yearningly at the menu. Black olives, artichoke hearts, pesto. She adored those toppings, but Jack couldn't stand them. "That's all."

"You got it." The boy floured up his hands and went to work.

Sarah felt a faint tug of regret. She should at least get black olives on half the pizza. But no. Especially during his treatment, Jack had become an extremely picky eater, and just the sight of certain foods turned him off. A big part of cancer treatment was all about getting him to eat, so she had learned to cater to his appetite until she practically forgot her own preferences.

He's not sick anymore, she reminded herself. *Order the damned olives.*

She didn't, though. What no one told you about a loved one getting cancer was that the disease didn't happen to just one person. It happened to everyone around him. It robbed his mother of sleep, sent his father to the neighborhood bar each night, brought his siblings jetting in from wherever they happened to be. And what it did to his wife… She never let herself dwell on that.

Jack's illness had stopped everything for her. She'd put her career on hold, shoved aside her plans to paint the living room and plant bulbs in the garden, squelched her longing for a child. All of that had gone by the wayside and she had parked it there willingly. With Jack fighting for his life, she had bargained with God: *I'll be perfect. I'll never get angry. I won't miss our old sex life. I'll never complain. I won't wish for black olives on my pizza ever again, if only he'll get better.*

She had held up her end of the bargain. She'd been uncomplaining, even tempered, utterly dedicated. She hadn't made a peep about their sex life or their lack of one. She hadn't eaten a single olive. And presto—Jack's treatments ended and his scans came back clean.

They had wept and laughed and celebrated, then woke up the next day not knowing how to be a couple anymore. When he was sick, they had been soldiers in battle, comrades in arms fighting their way to safety. Once the worst was behind them, they weren't quite sure what to do next. After surviving cancer—and she didn't kid herself; they had both survived the disease—how did you start being normal again?

A year and a half later, Sarah reflected, they still weren't sure. She had painted the house and planted the bulbs. She'd rolled up her sleeves and plunged into her work. And they had resumed trying for the baby they'd promised each other long ago.

Still, it was a different world for them now. Maybe it was just her imagination, but Sarah sensed a new distance between them. While he was sick, Jack had days when he was almost entirely dependent on her. Now that he was well, it was probably natural for him to reassert his independence. It was her job to allow that, to bite her tongue instead of saying she was lonely for him, for his touch, for the affection and intimacy they once shared.

As the aroma of baking pizza filled the shop, she checked messages on her cell phone and found none. Then she tried Jack, but got his "out of service area" recording, which meant he was still at the work site. She put away the phone and browsed a well-thumbed copy of the *Chicago Tribune* that was lying on a table. Actually, she didn't browse. She turned straight to the comic strip section to visit *Just Breathe.* There it was, in its customary spot on the lower third of the page.

And there was her signature, slanting across the bottom edge of the last panel: *Sarah Moon.*

I have the best job in the world, she thought. Today's episode was another visit to the fertility clinic. Jack was hating the story line. He couldn't stand it when she borrowed material from real life to feed the comic strip. Sarah couldn't help herself. Shirl had a life of her own, and she inhabited a world that sometimes felt more real than Chicago itself. When Shirl had started pursuing artificial insemination, two of her papers had declared the story line too edgy, and they'd dropped her. But four more had signed on to run the strip.

"I can't believe you think it's funny," Jack had complained.

"It's not about being funny," she'd explained. "It's about being real. Some people might find that funny." Besides, she assured him, she published under her maiden name. Most people didn't know Sarah Moon was the wife of Jack Daly.

She tried dreaming up a story line he would love. Maybe she'd give Shirl's husband, Richie, bigger pecs. A jackpot win in Vegas. A hot speedboat. An erection.

That would never fly with her editors, but a girl could dream. Mulling over the possibilities, she turned to the window. The rain-smeared glass framed the Chicago skyline. If Monet had painted skyscrapers, they would've looked like this.

"Regular or Diet Coke?" Donnie broke in on her thoughts.

"Oh, regular," she said. Jack could use the calories; he was still gaining back the weight he'd lost during his illness. What a concept, she thought. Eating to gain weight. She hadn't done that since her mother had weaned her as an infant. People who ate all they wanted and stayed thin were going to hell. She knew this because they were in heaven now.

"Pizza'll be right out," the boy said.

"Thanks."

As he rang her up, Sarah studied him. He was maybe sixteen, with that loose-limbed, endearing awkwardness that teenage boys possess. The wall phone rang, and she could tell the call was personal, and from a girl. He ducked his head and blushed as he lowered his voice and said, "I'm busy now. I'll call you in a bit. Yeah. Me, too."

Back at the worktable, he folded cardboard boxes and sang unselfconsciously with the radio. Sarah couldn't remember the last time she had experienced that kind of floating-through-the-day, grinning-at-nothing sort of happiness. Maybe it was a function of age, or marital status. Maybe full-grown, married adults weren't supposed to float and grin at nothing. But hell, she missed that feeling.

Her hand stole to her midsection. One day, she might

have a son like Donnie—earnest, hardworking, a kid who probably left his dirty socks on the floor but picked them up cheerfully enough when nagged.

She added a generous tip to the glass jar on the counter.

"Thank you very much," said Donnie.

"You're welcome."

"Come again," he added.

Clutching the pizza box across one arm, with the drink in its holder balanced on top, she plunged outside into the wild weather.

Within minutes, the Lexus smelled like pizza and the windows were steamed up. She flipped on the defroster and made her way westward through winsome townships and hamlets that surrounded the city like small satellite nations. She glanced longingly at the Coke she'd ordered for Jack, and another craving hit her, but she tamped it down.

Twenty minutes later, she turned off the state highway and wended her way to a suburb where Jack was developing a community of luxury homes. She slowed down as she drove through the figured concrete gates that would one day be operated by key card only. The tasteful sign at the entrance said it all: Shamrock Downs. A Private Equestrian Community.

This was where millionaires would come to live with their pampered horses. Jack's company had planned the enclave down to the last blade of grass, sparing no expense. The subdivision covered forty acres of top-quality pastureland, a pond and a covered training arena, lighted and lined with bleachers. The resident Thoroughbreds and Warmbloods would occupy an ultramodern, forty-stall barn. Bridle paths wound through the wooded neighborhood, the surfaces paved with sand to reduce impact on the horses' hooves.

In the late-afternoon gloom, she saw that all the work crews had gone for the day, driven away by the rain. There was a Subaru Forester parked at the barn, but no one in sight. The foreman's trailer looked abandoned, too. Maybe she had missed Jack and he was heading home. Perhaps he'd had an attack of conscience and left his meeting early to be with her at the clinic, but had gotten stuck in traffic. There were no messages on her mobile, but that didn't mean anything. She hated cell phones. They never worked when you needed them and tended to ring when you wanted peace and quiet.

The unfinished houses looked eerie, their skeletal timbers black against the rain-drenched sky. Equipment was parked haphazardly, like giant, hastily abandoned toys in a sodden sandbox. Half-full Dumpsters littered the barren landscape. The people who moved to this neighborhood would never realize it had started out looking like a battle zone. But Jack was a magician. He could start with a sterile prairie or a reclaimed waste disposal site and transform it into Pleasantville. By spring, he would turn this place into a pristine, bucolic utopia, with children playing on the lawns, foals gamboling in the paddocks, women with ponytails and no makeup and thigh-hugging riding pants heading for the barn.

Darkness deepened by the minute. The pizza would be cold soon.

Then she spotted Jack's car. The custom-restored GTO was the ultimate muscle machine, even though legally, it belonged to her. When he was ill, she'd bought it to cheer him up. Using her earnings from the comic strip, she'd managed to save up enough for a lavish gift. Spending her life savings on the car had been an act of desperation, yet she had been willing to give anything, sacrifice anything to make him feel better. She only wished she could spend her last cent to buy him back his health.

Now that he was well, the car remained his prize possession. He only drove it on special occasions. His meeting with the client must have been an important one.

The black-and-red car crouched like an exotic beast in the driveway of one of the model houses. In its nearly finished state, the home resembled a hunting lodge. On steroids. Everything Jack built was bigger than it had to be—wraparound deck, entryway, four-car garage, water feature. The yard was still a mud pit, with great holes carved out for the fully grown trees that would be installed. *Installed* was Jack's word. Sarah would have said planted. The trees looked pathetic, like fallen victims, lying limp on their sides with their withered root-balls encased in burlap.

It was pouring harder than ever when she parked and killed the headlights and engine. A gaslight on a lamppost faintly illuminated a hand-lettered sign: "Street of Dreams." There were at least two river rock gas fireplaces that she could see, and one appeared to be working, evidenced by a deep golden glow flickering in the upper-story windows.

Balancing the Coke on the pizza box, she opened her push-button umbrella and got out. A gust of wind tugged at the ribs of the umbrella, turning it inside out. Icy rain battered her face and slid down inside her collar.

"I hate this weather," she said through gritted teeth. "Hate it, hate it, hate it."

Rivulets of water from the unplanted yard ran down the sloping driveway and swirled away in muddy streams. The nonfunctioning sprinkler system tubes lay in a tangled mess. There was no place to walk without getting her feet soaked.

That's it, she thought. I'm making Jack take me home to California for a vacation. Her hometown of Glenmuir, in Marin County, had never been his favorite place. He favored the white sand beaches of Florida, but Sarah was starting to feel it was her turn to choose their destination.

The past year and a half had been all about Jack—his needs, his recovery, his wishes. Now that the ordeal was behind them, she let her own needs rise up to the surface. It felt a tad selfish but damned good all the same. She wanted a vacation away from soggy Chicago. She wanted to savor each worry-free day, something she hadn't been able to do in a very long time.

A trip to Glenmuir wasn't so much to ask. She knew Jack would balk; he always claimed there was nothing to do in the sleepy seaside village. Battling her way through the wild storm, she resolved to do something about that.

No locks had been installed yet on the prehung doors of the huge, unfinished home.

She smiled as she pushed open the front door and sighed with relief. What could be cozier than sitting in front of the fire on a rainy afternoon, eating pizza? Quite possibly, this house was the only warm, dry place in the neighborhood.

"It's me," she called, stepping out of her boots so as not to muddy the newly finished hardwood floors. There was no reply, just the tinny sound of a radio playing somewhere upstairs.

Sarah felt a twinge of discomfort in her belly. Cramping was a side effect of IUI, and Sarah didn't mind. The fact that there was pain lent an appropriate sense of gravitas to her mission. It was a physical reminder of her determination to start a family.

Shaking off the raindrops, she padded in stocking feet

to the stairs. She'd never been here before, but she was familiar with the layout of the house. Though it wasn't obvious to most people, Jack worked with only a few floor plans. The massive size and luxurious materials aside, he built what he unapologetically called "cookie-cutter mansions." She had once asked him if he ever got bored, building essentially the same house, over and over again. He had laughed aloud at the question.

"What's boring about netting a cool million on a tract home?" he had countered.

He liked making money. He was good at it. And she was lucky, because so far, she was terrible at it. Each year when they filed their income tax return, he would look at the revenues from her comic strip, offer her a generous smile and joke, "I always wanted to be a patron of the arts."

At the top of the stairs, she turned toward the sound of the radio, her raincoat brushing against the machine-turned banister. "Achy Breaky Heart" was playing, and she winced. Jack had terrible taste in music. So bad, in fact, it was actually endearing.

The door to the master suite was ajar, and the friendly glow of the fire glimmered across the freshly carpeted floors. She hesitated, sensing…something.

A warning, beating like an extra pulse in her ears.

She stepped into the room, her feet sinking into the deep pile of the carpet as her eyes adjusted to the soft, golden light. The diffuse, kindly glow of the lifetime-guaranteed Briarwood gas logs flickered over two naked bodies entwined on a bed of thick woolen blankets spread in front of the hearth.

Sarah experienced a moment of complete and utter confusion. Her vision clouded and she felt light-headed and nauseous. There was some mistake here. She had walked into the wrong house. Into the wrong life. She fought against the panicky random thoughts playing Ping-Pong in her head. For a second or two she simply stood immobile, assaulted by shock, forgetting to breathe.

After endless seconds, they noticed her and sat up, gathering blankets to cover themselves. The song on the radio switched to something equally appalling—"Butterfly Kisses."

Mimi Lightfoot, Sarah realized, was exactly as Jack had described her: the horsy type—dry skin and no makeup, hair in a ponytail. But with bigger boobs.

Finally, Sarah found her voice and spoke the only coherent thought in her head: "I brought you a pizza. And a Coke. Extra ice, the way you like it."

She didn't throw the pizza or spill the drink. She set everything carefully on the built-in media console next to the radio. She was as discreet and efficient as a room service waiter.

Then she turned and left.

"Sarah, wait!"

She heard Jack calling her name as she skimmed down the stairs with the speed and grace of Cinderella at the stroke of midnight. Shoving her feet into her boots barely slowed her down. In seconds, she was outside with her broken umbrella, heading for the car.

She started the engine just as Jack burst outside. He wore his good pants—the ones with the creases she had admired this morning—and nothing else. She could see his mouth working, forming her name: *Sarah.* She put the headlamps on bright and turned the car, feeling a satisfying crunch as the rear bumper of the Lexus toppled the custom river rock mailbox. Her high beams washed across the front of the house, illuminating the porch timbers and fine wooden window casements, the Andersen glass and the grand front entranceway.

For a moment, Jack appeared pinned by the glare, a prize buck frozen in the headlights.

What would Shirl do? Sarah asked herself. She gripped the steering wheel, threw the car into gear and floored the accelerator.

Part Two

JUST BREATHE

Two

After creaming the newly constructed mailbox and mowing down the "Street of Dreams" lamppost, Sarah actually contemplated nailing Jack, too. Just for an insane moment, she allied herself with the crazed women you saw on TV being interviewed behind bars: "I didn't think. My foot just pressed down and he hit the pavement..."

Somehow, she managed to aim the SUV away from him and toward the highway. She didn't know what else to do and couldn't think straight, so she headed home, exceeding the speed limit, like a horse sensing the barn after a long trek.

Predictably, her mobile phone rang right away. Jack was probably still half-naked. He probably still stank of Mimi Lightfoot's scent of sex. Sarah killed the power on the phone and pressed the accelerator harder. She needed to get home, give herself some breathing space and figure out what to do next.

As she pulled into the landscaped, circular driveway, it struck her that this had never felt like her home; it just happened to be where she lived. This was the House that

Jack Built, she thought, hearing the singsong rhythm of the old children's story in her head. And this was the wife who lived in the house that Jack built. And there was the mistress that screwed the husband that ignored the wife who lived in the house that Jack built….

It was nestled amid similar houses in the exclusive lakeside subdivision. The trees that shaded the lane were spaced perfectly apart, the mailboxes all matched and every home's entryway lay a uniform distance from the curb. The neighborhood had been planned by a designer who worked for Daly Construction.

She wheeled into the spacious garage, nearly grazing Jack's work truck—a custom F-350 Ford pickup—and hurried inside. Then she stopped cold. *Now what?* She felt so strange, almost traumatized, as though she'd been the victim of a violent assault.

She looked at the wall phone in the kitchen. The message light was blinking. Maybe she ought to call… who? Her mother had died years ago. Her friends…she'd allowed herself to drift away from people back home, and her Chicago friends belonged more to Jack than to Sarah.

What would Shirl do? she wondered, plucking the thought from the panic swirling through her head. Shirl was smart. Tough-minded. Shirl would remind Sarah to focus on practical matters, like the fact that she had a separate bank account. This was something they had set up during Jack's illness, so she'd have access to funds if the unthinkable happened.

Well, the unthinkable *had* happened. Not in the way she had feared, though.

Her stomach cramped, a sensation she would ordinarily welcome after the procedure, as it meant that biology was at work. Now the discomfort meant something altogether different.

The phone rang. Seeing Jack's number on the caller ID, she let it kick over to voice mail.

She sat in the dark house for a while, her sodden coat and boots still on. It was such a strange puzzle. Husbands cheated on their wives all the time; daytime TV was filled with dewy-eyed betrayed women seeking solace on national talk shows. The problem was as familiar to anyone as ring around the collar. Yet the issue had always brushed past Sarah like a wind pattern on a weather map from another part of the country. She could recognize it, imagine what it was like. She thought she understood.

What the talk shows never explained—what no one ever explained—was what, precisely, you were supposed to do the exact moment you made the dread discovery. Probably you didn't leave them a pizza.

She was familiar with the stages of grief: shock, denial, anger, bargaining… She had experienced them all when she'd lost her mother, and when her husband was diagnosed with cancer. This was different. At least in those instances, she had known how she was supposed to feel. It was horrible, but at least she knew. Now she saw a world turned upside down. She was supposed to be moving from the shock to the denial phase, but it wasn't working. This was all too real.

Late into the night she sat mulling over her options—drinking, hysterics, revenge—but nothing felt quite right. Finally, exhaustion claimed her and she went to bed. She lay still, bracing herself for a storm of inconsolable tears. Instead, she stared dry-eyed at the shadows on the wall, and eventually fell asleep.

* * *

Sarah was awakened from a fitful sleep by the sound of running water. She turned over in bed, seeing that Jack's half was a vast, deserted wasteland. He had come home, but not to her bed. The events of the day before crashed down on her and drove away all possibility of going back to sleep.

In the past year, she had gone to bed alone nearly every night while Jack worked late. How many marriages crashed and burned on the altar of "working late"?

I'm an idiot, she thought. She got up and brushed her teeth, pulled on her robe. On the bathroom counter was the bottle of prenatal vitamins she'd been taking. Normally, the morning after artificial insemination, she would cheerfully gulp down the pills, filled with hope and possibility. She wondered when she had begun to think of artificial insemination as normal.

Now she stared at the bottle in dull horror. "I'd better not be pregnant," she whispered.

Just like that, the dream of having a baby evaporated like a snowflake hitting a skillet. *Ssst.*

The good news was, she thought, combing her fingers through her hair, they had failed to make a child no matter how many times she made the trek to Fertility Solutions, so she was in little danger of being pregnant now. A small blessing, but probably a blessing all the same.

She phoned the clinic and left a voice mail: she would not be coming in for the second part of the procedure today. With a determined air, she unscrewed the top of the bottle and shook the vitamin pills into the toilet. Then, as though of its own accord, her hand snatched the bottle upright. She clutched it hard, saw that there were a few pills left. Slowly, deliberately, she put the cap back on the bottle. She should probably keep a small supply. Just in case.

She stuck her feet into scuffs and followed the sound of running water to the guest suite. Jack had come home late. She'd felt him looking in on her, but she'd lain still, feigning sleep, aware that he knew she was faking. There was much to discuss with him, but she hadn't wanted to engage at 2:00 a.m. Now, in the light of day, she felt…not stronger. But the shock and denial had worn off, giving way to a cold rage she'd never felt before, a sensation of such violence it frightened her.

She stepped inside to find Jack freshly showered, a towel slung around his slim hips. Under normal circumstances, she would find him sexy. She might even try some seductive moves on him, not that those moves had done her any good in a long time. Now that she was beginning to understand the real reason behind his lack of desire, she saw him through new eyes. And he didn't look sexy at all.

"So," she said. "Who wants to start?" When he said nothing, she asked, "How long has this been going on? How many times a week?" A dozen more questions pushed to the fore, but Sarah realized her main question was for herself. Why hadn't she seen or known?

He hung his head. Ah, shame, she thought. That might be promising. But if she was honest with herself, she had to admit that she didn't want him to grovel and beg her forgiveness. She wanted…she wasn't sure what she wanted.

When he looked up, she didn't see disgrace, but hostility in his eyes. All right, she thought, so he's not ashamed.

"Just a sec," he said, and ducked into the bathroom. He emerged a moment later wearing a white terry cloth robe, one they kept in the guest bath for company. His arms protruded from the too-short sleeves, and his legs were bare from the thighs down.

There was probably no dress code for the breakup of a marriage. Robes would have to do. At the very least, it would prevent them from running out of the house in a screaming rage. Or maybe not. At the moment, she would rather be anywhere but here.

"We've both been unhappy," he told her abruptly. "You can't deny it."

Oh, she wanted to. She wanted to swear her life had been perfect. That would make him responsible for causing it to collapse in an instant. Instead, she realized she'd been battling a pervasive disappointment, little sinking steps downward, so incremental they were easy enough to ignore until failure, wearing a ponytail and nothing else, held up a mirror.

"I won't deny it," she said, "as long as you won't deny you chose pretty much the worst possible way to express your unhappiness."

He didn't. He acted as though she hadn't even spoken. "I didn't ask to get sick. You didn't ask for a husband with cancer. But it happened, Sarah, and it screwed up everything."

"No, *you* screwed up everything."

He narrowed his eyes at her, coldly handsome. "When I was sick, when things were at their worst, it changed us. We weren't like man and wife anymore. We were like…parent and child. I couldn't get past that. When I'm with you, I see myself as a guy with cancer."

Her stomach tightened, and for a moment, she focused all her bitterness on the disease. It was true, the cancer and its treatment had taken away his dignity, rendering him helpless. He wasn't helpless now, though, she reminded herself. "That's over," she stated. "We're supposed to learn to be man and wife again. I don't know about you, but I've been working on exactly that. Apparently, you've been working on being a man again, only without the wife."

He flung her a look of unexpected venom. "You've spent the past year trying to get pregnant," he retorted, "with or without my help."

"You've been telling me since we got engaged how much you want kids," she reminded him.

"I never let it turn into an obsession," he said.

"And I did?"

He gave an angry laugh. "Let's see. Let's just see." Striding past her, he left the room and went to the master suite, barging into her mirrored dressing room. Feeling queasy, she followed him. He ripped a calendar off the wall and dropped it to the floor. "Your ovulation calendar." He moved on to another wall hanging. "Temperature chart." He ripped it down and threw it on the floor, then moved to the dressing table. "Here we've got your thermometers—looks like you've got one for every orifice—and fertility drugs. I figure your next step was to install a Web camera in the bedroom so you can record the exact moment it's time for me to do my part. Isn't that what they do at stud farms?"

"Now you're being absurd," she told him. Her cheeks felt hot with humiliation. Defend yourself, she thought. Then she realized that wasn't her job.

"What's absurd," he said, "is trying to be married to you when you're so focused on having a baby that you forget you have a husband."

"I changed my whole life for you," she said. "How can you say I forgot I have a husband?"

"You're right. You didn't forget. When it's time to fertilize the egg, you demand a performance, and failure is not an option. Can't you see how that might lead to a little anxiety on my part, every time you came after me?"

"Came after you? Is that how you see it?"

"Christ, no wonder I couldn't get it up for you. But I have to hand it to you, Sarah. You didn't let that stop you. Why bother with a husband when you've got a lifetime supply of viable sperm samples available?"

"Going to the clinic was your idea. You sat there and held my hand, month after month."

"Because I thought it would get you off my back."

Oh, God. She'd tried to be sexy for him. Desirable. Understanding. "Why didn't you say something?"

"It wouldn't have made a difference, and you know it. Listen, Sarah," he said, anger flashing in his voice. "Maybe I was the one who strayed—"

"I would say definitely, not maybe."

"These things don't happen in a vacuum."

"No, they happen in half-finished houses." She felt as though she was being smacked around by both of them and there was no stopping it, no laws to protect her from the agony, the humiliation, the sense of complete violation. She emitted a bitter sound, not quite a laugh. "I guess now I know where all your erections went. I was wondering. And does it bother your clients? To know their house had been christened by you fucking the stable girl?"

"Mimi's not—"

"Don't even." She held up a hand to stop him. "Don't tell me she's not a stable girl, a slut, a home wrecker. Don't tell me she's the Robert Trent Jones of arena design. Don't tell me how warmhearted and understanding she is."

"Why, because you're going to tell me *you've* been understanding? News flash—playing stud to your mare was not exactly a turn-on. Maybe if you'd been there for me outside the window of conception—"

"Oh, 'you weren't there for me,'" she said. "That's a classic. At any point, you could have come to me, talked about this. But I guess it's just easier to blame me for your choices."

"Okay, I can see you're not ready to acknowledge your part in this yet."

"My part? I have a part? Oh, goody. Well, guess what? I'm on center stage now."

He tilted his head to one side. "Fine. Go for it. Let me have it. Don't stop at backing the Lexus over a mailbox. Do your worst."

"That's your specialty," she shot back, wickedly pleased that he'd mentioned the Lexus. "What could be worse than what I walked in on yesterday?"

Jack fell silent for a moment. Then he said, "I'm sorry."

Here it comes, she thought, ready to go limp with relief. Finally, a little show of remorse.

Stepping over the discarded things on the floor, he walked into the main room, his hands shoved into the pockets of the robe. "I mean that, Sarah," he went on. "I'm sorry you had to find out like that. I wish I'd told you sooner."

Find out...told you... Wait a minute, she thought. This was supposed to be the apology segment of the crisis. The we-can-work-it-out phase. Instead, he was telling her that this was not an anomaly, a one-time slipup. It had been going on for a while. Sarah's stomach lurched. "Told me what?"

He turned around, looked her in the eye. "I want a divorce."

Congratulations, she thought, forcing herself to hold his

gaze. You just scored a technical knockout. But somehow, she was still standing. Still calm. "That's supposed to be my line," she said.

"I'm sorry this hurt you."

"This is still not remorse, Jack. You're sorry you got caught. You're sorry my feelings got hurt. How about being sorry you destroyed us? Oh, and here's a concept. How about letting me in on your little secret *before* I suffer through a year of fertility treatment, huh? Or were you going to change your mind if I got lucky and turned up pregnant?"

"God, I didn't think." He splayed his hand through his hair.

"You didn't think? You dragged me into Fertility Solutions month after month and it never occurred to you to think about whether or not this was what you wanted?"

"You wanted it so badly, I didn't know how to tell you I was having second thoughts. Listen. I'll go someplace else for a while," he said.

"Don't be ridiculous. This is your house." She gestured around the pristine home, indicating the warm, quiet elegance of the decor. Jack had once called it her dream house, but it had never been that. It came preplanned, prepackaged, like a magazine layout. She had simply moved in and unpacked her things like a temporary resident. It was filled with expensive things she had not picked out and had never wanted—tasteful artwork and collectibles, luxurious furniture. Deep down, she knew this was a place she had never belonged. She could picture herself leaving it behind like a hotel guest checking out of a luxury suite.

Leaving. The idea was there. It was not a decision she had worked herself up to. It just appeared fully conceived in her mind. The betrayal had occurred; now the next step was to leave, simple as that.

Or, Sarah thought, she could stay and fight for him. Insist on getting help, exploring their issues together, healing together. Couples did that, didn't they? It all sounded terribly exhausting to Sarah, though. And the cold feeling in the pit of her stomach seemed to contain a terrible truth. He might be the one asking for a divorce, but she was the one who wanted to leave. When had everything gone off track for them? She couldn't pinpoint the moment. She used to feel so lucky, wanting for nothing. Now she wondered where her luck had gone. Maybe she and Jack had used up all their cosmic Brownie points on the cancer.

"This is your life," she said to him. "You can't walk away from your own life, Jack."

"I just meant—"

"But I can." There. She'd said it. The words were out, a gauntlet flung to the ground between them.

"What's that supposed to mean?" he asked. "Where will you go? You don't know anybody. I mean…"

"I know what you meant, Jack. There really isn't any point in being diplomatic now, is there? This whole marriage has always been about your life, your hometown, your job."

"This *job* made it possible for you to stay home all day and draw pictures."

"Well, gosh, I guess I should be grateful for that. Maybe it was a way to deal with the fact that you were never home."

"I never knew you felt put out by the fact that my job kept me busy."

"You never knew how I felt about a lot of things. Take infidelity. If you knew how I felt about that, you probably would have left me *before* fucking someone else."

His cell phone rang again. "I have to go to work," he said, and went to finish dressing.

He emerged from his dressing room a few minutes later looking as neat and polished as an Eagle Scout. "Listen, Sarah," he said. "We have to deal with this. Just…take it easy. We'll talk about it some more tonight."

She stood at the window and watched his large, shiny truck disappear down the rain-slick road. After he was gone, she stayed there, looking out at the gray day. Her mind worked sluggishly, weighed down by disappointment and a slow-simmering rage. She sorted through the things Jack had said, and found a grain of truth in one thing: they had been so focused on wanting a baby that they didn't notice they had stopped wanting each other.

It was a lame, overused excuse for infidelity. And Jack was a grown-up. It didn't excuse what he had done, or justify his demand for a divorce.

She took a deep breath. So she was, what, supposed to hang around all day waiting for him to come home and kick her to the curb? *Good plan.*

Three

The empty prairie, crisscrossed by a grid of startlingly straight roads, rolled out like a vast wasteland in front of the hood ornament of the GTO. It was remarkable, Sarah thought, how quickly the suburban sprawl of Chicago gave way to the broad gray-and-white checkerboard of the heartland at its most bleak.

In the late afternoon, her phone sounded off with Jack's ringtone. She picked up without a greeting. "I'm leaving," she informed him.

"Don't be stupid. We agreed to talk about this." Jack's voice was sharp with both anger and distress.

"I didn't agree to anything, but I guess you missed that part." When had he stopped hearing her? she wondered. And why hadn't she noticed? "There's nothing to talk about."

"Are you kidding? We've barely begun to discuss this."

"The next time you hear from me, it'll be through my lawyer." As if she even had one at this point. She felt like such a phony, talking about "her" lawyer. But even just a day after discovering her husband with another woman, she had a clear vision of what her future held—legal counsel.

"Come on, Sarah—"

She gunned the engine to pass a semi.

"My God." Jack's voice squawked in disbelief. "Don't tell me you took the GTO."

"Fine. I won't tell you." She threw the cell phone out the window. It was a stupid, childish gesture. God knew, she would need a phone in the days to come.

She stopped at a RadioShack and acquired a cheap, pay-as-you-go phone, strictly for emergencies. She bought it with a brisk and icy calm, as if she did such things every day. As if she were not on fire with panic inside. There was a brittle outer shell around her and inside, a clockwork brain directing each step she took with passionless efficiency.

It was as if she had rehearsed the act of leaving her husband a hundred times before—pack a bag, burn CDs with all the personal data she might need, all the dark, sad-voiced music she might crave along the way. She'd had no trouble pulling the records—a simple step. She knew exactly where everything was. One of the terrible virtues of Jack's illness was that it had forced them to keep all their affairs in order and well documented. Now their affairs—all but the extramarital one—were still in perfect order, including her separate bank account and the title to the GTO.

Driving through nowhere, she spared a thought for some of the things she had left—Waterford crystal lamps. An Italian leather sofa, the Belleek china and serving pieces, a set of Porsche forged cooking knives, a flat-screen TV. Maybe one day she would miss some of those things, but so far, she didn't even want to think about them. Like a wild animal in a steel-jawed trap, she was willing to gnaw off a limb in exchange for a swift release.

Sarah stopped for gas in a town called Chance. She went to the ladies' room to change clothes and discovered that she had stuffed her suitcase with far too many A-line skirts and blazers and had forgotten certain key items, like a hairbrush and pajamas. Maybe she should have spent more time picking the right kind of clothes to bring on her journey. But when you're running out on your marriage, she thought, you didn't really take time to shop or plan ahead. You didn't even take the time to think.

She tugged a purse-sized comb through her hair, scowling when she hit a snag. Her hair was at that awkward in-between stage, neither impressively long nor sassily short. Jack claimed he liked her hair long and silky—"my California girl," he used to call her.

"Can you take a walk-in?" Sarah asked the woman at the counter of the Chance, Illinois, Twirl & Curl.

"What do you need, hon?" Heather, the stylist, scrutinized her in the mirror.

Sarah touched her hair. "I want to be ritually shorn of the person I never was to begin with."

Heather grinned as she led Sarah to a chair. "My specialty."

It was a relief to lie back over the sink, close her eyes and surrender to the warm stream from the hose and the creamy texture of the shampoo. The familiar perfume of the salon comforted her.

"You're a natural blond," Heather remarked.

"I was experimenting with being a redhead but it didn't work out. I've gone through every shade of brunette, too. Always looking for something different, I guess."

"And now?" The stylist finished with the shampoo, then combed smoothly and effortlessly through Sarah's hair.

Sarah took a deep breath and stared at her reflection in the big round mirror above the counter. The slicked-back hair made her look strange and unfinished, like a just-hatched chick. "Maybe I'll think better with short hair."

She heard the hungry rasp of the heavy scissors and with the first snip, she knew the decision was irrevocable. A cool breeze touched her neck, and a lightness lifted her, as though nothing anchored her to earth.

At a Wal-Mart outside Davenport, she bought a velour jogging suit to sleep in. The zip-up jacket and elastic-waistband pants were the perfect togs for terrible-looking roadside motels with sleepy desk clerks who had to be summoned by a bell on the counter.

At the state line, she caromed into a new-and-used car dealership so vast that its lot covered acres.

The GTO would fetch a handsome price, more than enough for a more appropriate car. She wouldn't miss the muscle car in the least and felt nothing when she explained that she wanted to trade it in. She had presented the car to Jack with so much love in her heart. Where had that love gone? Was it possible for it to simply disappear?

Poof, rubbed out like a mistake she made in her comic strip.

The question was, what car was appropriate? A car was a car, a way to go from point A to point B. All of a sudden, the issue seemed to matter. If she couldn't pick out her own car, what hope did she have of mapping out her own future?

Her footsteps dogged by an overeager saleswoman named Doreen, she strolled the lot, trying to tune out Doreen's constant, upbeat patter about the can't-miss attributes of every car they passed. "Here's a beauty," she said, indicating an ultraconservative Mercury Sable. "That's actually the same model I bought after my divorce."

Sarah ducked her head and tried to resist hunching her shoulders. Had Doreen somehow guessed that she was fleeing her husband? Was she wearing the unwarranted shame like a scarlet letter on her chest? She nearly ditched Doreen then and there. But she needed wheels, and she needed them now. At least, Sarah thought, she wasn't dealing with a guy wearing a plaid sport jacket and too much aftershave.

There was a slight reprieve when Doreen's phone rang. She glanced at the screen and said, "Sorry. I'm afraid I have to take this."

"You go right ahead," Sarah said.

Doreen turned aside and lowered her voice. "Mommy's busy," she said. "What do you need?"

Sarah slowed her steps as if to check out a silver hybrid. In actuality, she was checking out Doreen, who had been transformed in seconds from yappy high-pressure salesperson to harried single mom. Overhearing Doreen trying to referee a sibling dispute on the phone, Sarah realized there were worse things than being divorced. Like being divorced with kids. What could be harder than that?

All right, she thought, Doreen would get a commission from her. She grew more serious about her search, but all the cars seemed the same—bland, practical, ordinary. When Doreen got off the phone, Sarah said, "You've got every car in the world here. And none of them seems right."

"Why don't you tell me a little more about what you're looking for? Do you need four-wheel drive? A sports car…?"

The sodium vapor lights came on over the parking lot,

buzzing to life in the late-afternoon twilight. Sarah thought about Doreen's kids, waiting for her to come home from work.

"I'm leaving my husband," she said, the words frosting the air, seeming to hang there a moment like a speech balloon from Shirl's mouth. "I've got a long drive ahead of me." For some reason, it helped to tell this stranger the truth. "It seems like I should have the right car. I want…I'm not sure." She offered a self-deprecating smile. "Maybe I'm looking for a magic carpet. Or Chitty Chitty Bang Bang. With a drop top and a great sound system."

Doreen didn't bat an eye. "Hold that thought," she said, and consulted her electronic inventory tracker. "We need to hurry." Her voice was edged with urgency now. "This won't last another five minutes."

Mystified, Sarah followed her off the lot, back to a shop where cars were being prepped for market. "We've got a one-year waiting list for this. It was some woman's dream car, but she traded it in after owning it for just a few months."

They found a mechanic in an insulated jumpsuit under the hood of the cutest midnight-blue-and-silver car Sarah had ever seen. "You have a Mini," she said.

Doreen beamed like a proud parent. "My first. It's a Cooper S *convertible*—rare as hen's teeth. I'm sure it's promised to the top person on the waiting list but…gee…I just can't seem to find that list, and I'd hate to bother someone at the dinner hour."

They exchanged conspiratorial smiles. The little British-made car was adorable, like a windup toy. She could just hear Jack now, laughing and pointing out all the reasons a Mini Cooper wasn't practical or safe. It was a passing trend, overpriced, prone to breakdowns, he would say.

"It's perfect," Sarah told Doreen. "But I have to ask, why did she trade it in?"

"Right after she bought it, she found out she was expecting her third child. You can probably fit a family of four in a Mini, but five would be stretching it."

Plenty of room for me and my fax machine, Sarah thought.

"It's got autolock, which is an antitheft feature. It doesn't have OnStar, though," Doreen admitted.

"That's okay. I've never locked my keys in the car before, and I don't plan to start. I don't need a GPS, either. I know where I'm going." An hour later, she drove it off the lot. The car was crowded to the rear with her stuff, and the sound system didn't disappoint. She headed to the highway, darting up the on-ramp and merging into the stream of traffic headed west. In the middle lane, she suddenly found herself flanked by a pair of semis rising like steel walls and looming in close, ready to crush her. A terrible fear squeezed her heart. What the hell am I doing?

Sarah set her jaw and eased back on the accelerator, letting the trucks pull ahead. Then she turned up the radio and burst into song, "Shut Up and Drive" by Rihanna. She sang with a crushing sense of loss that mingled oddly with a terrifying exhilaration. She sang for the things she'd left behind. For a marriage she used to believe in, but didn't anymore. For the hope of having a baby, which was now as dead as her love for Jack. For the anonymous woman who had ordered the Mini and then traded it in when she realized her life was about to change radically.

Sarah found the first of a series of cheap roadside motels and lay staring at the blank ceiling of her room and listening to the sound of the highway. This felt like someone else's life, she thought, someone she didn't recognize at all.

* * *

Sarah drove west, her new car like a tiny bluebottle fly, flashing across the prairies, past endless seas of alfalfa and dried corn and deep emerald-green winter rye. By the time she reached North Platte, Nebraska, she made a terrible admission to herself. She had not been happy in a long while. This was not sour grapes. Humbly grateful for Jack's recovery, she had been afraid to voice her discontent. It would have seemed so petty and ungrateful. Instead, she had existed in a state that passed for happiness. Jack was well, they were financially comfortable, they lived in a lovely home in a nice neighborhood, they were trying to start a family to prove to the world that all was well. But happy?

That was the trouble with the human spirit, she realized as she drove the Mini across the mountains and finally to the edge of California. You could pretend all you wanted that you were happy, but discontent was bound to manifest itself. For Jack, it was in the arms of another woman. For Sarah, it was her dogged determination to get pregnant.

"So far, not so good," she said, her eyes fastened on the horizon.

On her final day on the road, she woke up at dawn and drove the final leg of the journey, along Papermill Creek through the murky, uninhabited forest of Samuel P. Taylor State Park, where the tall, thickly branched trees arched over the winding road, creating a canopy of shadows. Finally she reached the tiny hamlet of Glenmuir, on the western edge of Marin County, remote and nearly forgotten, surrounded by a wilderness so spectacular that it was protected by an act of Congress.

Emerging from a green tunnel of gloom, she passed rolling green hills dotted with dairy farms and ranches, through misty valleys to the gray-shrouded bay, where old dock pilings pierced through the fog. It was about as far as she could get from Jack without actually leaving the continent.

At the end of the journey, she found herself in a place she had not lived since heading off to college. She passed the dock where she used to stand, a pale shadow watching the world go by. Then she pulled up the drive and parked. She walked into the house by the bay where she had grown up, feeling the ache and fatigue of her marathon drive in her neck and shoulders. "I left Jack," she told her father.

"I know. He called me."

"He was screwing around."

"I know that, too."

"He told you?"

Her father didn't answer. He gave her an awkward hug—things were always awkward between them—and then she went to bed and slept for twenty-four hours straight.

Four

If she didn't know better, Sarah would have thought it was a bad idea to hire a divorce lawyer named Birdie. Birdie Bonner Shafter, to be exact. It sounded more like a porn star than an attorney.

She did know better, though she wondered if Birdie would remember her from high school. Probably not. Three years ahead of Sarah, Birdie had been too busy running the show—student council president, Girls State, volleyball team captain and Key Club were just a few of her roles—to spare a thought for lesser beings. The fact that she had been the meanest girl in the school was actually an asset now.

Sarah had been invisible to everyone who mattered in high school. Come to think of it, she had been invisible all her life, until she met Jack. Now she remembered why. It was safer to fly below the radar. She should have stayed that way—unnoticed, watching the world go by, drawing her private observations, making fun of the things she secretly envied. But no. She had to go and plunge into life—and into love—as though she belonged there. As though it was her right.

She got up and went to the window of the outer office, sending the receptionist a nervous smile.

"Can I get you something to drink?" the receptionist offered.

"No, thank you," said Sarah. "I'm fine."

"Ms. Shafter should only be a few minutes longer."

"I don't mind waiting." The tall casement window was surrounded by gingerbread molding. Some of the glass panes were original, judging by their slightly brittle, wavy quality. Birdie's law office occupied one of the historic buildings of downtown Glenmuir. Since Sarah had moved away, the main square had barely changed. It was a cluster of Victorian and carpenter Gothic wood frame buildings, some original, some knockoffs, the old ones built by nineteenth-century settlers who had come to fish the abundant waters of the secluded bay. A few local B and Bs attracted tourists from the Bay area, including May's Cottage, a private beach retreat that belonged to Sarah's great-aunt. The snug white bungalow was so popular as a vacation rental that it booked up months in advance. Most tourists, however, found the town remote and strange, hanging on the edge of nowhere, and they let the locals be.

When not festooned in fog, the area around Tomales Bay had a clarity of light she had never seen anywhere else in the world. The intense blue of the sky was reflected in the water. The placid water in turn mirrored the wooded wilderness that surrounded the bay. It looked exactly as it had five hundred years ago, when Sir Francis Drake had sailed in on his soon-to-be-legendary *Golden Hind,* to be greeted by painted members of the Miwok tribe.

Sarah smoothed her hands down her tailored blazer,

feeling overdressed in her Chicago outfit. People around here tended to dress in organic fibers and homely, supremely comfortable shoes. She didn't really own anything like that anymore. Jack liked her to dress like a Neiman Marcus catalog model, even when she protested that she worked at home, alone.

When they were first married, she liked to draw at her drafting table wearing a faded University of Chicago sweat suit and thick wool socks, her hair held back with a clip. "It helps me be creative," she had once told him.

"You can be creative in a sweater and slacks," he replied, and gave her a three-hundred-dollar cashmere cardigan set to make his point.

She gritted her teeth and focused on the bay in the distance. A seaplane came in for a landing, the lawnmower whine of its engine briefly filling the air. Sometimes the aircraft brought tourists to town but most of them came to pick up fresh oysters and transport them, still alive, to big-city restaurants. There was a boat out today, its full sails pulling it toward the horizon. Closer in, she could see the harvest skiffs her father used to take out three hundred sixty-four days a year, until he'd handed the business over to his son. Sarah's brother Kyle was as conventional as she was odd, and he'd been perfectly content to take over the family business. Meanwhile, their father had traded his cultivation trays for a 1965 poppy-red Mustang GT convertible in dire need of restoration. He lavished attention on the car, which seemed to occupy a permanent berth in Glenn Mounger's auto body garage.

A woman came in, breathless, and headed straight for the water cooler. Her athletic body was encased in gleaming black-and-yellow spandex. The chest-hugging top was covered with sponsors' logos. The stripe up the side of her skintight shorts read Trek. She wore an aerodynamic helmet and wraparound shades. In cup-heeled cycling shoes, her walk was stiff-legged, the toes pointing up.

She drank six cone-shaped cups at the water cooler and finally turned to Sarah. "Sorry about that. I used up my hydration pack."

"Oh." Sarah was at a loss. "I hate when that happens."

"Birdie Shafter," the woman said, taking off the helmet and shades. A riot of black hair and a supermodel face were revealed. "You're Sarah Moon."

Sarah covered her surprise. Somehow, she'd expected Birdie to have changed more from high school. "That's right."

"I'm training for a triathlon, so my schedule is pretty crazy these days." She held open a door marked with the nameplate Bernadette Bonner Shafter, Attorney at Law.

Sarah stepped into the office.

"Give me two minutes," Birdie said.

"Take five," Sarah offered.

"You're a peach." She ducked through a side door. Sarah heard the sound of running water.

Despite Birdie's unconventional appearance, the law office was all business. The array of framed diplomas and certificates did its job of instilling confidence in the client. Birdie had earned her bachelor's at USC and her law degree from San Diego State. She had numerous credentials displayed, and gold embossed stickers designated her a summa graduate from both schools. The State of California Bar Association empowered her as a member in good standing.

Dark wooden built-in shelves provided a wall of fame. Either Birdie was star-struck or she ran in exalted circles.

She had pictures of herself with the Governator and Diane Feinstein, Lance Armstrong and Brandi Chastain. There was a shot of her with Francis Ford Coppola in front of his winery and another with Robin Williams with the Coast highway in the background.

The photographs propped on the big tiger oak desk were more personal. There were shots of the Bonner Flower Farm, which Sarah recalled had been founded by Birdie's counterculture parents. Another photo showed Birdie and her husband, Ellison Shafter, whom Sarah's father said was a pilot for United.

There was also a picture of Birdie's brother, Will. Either it was an old photo, or he hadn't changed a bit. In Sarah's head, Shirl's voice asked, *Why should you change if you're already perfect?*

Of all the people Sarah remembered from high school, she remembered Will Bonner best. This was ironic, since he had probably never known her name. The framed photo triggered a flood of memories she didn't know she had. Standing there in the unfamiliar office, the antique pine plank floor creaking beneath her feet, she was surprised to discover old resentments festering in secret beneath the surface. Her life with Jack had formed a gloss over the past. Maybe that was why she'd married him. He took her away from people like this.

Now that he was out of the picture, there was nothing standing between her and old memories, and she fell into the past like Alice down the rabbit hole, grasping at stray roots on her way to the bottom.

She scowled in hostility at the picture of Will Bonner. He grinned right back at her. He had been in the same grade as Sarah, but unlike her, he was the epitome of high school perfection—a top-ranked athlete, blessed by all-American good looks. He had jet-black hair and the same twinkling eyes that used to make her knees melt when he looked at her. Not that he ever actually looked at her. Embarrassed by her futile and utterly predictable crush, Sarah had fought back the only way she knew how. In the underground comic book she self-published in high school on an old mimeograph machine in the basement, she'd depicted Will Bonner as a vain, bull-witted, steroid-abusing poster boy. He probably hadn't noticed her biting satire, either, but it had made her feel…not better…but vindicated. More in control.

No doubt he wasn't aware that she had sat in front of him in Honors English all four years, or that she made sketch after sketch of him, telling herself she needed the studies for her underground comics. Bonner had treated her as if she were a piece of furniture.

The years since high school had brought about at least one huge change, Sarah observed. In the picture, he was holding a dark-haired child whose face was buried against his burly shoulder. Some guys looked awkward with kids, like contestants on *Fear Factor.* Others, like Will Bonner, looked at ease and natural, approachable.

Under different circumstances, Sarah might be filled with questions about her high school obsession. Not now, though. Now, she had to explain her situation to Birdie and figure out what to do next.

Pulling her gaze away from the array of photos, she forced herself to wait quietly. The shock of leaving Jack had still not completely subsided, and that was probably a good thing, because it kept her numb. She was like a soldier with a limb blown off, staring uncomprehendingly at empty space. Later, she supposed, the pain would come. And it would be like nothing she'd ever felt before.

There was a fee schedule posted on the wall, like the specials menu of a restaurant, or a list of services at a beauty parlor, only it covered legal matters rather than hairstyles—family law, immigration, wills and probate, elder law. Sarah tamped back a feeling of apprehension. Could she even afford a lawyer? She suspected that none of her transactions would be simple. Or cheap.

She couldn't let money—or a lack thereof—stand in her way, though. She had to reinvent her life. Starting now.

"Thanks for waiting." Birdie stepped into the office. She had shed the cycling getup and donned a more familiar look—unbleached cotton, Dansko clogs, no makeup and an open, guileless expression of earnestness. On Birdie, the look didn't seem contrived. She wore the natural style well, as though she had invented it.

Yet the sight of her, looking so sincere and inoffensive, gave Sarah second thoughts. What had become of the meanest girl in school? Had she gone soft, just when Sarah needed a hard-ass? She needed a lawyer who would protect her interests through this process—she couldn't quite bring herself to use the D-word yet—not Mother Earth.

"No problem," Sarah said. "Thanks for seeing me on short notice."

"I'm glad I could work you in."

A soft burble from the intercom box interrupted her. "Sorry to interrupt you, Ms. Shafter," said the receptionist, "but there's a deadline attached to this. It's Wayne Booth of Coastal Timber."

Sarah moved toward the door, but Birdie waved her back, covered the receiver mouthpiece and said, "I won't be a minute." Then her posture changed. She stood straighter, held her shoulders back. "Wayne, I've already given you my client's answer. If that's your best and final offer, then we'll let a judge do better." She paused, and an angry voice crackled at her. "I understand perfectly, but I'm not sure you do. We're not playing a game here..."

Sarah watched as the earth mother turned into a corporate dominatrix, chewing out the legal counsel of a major timber company, getting her way and then gently setting down the phone. When she turned her attention back to Sarah, she looked serene and unflappable, as though the exchange had never happened. Sarah knew she'd found the right lawyer after all. The mean girl had figured out how to harness her powers.

They shook hands and took their seats, Sarah in a comfortable upholstered chair and Birdie at her desk. Sarah took a deep breath and plunged right in. "I just got here from Chicago. I've left my husband."

Birdie nodded, her expression turning soft with sympathy. "I'm sorry."

Sarah couldn't speak. Birdie pushed a box of tissues closer to her but Sarah ignored them. She twisted her wedding set around and around her ring finger. She really should take it off, but it was from Harry Winston, three carats total weight, and she couldn't think of a safe place to keep it.

"Is this a recent development?" Birdie asked.

Sarah nodded. "As of last Friday." The clock in her car had read 5:13 when she had peeled away from Shamrock Downs and Jack and Mimi Lightfoot and everything she'd ever believed about her life. How many women knew the precise moment their marriage cracked apart?

"Are you safe?" Birdie asked her.

"I beg your pardon?"

"I need to know if you're safe. Is he violent? Have you ever had an incident of domestic abuse?"

"Oh." Sarah deflated against the back of the chair. "Oh, God, no. Nothing like that." In truth, she felt as though a violent act had been committed against her, but it wasn't the sort you could report to the police. "He was unfaithful."

Birdie sent her a matter-of-fact look. "You should get tested, then."

Sarah regarded her blankly, uncomprehendingly. *Tested.* Then it dawned on her. Tested for STDs. For HIV, even. *Son of a bitch.* "I, er, yes, of course. You're right." A cold ball of fear formed in her gut. The realization that he'd put her in physical danger added fresh horror to the betrayal. "Sorry. That didn't occur to me until now. I still can't believe Jack did this."

"Jack." Birdie opened the laptop on her desk. "I'm going to make some notes here, if that's all right."

"Sure. This is all new to me."

"Take your time. So your husband's legal name...?"

"John James Daly," Sarah supplied. "I kept my maiden name after we married."

"And that was..."

"We've been married five years as of last June—2003. I met him when I was in college—University of Chicago—and married him right after graduation."

Birdie nodded. "The *Bay Beacon* ran a beautiful picture and did a little piece about it."

Sarah was surprised Birdie had noticed the picture and remembered it, but perhaps that had more to do with the uneventfulness of small-town life than to Sarah's importance. The twice-weekly local paper had always kept readers abreast of small matters—weddings and births, tides and the weather, roadwork and school sports. When she was in high school, Sarah had submitted some editorial cartoons to the *Bay Beacon,* but the paper's editor had declared them too edgy and controversial. Ironically, her drawings had poked fun at big-city developers vying for the chance to build shopping malls and condos right next to America's most pristine national seashore.

"I never saw the piece," Sarah said. "We live—I mean, I lived—in Chicago." She twisted the wedding set some more. "I wish I'd come back to visit more often than I did, but Jack never liked coming here, and time just seemed to slip by. I should have pushed harder. God, I feel like such a loser."

"Let's get one thing straight." Birdie folded her hands on top of the desk.

"What's that?"

"You don't ever need to justify yourself to me. I'm not here to judge you or to hold you accountable or anything like that. I'm not going to criticize any choice you've made, insult you or divulge details about your personal life to strangers."

Sarah's face burned with shame, because she knew exactly what Birdie was referring to. When Birdie was a senior in high school, she'd had a breast reduction. It was no secret; after all, she'd gone from having a triple D rack to wearing tank tops. Sarah had lampooned it in her underground comics. Why not poke fun at the meanest girl in the school? Now Sarah knotted her hands in her lap. "I'm sorry about that stupid high school comic book."

"Don't be. I thought it was funny."

"You did?"

"Yeah, kind of. Back then, I tended to like anything that was about me. I was awful in high school, with or without the boobs. To be honest, I sort of liked the attention of being featured in the funny pages. It was a long time ago, Sarah. Let's hope we've both moved on."

"I'm still drawing," Sarah admitted. "I have a syndicated comic strip, but I get my inspiration from my own life these days, not other people's."

"Good for you." Birdie shook her head. "Some people spend their whole lives filled with regrets about stuff that went on in high school. I've always wondered why that is. It's just four years. Four lousy years in a life that can span a century. Why do people get so fixated on those four little years?"

"Good question," Sarah said quietly.

Birdie took a form from the printer on the credenza behind the desk. "This outlines the terms of our agreement. I want you to read it carefully and call me if you have any questions."

The sheet was covered with dense legalese, and Sarah's heart sank. The last thing she wanted to do was wade through this. But she was on her own now, and she had to look out for herself. She studied the first paragraph, and her eyes started to glaze over. "Do you have a *Reader's Digest* version of this?"

"That's as simple as it gets. Take all the time you need." She waited while Sarah read over the document, seeing nothing questionable—other than the fact that this was going to cost a lot of money. She signed the agreement and dated it at the bottom. "Done," she said.

"Done. So let's get started. Mind if I record this interview?"

"I guess not. What are we going to talk about?"

"I need the whole story. Everything from the beginning."

Sarah glanced at the old-fashioned clock on the wall. "Do you have other appointments this afternoon?"

"I have all the time you need."

"He's in Chicago," she said. "Can I be here and, um, divorce him if he's in Chicago?"

"Yes."

Divorce him. It was the first time she'd actually said it aloud. The words came out of her yet she didn't understand them. It sounded like a foreign phrase. She was mimicking random syllables in a strange tongue. *Div Orsim. Divor Sim.*

"Yes," she repeated, "I do want a divorce." Then she felt sick. "That's like saying I want to disembowel myself. That's how it feels right now."

"I'm sorry," Birdie said. "It's never easy. But one thing I can tell you is that even though the loss hurts, it also creates new space in your life, new possibilities."

Sarah fixed her gaze on a spot out the window, where the waters of Tomales Bay flowed past. "I never meant to stay in Chicago," she said. "Never could get used to the god-awful weather there. After graduation, I planned to live in San Francisco or L.A., work for a paper while trying to get a comic strip into syndication.

"Then I met Jack." She swallowed, took a deep breath. "His whole family is in the construction business. He got a contract from the university to build a new wing for the commercial-art studio, and I was on the student advisory committee, with the job of supplying input for the designers."

She felt a smile turn her lips, but only briefly. "The students would feed them our pie-in-the-sky ideas and Jack would tell us why our plans wouldn't work. I drew a series of satirical cartoons for the student paper about the situation. When Jack saw them, I thought he'd be furious. Instead, he asked me out." She shut her eyes, wishing the memories were not so painful. But God, he'd been charming. Handsome and funny and kind. She had adored him from the start. Often, she'd wondered what he saw in her, but she didn't dare ask. Maybe she should have asked. She opened her eyes and stared at her knotted-together fingers.

"The family welcomed me with open arms. They treated me like their newest daughter." She still remembered her sense of wonder at the historic mansions in the shady neighborhood where Jack's family had lived for generations. "You have to understand, this was huge for me. After losing my mother, my dad and brother and I unraveled. It just felt so good to be with a real family once again. Jack grew up in the same place and had friends he'd known from nursery school. So I just…stepped in to this ready-made world. It seemed effortless. I suppose I was in love with him from the beginning and was changing my plans for the future by the third date."

From where she was now, she could look back and see that, for her, the process of falling in love had been an act of survival. She had lost her mother and was drifting out to sea. Jack—and all he stood for—was a solid object to cling to, something she could grasp with all her might and pull herself to safety.

Somewhere in the distance, a siren sounded, the throaty blast of a fire engine. Sarah's mouth was dry. She got up and went to the water cooler and poured herself two cups of water. When she turned back to Birdie, she felt momentarily disoriented. She sat back down and sipped the water.

"It's all right to cry," Birdie said.

Sarah pictured herself floating out to sea alone again, like Alice in Wonderland drowning in her own uncontrollable tears. "I don't want to cry."

"You will."

Sarah took a deep breath and another sip of water. She didn't feel like crying, yet her sense of loss was intense. She was coming to realize that she had lost so much more than a husband. Her ready-made community of family and friends. Her house and all her things. Her own identity as Jack's wife.

"We got married in Chicago," she reported to Birdie. Their wedding had been lopsided, the friends of the groom outnumbering the friends of the bride by ten to one, but Sarah hadn't minded. People adored Jack and she was proud of that. She had counted herself lucky to find a ready-made group of friends and a warmhearted family. "No assembly required," she had told him with a grateful smile. "We went to Hawaii for our honeymoon. I never did like Hawaii, but Jack just assumed I did."

She hadn't seen the truth then. She barely caught a glimmer of it now, but she was starting to understand. From the moment she met Jack, she was a satellite to his sun, reflecting his light but possessing none of her own. Her wants and needs were eclipsed by his, and it all felt perfectly fine to her. They lived in his world, did the things he wanted and became a couple according to his vision, not hers.

Every once in a while, she would make a suggestion: What about Mackinac Island instead of Hawaii? Or the Chateau Frontenac in Quebec City? He would pull her into his arms and say, "Yeah, right. It's Hawaii, babe. Cowabunga." And so it went. She found herself listening to country-western music that made her cringe, and learned to stay awake during White Sox and Cubs games.

"And the thing was," she told Birdie, "I was happy. I loved our life together. Which is probably crazy, because it was nothing like the life I would've chosen."

"It was the life you had," Birdie reminded her. "The fact that you liked it is a blessing. How many people endure a life they hate, every day?"

Sarah looked at her sharply. She suspected the rhetorical question was more about Birdie than about rhetoric.

"So here's the big irony about what happened next," Sarah said. "After our fairy-tale wedding and dream honeymoon, he wanted to start a family right away. For once, I asserted myself. I insisted on waiting a year or two, at least. I planned to focus on my career, so I lobbied hard to keep up the birth control a while longer."

"This is the twenty-first century," Birdie reminded her. "I don't think you're going to raise any eyebrows with that."

"Not at the time. I think it was the one decision in our marriage I truly owned. The one choice that belonged to me and me alone."

"Why do you say it's ironic?"

"Because that one decision almost killed Jack."

Five

Forty minutes before the end of Will Bonner's duty shift, the quick-call went off—"Battalion! Fire and Ambulance Stand By!"—followed by two tones, signaling an alarm. Will acknowledged immediately, summoned Gloria on the loud-speaker, then yanked the ticket from the printer. After years of following routine, he had the exit down to a bare minimum number of moves. He donned gear as he strode from the office, snatching HTs up off the charger. Then he was off, out the door in less than a minute, shifting seamlessly from where he was a moment ago to the place he was headed. That was the life of a firefighter; one minute, watching reruns of *Peyton Place* on the SOAP channel, the next, checking the area map, putting on his bunker gear, jamming his feet into boots.

The town of Glenmuir boasted a Seagrave rescue pumper, circa 1992, and a crew of captain, engineer and a rotating stable of volunteers. While Gloria Martinez, the engineer, cranked up the engine and the volunteer crew went to their on-board stations, Will and Rick McClure, one of the on-call volunteers, jumped into separate patrol vehicles and sped ahead to find the fire. That was the trouble with nonspecific reports, like the one that had just come in. Someone would call, reporting that smoke was visible. In these parts, the term "yonder" was considered a cardinal direction.

Locals were skittish about fires in these parts. The legendary Mount Vision fire of '95 still haunted the landscape with skeletal black trees, ruined structures, meadows choked with the nonnative fireweed that took hold after the disaster.

As he headed up a nameless road labeled Branch 74, he scanned the horizon for some sign of the reported glow or header of smoke. Although he stayed focused on the search, his mind flashed on a thought of Aurora. This was going to make him late to dinner. Yesterday, he'd missed career day at her school.

"No big deal," she'd told him. "It'll be just like last year."

"I missed last year."

"Like I said. It'll be just like that."

At thirteen, his stepdaughter had a tongue as sharp as her appetite for teen fashion magazines, which, by Will's judgment, she spent far too much time reading. When she was little and he had to leave her for a duty cycle, she used to throw a tantrum and beg him not to go. Now thirteen, she was either dismissive or brittle and sarcastic about his absences.

Will preferred the tantrums, if forced to make a choice. At least they were straightforward and over quickly. Being father and daughter used to be pretty effortless even though they were not related by blood. Will loved being her dad, and when Aurora's mother took off, that didn't change. If anything, it increased his devotion to her.

For a single parent, the job of fire captain was a mixed blessing. The schedule meant he got to be with her for long stretches of time, yet his absences were equally long. When he was on duty, she stayed with Will's parents or, occasionally, her aunt Birdie and uncle Ellison. The arrangement had worked for years; it was one of the reasons he stayed in Glenmuir. Without the infrastructure of his family, raising Aurora would be next to impossible. His parents considered it a joy and a privilege to care for her—a sweet-natured, bright and beautiful child who had come into their lives like an early springtime. Now that she was thirteen and at odds with the world, he wondered if she was becoming too difficult for them to handle.

If he dared to suggest such a thing, his family would think he'd lost his mind. His parents, who ran an organic flower farm, believed sincerely in karmic balance and the idea that life never gave a person more than he could handle.

Will spotted the black billows of smoke rising over a familiar ridge just beyond the hamlet of San Julio, then radioed Gloria with the milepost marker and sped to the scene. He wasn't sure whose property this was, a rolling spread of hay and alfalfa. No dwelling in sight, but a barn was on fire, the entire front a mask of flame. He slammed the truck into Park, leaving the keys in the ignition in case the vehicle was needed. Rick parked the other vehicle some distance away and ran to join Will, who was already surveying the area. A shadow flirted in his peripheral vision, and he turned in time to spy a stray dog.

He'd seen it around before, a collie mix with matted black-and-white brindled fur. The sight of Will and Rick in their helmet and bunker gear sent it racing away at top speed.

"I hope like hell this barn is used for storage, not livestock," he called to Rick.

"I hear you." Rick, a young volunteer just out of training, squinted a little fearfully at the building.

"I'm going to have to do a search of the premises," Will said, reminding himself that not so long ago, he'd been as green as Rick McClure. By the time the engine arrived, Will had donned his SCBA, though he didn't hook up the mask. He hoped he wouldn't need to put himself on air.

He went around the perimeter, radioing a report to his battalion chief. One good sign—he couldn't hear any sounds of trapped livestock. That kind of thing—it tended to etch itself on a firefighter's soul. With no rescue involved, saving the building wasn't the goal here; it was going up like tinder. But they needed to kill the fire to keep it from spreading to the surrounding wildlands.

The plan was to vent the blaze through a large panel door on sideways rollers. Will radioed task assignments to the engine crew. While the helmeted firefighters were pulling hose, he signaled for Rick to open the door and stand ready with the portable extinguisher. The goal was to vent in order to delay flashover—the transition from the fire's growth stage to the explosive eruption of the entire structure—until the hose line was in place. Then the fire would be pushed out through the front of the building. The blast of heat was always expected, yet always a surprise. When he was a rookie, it used to scare the crap out of him, that pressure pulsing against his face, an invisible force like the hammers of sound at a loud rock concert.

The fire was at the rollover stage, with lightning flashes of flame through the smoke. He heard a hiss and figured his air bottle was blistering in the heat. Cathedral-like, the tall Nordic-style barn was bathed in unholy light, the stacked bales of hay burning like a giant funeral pyre. I'm okay, he said, as he always did in these situations. I'm okay. In his mind, he made a clear picture of Aurora, his best reason to survive.

Birdie went to the window and lowered it to keep out the noise of a distant siren. Then she sat back down and leaned her forearms on the desk. "Sarah, I don't understand. Why do you say your decision to delay starting a family almost killed your husband?"

"If I'd agreed to try to get pregnant right away, like Jack wanted, we would have realized sooner there was a problem." Sarah cleared her throat. "How much detail do you need here?"

Birdie seemed to understand. "Don't worry about detail for now. Unless you think it's information I need in order to help you."

At some point, Sarah knew she would be forced to reveal the most intimate details of her marriage, opening them up like an unhealed wound to expose the raw nerves. She knew enough about divorce to realize this was part of the process. Knowing this didn't make it easier, though. Exposing her private pain behind the guise of her comic strip was one thing, but discussing it openly was quite another.

"Eventually, I wanted kids as bad as he did. Both of us seemed to be in fine health. So when we didn't get pregnant for a whole year, we checked things out. For some reason, we expected to find something wrong with me, not him." Determined to leave the wedding set alone, she picked up a pen and rolled it between the palms of her hands.

"I think it's a fairly common assumption," Birdie said. "No idea why, but it is."

Once it was determined that there were no problems with Sarah's fertility, Jack agreed to be checked out by his uncle, a urologist. Sarah braced herself for a report of low sperm count or poor motility or impaired delivery. In fact, the tests had revealed something far worse.

"Testicular cancer," she told Birdie. "It had metastasized to the lymph nodes in the abdomen, and to his lungs."

The oncologist's can-do attitude was reassuring. "Statistics and projections aren't going to turn this around. Fighting with everything we've got—that's what'll turn it around," the doctor had said. Jack was also lucky to have supportive friends and family. His parents and siblings had rallied around him the moment the diagnosis was made. People who had known him since nursery school came to see him, to hang out and add their good wishes to the seemingly bottomless pool of support.

"You have to understand," Sarah told Birdie, "when something like this happens, the whole world stops. You drop everything. It's like joining the military, and the disease is your drill sergeant. We started treatment right away, aggressive treatment. Thanks to his age and general good health, they went at it hard."

"Interesting that you say *we* started treatment. Not *Jack* started treatment."

"We were a team," Sarah explained. "The disease invaded every moment of our lives, waking or sleeping." She flicked the pen tip in and out, in and out. "Actually, I'm not sure if this is important now or not—we took care of one small detail before we started treatment."

"And the one small detail?"

"It was the doctors' suggestion. Jack and I were too panicked and scattered to think of it. Jack was advised to preserve some sperm samples. The treatment carried a risk of infertility so this was a precaution." She smiled a little. "Jack was always a bit of an overachiever. He preserved enough sperm to populate a small town. And up until last week, this story had a happy ending." More or less, she thought. Jack's performance at the sperm bank had been far more productive than his performance had been with her.

"Sorry, I need to clarify. You were his chief support during the treatment?"

"Financially, no. Fortunately, Jack and his family are extremely well-off. I barely had a career."

"The comic strip you mentioned earlier?"

Agitated, she continued clicking the pen up and down, up and down. "Yes. It's called *Just Breathe.*"

Birdie leaned back in her chair. "It sounds terrific, Sarah. Really."

"It'd be better if I was actually making a living wage. For the time being, I'm self-syndicated, which means a lot more work for me but ultimately, more independence and a bigger share of the earnings. When Jack was sick, I put aside the syndication work and did advertising art and greeting cards. I never stopped drawing my strip, though. In fact, during the worst days of the treatment, I did some of my best work. But I can't honestly say I contributed financially in any major way."

"How about moral and emotional support? And in the area of his care?"

"I did things I never thought myself capable of." She stopped, surprised to feel a wave of emotion as she was swept back to the endless, anguished postchemo nights, when even love and prayers were not enough to comfort him, when she held him while he shook with chills, when she cleaned up his puke and changed his bed as he moaned in agony. "I'll spare you the details of that. Suffice it to say I was steadfast, and anyone who tries to deny that I supported him is a liar."

"And the happy ending?"

"Before all this happened, I would've told you our happy ending was the day he was found to be cancer free and his treatments were stopped. I guess there's no such thing as a happy ending. Life is too damned messy for that. Things don't ever end. They just change." She looked down to see that she had completely disassembled the pen in her hands.

Birdie folded her arms on the desk and pretended not to notice. "So was there any point when you suspected your marriage was in trouble?"

Shamefaced, Sarah lined up the broken pieces of the pen on the desk—the cartridge, the tiny spring, the tube, the pocket clip. "It was the last thing on my mind. The last thing I was looking for. I was so full of gratitude and sheer elation over Jack's recovery that I couldn't see straight. I swore then, to myself and to Jack, that I was ready for a family. More than ready. It's stupid to postpone something you know you want. Life's too short. At the time, I had no idea that trying to get pregnant was a sign of desperation. I thought if I could make us look like a happy family by having a baby, then we would magically be a happy family." She carefully threaded the cartridge through the coil. "We tried both ways."

"Both ways?"

"Naturally and by artificial insemination. After treatment, Jack had a good chance of regaining fertility, so we both had high hopes. But…we didn't have much intimacy during or after his illness. He, um, couldn't perform and eventually quit trying." Sarah screwed the two parts of the pen tube together. "He still claimed to want a family. In fact, it was his idea to keep up the fertility treatments and the artificial insemination. Our lack of success turned out to be a blessing in disguise, I suppose. Bringing a child into our mess would be a disaster." The pen's clicker didn't work. She would have to take it apart and try again.

Sarah had come to realize that the rift had existed long before it was discovered. It had progressed and spread out of control by the time Mimi Lightfoot came along.

"After the illness," she said, "I kept reminding myself I was in a posttrauma state. We both were. So while I was going to the fertility clinic every time I ovulated, Jack was dealing with the trauma in his own way. I don't know when he hooked up with Mimi Lightfoot, but I bet it was a while back." The name tasted bitter in her mouth.

"This is the woman he was unfaithful with," Birdie prompted.

"Yes. He started a huge building project about eight months ago—luxury homes in a neighborhood designed for equestrians, and he was incredibly busy all the time." Sarah couldn't believe what a dupe she'd been. It had all the sorry hallmarks that had become clichés—late, vaguely described meetings, canceling engagements with her. Begging off sex with her. "I thought he needed more time to come to terms with what happened to him, but I had faith that he'd get over it. And he did, I guess. Just not with me."

She took a deep breath and told Birdie the worst part—the events of that cold and rainy day, her last as a happily married woman. She told about her loneliness for her husband after going to the fertility clinic by herself. She told about stopping for pizza on the way to visit him at the work site, because he loved pizza and she wanted to surprise him. She even told about the moment she had walked in on every woman's nightmare.

The eerie calm that had enshrouded her since that night was growing threadbare in places as flashes of emotion crept in—anger at Jack, shame and humiliation, a sickening sense that she had lost her dreams. She felt bombarded by thoughts of the babies that would never be, the perfect home that had only been an illusion.

Until now, dazed shock had insulated her from facing the hard questions about what might have been had she done something differently. Numbness dulled the embarrassment of having to air her dirty laundry to a virtual stranger, muffled the body blow of knowing the life she'd taken such satisfaction in was a sham.

Forced to describe her husband's infidelity, she felt her womanly pride bleeding on the floor. She struggled through this, the hardest part of her narrative. "So there you go. The end of happily-ever-after." Slumping back in the chair, she sensed fatigue sneaking up to conquer her. She had buzzed across the country on an adrenaline rush. Finally, exhaustion spread over her, pressing down.

"You know," she concluded, "I do have one big regret."

"What's that?" asked Birdie.

"I wish I'd ordered black olives on the damn pizza."

Six

Will Bonner walked around the smoldering barn, studying the ruined structure in silence. He took a bandanna from his back pocket and wiped his face. He should be home already, fixing supper with his kid. Unfortunately, people who started fires showed no regard for the captain's duty schedule. He was counting his blessings, though. The barn had been vacant.

Vance Samuelson, one of the volunteers, and Gloria Martinez, the engineer, were putting the truck back in order.

"Well?" asked Gloria, loosening her suspenders, "what's your assessment?"

"Deliberate," Will said, motioning her to the middle of the floor. The roof lay in corrugated metal sheets around them. The surface was still hot beneath his feet. "That's what the arson investigator will rule. But they can only figure out so much. To find out who's doing this, we'll need you and me. Hell, we'll need the whole county." He stuck the bandanna in his pocket and led the way out of the wreckage of the barn. "I'm pissed off, Gloria. This reminds me of that incident almost five months ago, the one I haven't figured out yet."

"It's the arson investigators' job to figure it out, not yours. You've got your own job to do."

He nodded and peeled off his protective jacket, which now felt like a sauna. "In theory. We know this community. We know who's doing what, who's feuding with his neighbors, who has money troubles, whose kids are out of control. We'll be the ones to figure out who's setting these fires."

"Sooner rather than later, I hope." She scuffed her boot in the black cinders around the foundation of the barn. "Same culprit with both fires?"

"Probably. I think he used different accelerants for number one and number two."

"Just what we need. A smart arsonist."

"He's not supposed to be smart," Will reminded her. "According to profile, he's got below-average intelligence."

"Maybe he's addicted to crime shows. You don't have to be smart to copy something they demonstrate step-by-step on TV."

"Crime shows provide such a valuable public service," he said, feeling weariness settle into his bones. "They make our job so much easier." He rolled back one sleeve, checking his forearm for a burn. The skin was bright red, appearing slightly sunburned. The dragon tattoo, imprinted on a much younger, much stupider Will Bonner, was unscathed. He checked his watch, then put on his dark glasses. "I'm going to be late getting home. Again. You want to have dinner with us?" He often invited her, and not just because he liked and respected her. So did Aurora, and lately, his stepdaughter seemed to prefer discussing shoe shopping with Gloria to hanging out with Will.

Gloria sent him a weary smile. "Thanks, but I have plans." She patted him on the sleeve. "See you around, partner."

The Mini still had that new-car smell even though Sarah was its second owner. Following her meeting with Birdie Shafter, she got behind the wheel, feeling wrung out. She didn't know what to do next and didn't really have a road map.

She told herself there was no shame in being back in Glenmuir. Soon the whole town would know she had returned home in defeat—a woman betrayed—and that her perfect life in Chicago had been a sham. But so what? People started over all the time.

Her phone was ringing. She checked the screen, tamped down a jolt of panic and took the call. "How did you get this number?"

"We should talk," Jack said, ignoring her question. "My folks think so, too. Everybody does."

"I don't. My lawyer doesn't." Actually, Birdie hadn't said so specifically, but she had advised Sarah not to give him any more information than necessary at this point.

"You have a lawyer?" Jack demanded.

"And you don't?" She suspected he had called Clive Krenski the moment—the very second—he had thrown on his clothes that day, still sticky with Mimi Lightfoot. His hesitation confirmed it.

"I already gave her Clive's number," Sarah said. From the brick-paved town parking lot, she had a view of the harbor and of Glenmuir's picturesque square. It looked as quaint and pristine as the set of a nostalgic movie, with striped awnings over the shop fronts, bowls of water set out for any dog that might pass, lush flower baskets suspended from the light poles and businesses that respected the town's resistance to change. There were no franchise stores or glaring signs, just an air of simpler times past.

"Don't do this." Jack sounded drained and stressed-out.

Her old habit of worrying about every breath he took threatened to kick in. She stiffened her spine against the seat back. "Her name is Bernadette Shafter—"

"Oh, perfect—"

"—and I'm not going to discuss certain things with you."

"Then how about you listen?"

She stared out at Tomales Bay. A flotilla of brown pelicans bobbed on the water under a late afternoon sky of layered blue and cotton candy clouds. Jack hadn't liked Glenmuir. He considered it a backwater, a place where old hippies might go to die…or become oyster farmers. Though years had passed, she still remembered that jab at her father. It had bothered her then and it bothered her now. The difference was, now she was doing something about that and all the other little hurtful things he'd said and she'd swallowed while making excuses for his lack of consideration.

"I'm listening," she said.

"You can't just piss away five years of marriage—"

"No, you did that." She watched some seagulls rise in a flock, creating a shadow on the water. "How long have you been with her?" Sarah asked.

"I don't want to talk about her. I want you to come back."

Sarah was stunned, not just by his words but by the fear in his voice. "You want me to come back. What for? Oh, here's an idea. We can get tested together. Yes, Jack. As if being cheated on isn't bad enough, I'm going to have to get tested for STDs. We both are." She blinked back tears of humiliation.

"That's not a factor. Mimi and I are exclusive."

Are. Not were. "Really? And you know this…how?"

"I just know, okay?"

"No, it's not okay, and you have no idea who she was with before you."

"She was—" Jack fell silent for a moment. Then he said, "Sarah, can we not just throw this away? I'm sorry I said I wanted a divorce. That was stupid. I hadn't thought anything through."

Oh, my. Apparently Clive had explained the fiscal pitfalls of running off a perfectly good wife. "So are you saying you've changed your mind?"

"I'm saying I never meant it in the first place. I was scared, Sarah, and embarrassed and guilty. To hurt you that much…it's the last thing I wanted. I was in panic mode, and I handled it badly."

She actually felt torn, she noted with an unpleasant jolt. Although she was clearly the injured party, she was at war with herself. The part of her that was conditioned to love him, the part that had carried her through his cancer treatment and her fertilization attempts melted at the sound of his voice. At the same time, the part that had just endured the overwhelming humiliation of the attorney's office was still choking on the devastating memory of seeing her husband screwing another woman.

"I have a headache, Jack. It doesn't matter to me whether you handled it well or badly."

"Forget what I said that morning. I didn't mean it. We can get through our problems, Sarah," he told her, "but not this way."

The flock of birds disappeared, leaving the bay flat and empty, beautiful in the afternoon light.

"Well, guess what?" she asked. "I'm doing this my way for a change."

He hesitated. "We need to talk about us," he said. "About you and me."

"You have no idea what I need." Sarah wasn't angry. She was so far past anger that she had entered a red zone of emotion she had never felt before, didn't even know existed. It was a tight, ugly place with dark corners where rage festered and gave rise to images she never realized she could conjure. These were not pictures of her doing horrible things to Jack, but to herself. That was what frightened her most of all.

"Sarah, come home, and we'll—"

"We'll what?"

"Deal with this like people who care for each other instead of communicating through lawyers. We can't just call it quits. We can fix this, go back to the way things were."

Ah. Initially he'd spoken from an angry, impulsive, honest place. After the lawyer explained what this would cost him, he was filled with remorse.

She saw a chartreuse-colored pickup truck merge onto Sir Francis Drake Boulevard and troll slowly northward. The side door bore the seal of the city of Glenmuir, established 1858. There were red conical lights on the top, a big tank with some sort of pump in back. A sun-browned, tattooed arm, with the sleeve rolled back, was propped on the edge of the window. The driver turned a little and she caught a glimpse of a baseball cap and dark glasses.

"Why would I want that?" she asked Jack. She'd spent most of the cross-country drive thinking about the way things were. The hours and hours of driving alone had forced her to confront the harsh truth about her marriage. She'd been fooling herself for a long time about being happy. She'd been acting like a contented, fulfilled wife, but that wasn't the same as being one. It was such a lousy thing to realize about yourself. She took a deep, steadying breath. "Jack, why would I want to go back to the way things were?"

"Because it's our life," he said. "Jesus—"

"Tell me about the bank accounts. All four of them." A strange feeling came over her. Deep inside, she discovered a core of calmness that radiated outward like a general anesthetic. "How soon did you put a freeze on them? Did you remember to zip your pants first?" Actually, she knew the answer. He had made his move within hours of the pizza delivery. In Omaha, she had stopped at an ATM to make a withdrawal from their joint checking account, only to find that the card was declined. The same was true of the other three accounts. Fortunately for her sanity, she had a credit card she used for syndication business. And, though she had never seen it that way before, she had an ace in the hole. There was a large sum of money in an account she held in her own name. On the advice of their CPA and Clive—who, up until now, she had considered a friend—she had opened the account when Jack's cancer had been discovered. If the worst happened, there might be some decisions she would have to make on her own.

The decision to divorce her husband had not occurred to her back then.

"I did that to protect both of us," Jack said.

"Both of us? Oh, I see. You and your lawyer, you mean."

"It's clear you're not thinking straight. I got a call from the bank about a transaction with State Line Auto Sales—"

"Ah, so that's what's got you worried," she said, suddenly realizing the true reason for his call. "And here I thought you called about me."

"Now you're trying to avoid the subject."

"Oh, sorry. I traded the GTO for a car I actually want."

"I can't believe you did that. Of all the childish, immature things... You had no right to trade in my car."

"Sure I did, Jack. I bought the thing, remember? The title's in my name."

"It was a gift, dammit. You *gave* it to me."

"Boy, you sure know how to scold a girl about a car," she said. "I'd like to hear what you have to say about something *really* bad, like...oh...infidelity?"

He didn't bother responding to that. How could he? "I wish I could take back what I did, but I can't. We have to move on, Sarah—together. We can heal from this. I need a chance to make it up to you. Please come home, sugar-bean," he said, using his pet name for her in a voice that used to beguile her.

Now it just made her queasy. With a curious feeling of detachment, she stared at the scene in front of her—a sleepy seaside town. Two women chatting on the sidewalk. A shy-looking mongrel flashed around a corner, furtively looking for scraps.

"I *am* home," she said. Birdie had explained that there was an advantage to initiating the divorce from California, a community property state. She had warned Sarah that Jack's lawyer would probably fight it tooth and nail.

"What about everything I gave you?" Jack reminded her. "A beautiful home, anything you wanted or needed. Sarah, there are women who would kill to have those things..."

Jack was still talking when she turned off the phone. He just didn't get it and probably never would. "Those things were worthless." Her hand shook a little as she fitted the key into the ignition. Nerves, she thought. Rage. She knew enough about divorce to realize she was in for the entire painful spectrum of emotions. She wondered how and when they would strike. Would she be smacked down as though hit by a truck, or would the pain creep up on her and lodge like a virus under her heart? Now, for the first time, she fully understood how Jack had felt before undergoing his first treatment. The absolute terror of what she was about to do was excruciating.

She sat and watched the only traffic signal in town turn from yellow to red. At the main intersection, a school bus lumbered to a halt and its stop signs cranked open like a pair of large ears. Sarah suspected it was one of the same buses she had ridden all her life. The sides were stenciled West Marin Unified School District. Judging by the ages of the kids who emerged from the bus, this was from the junior high. She watched a group of schoolkids with backpacks walking down the streets, pausing in front of the candy store to dig through their pockets for change. Some of the boys were smooth-cheeked while others sported a five o'clock shadow. The girls, too, came in a variety of shapes and sizes, their manner ranging from awkward to cool.

One of the cool ones—Sarah could spot them a mile off—was a self-possessed blond demigoddess who made a big production of lighting a cigarette. Sarah flinched, wondering where this girl's mother was and if she knew what her daughter was up to.

Once again, Sarah told herself it was a good thing her quest to get pregnant was over. Kids were a constant challenge. Sometimes they were downright scary.

The last to emerge from the bus was a remarkable-looking girl. Small of stature, she had shining jet-black hair, pale skin and the perfect features of a Disney princess. There was a flawless, other-worldly quality about her that made Sarah want to stare. The girl was Pocahontas, Mulan, Jasmine. Sarah half expected her to burst into song at any moment.

She didn't burst into anything, of course, but walked over to the fire department pickup truck. The driver was talking on the phone or a radio. The girl got in, slammed the door and they drove off.

Sarah was a watcher, not a doer. She'd always been that way, watching others live their lives while she lived inside her own head. And it struck her—hard and against her will—that even though she was the wronged party in her marriage, she wasn't blameless for its demise. Ouch.

The black-and-white dog feinted away from a group of boys horsing around, and darted out into the street. Sarah jumped out of the car and dashed toward the mongrel. She shooed it back onto the sidewalk. At the same moment, she heard the thump of brakes locking up. She froze in the middle of the roadway, a few feet from the chartreuse pickup.

"Idiot," the driver called. "I almost hit you."

Embarrassment crept over her, quickly followed by resentment. These days, she was bitter about all men and in no mood to be yelled at by some tattooed redneck in a baseball cap. "There was a dog…" She gestured at the sidewalk, but the mongrel was nowhere in sight. "Sorry," she muttered, and headed back to her car.

This was why she was a watcher and not a doer. Less chance of humiliating herself. Yet now, thanks to Jack, she had discovered that there were worse things than humiliation.

Seven

Flames leapt at the face of Will's daughter. Each individual golden tongue seemed to illuminate a different facet of her pale skin and shiny black hair. The overfed charcoal fire roared at her, seeming to lick her eyelashes.

"Jesus, Aurora," he said, running to the patio to clap the lid on the barbecue grill. "You know better than that."

For a moment, his stepdaughter merely stared at him. Since coming into his life eight years before, she'd owned his heart, but when she did things like this, he wanted to shake her.

"I was firing up the barbecue," she said. "Did you pick up the stuff for the Truesdale Specials?"

"Yes. But I don't recall saying it was okay for you to start the grill."

"You took too long at the store. I was sick and tired of waiting."

"You're supposed to be doing homework."

"I finished." Her eyes, lavishly surrounded by dark lashes, regarded him with reproof. "I was only trying to help."

"Aw, honey." He patted her on the shoulder. "I'm not mad. But I figured you knew better than to start a fire. Think of the headline in the *Beacon* if anything happens—Fire Captain's Daughter Goes Up In Smoke!"

She giggled. "Sorry, Dad."

"I forgive you."

"Can we still make Truesdales?"

The burgers were their special meal, and theirs alone—mainly because no one else would touch them. They were made of SPAM, Velveeta and onion forced through a meat grinder, then grilled and served with a sauce of tomato soup. Heaven on a bun. Aurora was the only person Will had ever known who would eat them with him.

He lifted the black dome of the lid. "No sense letting a perfectly good fire go to waste."

Over the years, of necessity, he had learned to cook. Round-the-clock shifts at the firehouse gave him plenty of time to learn the craft. He was famous for his fluffy pancakes, and his savory beef stew had once won a fire district prize. For someone who'd once expected to be drafted by a pro baseball team, firefighting was an unusual career choice. And for a single stepfather, it was risky, but for Will, it wasn't even a choice. It was a calling. Years ago, he had discovered that rescuing people was what he did best, and risking himself was simply part of the job. And when it came to keeping himself safe, Aurora—his heart—was more powerful than body armor. Failing to come home to her was not an option.

With the burgers sizzling on the grill, he and Aurora worked side by side, putting together a macaroni salad. She chattered about school with the kind of breathless urgency only a seventh grade girl could convey. Each day was packed with drama, rife with intrigue, romance, betrayal, heroism, mystery. According to Aurora, it all happened in the course of a typical day.

Will tried to follow the convoluted saga of someone's text message sent to the wrong phone, but he was preoccupied. He kept mulling over the barn fire, trying to figure out why it had been set, and who had done it.

"Dad. *Dad.*"

"What?"

"You aren't even listening. Geez."

She was getting too good at catching him. When she was little, she didn't notice him zoning out. Now that she was older, she had a well-developed sense of when she was being ignored.

"Sorry," he said. "Thinking about a fire today. That's why I nearly missed picking you up at the bus this afternoon."

She quickly turned, took a jar of mustard from the refrigerator and set it on the table. "What fire?"

"A barn up on one of the branch roads. Deliberately set."

She carefully folded a pair of napkins, her small hands working with brisk efficiency. "By who?"

"Good question."

"So are you, like, totally clueless?"

"Hardly. There are tons of clues."

"Like what?"

"Footprints. A gas can. And some other stuff I can't talk about until the arson investigator finishes his report."

"You can tell me, Dad."

"Nope."

"What, don't you trust me?"

"I trust you completely."

"Then tell me."

"No," he said again. "This is my job, honey. I take it a

hundred percent seriously. You heard anything?" He glanced at her. Kids at school talked. Arsonists were proud of the work they did, and typically enjoyed a sense of notoriety. They could never keep quiet about anything for long.

"Of course not," she said.

"What do you mean, of course not?" He slid two SPAM burgers onto grilled buns and brought them to the table.

"I mean, you're assuming someone at school would actually talk to me." She spoke flippantly, almost jokingly, but Will sensed real pain beneath the remark.

"People talk to you," he said.

She neatly tiled her burger with a layer of pickle slices. "And you would know."

"What about Edie and Glynnis?" he asked, naming her two best friends. "You talk to them all the time."

"Edie's busy with her church group and Glynnis is all freaked out lately because her mom's dating Gloria."

"Why is she freaked out?"

"Come on, Dad. I mean, when it's your own *mom*..." She wrinkled her nose. "Kids don't like their parents dating anyone."

He glowered at her. "Present company included, I assume."

"Hey, if you want to go out with some woman—or some guy, even—don't let me stop you."

"Right." Will knew she had a million tricks up her sleeve for keeping him from dating. Given the roughness of her early years, her clinginess was understandable. No big deal for the time being, though. He wasn't seeing anyone.

"Maybe I set the fire," she suggested. "Out of boredom."

"Don't even joke about that."

"My life's a joke. And I *am* bored. Edie and Glynnis live too far away. I don't have a single friend right here in Glenmuir."

He pictured her at the big glass-and-brick school, a long bus ride into alien territory. Only a handful of kids lived in Glenmuir, but naively he had hoped she would make other friends and head into high school with a bigger peer group. "Hey, I grew up here, too. I know it can be hard."

"Sure, Dad." The look she gave him spoke volumes. She poured warm tomato soup over the burger, then centered the top bun on it. She took a large bite and slowly chewed. Despite her delicate beauty, her fingernails were lined with dirt.

Will knew instinctively that now would be a bad time to make her wash her hands. Lately, he wasn't so hot at reading her mercurial moods, but he knew that much. He had practically made a career out of reading parenting books, even though they all seemed to give conflicting advice. One thing they agreed on was that rebellion stemmed from a need to escape parental control, running up against a need for boundaries and limits. Not that it made dealing with a thirteen-year-old any easier.

"What, you think I had it made?" he asked.

"Hello? Granny and Grandpa told me pretty much your life story. Including the fact that you were this big basketball and baseball star, and a straight-A student."

He grinned. "In their totally objective opinion. Did they tell you I used to bike to school instead of taking the bus because I was scared of being picked on?"

"Like that's supposed to make me feel better?" She ate methodically, without a single wasted movement.

He was grateful to see her eating. According to the

reading he'd done, Aurora was definitely at risk for an eating disorder. She fit the profile perfectly—beautiful, intelligent, driven to succeed…and a loner with self-esteem issues. Abandonment issues, too, given her history.

"How about we discuss things you can do to be happier at school?" he suggested.

"Sure, Dad," she said, stabbing her fork into the macaroni salad. "I could try out for the cheerleading squad or the chess club."

"Either one would be lucky to get you," he pointed out.

"Yeah, lucky them."

"Damn, Aurora. Why do you have to be so negative?"

She didn't answer right away, but took a long drink of milk, then set her glass on the table. A pale mustache arched over her lip, and Will was struck by a jolt of sentiment. He suddenly saw her as the silent child who had come, uninvited, into his life eight years before, clinging to the hand of a woman who had wreaked havoc on both of them and left a raft of emotional wreckage in her wake.

Then, as now, Aurora's looks had been striking, wide brown eyes and glossy black hair, creamy olive-toned skin and an expression of bewilderment at a world that had treated her harshly. From the first moment he saw her, Will had made it his mission to atone for the sins committed against this child. He had given up his dreams and plans for the future in order to protect her.

And not once, not for a single second, did he regret any of the sacrifices he made.

Or so he told himself.

She wiped her mouth with her napkin and suddenly she was thirteen-year-old Aurora again, half-grown, her appearance turning womanly in a way Will found intimidating.

"She's Salma Hayek," Birdie had remarked last summer after taking Aurora shopping for swimsuits.

"Who's that?"

"Latina actress who looks like a goddess. Aurora is absolutely gorgeous, Will. You should be proud of her."

"What, like I had one damn thing to do with the way she looks?"

Birdie had conceded his point. "What I mean is that she's growing into her looks. She's going to get a lot of attention because of it."

"And getting attention for looks is a good thing."

"It was for you, little brother," Birdie had teased. "You were the prettiest thing the high school ever saw."

The memories made him wince. He had been so full of himself, he was probably swollen like a tick with unearned pride.

Then Aurora had come into his life, helpless as an abandoned kitten, and everything else had ceased to matter. Will had dedicated himself to keeping her safe, helping her grow, giving her a good life. In turn, she had transformed him from a self-centered punk into a man with serious responsibilities.

"Why do I have to be so negative?" Aurora mused, finishing every crumb on her plate. "Gee whiz, Dad. Where do you want me to start?"

"With the truth. Tell me from your heart what's so intolerable about your life."

"Try everything."

"Try being a little more specific."

She stared at him, mutiny in her eyes. Then she pushed back from the table and went to get something from her backpack—a crumpled flyer printed on pale pink paper. "Is that specific enough for you?"

"Parents' night at your school." He knew exactly why that upset her, but decided to play dumb as he checked the date. "I can make it. I'm not on duty that night."

"I know you can make it. It's just that I hate it when they expect parents to show up."

"What's so bad about that?"

She plunked herself back down in her chair. "How about I have no mother. No idea who my father is."

"He's me," Will said, fighting now to keep anger down. "And I've got the adoption papers to prove it."

Thanks to Birdie, the family's legal eagle, he had a father's rights. Those had never been challenged—except by Aurora, who sometimes dreamed her "real" father was a noble political prisoner pining away for her in some Third World prison.

"Whatever," she said, her inflection infuriating.

"Lots of kids have single parents," he pointed out. "Is it really that bad here?" He gestured around the room, indicating their house. The wood-frame house, built in the 1930s, was nothing fancy, but it sat a block from the beach and had everything they needed—their own private bedrooms and bathrooms, a good stereo system and satellite TV.

"All right," she said. "You win. Everything is just super."

"Is this some new class you're taking in seventh grade?" he asked. "Sarcasm 101?"

"It's just a gift."

"Congratulations." He clinked his beer can against her milk glass. During his duty cycle, there was no drinking, of course, but on his first night off, he always had one beer. Just one, no more. Heavy drinking meant nothing but trouble. Last time he'd really tied one on, he had wound up married, with a stepdaughter. A guy couldn't afford to do that more than once in a lifetime.

"So spill," he said. "What'll make you happy, and how can I give it to you?"

"Why does everything have to be so black-and-white with you, Dad?" she asked in annoyance.

"Maybe I'm color-blind. You should help me pick out a shirt for parents' night."

"Don't you get it? I don't want you to go," she wailed.

He didn't let on that her attitude was an arrow to his heart. There was never a good time for a child to be left by her mother, but Will figured Marisol had picked the worst possible age. When Marisol took off, Aurora had been too young to see her mother for what she was, yet old enough to hold on to memories, like a drowning victim clinging to a life raft. Over the years, Aurora had gilded those memories with a child's idealism. There was no way a flesh-and-blood stepfather could measure up to a mother who braided hair, served pancakes for dinner and knew all the words to *The Lion King*.

He'd never stop trying, though. "I hate to disappoint you, but I'm going," he told her.

Aurora burst into tears. This, lately, had become her specialty. As if cued by some signal he couldn't see, she leaped up and took off. In a moment, he'd hear a *thud* as she flung herself on the bed.

Will thought about having another beer, but decided against it. Sometimes he felt so alone in this situation, he had the sensation of drifting out to sea. He went over to the slate message board by the door. He and Aurora used it for reminders and grocery lists. Picking up the chalk, he wrote, "Parents' night—Thurs." so he wouldn't forget to attend. Upstairs, Aurora landed on her bed with an angry thump.

Eight

As she drove away from town, Sarah told herself not to dwell on Jack and the things he'd said. Instead, her mind worried the conversation as though seeking hidden meaning in every syllable and inflection: *You're not ready to acknowledge your part in this yet.*

Of all the things he had said, that was surely the most absurd. What was she guilty of? Trading the gas-guzzling GTO for a Mini?

Please come home, Jack had urged her.

I *am* home.

She didn't feel it yet. She had never been comfortable in her own skin, no matter where she lived. Now she realized something else. Her heart had no home. Although she'd grown up here, she had always looked elsewhere—outward—for a place to belong. She'd never quite found that. Maybe she would discover that it was a place she'd left behind. A place like this.

It was a land of lush abundance and mysterious wilderness, demarcated by flat-topped cypress trees sculpted by the wind, gnarled California oaks furred with moss and lichen, forget-me-nots growing wild in hilly meadows and ospreys nesting atop the light poles.

Her father lived in the house his father had built. The Moons were an old local family, their ancestors among the town's first settlers, along with the Shafters, the Pierces, the Moltzens and Mendozas. There was a salt marsh behind the home and a commanding view of the bay known locally as Moon Bay, even though no printed map ever designated it as such. At the end of the gravel road was the Moon Bay Oyster Company, housed in a long, barn-red building that projected partially onto a dock. The enterprise had been started by Sarah's grandfather after he came home wounded from World War II. He had been shot in the leg by a German in Bastogne during the Battle of the Bulge, and he walked with a permanent limp. He had a good head for business and a deep love of the sea. He chose to grow oysters because they flourished in the naturally clean waters here and were prized by shops and restaurants in the Bay Area.

His widow, June Garrett, whose married name—Moon—made her sound like a Dr. Seuss character, was Sarah's grandmother. She still lived in what the family called the "new" house simply because it was built twenty years after the original one. It was a whitewashed bungalow with a picket fence at the end of the lane, a hundred yards from the main house. After Grandpa had died, Gran's sister, May, had moved in with her. The two sisters lived together, happy in their retirement.

Sarah decided to stop in at Gran's before heading to the main house. She had arrived in a whirlwind of fury and grief, and hadn't seen Gran and Aunt May yet. Now that she'd consulted a lawyer and rebuffed Jack's attempt to change her mind about the divorce, she felt more in control. She turned down the lane toward her grandmother's house, the tires of the Mini crunching over the oyster shell gravel of the driveway.

The sounds and smells of the bay and tidal flats caused the years to peel away. With no effort at all, she regarded this place through the filter of memory. For a child, this was a magical realm, filled with dreams and fairy tales. With the sturdy, handsome house by the bay as her home base, and her grandmother's cottage a short walk away, she'd been surrounded by security. She had explored the marshes and estuaries; she'd raced the tide and tossed homemade kites to the wind. She'd lain in the soft grass of the yard and imagined the clouds coming to life. In her mind's eye, she'd turned the clouds into three-dimensional speech bubbles filled with words she was too shy to say aloud. This had been her dreamworld, scented with flowers and alive with blowing grass and the buzz of insects. As a child, she'd been a great reader, finding the ultimate escape within the pages of a story. She learned that opening a book was like opening a set of double doors—the next step would take her inside to Neverland or Nod, Sunnybrook Farm or Mulberry Street.

When she started high school, Sarah's attitude changed. That, she suspected, was when her heart had come unmoored from this place. She became self-conscious about the family business. Other kids' parents were dot-com millionaires, lawyers, rich movie execs. Being an oyster farmer's daughter made her a total misfit. That was when she taught herself to disappear. In her many sketchbooks, she designed special places of her own, filling them with everything she wanted—adoring friends, puppies, snow at Christmas, floor-length dresses, straight-A report cards, parents with normal jobs, wearing business suits to work instead of rubber aprons and gum boots. She let herself forget the magic; it was teased out of her by kids who made fun of the very idea of living in this rustic, seaside family compound.

Reflecting back on those days, she realized what a dumb kid she'd been, letting someone else's perception dictate the way she felt about herself. Independent and solvent, her family was living the dream, an American success story. She'd never appreciated that.

"It's me," Sarah called through the screen door.

"Welcome home, dear," Gran said. "We're in the living room."

Sarah found her grandmother waiting with open arms. They hugged, and she shut her eyes, her senses filling with the essence of her grandmother—a spicy fragrance redolent of baking, soft arms that felt delicate, though not frail. She stepped back and smiled into the kindest face in the world. Then she turned to Aunt May, Gran's twin, every bit as sweet and kind as her sister. She almost wished they were not so sweet; for some reason, their sweetness made her feel like crying.

"So did Dad tell you?" she asked.

"He did indeed, and we're very sorry," Aunt May said, "aren't we, June?"

"Yes, and we're going to help you in any way we can."

"I know you will." Sarah shrugged out of her sweater and sank into an ancient swivel rocker she remembered from her childhood. "I survived my first meeting with the lawyer."

"I'll make you a chai tea," Gran said.

Sarah sat back and let them fuss over her. She took comfort in their homey clucking and in the fact that they never changed a thing in their house. They had the same cabbage rose carpet on the floor, the same chicken-print tablecloth. As always, Gran's area of the living room was a storm of clippings and magazines piled haphazardly around her chair. Sketchbooks and an array of drawing pencils littered a side table. By contrast, Aunt May's side of the room was painstakingly neat, her knitting basket, TV remote and library stack arranged just so. This had always been a place of familiar things, where she could always find a homemade fig-filled cookie, or lose herself in Gran's display of World's Fair souvenirs, or simply sit and listen to the twins' murmured conversation. It was soothing, yet at the same time there was something stifling about this place. Sarah wondered if the sisters ever felt trapped here.

Because they were twins, the sisters were considered a bit of a novelty, and always had been. Growing up, they had enjoyed the peculiar social status afforded young ladies who happened to be pretty, popular, well-mannered and nearly identical. The story of their birth was the stuff of legend. They were born on the last day of May, at midnight during a terrific storm. The attending doctor swore that one twin was delivered a minute before midnight, and the second a minute after. Hearing this, their parents named them May and June.

Although biologically they were fraternal twins, most casual observers had trouble telling them apart. They had the same graceful drifts of white hair, the same eyes of milk glass blue. Their faces were all but indistinguishable, like two apples side by side, drying in a bowl.

Despite their physical resemblance, the sisters were polar opposites in many ways. Aunt May was conventional and neat as a pin. Gran was considered bohemian in her day; she preferred painting over housework and raising a family. More traditional, Aunt May dressed in calico cotton prints and crocheted shawls; Gran favored overalls and tribal print smocks. Both women, however, spent their lives fanatically devoted to family and community.

"You probably don't want to talk about your meeting," Aunt May suggested.

In this family, denial was a fine art. "I'll spare you the details."

Gran served the chai in a Raku-fired mug. "You probably need a break from brooding about all this nonsense, anyway."

Sarah tried to smile back. Relegating her shattered marriage to "all this nonsense" did seem mildly amusing at that.

Her grandmother and great-aunt willingly changed the subject. They chattered on about the things that filled their days. Gran and Aunt May seemed to be completely without ambition or curiosity about the world beyond the quiet, protected bay. They organized things—the annual Primrose Tea. The Historical Society's benefit banquet. They presided over a monthly bridge tournament and faithfully attended meetings of the garden club. Currently they were preoccupied with projects and plans, as always, working on their presentation on bulbs for the Sunshine Garden Club. And if that didn't keep them busy enough, they had to get the place ready to host their weekly potluck and bunco game.

Sarah marveled at how seriously they took these social functions, as if they were matters of life and death.

The old women studied Sarah, then exchanged a glance filled with meaning. What was it with twins? Sarah wondered. They had some crazy Vulcan mind link, and seemed capable of holding whole conversations without saying a word.

"What?" Sarah asked.

"You don't appear to have much patience for things like garden club meetings and bunco evenings."

"I'm sorry, Gran. Just preoccupied. And tired, I guess." She tried to look interested. "But if they're important to you—"

"They're important to all of humankind," Aunt May said.

"Garden parties?" Sarah squeaked. "Bunco games?"

"Oh, dear. Now she's irritated," Gran said to her sister.

"I'm not irritated. Mystified, maybe, but not irritated." Deep down, she wondered how it could possibly mean a thing that Reverend Schubert's birthday party had fresh flowers or that they put out the good china for their potluck.

"Showing respect and thoughtfulness to those we care about is the part that matters. It's what separates us from the beasts of the field."

"The cows in Mr. Prendergast's pasture seem pretty content to me."

"Are you saying you'd rather be a cow?"

"At the moment, it sounds very appealing to me." As a cheeky, awkward teenager, Sarah had unleashed her pen, drawing comic satires of the Historical Society's display of the Drake landing, or creating send-ups of the women of the garden club, chattering away while birds built nests in their fantastically ornamented straw hats.

"Someday you're going to tick off the wrong person," her older brother, Kyle, had warned her. He had dedicated his life to pleasing his parents. Every time Sarah attempted to do this, she failed.

But mostly, she realized, she'd failed herself. When you lived your life to please others, there were hidden costs that often outweighed the rewards. Years later, in the wake of the ultimate failure—her marriage—she was finally waking up to that fact. Looking around her grandmother's house, she wondered if she was seeing a glimpse of her future. The thought depressed her, and she felt the old ladies studying her.

"You're home, dear," said Gran.

"Home where you belong," Aunt May added.

"I never really felt like I belonged here."

"That's your choice," Gran pointed out. "Deciding where you belong is a choice."

Sarah nodded. "But…I don't want to be that divorced woman who moves back to her father's house. That's just…pathetic."

"You're entitled to be pathetic for a while, dear." Gran smiled gently at her. "No need to rush into anything."

With her grandmother's permission to be pathetic, Sarah made her way down the lane to her father's, passing marshes fringed by wild iris, with the green-draped coastal hills looming in the distance. She parked in the driveway and went into the garage, a handyman's nirvana with an adjacent workshop. Generations of tools hung on the walls and littered the workbench, and the sharp odor of motor oil tinged the air. A half-dozen projects occupied benches and sawhorses, all related to her father's new passion—restoring his 1965 Mustang convertible.

"Dad," she called out. "Hello?"

There was no answer. He'd probably gone into the house. Sarah hesitated, haunted by memories she hadn't thought about in a very long time.

Her mother used to work in the well-organized garage annex. Jeanie Bradley Moon had been a master spinner and weaver, known for her textiles of cashmere and silk, created on a counterbalance loom of cherrywood. She and Sarah's father, Nathaniel, had met at a local artisans' market and were married only a few months later. They'd made a life here together, raised Kyle and Sarah. She still remembered the long, late-night girl-talks with her mom—her rock, the most steady thing in her life. Or so she thought. Now she yearned to talk with her mother again, and the wish felt like a rock crushing her chest. How could her mother just be gone?

Sarah took a deep breath and stepped into her mother's world, a place of shadows and skeletons now. This was the hardest spot on earth for Sarah to be, because it was where memories of her mother burned the deepest. At the same time, she felt the irresistible pull of remembrance as she looked around the room. It used to be a hive of activity, alive with the clack of the loom and the smooth, quick rhythm of the treadle. But all that had changed eight years before.

Sarah had been a sophomore at Chicago when the call came from her sister-in-law, LaNelle. Kyle and Nathaniel were in shock, so it had fallen to LaNelle to give Sarah the devastating news.

She'd lost her mother.

Sarah had never understood why people used the term "lost" when somebody died. She knew exactly where her mother was—unreachable, untouchable, felled by an aneurysm that was as heartless and indiscriminate as a bolt of lightning. What did you do when the mooring you'd been clinging to was suddenly taken away? What were you left holding?

She still hadn't found the answers. Yet here in the shop, it looked as though Jeanie had stepped out for a minute to check the mail. Everything was the same as she'd left it eight years before—the balls of spun yarn tucked neatly in their cubbies, a peony-pink swath of fabric still hanging from the loom, waiting for the next row to be woven.

Sarah was the one who was lost. It was as if someone had pulled a dark hood over her face, spun her around until she was dizzy, then thrust her forward, to grope her way blindly through life, praying she would find something to hold on to.

Eventually she had—Jack Daly. She had held fast to him, hauling him home like a trophy for having survived her loss. She held him up as proof that she had transformed herself from an oyster farmer's daughter into a career woman, adored by the likes of Jack Daly. She wanted to shout to the world—look at what I've made of myself. *Look at the man who loves me—a prince from Chicago.*

She had taken pride in showing off her handsome, successful fiancé to a town that considered her a loser. Like Cinderella, she wanted the world to know she'd found the mate to her favorite pair of shoes, and was about to marry a prince. She had it all—the glass shoes, the hot guy, the golden future.

To give him his due, Jack had played his part. Everyone could see how good-looking he was. They had visited the town at the height of springtime's Primrose Days, when the eucalyptus trees festooned themselves in long, willowy foliage, the hills exploded with wild iris blossoms and lupine, and the steelhead were running in the mountain streams. The pristine inland sea of Tomales Bay and the craggy western shores that edged the Pacific created a dramatic backdrop for her triumphant homecoming.

And again, in true fairy-tale fashion, her boastfulness had unintended consequences.

"When am I going to meet your friends?" Jack had wondered.

He had to ask. There were people who knew her, acquaintances of her parents, former classmates, employees of the Moon Bay Oyster Company, Judy the Goth, a clerk at Argyle Art & Paint Supply. Sarah had run around with a group of other misfits, but hadn't stayed in touch with them after high school. She'd fumbled through an explanation. "I was never very social…."

"You must've had friends." To a guy like Jack, who was surrounded by a vast and happy group of friends—good friends, real ones—this was unthinkable. There was no way Sarah could explain this to him. No way he could understand that her entire adult life was spent trying to escape her adolescence, not relive it.

Unable to produce a vibrant social group from her past, she suggested they leave Glenmuir a day sooner than planned, ostensibly to play tourist in San Francisco but actually to get away from reminders of the person she'd been. After that, she embraced Jack's world and it had embraced her. His parents were like a latter-day Ozzie and Harriet. He had enough close friends to populate a small town. At his side, she was liked and accepted, even admired.

The idea of coming home after that, to the empty house on the bay and her father looking lost, was flat-out painful. She made subsequent visits home without Jack, spending quiet hours wishing she could ease her father's agony, but failing at that. Her father soon took to visiting her in Chicago, and his company was a comfort to her during Jack's illness.

Now she felt like a stranger here, her footsteps sounding hollow in the empty workshop. She studied the ball of bright pink cashmere yarn still on the spool, remarkably untouched even now, as though endlessly waiting. I still see you in dreams, Mom, she thought. But we never talk anymore.

She touched the top of the spindle with the tip of her finger. Suppose she were to prick herself and bleed, and then fall asleep for a hundred years?

Good plan.

"I'm home," she said, putting her purse and keys on the Formica counter in the big, sunny kitchen of her father's house.

"In here," he called out. In his easy chair, with catalogs spread out on the coffee table in front of him, Nathaniel Moon looked like a man of leisure. He had certainly earned the privilege. Before retirement, he had the business to grow and teach to Kyle. Now that he'd stepped back, he spent most of his free time researching and restoring the Mustang.

"You look busy," she said.

"I've been reading up on how to repair an intake carburetor," he said.

These days, his passion consumed him. When not over at Mounger's garage, working on the car, he was surfing the Internet for parts or watching car restoration shows on television. Sarah saw him disappearing into the car the way she disappeared into her art.

Embarrassingly enough for his children, he had become a babe magnet since being widowed at a relatively young age. He was a kindly, tolerant man, unfailingly polite as he rejected the women vying for his attention.

Everyone in town knew Nathaniel Moon, and everyone liked him. "Such a nice, good-looking man," people often said.

Sarah could not disagree with a single thing that was said. Yet she felt now, as she had all her life, that she didn't really know him. He was like a TV dad—well-groomed, sympathetic, benign and ultimately unknowable.

"Does this town have an animal control department?" she asked him.

"I think so. Why? Did you spot an animal out of control?"

"A stray dog. I saw it nearly get hit in the middle of downtown."

"We're a progressive area," he said. "We have a no-kill shelter."

"That dog better hope you have no-kill drivers."

"I'll see if I can find a number for you. How did your meeting go?" he asked without looking up from the catalog he was studying.

"It went. I was surprised Birdie Bonner remembered me."

"She's Birdie Shafter now," he reminded her. "Why surprised?"

"Because we weren't friends," Sarah said. "We went to the same school, but we weren't friends. I never had many friends."

He flipped a page. "Sure you did, honey. There were kids over all the time when you were young."

"Those were Kyle's friends. Remember him? My perfect brother? The only time people came to see me was when Mom put the squeeze on their mothers and they were forced, or bribed."

"I don't remember that at all." He flipped another page.

She studied her father, saddened by the distance between them. There was plenty more she could say. She wished she could ask him if he missed her mother the way she did, if he still saw his wife in his dreams, but she felt used up, too emotionally frazzled to deal with her father's curious distance.

"Come on," he said, standing up with an unhurried motion. "Let's take the boat out. I'll bring something to eat."

She wanted to say she wasn't hungry, she'd never eat again. The fact was, she was starving. Betrayed by her own primal greed.

Within fifteen minutes, they were out on the water, the Arima Sea Chaser pushing up a V-shaped wake behind them. They pulled out into the channel and slowed down to trolling speed so the motor would run quietly. Powerboats were restricted on the pristine bay, but as a local oysterman, her father was exempt. The feel of the soft vinyl-covered seat, the rich smell of the tidal flats and the taste of the air evoked a feeling of days gone by. For a short while, time flowed away. The marriage and Jack's illness and his final betrayal might have happened to someone else.

Her father opened a beer and offered her the can. She reached for it, then hesitated.

"Not your brand?" he asked.

In the pit of her stomach, she felt a swift, dull terror as the illusion shattered. Those years had happened to her.

Her father studied her face. "Did I say something wrong?"

"No, I just… It's been a while since I've had a drink. Before all this happened, we were trying to get pregnant."

He looked supremely uncomfortable, his eyes crinkling behind his shades. "So, um, are you…?"

"No." Part of her wanted to tell him about the clinic visits, the drugs and discomfort and nausea. Another part wanted to keep her pain private. "After Jack's treatments ended," she went on, "getting pregnant was my main goal in life." Hearing herself speak the words, she felt a twinge. When had her priorities shifted from her marriage to her reproductive system?

"Anyway, I'm not," she said quickly, knowing this conversation was going to be a challenge, "and I'll take that beer." She took a swig, savoring her first gulp. God, it had been too long. "For the past year, I've been undergoing artificial insemination."

He cleared his throat. "You mean Jack couldn't… because of his cancer?"

She looked out across the water. "The doctors always encouraged us to set positive goals during treatment, the logic being that every reason for him to get better reinforced his recovery."

"I'm not sure it's a baby's job to be that reason."

Sarah felt a stirring of defensiveness. "We wanted to start a family, same as any other couple." After all that had happened, she was forced to examine her real motives. Deep down, she had known for a long time that something was wrong, something that having a child would not fix.

"So anyway," she said, trying to get the conversation back on track, "I might as well celebrate my new freedom." She tipped her beer in his direction. "And I promise, that's all the detail you'll get from me."

Clearly relieved, he slumped back on his seat. "You've had a tough break, kiddo."

"I hope it's not too weird, me telling you this stuff."

"It's weird," he admitted. "But I'll deal with it."

She ducked her head to hide a smile. Her father was a Marin man, through and through, trying to be sensitive.

"You warm enough?" he asked.

She savored the flow of the breeze over her face and through her hair. "I've been living in Chicago, Dad. Your worst weather feels like a heat wave to me." She pictured herself in Chicago, shoveling snow off the driveway in order to get her car out. She had once drawn Shirl digging her way out of a second-story window and escaping to Mexico.

"What's funny?" her father asked, steering the boat around a landmark known as Anvil Rock.

Watching the undulating green hills go by, she said, "Nothing, really. Just amusing myself with my own thoughts."

"You were always good at that."

"Still am. Birdie offered to give me the names of some therapists but I kind of like psychoanalyzing myself."

"How's that working for you?"

"It's not that hard. I'm not a very complicated person." She hugged her knees to her chest. "I feel so stupid."

"Jack's the one who ought to feel stupid."

"I bargained with God," she confessed to her father, speaking up midthought as if he had been in on her private reflections.

And maybe he had been. He said, "What'd you bargain for?"

"Jack to recover."

He nodded, sipped his beer. "Can't say I blame you."

"So is this my punishment? God spares Jack's life, and I have to lose Jack?"

"God doesn't work that way. He didn't cause this. Your shit-for-brains, two-timing husband caused this."

She doubted Jack would see it that way. He was surrounded by friends and family who adored him, whose regard ran strong and deep. The same people who had rallied around him when he'd fallen ill were undoubtedly there to support him through his marital crisis. They would persuade Jack that he was as blameless in this as he had been in getting sick, that his wife had backed him into a corner, pressuring him to make a baby. She wasn't there to observe this but she knew it was true because she knew Jack. The people in his life were his means of validation. He needed them in the same way she needed ink and paper to draw. Sarah used to think she was the one he needed most, but that was not the case, obviously.

Jack claimed that she shared responsibility for the demise of their marriage, and in a traitorous part of her heart, she had to wonder if that was true. Had she played a part? In her dogged quest for a baby, had she put undue stress on Jack? One of the issues she'd had to face was the fact that their marriage had been in trouble long before she found out about Mimi. Yet despite the facts staring her in the face, Sarah still resisted the notion, digging in her heels and denying there was anything wrong.

"Thanks for saying that, Dad," she said, watching the majestic scenery. As an angry teen, she'd lost her appreciation of the dramatic beauty of the forests and cliffs reaching down to the sea. It was only when she settled in Chicago that she could look back and see that the prison of her adolescence, which had seemed so oppressive to her, was finally revealed to be a paradise. In Chicago she'd been like a tree uprooted and then planted in the wrong spot, a place where it wasn't getting enough light or water. She tipped back her head and felt the sun's warmth on her cheeks.

"I'm too calm," she told her father.

"What's that?"

"About Jack. I'm too calm."

"And this is a bad thing?"

"It would be normal to fall apart," she said. "Don't you think?"

"Normal for what?"

"For me. For anybody."

"I honestly don't know, honey."

The comment awakened an old ache inside her, of the reality of her relationship with her father. In the deepest possible way, they simply did not know each other; they never had. For no reason she could think of, they had never done the work of building a relationship. Maybe this was their chance to do that. In the suck-ass situation she found herself in, perhaps there was an unexpected opportunity.

"Dad—"

"It'll be dark soon." He brought the Sea Chaser around and headed back toward home. "Hang on."

Nine

In the wake of Aurora's outburst, Will finished his dinner unhurriedly. Experience had taught him that it was pointless to follow her to her room when she was like this. She'd just wail about the injustice of the world and refuse to listen to a damn thing he said. She needed time to cool off; then he'd sift through the ashes of her mood and try to determine the cause.

After a long shift, he liked to come home to a little peace and quiet, catch up on the mail and bills, maybe play a round of one-on-one with his daughter in the driveway. Lately, however, he never knew what to expect when he got home. His cheerful, predictable daughter was going through growing pains, and he was seeing more pain than growing. She had learned to push his buttons by bringing up the subject of her mother. He couldn't tell if she was truly tormented by what Marisol had done, or if this was a way to get to him.

Feeling weary, he got up and took his dishes to the sink, leaving Aurora's on the table. She could put her own supper dishes away. That was the rule, and he'd be damned if he'd change it just because teenage aliens were taking over her body.

Yeah, that was it. His sunny, funny daughter, whose face used to be as open as a flower in springtime, had been hijacked. In her place was this moody stranger who argued and challenged, whose secretive silences perplexed him, whose wounds he could neither see nor heal.

Damn. She scared him, a fact he could barely admit to himself. It was true, though. Will Bonner, fire captain and ace public servant, was terrified that he was going to do something wrong or irreparable with this child, who had come to him so damaged and needy. This was a life, not a toy, and everything mattered so very much. He was scared because he didn't want to blow it. He was constantly questioning himself. Am I being too harsh with her? Too lenient? Should I change this crazed schedule, find her a therapist? A mother?

The notion poked at him as it sometimes did when Aurora brought up the topic. He used to have no problem being everything she needed in a parent. Then puberty hit her, and a new, tense dynamic arose. The young woman inside Aurora was a stranger to him, and she seemed to need things he couldn't give her. But a mother wasn't something he could provide by the sweat of his brow, like a roof over her head.

Restless with worry and discontent, he caved in and cleaned up her side of the table. There was no crew or team of investigators to help him solve this one. He wanted to protect his daughter and give her a happy life, but despite his best efforts, she seemed to be slipping away from him, and he didn't know how to get her back.

"Special delivery," called a voice through the back door.

Will went to open it for his sister. Preceded by a giant bouquet of white peonies, Birdie came into the kitchen and set the pail of flowers on the counter. "Left over from that wedding in Sausalito," she explained. Their parents' flower farm did a brisk business in weddings. "I thought Aurora might like them."

"Thanks, but Aurora doesn't like anything these days."

"Aren't we in a good mood," she observed.

"We're in a shitty mood," he admitted. "That kid could pick a fight out of thin air. Tonight she played the you're-not-my-mother card and got all pissed off about..." He could hardly remember. "About nothing," he concluded.

Birdie found a pair of mason jars under the sink, spread a newspaper on the table and took out a pair of scissors. Watching her, Will felt a glimmer of insight. A guy knew flowers were pretty enough in their own right. He would have left the pail on the counter and that was that. It would never occur to him to arrange the flowers in a vase or jar. The more Aurora acted like a girl, the harder she was to comprehend.

"You know, little brother," Birdie said over her shoulder, "I don't call myself an expert on child rearing, but this seems like normal teenage behavior to me."

"What's normal about being miserable?"

"It goes away, like the fog in the morning. You watch. In a few minutes, she'll be back to her old self."

"For how long? I might look at her the wrong way and she's back to hating me."

"I'd say that's actually a healthy thing."

"What, hating me?"

"Think about it, Will. She's perfect in every other area of her life. Perfect in school, perfect when she's with Ellison and me, perfect when she's with Mom and Dad. And yet she's human. She has to have some way to express things that are less than perfect. A safe way." She snipped off the flower stems to a more manageable length.

"And I'm that way."

"I think so. On some level, she knows that no matter how bad she is, how angry or rebellious, you'll never leave her. You're her soft place to fall." She stepped back to study the flower arrangement, tweaking them here and there.

Will was quiet for a moment. Maybe Birdie was on to something. Maybe Aurora did save all her bad behavior for him. He'd never, ever leave her, and she knew it.

"I'll talk to her," he told his sister.

"Let me know if I can help," Birdie said. She paused and looked at the spread-out paper. It was open to the comics section. "Ever read the funny pages?" she asked.

"Sure. Doesn't everybody?"

"I guess."

"Why do you ask?"

"My newest client is a comic strip artist. Remember Sarah Moon from high school?"

"Heard of the Moon family, of course." He frowned, trying to recall someone named Sarah.

"She was in your graduating class, moron. She drew that anonymous comic strip everyone was obsessed with, the one that satirized practically everyone in the school."

Will clapped his hand on his forehead. "I remember her." He flashed on an image of a sharp-featured, skinny blond girl, slipping around corners when you least expected her, owlishly observing everything with a critical eye. She had drawn blistering parodies of Will in high school, depicting him as a brainless side of steroid-pumped beef. "She was a nightmare. So what about her?"

"She just moved back to Glenmuir."

"Oh. Is she in some kind of trouble?"

"I wouldn't tell you if she was."

Didn't matter, Will thought, not in a town like this. He'd find out the whole Sarah Moon story through the mysterious and invisible grapevine, sooner rather than later.

Part Three

JUST BREATHE

Ten

Sarah woke up in her childhood bedroom, her heart pounding with terror. Since returning to Glenmuir, she had been stalked by unremembered nightmares—nameless, faceless fears that plagued her sleep and caused her to awaken drenched in sweat and gasping for air. She struggled to calm herself, trying to focus on the familiar details of the room.

For a few moments, the sense of unreality was profound. The softly draped, white iron-railed bed felt like a raft set adrift in time. Practicing a set of breathing exercises she'd learned in a yoga class, she floated beneath a duvet cloud.

The sweat gradually evaporated and her heart slowed down. There was a time when she might have tried to recapture her nightmares, pick them apart, try to discover the meaning hidden within. These days, she didn't want to remember. She just wanted to escape. And she knew damned well what the meaning was. She had cut the moorings of her old life and she was lost at sea. She was grief-stricken, mortally afraid, physically ill. Depressed.

Being aware of the condition didn't make it bearable,

unfortunately. It simply made her feel more powerless than ever. At some point, she should probably drag herself to the doctor, get some meds for it. When Jack was sick, she'd been offered a menu of ways to cope, with pills at the top of the list. She hadn't taken advantage of any of it. Weirdly, she felt compelled to suffer. Her husband had cancer, and trying to escape through a little hexagonal pill seemed artificial and cowardly. Instead, she had disappeared into her art, drawing, working her emotions through made-up figures on a blank white page.

She didn't have to suffer for Jack anymore. She didn't have to suffer at all. She needed to see a doctor, go on medication, but she was too depressed to get out of bed.

She had no idea she possessed the capacity to sleep so much. Normally, she loved getting up early. In Chicago, she would awaken at the crack of dawn with Jack, fix a pot of coffee for him. With *Morning Edition* playing on the radio, they'd each go through "their" sections of the paper. Business and sports for him, editorial and lifestyle for her, with special attention paid to the comics section.

This had not been the scenario in the very earliest days of their marriage. Back then, the morning news had been the last thing on their minds. The radio would be set to sexy blues or gentle cabaret music, a sound track for their newlyweds' lust. They used to make love for an hour or more, until Jack realized he was going to be late for work. Then, with Sarah laughing at his haste, he'd rush through his shower and make a dash for his car, an English muffin clamped between his teeth, a thermos of coffee in hand and the twinkle of a satisfied husband in his eyes.

Then, along with illness came an end to those early days. Instead of massage oils and muted jazz tunes, their nightstands became littered with bottles and blister packs, trays for catching vomit, crumpled instruction leaflets from the medical team and reams of seemingly endless paperwork related to Jack's treatment and its cost.

There was no returning to the couple they'd been as newlyweds. Sarah thought she'd accepted that. She pretended not to mind the more tame morning routine they followed—traffic reports on the radio, the crinkle of newspaper pages turning.

"I'm an idiot," she whispered to the sloping ceiling of her bedroom, her gaze idly tracking a bar of sunlight that seeped through a gap in the drawn curtain. She had told herself she and Jack were maturing as a couple, not drifting apart. Somehow, she had managed to delude herself that this distance was a normal phase in any relationship.

But she had never managed to convince herself to be happy about the gradual shift. Her subconscious kept whispering that something was wrong. She tried to shut it up as best she could, burying herself in work, dreaming about the family they'd have one day and trying to think up ways to revive her intimacy with Jack.

What a waste of time, she thought now, reaching for her sketch pad and favorite drawing pencil, which she always kept on the nightstand beside her. She made a rough sketch of Shirl telling her mother, Lulu, "I should learn to listen to my subconscious."

And Lulu, a wisecracking divorcée recovering from a boring thirty-year marriage, replied, "Dear, you don't need a subconscious when you have me."

"Oh, man," Sarah said, the sketchbook slipping from her fingers and flopping on the floor. "Don't do it, Shirl. Do not do what I think you're about to do."

She burrowed under the covers and shut her eyes. Shirl sometimes had a mystifying habit of exhibiting a mind of her own. Losing control of a figment of her imagination was probably a form of insanity, but Sarah couldn't deny that it happened. She never knew what Shirl was going to do until Shirl made up her mind.

Sarah decided to sleep some more. But she knew when she woke up again that her comic strip was about to take a turn in a direction she had not planned. After splitting up with Richie, Shirl was going to move in with her mother.

"At least that means I haven't gone completely bonkers," she told her editor on the phone, when Karen Tobias called her later that week.

"How so?" Karen asked. She was the comics page editor for the *Chicago Tribune*, which carried *Just Breathe*, and she'd given Sarah her biggest break to date.

"Well, a lot of the story line was starting to look like my life, maybe too much so. But with Shirl moving in with her mother, well, that's completely different. My mother's been gone for several years, so if I were to move in with her, that would be sort of tragic, you know?"

"Not to mention gross."

Sarah yawned, wondering how she could feel so exhausted after a nap. "Anyway, I'm happy about this new development. It proves Shirl and I are completely separate entities."

"Because she's going to live with her mother."

"Right."

"And at the moment, you are living where?"

"Glenmuir, California, remember? I told you, I came back home and moved in with my father."

"And this is different from Shirl…how?"

"Now you're being sarcastic. You're not my therapist."

"True. If I was that, I'd actually know what advice to give you."

"I don't want any advice. Didn't Virginia Woolf say, if I quiet the voices in my head, I would face the day with nothing to write."

"Did Virginia Woolf say that?"

"Maybe it was van Gogh."

"And things worked out so well for them." Karen cleared her throat. Then Sarah heard a pause and an inhale, and she pictured her editor lighting a cigarette. This was not good. Karen only smoked in times of extreme stress. Sarah braced herself.

There was another inhale, followed by a lengthy exhale. "Sarah, listen. We're doing some reorganizing of the page."

Sarah wasn't naive. She'd been in the business long enough to know what that meant. "Ah," she said, yawning again. "You're cutting the strip."

"If it was up to me, I'd keep you on. I love Lulu and Shirl. But I've got a budget to make."

"And some syndicate is offering you two cheesy, factory-drawn, brain-dead strips for the price of one."

"We've had some complaints. You know that. Your stuff is edgy and controversial. That sort of thing belongs in editorials, not the funny pages."

"Which, by the way, are not exactly funny if you fill them with bland, inoffensive tripe," Sarah pointed out.

Karen exhaled again into the receiver. "You know what's sad?"

"Getting divorced and fired in the same month," Sarah said. "Believe me, that's way sad."

"What's sad," Karen said as if Sarah hadn't spoken, "is that I don't have the budget to keep a strip I love. Sarah, you should consider going with a syndicate. That way, you don't live or die by one paper."

"And I don't have to be fired to my face."

"Well, there is that."

"How long?" Sarah asked.

"I didn't make this decision lightly. I was forced into it."

"How long?" Sarah asked again.

"Six weeks. It's the best I can do."

"I'm sure it is."

"Hey, I'm under a lot of pressure here."

"And I'm tired. I need to sleep." Sarah hung up the phone and drew the covers over her head.

Eleven

"What's with all the parental controls on your computer, Aurora?" asked Glynnis Ross, who was in a three-way best friendship with her this year. The third leg of the triangle was Edie Armengast, who sat on Aurora's other side as the girls studied the computer screen.

"My dad has it rigged that way," Aurora said. "Keeps me from checking out porn and gambling sites."

"Keeps you from downloading songs, too," Edie said, glaring at the screen in frustration.

"How are we going to hear the new Sleater-Kinney?" Glynnis asked, twisting a bright yellow LiveStrong bracelet around and around her wrist.

"We'll do it at my house tonight," Edie said. "You're still planning on sleeping over, right?"

Reaching across Aurora, they gave each other a high five. She slumped back in her chair. A three-way friendship had its drawbacks. Sometimes two could band together to make the third member feel left out. They didn't do it on purpose. In this case, simple geography was the culprit. Glynnis and Edie lived in San Julio, across the bay from Glenmuir, and their houses were walking distance apart. They slept over at each other's practically every Friday and Saturday night. Aurora couldn't wait until she was good enough at sailing to make the crossing by herself in the catboat. Then she'd join in the sleepovers anytime she wanted.

"We're supposed to be picking topics for our social studies reports," Aurora said. The assignment was to interview somebody in the community about their job. "Have you done that?"

"I figure I'll talk to my uncle, the DJ," Glynnis said.

"Can't," Edie told her. "Didn't you read the assignment? It can't be anybody you're related to."

"Then Aurora could do her dad," Glynnis said with a snicker.

Aurora felt a chill, as if she'd swallowed a scoop of ice cream too fast. "I can't believe you said that."

"I was only joking."

"It's not funny," she said. Glynnis had a nasty streak sometimes.

"It's *really* not funny," Edie said, siding with Aurora. "It's totally mean."

Glynnis sniffed. "You have to admit, it's kind of weird that you live with your stepfather, Aurora."

She hated when people commented on the situation. When pressed, she did her best to make her biological father sound special. He was a political prisoner. A government agent. A humanitarian dissident in hiding.

She couldn't do much about her mother's story, not here in Glenmuir, anyway. Most people in town knew the situation. A lot of them probably knew more than Aurora herself.

"You and I both have single moms, Glynnis," Edie said.

"So do lots of kids, but they usually live with their mother or sometimes their father. A stepfather is definitely considered weird," Glynnis maintained.

Glynnis tried hard to be cool about the fact that her mother was gay, even though she was obviously skeezed out about it. At least Glynnis *had* a mother.

Aurora figured that to outsiders, it must look as though she didn't have even one real parent who wanted her. It looked that way to Aurora, too, when it came down to it. By now, she'd heard every nosy question in the book. *What happened to your real parents? Don't you have any blood relatives? Or the kicker, How come your stepfather is only fourteen years older than you?*

So is my mother, Aurora would think when someone asked her that, but she never said so aloud. She tried not to dwell on the fact that she was now the same age her mother had been when she got pregnant with Aurora.

Long ago, Aurora had stopped asking her father why her mother had left. But she'd never stopped wondering. Mama had worked at a demanding job. She kept house for Gwendolyn Dundee, whose giant barge of a Victorian mansion sat up on a hillside overlooking the bay. Heiress to a timber fortune, Mrs. Dundee employed a small staff to keep her estate running smoothly. And she worked them hard. Mama often came home cranky and exhausted, filled with complaints about Mrs. Dundee's fussiness over her Erté crystal collection or her annoyingly perky cockapoo.

"You might be getting a stepmom of your own one of these days." Edie nudged Glynnis in the ribs.

Glynnis shuddered. "Don't get me started." As if eager to change the subject, she clicked another link on the computer. "Maybe one of us could interview Dickie Romanov. He's supposedly related to the Czar of Russia."

"There is no Czar of Russia," Aurora said.

"Not anymore," Glynnis agreed, scrolling through the high school alumni list. "Some of the Romanovs escaped and came to America and went into the fur trade."

"My mother says Dickie has a head shop," Edie said. "Last I checked, they didn't sell fur at head shops. Just roach clips and bongs and stuff." She acted as if she knew what she was talking about.

"One of us could talk to that woman who owns the art supply and paint store," Aurora said. "Judy deWitt. She did those metal sculptures in the town park." The idea of interviewing an artist appealed to her, since art was her favorite subject.

"We could ask her where she got her tongue pierced," Edie said with an exaggerated shudder.

"What's wrong with getting your tongue pierced?" Aurora asked.

"It's a sign of brain damage," said her dad, coming into the room. "At least, that's what I've heard." He tossed Aurora a sack of Cheetos and handed out cans of root beer. "Hey, rugrats."

Aurora flushed. He'd been calling her friends rugrats for about a hundred years and they were probably as sick of it as she was. "You've got a tattoo," she pointed out. "What's that a sign of?"

He absently rubbed his arm. His shirt concealed the long-tailed dragon etched into his flesh. "Of being young and stupid."

"Why not get it removed?"

"It's a reminder not to be stupid," he said.

"Hey, Mr. Bonner," Glynnis said in her teacher's-pet

voice. "We have to interview someone from our community for social studies. Can I interview you?"

"My life's an open book."

Uh-huh, thought Aurora, remembering all the times she'd asked about her mother. There was some secret about her, something her dad didn't like to discuss, about Tijuana, where Aurora and her mother came from, and what their life had been like before he came along. He always acted as though there was nothing to tell. "Bringing you to the States gave you a chance for a better life," was his favorite explanation. When she wanted to know what was wrong with their old life in Mexico, he just said, "It wasn't healthy. Too much poverty and disease."

"When's a good time for you?" Glynnis asked.

"What about now?"

She looked startled for a moment, then shrugged her shoulders. "I'll get my notebook."

Glynnis and Edie hung on every word Aurora's dad spoke as he talked about growing up in Glenmuir, and how when he was in high school he'd been one of the volunteers who fought the Mount Vision fire, and how maybe that experience led to his later becoming the youngest fire captain in the district.

Aurora knew that lots of other kids had volunteered when the Mount Vision fire broke out, but none of them became firefighters. Something else drove him, though he'd never explained just what that was.

She took out her sketchbook and worked on her drawing of Icarus, who was so exhilarated with flying that he ignored his father's warning and flew too close to the sun, causing his wings to disintegrate. She was drawing him in the moments before that, when he had no clue he was about to plunge into the sea and drown. She kept wanting to have him remember his father's warning at the last second, and swoop to safety, but you couldn't mess with ancient myths. Things happened the way they happened, and no amount of wishful thinking could change anything.

In English class, they were studying the Greeks and the archetypes that came from mythology. She knew exactly who her dad was. When Achilles was born, he was prophesied to be a perfect warrior. His goddess mother held her baby by the heel and dipped him in the River Styx, knowing this would protect him from injury. He grew up shielded from all danger, just like her dad on Bonner Flower Farm. Great things were expected of him. He didn't even know about that one tiny spot on his heel where he hadn't been dipped in the magical river. He had no idea he was vulnerable there. The powers that be didn't tell him. If he knew he had a weak spot, the knowledge would undermine his courage and keep him from taking the risks a warrior had to take.

The whole point of the myth was that everyone was vulnerable, no matter how strong they appeared. In the case of her father, Aurora knew what his Achilles' heel was. It was her. He never said so. He didn't have to. In a small town, where everyone knew everyone else, she'd heard several versions of the story. Her dad was all set to go to college on a scholarship or play for some baseball team and become rich and famous, maybe marry a starlet or heiress. Instead, he ended up with Aurora and her mom, a dangerous job and a bunch of bills to pay.

In junior high, Aurora had met several teachers and coaches who had helped her dad get all the scholarships and stuff, and were obviously disappointed when he didn't follow the prescribed path. The way they said, "He went to Mexico and came back with a wife and child," you'd think Aurora and her mother were cheap souvenirs or stray cats.

"What's the hardest part of your job?" Glynnis asked him.

"Being away from my daughter," he said without hesitation.

"I mean about fighting fires."

"We've had some arson incidents this year. Those can be pretty tough to figure out sometimes."

She leaned forward, her eyes narrowed. "Arson?"

"Yes. Deliberately setting a fire. Sometimes for insurance purposes, sometimes for the thrill."

"You mean somebody just lights a match, and up it goes?"

"Sometimes there's a delay device. And usually there's an accelerant."

"Like what?"

"A delay device can be something as simple as a cigarette with matches rubberbanded to it. When the cigarette burns down to the match heads, they ignite. Accelerants are things like gas, kerosene, paint solvents. Marine resins and varnishes—plenty of that around here. We can detect them by using a trained dog. In our district, we have Rosie, a Lab who can sniff out residue down to one part per trillion. We also have a photoionization detector." He paused and spelled it out for her. "It's known as a broad-spectrum monitor. The investigator uses the probe to sniff around places where accelerant might be present." Ten minutes later, her dad finished the interview and half the bag of Cheetos. "How'd I do?"

"I'll let you know when I get my grade," Glynnis said, finishing up her notes with a flourish. "Thanks, Mr. Bonner."

"No problem. I'll be out in the garage, Aurora."

After he left the room, Glynnis closed her steno pad. "Your dad is so hot."

"Don't even go there," Aurora warned her. It wasn't the first time one of her friends had pointed this out. Her dad? Hot? Ew.

To change the subject, she said, "I still have to find someone to interview."

Edie clicked to a comic strip Web site Aurora had never seen before. "Check it out. This is one of my mom's former students." Edie's mother was head of the English department at the high school, and Edie was always the first to know school gossip.

Aurora felt a quick burn of envy for Edie—for anyone—who had a mother to gossip with.

"A cartoonist," Glynnis said with a bored sigh. "What's so big about that?"

"Nothing," Edie said, "but in a town full of nobodys, she's practically somebody."

"Sarah Moon," Aurora said, scanning the page. There was an artsy black-and-white photo of some woman, her face half-hidden in shadow, a fall of light hair obscuring her features. The photograph was frustrating, designed to obscure her features like a shot from a film noir. "I bet she's related to the Moon Bay Oyster Company guys." The drawings were boldly sketched, with the main character saying things like "In my world, chocolate is a vegetable." The comic strip was called *Just Breathe*. A sample episode showed the main character, Shirl, getting her belly button pierced.

Aurora's interest was piqued. Mr. Chopin, the art teacher, said she had a real talent for drawing. It might be interesting to meet someone who made a living doing art.

"'About the artist,'" Edie read aloud. "'Sarah Moon is a native of West Marin County, California. A graduate of the University of Chicago, she now lives with her husband in Chicago.'"

"So how am I supposed to interview her? It says she lives in Chicago."

"According to my mom, that's changed," Edie informed them. "She lives here now. She's your aunt's client, you know."

Aurora's aunt Birdie practiced family law, and divorce was a huge part of that. She never, ever talked about her cases, but if a woman became her client, chances were she was getting a divorce. Aurora didn't have to ask why Sarah Moon had come back to Glenmuir, because she knew the answer. A woman moved away when her marriage ended. That was the law.

After her friends left, Aurora found her father in the garage, working on the catboat. It was the same boat he and Aunt Birdie used to race in regattas on the bay when they were kids, so it was like this family heirloom thing. The boat was about fourteen feet long, and had been brought all the way from Cape Cod by her grandpa Angus.

"What are you doing, Dad?" she asked.

He didn't look up, but kept messing with a clamp, the glow of the sunset through the dusty window illuminating his broad shoulders. She remembered hanging on to those shoulders when she was little, going along for the ride as he did his daily set of chin-ups. He was able to raise and lower them both as though her weight added nothing. Feeling lonely, she waited for him to pause in his work, but he didn't.

"Dad?"

"Trying to repair a cracked spar. It really needs to be replaced, but I don't think they make them out of spruce anymore."

"Oh, that's important." She tapped her foot.

"I thought you wanted to win the next regatta."

"No, *you* wanted to win it. You have no idea what I want," she said with a dramatic flourish.

"Something I can help you with?" he said, still without turning.

"Oh, yes. I just noticed that my eyes are bleeding."

"Ha ha."

"And my hair's on fire."

"I see."

"And I'm pregnant."

"Hand me that other clamp, Aurora-Dora." He half turned and held out his hand.

Aurora weighed her options. She could use his preoccupied mood as an excuse to get mad at him—again. Or she could spend some time with him before he went back on duty in a couple of days.

"Please," he said.

She handed it over and watched him work for a few minutes.

"How come you didn't talk about my mother when Glynnis interviewed you?" Aurora asked, although she was pretty sure she knew the answer.

"The topic was my job," he said.

"You never talk about my mother."

"She hasn't really stayed in touch since she moved to Vegas," he reminded her. "You know that. Now, pull up a stool."

She debated about whether or not to keep on about her mother but decided to abandon the topic. She scooted her stool next to the work area and rolled up her sleeves. Regattas were a time-honored tradition on the bay, and her dad had taught her to sail the small, sleek catboat, promising that if she learned to read the wind and water, she could win the race one day. The boat was old, though, and needed work. It was the same boat her dad had sailed when he was her age, and there was something comforting in the sense of continuity she felt. She was glad she'd decided to get along with him. He had the warm dad smell, the one that always made her feel safe and protected. She paged through the marine supply catalog, looking up spars. "How about you replace the spruce with the carbon fiber version." She angled the page toward him.

"How did you get so smart?"

"I take after my dad."

He ruffled her hair and she pretended to mind, but she didn't, not really. When he acted like this, Aurora loved her father so much that she wanted to cry. Which was stupid. Loving someone was supposed to make you happy. Or so people said.

She leaned over next to him, remembering how safe and secure she had felt as a little kid when he held her. Sometimes he used to hold her sideways like a barbell and press her up and down until she screamed with laughter.

She was too big for that now. He patted her on the head, pulled away and stood up. "All right, kiddo. I need to get some things from the lumberyard and the marine store. You want to come along?"

This was how she'd been raised, tagging along to the lumberyard or hardware store. While her friends were shopping with their moms, Aurora's dad was teaching her how to pitch a fastball or change the oil in the pickup truck. Sometimes he made clumsy attempts to do girl stuff, like painting her fingernails or doing her hair, but it always felt forced. She sighed and nodded her head.

He headed for the combination mudroom and laundry room to grab his coat. His hand touched the doorknob, and he yanked it back as though it had burned him. "Jesus, Aurora," he snapped. "How many times have I told you not to leave your stuff hanging around?"

"Chill, Dad," she said, snatching the purple bra from the doorknob and wadding it in her fist. "Some of my things are too delicate to go in the dryer." She collected a few more items she'd left draped around the laundry room.

"Yeah, well, I'm too delicate to deal with that stuff," he said, "so hang your underwear somewhere else to dry. Like where I can't see."

"Geez. I never saw someone so freaked out by clean laundry." She lifted her chin defensively. "At least I *do* my own laundry."

He glowered at her, and his cheekbones were red. "Are you coming or not?"

"Forget it," she said, the mood ruined. "I'm going to stay home and fold my underwear."

"Don't get all pissy with me."

"Why not? You're pissy with me." She was totally embarrassed that he'd said something instead of pretending not to notice.

"I'm just asking you to show a little discretion, that's all."

"What is your problem?" She already knew the answer, though. He couldn't stand to connect his little girl with grown-up woman stuff.

"I don't have one." He shoved his arm into the sleeve of his jacket. "So you don't want to come to the lumberyard?"

"No." She tossed her head and added, "Thanks."

"I don't know why the hell everything has to be a fight with you."

"I'm not fighting. I'm going to watch one of the DVDs we rented."

He looked as if he was debating saying something else. She almost wanted him to make her go. But he said, "Suit yourself. I'll be back in a while."

He walked out the door, and she picked up a DVD from the coffee table—*13 Going On 30*. How appropriate. She stuck the disc into the player. As the opening credits rolled, his truck started with a blast of exhaust. Aurora scowled at the screen and wished she'd gone with him after all. A trip to the marine supply store or the lumberyard with your dad hardly qualified as Friday night fun, but at least it was something. She was always complaining that her dad ignored her or took her for granted, and then she proceeded to blow him off.

She glared at the phone. Maybe she could invite a friend over to watch the movie with her. Besides Glynnis and Edie, her only other friend was Janie Cameron. But she was out. To the envy of the rest of the seventh grade girls, she had a real actual boyfriend. They went to the movies together and held hands in the school yard, and they always looked as though they had a secret.

Aurora's dad had decreed that she was not allowed to have a boyfriend until she was sixteen. She acted outraged about the rule, but was secretly relieved. She wouldn't know how to act with a boyfriend.

Not even Zane Parker, she thought, picturing the cutest boy in Glenmuir.

In the meantime, she wished she knew what it was that made some girls so appealing. Mandy Jacobson, the most popular girl in the school, was the one Aurora really wanted to be best friends with. Mandy lived in one of the nicest houses in town and eased through every day like a soap bubble floating on the breeze. She made life look fun and simple. Unfortunately, Aurora hadn't managed to fit into her circle of friends. The closest she came was lending her homework to Mandy and her sidekicks, Carson and Deb. It was wrong to let them copy it; Aurora knew that. But it was also wrong to feel lonely all the time. Ages ago, Mama used to say, *You survive by using what you got.* In Mama's case, it sure as heck wasn't book smarts, but that was what Aurora had going for her. She was a straight-A student. Getting good grades was a cinch compared to the really hard stuff, like figuring out why your life sucked.

Restless with a pervasive discontent she couldn't name, she picked up the TV remote and scrolled through the menu. The cursor seemed stuck on the option *En Español.* She pressed Enter, and the movie began with an opening scene of kids at school, chattering together in rapid-fire Spanish.

Aurora understood every syllable and inflection. This was her first language, her mother tongue, the only one she knew until she moved to el Norte. Outside of Glenmuir, almost no one realized she was bilingual and she sure as heck didn't advertise that little tidbit. It was one of the things that made her different from everyone else. There were already too many of those.

She switched the movie to English. At least the actors' lip movements matched the words they were saying. But Aurora couldn't concentrate on the movie. Eventually, she turned it off and went out on the porch, stepping over sports equipment and squeezing past bikes. Her grandmother and Aunt Birdie were always bringing over blooming plants and afghans and stuff to make the place look "homey," but the look never took. The plants eventually died of neglect, the afghans usually ended up wadded in a cupboard somewhere, and the sports equipment prevailed. You might as well hang out a sign that said, No Woman Lives Here.

Sticking her fingers in the back pockets of her jeans, Aurora paced back and forth. It was so stupid of her to get all mad and refuse to go with her dad. Because despite the fact that they had a weird family situation, she couldn't imagine life any other way. She and her dad were a team. They were inseparable. Being without him would be like being without air to breathe.

Feeling guilty, she put the clean laundry in a basket, including the lacy undies and bras she had hung up to dry. She pretended not to understand why her dad didn't want to see such things hanging around, but she knew. He didn't like being reminded that she was growing up. Things were much simpler when she was a little kid.

She wondered why she did stuff to tick him off when really she loved him so much.

It was just that whenever they seemed to be drifting apart, she panicked.

She couldn't afford to lose him, too.

Twelve

Sarah could feel the surface of the bed molding to her body as she lay there, trying her best to lose count of the hours and the days. She wished there was a way to ignore the cycle of light and dark that marked the passage of time. She also wished she knew what to do with herself.

She never expected to be starting her life over. For the first time ever, where she went and what she did was totally up to her. Right out of high school, her route had been mapped by her acceptance to the University of Chicago. Following that, she'd been enfolded into Jack's life. There had been no decision-making process on her part except to follow along.

She'd been an excellent follower, but now that she'd left Jack, she looked ahead and saw no one leading her. To her dismay, she found this utterly terrifying. Maybe she should have stayed, fought for him. Infidelity was something a marriage could survive, or so said all the experts. He claimed he wanted to give it another shot, although she strongly suspected his backpedaling came at the advice of his lawyer.

She stared at the ceiling of her room, which she had

gotten to know in appalling detail. Dormer windows and window seats with plaid cushions. Lace curtains her mother had hung before she was born. Sarah could picture her mother, rounded with pregnancy, threading the curtain onto the rod, then fluffing it out just so. She imagined her pausing to rest at the window seat, gazing out at the water while caressing her belly and thinking about the baby.

The walls slanted over her like protective arms. Made of old-fashioned lath-and-plaster construction, the chalky surface was hand finished and painted a delicate robin's egg blue. Unfortunately, there were a good many cracks here and there that needed repairing.

Maybe she would be a plasterer, Sarah thought. She would be good at it.

She imagined mixing up a creamy batch of plaster, swirling it gently in a bucket and then spreading it oh-so-expertly across the scarred and damaged surface. She would cover all the imperfections with a smooth new skin, and no one would know what a mess it was underneath.

"Sarah?" A light tap sounded on the door.

She stifled a groan. "What is it, Gran?"

"Your aunt May and I came to see how you're doing." Without waiting for an invitation—which Sarah would not have extended—Gran pushed open the door. She came in, carrying a cardboard box. Aunt May was with her, bearing a vase of freshly cut flowers.

"Oh, hi," Sarah said lamely. It took every ounce of her energy to push herself up to a sitting position. The sisters were as kind and colorful as the bouquets they expertly arranged. Gran wore a tunic of barkcloth with a tribal print, a getup that oddly complemented her snow-white hair. The more conventional May was in yellow calico, her narrow shoulders wrapped in a crocheted shawl. Despite their different taste in clothes, they both wore the most extraordinary shoes. Sarah couldn't help but stare.

"Like them?" Gran pointed her toe and turned her foot this way and that.

"Your grandmother made them," Aunt May added, "so the only possible answer is yes."

"I love them."

The shoes were hand-painted Keds canvas sneakers. May's were decorated with sunflowers, and Gran's with wisteria. And they were not just splashed with fabric paint. These sneakers were works of art, the flowers as intricate and beautifully rendered as old masters' still lifes.

"You get your talent at art from me." Gran placed her box in Sarah's lap. "These are for you."

"We had your father bring us a pair of your shoes so we could get the proper size," May explained.

Sarah opened the box to find a pair of size-seven Keds, gorgeously painted with multicolored primroses. "These are just beautiful," she said. "Did you know primroses are my favorite flower?"

Gran nodded. "I remember. When you were a little girl, you used to say it's because they're like Life Savers candy. They come in all colors, and all colors are good."

Sarah cradled the sneakers. "These are too nice to wear. I should put them on display."

"You'll display them every time you wear them, dear."

Sarah shook her head. "I can't get over you two. How can I compete with your tactics?"

"You know what they say about old age and treachery," Gran said.

Aunt May patted Sarah's arm. "This is a symbolic offering. Here's to you getting back on your feet."

Sarah pressed herself against the pillows. "God, that is so—"

"Manipulative?" Aunt May suggested.

"We're using everything we've got," Gran admitted.

"We have quite an arsenal," Aunt May said.

Gran and May exchanged a glance that was weighty with concern. "What are you doing, Sarah?"

"Actually, I was contemplating a new career. What do you think of a future in plaster?" She indicated a crack in the wall.

"Don't be silly." Aunt May set her vase on the dresser and fussed with it for a moment. She was one of those women who had a magic touch. A few seconds of plucking, and the flower arrangement looked like a miniature English garden.

"What's silly about plastering?" Sarah asked. She figured it was no sillier than arranging flowers and painting sneakers.

"You're an artist," Gran said. "Not an artisan. There's a difference."

She and May sat on the end of the bed, on opposite sides. Sarah thought they looked as pretty as a picture, backlit by a soft glow from the window, filtered through the lace curtains. Seeing them together made Sarah wish she had a sister, or even a best friend.

"Maybe I don't want to be an artist anymore," Sarah said.

"Why would you say such a thing?" Gran looked aghast.

"It's too hard to make a living. And too easy to get your heart broken."

"Heavens to Betsy. If you're afraid of a broken heart, you're afraid of life itself." Her grandmother was a walking Hallmark commercial.

"I'll worry about my heart later. For the time being, I need to find a stable job and quit dreaming about making it as an artist."

"You don't sound a thing like the Sarah we know."

"The Sarah you know is gone—cheated on by her husband and dumped by her biggest paper."

"Oh, dear, the paper?"

"My comic strip was dropped from the *Tribune*. Working at the oyster farm doesn't look so bad to me now."

"You always hated working at the farm," Gran pointed out. "Don't pretend you didn't. And we're sorry about the *Tribune*, but there are thousands of other papers and you mustn't give up. You've had a huge loss. One of the biggest losses a woman faces. Your husband was unfaithful. He took away your sense of trust and security. But don't let him take away your dream, too."

Aunt May bobbed her head in agreement. "We know it's risky—"

Sarah plucked at a fluff of chenille on the bedspread.

"Taking an emotional risk calls for a special kind of bravery," Gran said.

Sarah couldn't help herself. She burst into laughter. It was the first time she'd really laughed since leaving Jack, and it felt great, a surge of emotion so strong that it left her spent and limp against the bank of pillows.

"That's me," she said. "Fearless Sarah Moon." She dabbed at her eyes with a corner of the bedspread. "You girls crack me up. You really do." When they didn't respond, she finished drying her face. "Did you know I haven't washed my hair in ten days?"

"How very fascinating," Gran said.

"I'm letting the natural oils repair the damage."

"And clever, too," Aunt May chimed in.

"I could use a little sympathy here. What do you say?"

"Oh, Sarah," Gran began. "You don't need sympathy. You need a life."

"What for? So I can screw it up some more?"

"Well. With an attitude like that, you're doomed."

She glared at the sisters. "Even the doomed need sympathy. You're supposed to tell me that you love me and you want to see me finding new ways to be happy, and that's why you're giving me advice. And you'll point out that you've both suffered your share of pain in this life so you know a little about how I'm feeling."

The sisters exchanged a meaningful glance. "Such a smart girl," said Aunt May.

"We always knew it," Gran agreed.

"This is not helping," Sarah said.

"Talking about your troubles with people who care always helps."

Sarah blew out a sigh and folded her arms across her chest. "I give up. What do you want from me?"

"We want you to start by getting out of bed. You've scarcely left this room. It's not healthy."

"I don't care about being healthy."

"Nonsense, dear. Of course you do."

My God, Sarah thought. They were like the girls in *Arsenic and Old Lace.* Completely dotty but convinced they had all the answers.

"You're still so very young," Gran said. "You have so much ahead of you. We want you to go out and embrace that, Sarah. Not hide away and sleep."

"We think you want that, too." Aunt May took a key from her crocheted handbag and set it on the bedside table. The key chain was a plastic dime-store figure from the cartoon *Lilo and Stitch.* Sarah had always liked that character. She surfed her way through life and sang in the face of trouble.

"What's that?" she asked.

"The keys to May's Cottage," Aunt May said. "I'm giving you a lease on it, with the first year rent free."

The cottage by the sea had been in the Carter family for nearly a century. Elijah Carter, who'd made a modest fortune fishing the rich waters of the bay and the ocean beyond the point, had built it for his new bride, whom he had brought from Scotland.

"The lease is in the house," Aunt May said, "on the kitchen table. I'm charging you one dollar for the first year's rent, just to make it official. You simply need to sign the paper and bring it to me."

"I don't understand. Why are you doing this?"

"Like we said, it's to help you get back on your feet," Gran explained with exaggerated patience.

"You need a place of your own," Aunt May added.

"We think it's healthier," Gran said.

"And it's close to town and has a high-speed Internet connection," Aunt May said.

"You're kidding."

"No. Broadband was requested numerous times by my guests, so I finally had it installed." Aunt May spoke as though she knew what she was talking about.

"I can't live at the cottage," Sarah said. "It's a huge source of income for you." With its vintage furniture and period decor, the cottage was rented to well-heeled tourists for $500 per night in the high season, and harried San Franciscans flocked to pay it.

"I don't need that, I assure you," Aunt May said. "And I've been thinking of finding a tenant for quite some time."

The bungalow was an artist's dream, Sarah thought. Quiet and private, with a spectacular view of Tomales Bay, yet still close to town. High-speed Internet.

"I don't know what to say," she told her great-aunt.

"A simple thank-you will do."

Sarah turned on her side and stared at the key. A part of her wanted to reach out and seize the offering before the opportunity was snatched away. Yet another part recoiled at the idea of setting herself up in a place of her own.

"I can't live at the cottage," she whispered.

"Of course you can," Aunt May said. "It's perfect."

"I don't want perfect. I want…normal. At least if I stay here, in bed at my father's house, I can maintain the illusion that my situation is temporary. That I'll wake up one morning, come to my senses and reclaim my life."

"Is that what you want?" asked Gran.

"I keep trying to convince myself to forgive Jack. That's what he wants me to do. To reconcile with him."

"I didn't quite catch your answer," Gran said. "Is that what you want?"

Sarah stretched the bedspread into a tent across her knees. Jack had conveniently forgotten that he was the one who'd said it first: *I want a divorce.* He had spoken those words before the idea had ever occurred to her. Now he wanted to take back what he'd said.

Yet hearing the words spoken aloud had unraveled something in Sarah, a deeply hidden discontent, and now there was no reeling it back in. He had expressed something she wanted before she even knew she wanted it.

"I miss being in love," she confessed to her grandmother and great-aunt. She missed the happy warmth in her heart of being part of a couple. She missed snuggling up to him, feeling his arms wrapped around her, breathing in his scent.

But although she missed these things, she could not persuade herself to love him again.

Could love be killed in an instant? she wondered. Could it exist one moment, and then die like a person taking a bullet to the heart? Like a blood vessel bursting in the brain of a person who was in the middle of weaving a blanket?

The demise of Sarah's marriage wasn't so instantaneous, she forced herself to acknowledge. One of the hardest truths she had to face was that their marriage had been on life support for a long time prior to that final betrayal. Finding him naked—and erect—with Mimi had merely been a formality.

"It was way too easy to stop having feelings for him," she said. "Like turning off a switch. Makes me wonder if I'm all that good at relationships."

"You *are* good at relationships," Gran contradicted. "Look at all you've done for love. Lived in Chicago when all you wanted was to be by the sea, away from the wind and the snow."

"The right clothes can make any climate bearable."

"You were steadfast through his illness. You did it all."

"That's devotion, which is different from the way I loved him in the beginning. Deeper and God knows more personal. But not passionate." A bleakness settled over her. That passion, that heart-pounding he's-the-one feeling, had never returned after Jack's cancer treatment. They had each gone in different directions, looking for something to replace the lost passion—she to a fertility clinic, he to another woman's arms.

"Enough of this gloomy talk," Gran declared, dusting her hands together as if she'd just taken out the rubbish. "Time to move on."

"This is my marriage," Sarah said. "My life. Not just some gloomy talk."

"We know that. We don't want you to turn into one of those insufferable and bitter divorced women."

"Fine, then what do you want me to turn into?"

"A happy, productive, well-adjusted divorced woman."

"Great. I'll get right on that."

"Who dates," Aunt May added.

Sarah flopped back on the bed and pulled a pillow over her head. "I don't believe you people."

She felt a friendly pat on her leg and lay quietly until she was sure they were gone. Then, like a soldier in enemy territory peeking out of a foxhole, she moved the pillow to see if the coast was clear. They were gone but had left the curtains wide-open to the late-morning light. A slanting golden bar fell across the bed and touched on the white wicker nightstand, where the key to May's cottage gleamed.

Sarah took a deep breath. She suddenly felt ravenously hungry. She got up, and a wave of light-headedness washed over her.

"Yikes," she muttered. "I need to eat more or sleep less."

What were the old ladies thinking? she wondered. It was too soon to be making a decision like this. She picked up the Lilo key chain. The golden key was etched with the warning Do Not Duplicate.

Thirteen

"Something's going on at May Carter's cottage," Gloria observed as she and Will returned to Glenmuir from Petaluma.

Gloria decelerated and trolled past the seaside bungalow. In the falling light at day's end, the historic cottage resembled an illustration in a storybook or tourist brochure. Surrounded by a moss-covered picket fence, its flower boxes spilling color, it had a timeless charm that had made it a coveted beach rental in the area.

In the front hung a weathered oval sign, discreetly flapping in the breeze. May's Cottage, the sign read. Circa 1912. Weekly Rates.

"Looks like another batch of tourists to me," Will said.

"That car belongs to Nathaniel Moon's daughter. It's the only blue Mini in town."

"I'll call a press conference."

"Very funny." Gloria's glance flicked over at him; then she turned back to the road. "I hear she's single."

"I hear she's married."

"Not for much longer."

Will almost felt sorry for Sarah Moon. The trouble with living in a small town where nothing ever happened was that everyone kept track of everyone else's business. Secrets didn't last long in Glenmuir.

Sometimes there were exceptions, though. He flipped through a file from the arson investigator they'd met with this afternoon. They had a dossier of evidence in both hard copy and digital form, which covered two separate incidents of arson in two successive months. Yet despite all the evidence, there was one thing lacking—a suspect.

Gloria kept her eyes on the road, though a knowing smile curved her mouth. "Weren't you and Sarah in the same grade, coming through school?"

"I think we were," he said, and although he knew where the conversation was leading, he added, "I barely remember her. So?"

"So nothing," she said. "Just an observation. She's single. You're single—"

"Shut up, Gloria."

"Aw, come on. You are the town's most eligible bachelor, and available women don't exactly grow on trees around here."

"Maybe that's why I like it here."

"Bullshit. I know you, Will. You want to find someone. Marisol's been gone five years."

"Drop it, Gloria." He tried not to think about all the lonely nights when his arms ached to hold someone.

"I'm just saying, nature abhors a vacuum. Trying to match you up with someone has become a favorite pastime around here."

"Great. Well, guess what, Gloria. I'd just as soon be

taken off your list, if you don't mind. Find some other bachelor to fix up."

"Like who?"

He thought for a moment. "Darryl Kilmer's single."

"Give me a break. He doesn't have it."

"Have what?" he demanded in exasperation.

She turned the vehicle into the station parking lot. "Let's see. Dental work?"

"Very funny, Gloria."

"Don't pretend you don't understand."

"I'm not pretending. I really don't get why people are always trying to pair me up with someone."

She cut the engine and put her hand on his arm to keep him in his seat. "People want the best for you, Will. You're the kind of old-fashioned, stand-up guy nobody ever seems to meet these days, not in real life. You're a good man with a heart full of love. It doesn't seem right that you're alone and Aurora doesn't have a mom."

"Hell, Gloria, now I want to marry *you*." He leaned across the seat and kissed her cheek. "What do you say? We can make it to the state line by sunset. Better yet, my aunt can fly us to Vegas in an hour." To Will's surprise, Gloria reached up and brushed a sweat-soaked lock of hair off his forehead.

He was too startled to move, to do anything but stare. He swallowed, cleared his throat, found his voice. "Gloria?"

"You break my heart, Will," she whispered. "You always have."

"I don't know what you're talking about. I never—"

"It's not your fault. You can't help who you are any more than I can."

He frowned. "Why are you being so nice to me?"

"I'm always nice to you. And everybody who knows you wants to see you happy. Ruby and I were talking about it. We were wondering what it would take to make you happy."

"Let me watch?" he suggested.

She shoved him back. "Pervert. That will teach me to get all sentimental over you." She climbed out of the truck.

Will called after her, still teasing. "What about me, Gloria? What about my heart full of love?"

She turned and looked back at him. "Find someone to give it to, Will. Just a bit of friendly advice."

Juggling two full grocery sacks, Sarah opened the door with her hip and headed for the kitchen counter. With mechanical efficiency, she put away the groceries. Milk, bananas, Pop-Tarts, frozen dinners, a package of fresh batteries for the smoke alarms. She had promised Aunt May she'd replace them. The local paper had reported a recent incident of arson. Most likely, the culprits were vandals committing mischief, but you couldn't be too careful.

On a whim, Sarah had bought a bouquet of fresh-cut flowers, a beautiful profusion of candy-colored snapdragons, primroses and pale green Bells of Ireland. As she took them from their cellophane wrapper, she recognized the logo on the small gold sticker. Bonner Flower Farm.

Birdie's parents, she thought. The parents of Birdie and Will.

Other than mentioning he had a daughter, Birdie hadn't said anything else about her brother. Sarah assumed he was married to someone fabulous and long gone from Glenmuir, chasing dreams of glory somewhere glamorous. She could picture him living in one of those big-money enclaves that attracted professional athletes and their expensive toys, like yachts and motorcycles and Cessna planes.

She arranged the flowers in a vase and placed it in the middle of the table in the kitchen nook, admiring the way the light from the windows behind made the flowers glow in a halo of color.

She hoped she was doing the right thing by accepting Aunt May's offer. In practical terms, it was ideal. The cottage was perfectly appointed, with durable but cozy furniture, a fine array of dishes and utensils in the kitchen. Sarah had set up her drafting table and computer in the smaller bedroom, and was managing to keep up with her deadlines—just barely. If she was going to make a living on her own, she'd need wider syndication. Contracting with a syndication service was probably the wise move now.

But being practical had never been her strong suit, and most days, she muddled through without making a decision. She constantly felt restless and scared, her mind going in all different directions. She was truly on her own for the first time in her life, and to her dismay, she wasn't handling it well.

No, she was terrified. She'd never had to face the future relying solely on herself. The prospect thoroughly intimidated her, the specter of failure looming large.

Exasperated with herself, she grabbed the most recent volume from a small display of guest books on a shelf under the window. This one was an oversize hand-bound book with entries dating back a couple of years.

"We had a fabulous stay to celebrate our twenty-fifth wedding anniversary," was written in a large curly script, and the entry was signed by Dan and Linda Davis.

The Norwood family from Truckee reported that they'd had an "unforgettable family vacation, just magical."

"This is the kind of place we want our kids to experience, so they can discover the beauty of unspoiled nature," wrote Ron van der Veen of Seattle, Washington.

Sarah paged through the comments, skimming rudimentary sketches and happy faces, effusive statements supported by multiple exclamation points.

"What's wrong with you people?" she asked, still browsing. "Didn't anybody have a lousy time? Days on end when the fog never lifted? A painful sunburn? Getting stung by a bee or a rash of poison ivy? Come on, people. How about a fight? A nice, big knock-down, drag-out domestic dispute, maybe one that culminated in a call to the police."

She shook her head and mocked an entry that sounded like a chamber of commerce ad: "Food, fun, friends and family—it doesn't get any better than this."

"I would love to see just one honest entry," she said. "Like some guy writing that this is the perfect spot to bring his mistress to avoid all danger of getting caught by his wife. Or some woman admitting that the sex was terrible." She took out a Blackfeet Indian pencil and doodled on a blank page. "I won't hold my breath waiting for that one."

A vacation was supposed to be a time to renew and heal. When Jack's treatments were finished, they had made a trip that was supposed to refresh them and prepare them for a bright future. They stayed at a historic boutique hotel, the Inn at Willow Lake, in a town called Avalon, in upstate New York. She'd chosen the location based on the fact that the tiny local paper carried her strip. She had found the inn online. They were supposed to get away from it all, but Jack had stayed tethered to work by cell phone and BlackBerry. They'd made love, and she'd dared to hope she was pregnant at the end of the trip. Instead, they'd returned to

Chicago with a vague, unsettled distance between them. Jack threw himself into working on Shamrock Downs. And into shagging Mimi Lightfoot.

Looking down, she saw the doodle resolve itself into a sketch of Shirl, bringing home a bored-looking goldfish in a clear plastic bag. "Having one of those days?" asked the goldfish. And Shirl's response: "Having one of those lives."

"Too much time on my hands," Sarah said, shutting the book and turning her attention back to the groceries. She frowned at the bottom of the bag. "I can't believe I bought this. I don't even remember putting it in the cart."

At some point, with her brain on autopilot, she had bought Jack's favorite snack—a can of King Olaf kippered herring and a box of Ritz crackers.

"I don't even want to think about why I did that." She carried the items to the trash can but decided that wasn't far enough. She marched out to the beach instead, lifting her legs high over the dune grasses and making her way to a heap of driftwood logs deposited by a storm.

There, she used the key to roll the top off the can of kippered herring. The smell alone threatened to knock her off her feet. Since moving into the bungalow, she seemed to have developed an extra sensitivity to smells. The fishy, oily odor of the herring made her nauseous.

The smell reminded her of Jack, who liked to snack on the foul stuff while watching television.

She emptied the can and the box of crackers on the beach, then sat back to watch the show. Seemingly within seconds, the seagulls came, wheeling in and screeching as they fought over the feast. It took them only moments to devour the fish and snap up all the crackers, gobbling them right then and there or carrying off morsels to far places.

Sarah felt a strange and curious thrill as she observed the feeding frenzy. It was over within minutes, and there was not a single crumb left that she could see.

After she'd retrieved the empty can and cracker box, she felt a familiar pair of eyes on her. "You again," she said.

It was the stray dog she'd spotted her first day in Glenmuir and many times since. The dog kept coming around, too wary to let her near but always keeping her in sight. She thought of the dog as the lion to her Androcles, and started leaving a bowl of water and kitchen scraps on the stoop behind the bungalow. She never saw the dog there, but the water and scraps always disappeared when she wasn't looking. The mongrel was a lost soul drifting around, as though hunting for a place to alight.

She and the homeless stray had been doing this dance of trust like shy teenagers at a school social. They would brush close and then retreat, never quite able to relax around each other but bound by some mutual affinity.

Sarah had complained to her father, her grandmother and great-aunt, even to Birdie about the stray. She was terrified that it was going to get hit by a car. Glenmuir didn't have an animal control division, but there was a rescue farm out on Branch 62. The trouble was, this particular mutt was too clever to be rescued. It had a way of disappearing when anyone came looking for it. The one time a volunteer had managed to transport the dog out to the farm, it had escaped and run five miles back to town.

"Don't tell me," she said, now used to being shadowed. "You're hungry, too. You should have said something."

Exasperated, she managed to pry the last cracker from its waxed paper tube. She held it out to the dog. Predictably, the mutt regarded it with longing but refused to take it from her hand. The dog crept forward, its nostrils quivering, its eyes intent as though determined to hypnotize the cracker from her hand to its mouth.

Sarah took a step closer. The dog feinted back.

"Don't you think I've already suffered enough rejection?" she said impatiently.

The dog whined and licked its chops, but held itself poised to flee.

Sarah looked at the velvety brown eyes. It had actual eyelashes. She didn't even know dogs could have eyelashes. "Come on, pooch," she cajoled. "You know you want this. And I would never hurt you."

The dog strained its neck and sniffed at the cracker, all but shaking with desire. Closer…come on, thought Sarah. Come on, come on, come on. She leaned down, desperate to make a friend of the mutt.

The dog skittered back, tail between its legs.

"Fine," Sarah said. "Suit yourself. Starve, if you'd rather." She tossed the cracker to the ground and marched back to the cottage. On the back porch, she turned to see that the dog had finished the cracker and now sat at attention, tail gently wagging as though blown by a breeze.

The mutt was annoyingly cute, its face half black and half white, eyes sharp with what Sarah could only describe as a penetrating intelligence.

She refilled the big mixing bowl with water, set it on the stoop and went back inside, determined not to care whether the dog stuck around or took off. Besides, she was desperate to wash the odor of kippered herring off her hands.

Fourteen

"This is starting to make us look like idiots," Will admitted, circling the gardening shed behind the elementary school. Another fire had occupied their shift, and in its aftermath, they were probing around in the wreckage.

"Could be we *are* idiots," Gloria explained. "Somebody is setting fires right under our noses and we can't stop him."

Frustrated, he poked at an old can of paint thinner. Once again, it was a lucky break that no one was harmed by the fire. There was just property damage. Will didn't want to count on luck alone to keep people safe. He wanted to nail this asshole.

"So how certain are we that it's the same guy?"

"We're not, but my gut tells me it is. Still, there's no consistency," he said. "The days and times are all over the map. The intervals between attacks are random, and the accelerant varies every time. How the hell is the arson investigator going to profile this character?"

"Not our problem."

"But it's happening here. In a place this small, a guy

can't sneeze without the whole town hearing it. How is somebody getting away with this shit?" He knew of arsonists who operated for five, six, even ten years without being nailed.

"We're overlooking something."

"No kidding." Will studied the file for what seemed like the thousandth time. Arson investigation techniques were sophisticated, but the department was spread thin. So long as there was only minor damage, this case wouldn't be at the top of the priority list. He stared at dates, times and details until his eyes watered. He kept thinking there had to be something significant about the cases as a group. But there was nothing. Nothing but…

"Every one of these fires was set on our watch," he said.

"There's a one in three chance that any fire will take place on our watch."

"But three in a row?" asked Will.

"So what do you make of it? Is somebody out to get one of us? Both of us?"

"It's something to think about," he said to Gloria. "So. Who have you pissed off lately?"

He was kidding, but Gloria's cheeks reddened and she ducked her head and muttered something.

"What was that?"

"My ex," she said without looking at him. "Our house finally sold, and he was terrible all through the settlement. He contested every last nickel and dime."

Will had only met Dean a few times. His impression had been that the guy didn't appreciate his wife or recognize how desperately unhappy she was. "Do you think he'd go around setting fires?"

"He's a lazy-ass son of a bitch. Committing arson is too much work."

"Maybe he's not out to hurt you," Will suggested. "Maybe Ruby?"

Gloria shook her head. "She doesn't have an ex. Just that bratty daughter."

"Glynnis? Never seemed bratty to me," Will said.

"Yeah, well, you were never dating her mother." Gloria picked up a metal implement, warped beyond recognition. "The fires were set on my watch, it's true," she said. "But they also occurred on yours."

"Yes." Will had already racked his brains over that one.

"Your ex is no picnic, either."

He didn't deny it. He had never done a blessed thing to the woman except give her and her child a stable home and a settled life. In the end, even that had not been enough to make Marisol stay clean and sober. Being safe was no substitute for being happy.

"She'd have a long commute to set these fires," he said. "And she never learned my work schedule when we were together so I don't see how she'd know it now. Besides, isn't one of the main motives for arson a bid for attention? I guarantee, she never wanted that from me."

A skip loader rumbled into view, the service contracted to clean up the debris. "Let's get everything packaged and sent to the lab, Captain. I want to get off duty on time and wash the smoke out of my hair. I've got a support group meeting tonight."

"What kind of support group?" This was Marin; there was something for everybody here. "I mean, if you don't mind saying."

She laughed. "Like I have any secrets from you. I go to a divorce support group once a week. Want to come?"

He frowned. "Right."

She shrugged. "I still have issues. Don't we all?"

"I'd rather spend the time with Aurora."

She eyed him as if she was about to say something else. Instead, she walked toward the showers, peeling off gear as she went.

In the rose-entwined cottage by the sea, Sarah Moon slowly unraveled. She recognized that she was losing her mind. Like a victim of progressive dementia, she could intellectualize about the process. She even made it the focus of her comic strip, when she remembered to draw it and send in each week's worth of digital files.

She wasn't a raving lunatic, which became a source of great relief and misplaced pride. She was a quiet, unobtrusive nut cake. Subtle, even. She'd taken to eating Fluffernutters in the middle of the night and listening to her great-aunt's Edith Piaf collection, singing along in nasally French—and she didn't even speak French. She had watered the plants in the window boxes to death, drowning them in her overattention.

Sometimes her lunacy was not so subtle, she acknowledged with a sigh, standing outside the Magic Bean. The coffee shop and newsstand was a ten-minute walk from her house, and she went there daily to pick up newspapers, magazines and paperback novels.

This morning she had gotten up early, determined to have a normal day. She had taken a shower, put on makeup and an actual outfit—black jeans with half boots, a beige sweater—and walked to town for a latte and scone and to buy a paper. At the cash register she noticed the clerk studying her with an odd look on his face.

"Everything all right?" he asked.

"Just grand." Sarah paid him and went outside. At that moment, she caught a glimpse of her reflection in the shop window and gasped. She was still wearing a towel, twisted like a turban, atop her head.

"Brilliant, Sarah," she muttered. "Oh, you are brilliant."

She tried to maintain her dignity as she unwound the towel. What an idiot. What a complete moron.

She shook out the towel, already sketching a comic strip in her head. Shirl would have a field day with this. Was this a new stage of her meltdown? A mental breakdown? Early onset dementia?

Sarah walked to Sunrise Park, a little oasis with tree-shaded benches and a view of the bay. There was not a soul in sight, which suited her just fine. Taking a sip from her travel mug, she shut her eyes. Gran and Aunt May insisted she'd be happy at the bungalow, that it would be the perfect way to get back on her feet.

Unfortunately, she was still stumbling around with a stupid towel on her head.

A chill slipped over her. Even though she stood with her eyes closed, she had a premonition.

Someone was watching her.

She snapped open her eyes to find herself looking into a soulful, brown-eyed gaze.

"What do you want from me?" she asked.

A worried frown deepened the crease between those soft, pleading eyes. Sarah let out a sigh and sat down on a bench. "You just won't take no for an answer, will you?"

With a Lassie-like whine, the mutt sat at attention in front of her. Even though Sarah pretended to be exasperated by the stray, she secretly found it charming, its attention flattering, which caused her a bit of worry about the state of her social life.

She took out the scone, broke off a corner and held it

out. This had become their daily ritual, and each morning, the dog grew a little bolder and came a little closer. Today the mutt got up and took a step forward to sniff the morsel and wag its tail. Then it feinted back, giving another soft, urgent whine. A flock of seagulls, more aggressive than the dog, ventured close to wait for crumbs.

"Oh, come on," Sarah murmured. "When are you going to quit with the *Dances With Wolves* routine?"

The dog licked its chops and stared at the food intently. A clear string of drool spun from its mouth.

"You know," Sarah said, opening her hand fully, "we really must stop meeting like this. People are going to start to talk."

Its gaze never wavering, the mongrel lowered to a crouch, front paws extended.

This was a new posture, Sarah realized. She had studied up on dogs and learned that this was a more relaxed stance, indicating trust.

"I've been patient long enough," Sarah said, "and I don't know why I waste my time. I have bigger problems than you, anyway. My marriage is over. My career's on the skids. I just bought coffee with a towel on my head. I'm having some kind of mental breakdown. Dealing with you isn't going to help a thing."

The dog was a good listener. Sarah would allow that.

Still holding the offering in her hand, she found herself, as usual, thinking of Jack. "My husband was a lousy listener from Day One," she told the dog. "Now I look back and wonder if he ever heard a word I said. And maybe I wasn't hearing him, either. Maybe I was so obsessed with getting pregnant that I stopped hearing him. I figured if we couldn't be a happy couple anymore, we could be a happy family. Stupid, huh? I'm supposed to be a smart person.

You'd think I'd be able to see that we were losing each other."

She felt a terrible heat washing through her. For a moment, she thought she was choking, unable to draw air into her lungs. Then, finally, she recognized the sensation of sobs building in her throat, of tears spilling down her face.

For the first time since leaving Chicago, she cried. Really cried. Grief came from the deepest part of her heart, from a well of pain that made each breath she took a torturous journey. The tears scalded her face in a sudden, salty flood. She had no control over this, and couldn't hold back the pain. It was a force of nature, brutal and insistent, carrying her off in a bitter tide. She didn't know how long she sat alone and wept. She couldn't stop. She would never stop because she would never, ever get over the agony of her broken marriage.

The dog chose that moment to sniff her hand, then give her a nudge. Sarah didn't believe in everyday miracles anymore, though. She knew the dog was simply going for the bit of ginger scone clutched in her fist. Still, it was the first time she and the mongrel had connected. Slowly, watching the patiently lapping pink tongue, she opened her fingers and let the dog eat the crumbs stuck to her palm.

"I had a perfectly good meltdown going." She offered the broken scone. "You might as well have the rest of it. I don't want to eat out of this hand, that's for sure."

She broke off pieces bit by bit, and the dog finally ventured close enough for Sarah to discern that it was a female. She accepted the food with unexpected grace and delicacy. She didn't snap them up and gobble them, but ate daintily and steadily until the last morsel was gone. Afterward, she didn't sidle away but sat close enough for Sarah to touch her fur with a tentative, open hand. The dog didn't seem to mind. The tip of her tail quivered.

Sarah used the damp towel to wipe her tears. Her coffee had turned cold, so she took both the cup and the wadded-up napkin and bag to the trash can and threw them away. Normally, the dog would skitter away at this point, but today she followed Sarah.

As she walked back home, Sarah could hear the click of the dog's nails on the pavement close behind her. The morning fog was thinning and breaking apart to reveal patches of blue. She tilted her face up to the sky to catch the first of the sun's warmth.

Fifteen

"I can't keep her." A week later, sitting on her father's deck, Sarah stroked the dog's silky head. "My life's in chaos right now and I can't have a dog. Come on, Dad—"

"Sorry," Sarah's father said, easing back in a chair on his deck. "Can't help you out."

Her stomach sinking with dismay, she tightened her grip on the retractable leash. She was with her family on the deck overlooking the oyster beds and processing sheds. Her father and Kyle were talking about tearing down the oldest shed, a long, low building with a rusting propane tank surrounded by rickety lattice. With a sigh, Sarah tried again. "Shc's a rcally nice dog. I've already given her a bath, and we have an appointment with the vet tomorrow—"

"I can't, honey," he said. "I can't take a dog."

"How can you resist this dog?" Sarah couldn't help feeling a surge of pride as she regarded the velvet-eyed mongrel. She was a female under the long, brindled fur, and was really quite beautiful now that her coat was clean and shiny. "A week ago she wouldn't let anyone near her. Now she wants to be everyone's best friend."

She turned to Kyle and LaNelle. Her sister-in-law didn't even pretend to consider adopting the dog. "We just installed two thousand square feet of ivory wool carpet," she said.

Sarah felt no surprise. They weren't about to let a dog interfere with their love of shopping for fine things. Thanks to Kyle's expert management and an economic surge in the area, they were prosperous beyond anyone's expectations. Business had waned when jarred oysters went out of fashion and whole ones in the shell came into demand, but Kyle was undaunted. He simply had a knack for feeding the market what it wanted.

"Gran and Aunt May," she said, gently stroking the dog's head, "you're my only hope."

The elderly sisters exchanged a glance. "We're not your only hope, and we're not taking that animal."

"But—"

"You are keeping it," Gran said simply.

"At Aunt May's cottage? No way. She'll ruin the yard."

"Anything she tramples or digs up can be replanted," Aunt May said.

"What about inside?"

"That place has survived tourists for years. A dog won't do anything that can't be fixed."

"But—"

"What' s the real reason you don't want this dog?" Nathaniel asked.

"She obviously adores you," LaNelle pointed out.

"I can't have a dog right now. I can't have anything that requires care and feeding. My life is a mess. The timing is all wrong." Sarah felt them all watching her. Their weighty silence pressed down on her.

This was her family, she reminded herself. She had been too long without them. She needed to learn how to let them into her life again. Maybe that included listening to them and taking their advice. But…a dog?

Taking a deep breath, she started with a terrible admission she didn't even like making to herself. "All right. The real reason I'm resisting adopting this dog is that Jack and I had always planned on getting a puppy for our kids. I'm trying to get past that time in my life, and having this fur ball in my face every day would remind me of…everything."

Kyle cracked open a beer and took a sip. "Don't play that card, Sarah. You're going to stew about what happened, dog or no dog."

That old, vaguely competitive feeling Sarah had for her brother crept into her heart. Kyle had always been the golden child. The perfect son, happy to plunge into the family business without feeling any of the resentment and anguish Sarah had experienced, growing up. Hard times had required them both to work the oyster farm as adolescents but while Kyle had embraced it, Sarah had seethed with shame. She'd hated going to school each day with ruined hands, red and chapped from the harsh work. She wished she'd been more like Kyle, finding not just acceptance but pride in the family enterprise.

"How do you know I'm going to stew about what happened?" she asked.

"You seem to pick the toughest way to deal with things," Kyle said mildly. "You always have."

She glanced at her father but already knew he wouldn't defend her. Everyone—herself included—knew there was a grain of truth in Kyle's observation. "The whole kids-and-puppy thing is a real sore spot with me. I can't believe

I was so naive about…everything. I still lie awake at night and wonder what it was Jack and I thought would happen once the kids materialized. And I feel like an idiot for not clearing up a few key issues, like why we even *wanted* a family when we barely knew each other anymore."

"My little sister's not an idiot." Kyle tipped his beer in her direction.

"Thanks, but isn't it true that most women ask themselves these questions before they embark on some giant campaign to get pregnant?"

LaNelle handed her a page torn from the *Bay Beacon.* "Don't take this wrong, Sarah. When I came across this, I thought of you."

There was a circled item for a divorce support group meeting in Fairfax, a half-hour drive away.

"I'm not the support group type," said Sarah. "This whole family—" she encompassed Kyle and her dad with a look "—we kind of avoid that sort of thing."

"This is West Marin. Nobody here avoids that sort of thing," LaNelle insisted.

Her brother and father shuffled their feet, united in male sheepishness.

"I've been away too long," Sarah said. "I'm more Chicago than Marin."

"So how do people in Chicago handle something like this?"

"It's hard to generalize. Some might go out and get drunk, or talk about the issue with people who have been their neighbors and friends for a hundred years." She pictured the neighborhood where she'd lived with Jack, the people as friendly and open as the Midwestern prairie. "It doesn't matter. I'm dealing with things on my own."

No one said anything to that, but Sarah could guess

their thoughts: And you're doing so well with it. These days, Sarah cried a lot. Anything might set her off—a certain song on the radio. A Hallmark commercial on TV. The sight of two people holding hands or worse—holding a baby.

"Besides, my personal life is not the issue here," she added. "I'm trying to give away this perfectly good dog."

"No, you're not," Gran said. "You're keeping it."

"I can't even keep the flowers in the window boxes alive."

"The dog doesn't know that," Gran said. "Sarah, listen. And pay attention, because this is important. Love comes into your life in its own time, not when you're ready."

Sarah knew her grandmother was right. She already loved this dog. Still, she was terrified of taking on such a huge responsibility when her life was a mess. "I ought to take the thing to the shelter in Petaluma," she pointed out. "They'll find her a good home."

"You wouldn't abandon this dog," her grandmother said.

"That's right." Aunt May nodded in agreement.

"And why would you want to, anyway, honey?" her father asked philosophically.

"You can't argue with your elders," Kyle added.

She didn't know whether to laugh or cry. Her family could be a stubborn, insistent bunch; she had nearly forgotten that about them. After the years in Chicago she had begun to think of Jack's large family as her own, but once she left him, she learned otherwise. No one from the Daly clan had called her, not even a sister-in-law by marriage. Like pioneers on the Great Plains, they had circled their wagons, determined to keep outsiders where they belonged—on the outside.

"What makes you think I won't take this dog to the shelter?"

"You're our Sarah," her father said indulgently. "You'd never do that."

"Her name is Franny," Sarah told the vet the next day. She and Franny had been busy. After surrendering to the idea that she had no choice but to keep the dog, she had spent hours grooming her and fixing her a soft bed of cushions in a corner of the house. The dog, starved for attention, seemed delighted by it all.

Though clearly eager and housebroken, Franny was otherwise untrained. Sarah had been watching *The Dog Whisperer* on TV, and she studied a book by the monks of New Skete, who were experts in dog behavior. So far, Franny had learned to sit and lie down, and Sarah had learned calm, assertive behavior. Franny was balky on a leash until Sarah took to keeping treats in her pocket and doling them out when the dog cooperated.

Dr. Penfield estimated that Franny was about two years old, and in excellent health. "Franny," the vet continued. "Any reason you picked that name?"

"Not really. I considered names from mythology, like Ariadne or Leda, but they all seemed pretentious for a dog."

"Not to mention hard to spell." Dr. Penfield grinned. "However, Leda would have been appropriate. She was the mother of Gemini."

Sarah pretended she was aware of that, though in reality, she wasn't much for constellations. "Why do you say it's appropriate?"

Dr. Penfield was gently palpating the dog underneath. "Because she's expecting, and there's definitely more than one."

It took Sarah a moment to process this information. "Oh, lovely," she said, her heart sinking. "I was going to ask about having her spayed."

The vet was quiet for a few seconds. "That is still an option," he said quietly.

"Not for me." A chill ran over Sarah. "I mean, I could never…I'll find a way to deal with the puppies when the time comes."

He nodded, regarding her kindly. "Nature does all the work. The pups will need to stay with her for about eight weeks after they're born. Then they can be adopted, and you can get your dog spayed."

Sarah stroked Franny under the chin. "An abandoned, unwed mother," she murmured. "No wonder you were so skittish."

The vet handed Sarah a sack of product samples. "I think she'll be all right now." She stopped in at her grandmother's house on the way home.

"I have a special delivery," she said to Gran and Aunt May, finding them in their garden cutting flowers. "And Franny has news. She's pregnant."

"Oh, my," Gran said, taking off her pink gardening gloves. "That's more than you bargained for."

"We'll be all right." Sarah slipped the dog a treat. She felt enormously tender for Franny, who had been through God-knew-what. "But, Aunt May, it's more than you bargained for, too. We can find someplace else to live."

"Don't even think about it," Aunt May said. "You're staying for as long as you need it."

Sarah handed her a framed drawing she'd done. "I thought you'd say that. This is a thank-you gift. For letting me use the cottage."

Gran and Aunt May admired the picture. It was a sketch

of them both, seated on their porch across from a cartoon Sarah. There was a speech bubble coming out of Gran's mouth that read, "The older you get, the smarter we get."

"Oh, that's just lovely," said Aunt May. "We'll put it up over the mantel."

"There's really no way to thank you," Sarah said. "I don't know what I'd do without both of you, and the cottage, and all your kindness. In the middle of the mess I've made of my life, you girls are a lifeline."

"Dear, you didn't make a mess," Gran said.

"I made some bad choices." Sarah watched a bee droning around a lily blossom. "I feel like my years with Jack were such a waste, after all this."

"Never say that," Gran told her in a firm voice. "No moment you spent loving someone is ever wasted. Your time with Jack enriched your life in ways you can't always see."

"She's right," Aunt May agreed. "Don't have regrets." She indicated the drawing. "Promise us that, all right?"

Sarah nodded, hoping one day she'd be able to think of her marriage without all the anger and raw pain. "I promise," she said.

Sarah still felt vaguely foolish, even a bit like a phony, walking a dog. Surely any onlooker would assume she was only playing at being a dog person. Dog people had settled lives and goals and regular jobs. They didn't live in borrowed beach cottages and keep weird hours and wonder what lay around the next corner.

Despite her reservations about keeping Franny, one thing was nonnegotiable. The dog had to be taken out. Staying inside like a hermit was no longer an option. Sarah's self-imposed isolation had come to an end. There was an area of the town park where dogs were permitted so long as they were kept on a leash. It was a great spot for people watching. Benches lined the walkways, which were shaded by massive oak and laurel trees. At concrete tables inlaid with chessboards, pairs of players often sat down to match wits. Near the swing set and teeter-totter, young mothers would stand together for hours, chatting away while their children played. Sometimes the kids would grow bored or cranky, but the mothers seemed reluctant to part. It didn't take Sarah long to realize that bringing the kids to the park was as much about the mothers' social life as it was the children's.

After an hour of chasing a driftwood stick, Franny lay in a patch of sunlight and was soon drowsing. Sarah flipped to a fresh page of her sketchbook. A few swift strokes of her pencil rendered the two young women across the way, seemingly absorbed in one another as their children dug in the sandbox. The sketch captured their absorption in the conversation as well as their watchful, protective stance over the children, the peculiar dichotomy of young mothers.

Drawing was one area where Sarah had plenty of confidence in herself. People were often startled by the differences between her comic strip, which created strong impressions with a few bold lines, and her studio art, done with considerable technical expertise and subtlety.

The afternoon school bus disgorged a group of half-grown kids. A slender, dark-haired girl approached Sarah. Franny, who had been dozing under the bench after a good run, lifted her head, then flattened her ears as a growl rumbled in her throat. The girl kept her distance as she shifted her backpack from one shoulder to the other.

"Sorry about her," Sarah said. "I just adopted her, and

she's still in training." She made a scolding sound at Franny and the dog went over on her side, instantly contrite. "Have a seat," she said.

In a flicker of recognition, she realized it was the schoolgirl she'd seen around, the one she thought of as a Disney princess. The girl sat tentatively at the opposite end of the bench and was craning her neck at Sarah's drawing.

She angled the drawing toward her. "I was making a sketch or two," she said.

Color surged to the girl's cheeks. "Sorry. Didn't mean to seem nosy."

"I don't mind."

"You're really good."

"Thanks." She deepened the shading around a key figure in the drawing. "My name's Sarah."

"I'm Aurora," said the girl. "And actually, I know who you are—Sarah Moon, right? You have that comic strip, *Just Breathe*."

Sarah lifted her eyebrows. "News travels fast."

"Don't worry. I'm not a stalker or anything. Nothing else happens around here. My friend Edie's mom, she teaches at the high school. Mrs. Armengast. She said she was your English teacher."

"I remember her." Mrs. Armengast was an anal-retentive, humorless taskmaster whose success record for AP English was legendary.

"She remembers you, too." The girl toyed with a zipper on her backpack. "Um, I'm doing this project for school, about jobs in our community. I'm supposed to interview somebody about their job. So I was wondering if I could interview you."

Sarah nearly choked on the irony of it. "I'm flattered, but the truth is, I barely have a job."

"Drawing a comic strip isn't a job?" Aurora looked crestfallen.

"You know what?" Sarah said, feeling a stab of defiance. Why let the kid think she was a loser? "It is. I'm self-employed, like a subcontractor. And yes, drawing the strip is my job and I'd be happy to tell you about it."

"Can I take notes?"

"Of course."

Looking adorably efficient, she scribbled down the vitals—Sarah's name and age, where she'd gone to college and what she'd studied there. As she gave Aurora a rundown on her career as an illustrator and comic strip artist, a curious thing happened to Sarah. She started feeling marginally better about herself and grew more animated, describing her computerized comic strip layout and her routine of writing in the morning and drawing in the afternoon, staying two months ahead of publication. When she mentioned that her handwriting had been digitized to create her own font, called "SWoon," Aurora's expression turned to something like awe, even after Sarah explained that it was common practice in the industry.

The conversation with this girl reminded Sarah that she had a long list of accomplishments, yet somewhere along the way, she'd stopped taking pride in them. She'd been so wrapped up in her marriage, Jack's illness and recovery, and her quest to get pregnant that she'd lost the dreamy-eyed artist she'd oncc been. She had even begun to buy into Jack's assessment of her career as an unstable and unprofitable pursuit to be regarded more as a hobby than a career.

"A lot of people think you can't support yourself doing art," she said. "Especially people outside Marin. I say it's possible, even though it might not be easy. Art has to be studied and practiced, just like everything else. Before that, you have to love it, plain and simple. You have to love it and let it mean something to you." Sarah couldn't remember a time when she wasn't trying to draw something. Her earliest efforts were stick figures scrawled on the backs of church collection envelopes. When she was tiny, her mother used to give her a pencil to keep her quiet during services. In high school, she had turned her lousy social life into fodder for an underground comic strip that had turned out to be more popular among students than the yearbook.

She let Aurora flip through her sketches. The girl paused at a swift rendering of Shirl with a think bubble over her head with the age-old question, "Paper or plastic?"

A burst of adolescent laughter sounded, and Sarah saw the girl's attention lift toward it.

"Friends of yours?" Sarah asked.

"Nope. Just some girls from my school." Yearning in her brown eyes.

So that's how it is, Sarah thought. She wondered how this gorgeous creature could ever be considered an outcast.

Aurora glanced over as Sarah was studying her.

"I didn't mean to stare," Sarah said, then frowned a little. "It looks like you have a bruise on your cheek." All sorts of possibilities flitted through her mind.

Aurora frowned. Using her sleeve, she rubbed at her face.

To Sarah's relief, the bruise disappeared. "Didn't mean to worry you," Aurora said. "I was doing a charcoal drawing in art class today. Art's my favorite subject."

"It was mine, too."

"That's what I thought." She blushed again. On the far side of the park, a blond woman in a Volvo pulled over to the curb and the group of laughing girls got in.

"My mother works in Vegas," the girl said, though Sarah hadn't asked.

"Oh. Is that where you live?"

The girl hesitated. "I'm staying with family here," she said. "Just until my mother gets settled, you know?"

"I bet you miss her," Sarah commented. "But it's great that you have family here, too. That's nice. It's lucky."

"Yeah, well, Vegas is all about luck."

Sarah watched the pair of young mothers rounding up their toddlers from the swing set and sandbox. She closed her sketchbook and took out a Kleenex to wipe her hands.

"We'll probably all move to Vegas pretty soon," Aurora said.

"All of you. Does that mean you have brothers and sisters?"

"Nope. It's just me and my dad. He really misses my mom." She twisted her small gold stud earring.

Sarah couldn't stand Vegas, although she could see how the glitter and flash might appeal to a kid, even someone too young to gamble. She felt a twinge of bittersweet envy at the girl's words. *He really misses my mom.* Having parents who loved each other gave a child such a sense of security.

"I better go," Aurora said suddenly, slapping her notebook shut and stuffing it into her backpack. "Thanks for the interview."

As the girl walked away, Sarah called after her. "Hey, see you around."

Sixteen

Sarah hesitated at the entryway of the Fairfax Grange Hall, a public facility used for meetings and the occasional special event. I can't do this, she thought. I don't belong here.

"Excuse me." A small, energetic woman brushed past her, the scent of shampoo wafting from her just-washed hair. At one end of the light-filled room, there was a stage hung with dusty-looking drapes. At the other end, Sarah could see a few people—mostly women—in folding chairs arranged in a semicircle or gathered around the coffee urn at a table. These were people of all ages, shapes and sizes. Even so, she couldn't imagine they had anything in common.

"Can I get by?" somebody asked from behind her.

She stepped aside for a man on crutches, his leg encased in a full-length air cast.

"Let me get the door," Sarah said, holding it wide.

"Thanks." The man hobbled in. He was Latino, compact and fit with a face that bore the lines of years in the sun. He passed by Sarah and turned to her. "Well? Are you coming?"

Sarah panicked. Now someone had noticed her. Now she was trapped. Her mouth was dry. "Do I have to?" she blurted out.

"No." He headed for the chairs, then pivoted on one crutch and turned back. "You can always go home and stare at the four walls instead, but who wants to do that?"

She caught the glint of humor in his eyes. "There go my plans for the evening."

She picked a chair near the door. "In case I need to make a fast getaway," she told the guy in the cast, pulling up an extra chair for him to rest his leg on.

"It gets easier."

"This isn't so hard," she said, even though she'd been seated less than a minute. "I think I'll just observe tonight, though. I'm not really into holding hands and praying."

"Wrong meeting," he said. "We don't do that here."

Sarah slumped in relief.

"We do the group hug instead."

She blanched.

He laughed aloud, drawing attention to them. "Kidding."

There were perhaps a dozen people present, and to Sarah's dismay, one of the women said, "We have a new face tonight."

Sarah felt pinned by their gazes. A frog on the dissecting tray. She managed to lift her hand in a feeble wave.

"Let's go around and introduce ourselves. I'm Imogene. My divorce was finalized a year ago."

Sarah couldn't keep track of all the names, but the common bond was clear now. Each person in the room was at some stage of divorce. That was the whole purpose of the group—to offer support for people facing divorce. Simply coming here was huge for Sarah, an acknowledgment that what was happening to her was difficult and she was having trouble dealing with it. When her turn came around, she wanted to bolt. I'm not divorced, she'd say. I don't belong here.

"I'm Sarah," she heard herself say. "I, ah, came here from Chicago."

To her intense relief, no one seemed to expect more. The topic switched after a few murmurs of welcome. "I'm Gloria, and I'd like to talk about authenticity," a woman said. "Today at work, my partner brought up something I've been thinking about. Just being a good person doesn't necessarily entitle you to a good life. It used to make me angry as hell, thinking about how hard I worked at being a good wife. It was completely frustrating because no matter how great everything looked on the outside, I was miserable on the inside. That didn't change until I understood that I have to surrender to who I am." She smiled, and her eyes softened. "Ruby and I will be celebrating our six-month anniversary together pretty soon. I wish I could tell you that we're living happily ever after, but that would be a lie. She's got a thirteen-year-old daughter who's having trouble accepting this. So we're living happily a day at a time."

Sarah decided this was definitely not the support group for her. How could she have anything in common with Gloria?

No matter how great things looked on the outside, I was miserable on the inside.

So, okay, Sarah thought. There's that.

Feeling less resistant, she leaned back and listened to forty-five minutes of talk. To her surprise and discomfiture, many of the things people said resonated through her. So many marriages went bad because someone was pretending. She wondered why. Why did people pretend? Why had she?

She'd come here thinking she'd never be able to relate to these people. Yet just like these strangers, she'd experienced the feelings of shock, frustration and isolation, of shame and disappointment and rage. She was all too familiar with the sense that things were slipping away, and with the denial that kicked in, enabling her to pretend things were fine—for a while, at least.

"Anyone else?" a woman asked, looking around the room.

Sarah's heart sped up. This was a group of strangers. She had no business sharing personal matters with them.

People were looking at watches. Chairs were scraping.

Good, she thought. Saved by the bell. She had never been socially gregarious. As a student, she never liked raising her hand in class or contributing to a discussion. When she was Jack's wife, she'd always been content to follow him to social functions and watch from the sidelines.

Her palms were sweating. Best to slip away and forget about this.

And then, just as people were starting to rise from their seats, someone said, "I'm scared to find out who I am without my husband."

The room fell silent. The words seemed to echo off the old, battered walls of the building.

Oh, crap, thought Sarah. That was me.

Her face heated uncomfortably and she fumbled for an explanation. "Um, I'm not sure why I blurted that out." She paused and looked around the room, expecting to see impatience or boredom. They were all staring at her. She attempted a self-deprecating grin. "Stop me if you've heard this one before."

The guy next to her—Luis—patted her arm. "My friend,

if you come to this group long enough, you've heard everything before. That doesn't matter. For you, this is all brand-new. That's what matters."

Part of her, the Chicago part, wanted to jump up and yell, "How can this matter to you people? You don't even know me. How can you care?" Yet deep down, she was grateful to be heard. Finally. She took a deep breath and laced her fingers together in her lap. "I married right out of college. I never really made a life for myself. I went from a shared dorm room to Jack's house. Back when it was all working, it felt fine. Then as time went on, it didn't. It felt like I was living a borrowed life. Something not my own, something I'd need to give back to its owner after a while."

Instead of feeling nervous or silly, Sarah relaxed. These people weren't here to judge her. They were here to listen. "He had already settled down before he met me. So the house we lived in was his. We called it ours but it was always his.

"Do you know, several times after we were first married, I drove right past that house when coming home? I didn't even recognize it as mine. How can you not know what your own house looks like?" She wondered how she'd stayed blind to so much for so long.

"When you work at home, like I did, you generally create a space that reflects who you are, right? Well, not me. My home office was a little study with built-in shelves and a drafting table. Jack kept his fly-tying equipment in there, and his gear was always parked right in front of the window, blotting out the light. And it never occurred to me that this was a problem." She glanced at her watch. "Anyway, a lot of other things happened. Things that may not shock you all but they sure as hell took me by surprise.

I'm glad I came here tonight. Thanks for making me feel welcome." She stopped, pulled in a deep breath, feeling cleansed. No, scoured raw. Which felt better than dragging herself around, half-alive, day after day.

They put their chairs away and cleaned up the coffee service. "I hope you'll come back," Gloria said.

"I wish I didn't need to," Sarah told her.

"Everyone needs friends."

"You're right, but it's not like they come knocking at the door."

"True. You have to take steps yourself. This—coming to a meeting—is one of them."

Sarah found a tea towel and dried the lid of the coffee urn. "Here's what scares me. I feel as though I've reached the end of my life, like there's nothing left for me to do."

"Don't think of it that way." Gloria wiped down the counters and sink. "Think of it as having a really long adolescence. And now you're finally ready to grow up."

Sarah felt drawn to Gloria's straightforward manner. "That's one way of looking at it. So how long have you been divorced?"

"Just a year. After a decade of trying to talk myself into being happy, I got divorced, fell apart and fell in love, all in the space of a few months. People say you shouldn't start a new relationship so soon after the marriage ends, but hell. Who cares what people say?"

Sarah put on her jacket as they walked out together.

"Come back next week," Gloria said.

Sarah hesitated, then felt like smacking herself. "I still have this habit of thinking of him. Someone extends an invitation, and I automatically think of Jack's schedule. Or I'll go to the grocery store and buy things he likes, without even thinking about it. I don't even know what kind of crackers I prefer. I always bought Ritz because those were Jack's favorites."

"I hope you took them right back to the store."

"Better than that. I went down to the beach and fed everything to the seagulls."

Seventeen

Aurora was tired of being an A student, but she didn't quite know how to go about changing her reputation. Her English teacher had assigned *War of the Worlds*, and she wanted to turn up her nose at it, but in all honesty, she couldn't. It was a great book, way better than the movie. Yet if she admitted this aloud, she'd be as uncool as a member of the chess club. Bummer. She liked chess, too.

Glenmuir was the end of the line for the school bus. At the intersection of Drake and Shoreline, the brakes hissed and it shuddered to a halt. Aurora looked up from *War of the Worlds* as Mandy Jacobson and her sidekicks moved forward to exit the bus, chattering and laughing all the way.

Aurora waited expectantly, hoping as she did each day that the girls would notice her, maybe invite her to come along for whatever it was they did every day. They always seemed to be having a hilarious time, even just walking down the street.

But today, like all days, they breezed past, leaving the scent of bubble gum and Juicy Couture body splash in their wake, ignoring Aurora as though she was a knapsack somebody had left behind.

You'd think she would learn, give up and move on after all this time. Yet their lives looked like such fun. It was hard not to want to be one of them. On the bus, they put on makeup and did each other's hair. Some days, they acknowledged Aurora, but only if they needed to copy her prealgebra or Spanish homework, because they knew she'd have hers done, and correct. And even though it made her heart pound and her palms sweat in terror of getting caught, Aurora obliged. She had no choice. If she refused, these girls would have nothing to do with her.

She got up slowly and slid her arm through one strap of her backpack.

"See you tomorrow, hon," said the bus driver.

Aurora thanked her and offered a half wave as the door clanked shut.

Mandy and her friends were gathered at the window of Vernon's Variety Store. Since Mr. Vernon had caught them shoplifting makeup last summer, they weren't allowed in the shop, something they seemed to find funny, rather than shameful.

"How about an ice cream?" someone asked.

Aurora was so startled, she nearly tripped over her own feet. "Huh?"

Seated at a stainless steel round table outside the Magic Bean, Sarah Moon was watching her. "I was just wondering if I could buy you an ice cream."

Aurora's cheeks heated. It was embarrassing to be seen following Mandy, Carson and Deb around like a lost puppy.

"Unless you've got plans with your friends?" Sarah asked this tentatively, and Aurora had the impression she understood the way things were.

Aurora decided to enlighten her. "They don't really want to hang out with me." She instantly wished she hadn't been so bluntly honest. She braced herself for Sarah's reaction.

Most adults would say, Nonsense, of course you have friends. Not Sarah, though. She didn't even act surprised.

"Why aren't you friends?" she asked.

Aurora shrugged.

"Let me guess. The ones you want to be friends with ignore you. And the ones who want to be your friends are too geeky to live."

"Pretty much," Aurora admitted, wondering how Sarah knew.

"I hate when that happens."

Aurora concealed a sigh of relief. Thank God she didn't say anything like, *I'll be your friend.* Way too many adults said stuff like that. She especially heard that kind of talk from women her dad dated. The tactic always backfired. It made Aurora feel as used as she did when Mandy copied her homework.

"Watch your step," Sarah said. "Franny has a knack for getting underfoot."

Aurora looked at the dog on the leash, lying under the table. She hesitated, remembering that the mutt had growled at her.

"How is the training coming?" she asked.

"Amazingly well, especially since I've never had a dog before."

"What made you decide to get one now?"

"I didn't exactly decide," Sarah explained. "I just sort of… ended up with her."

Aurora was extremely familiar with the concept but she didn't say so. She started to feel uncomfortable, remembering the lie she'd told Sarah Moon last time they met. She and her dad were moving to Vegas to be with her mom. *Yeah, right.*

"I call her Franny," Sarah explained, "after a character in a book."

"*Franny and Zooey*," Aurora said, relieved that Sarah didn't ask about her Vegas plans.

"You know that book?"

"Sure. I've read *Nine Stories* and *Catcher in the Rye,* too."

"I'm impressed."

Aurora shrugged again. Reading any book ever written—that was simple. Making friends with Mandy Jacobson and her gang—*that* was impossible.

"Would you like to have a seat?"

Aurora hesitated, just for a moment. Her dad was on duty until tonight, so she had to go to her grandparents'. She was about to politely decline when a boy came out of the coffee shop. It was Zane Parker, the heartthrob of Glenmuir. In a Magic Bean T-shirt and baseball cap, a black apron slung low around his hips, he greeted her with a smile. Aurora instantly sat down next to Sarah.

"Hey," he said. "Can I get you something?"

"Yes, please." She panicked, having no idea what she wanted. She couldn't remember her own name. "A Coke, please." As he headed back into the shop, she recalled that she didn't really like Coke.

"And how about an ice cream?" Sarah offered.

"No, thank you."

Sarah stuck her spoon into the stainless steel cup. "Normally, I don't even like ice cream but lately it's all I think about. I started trying weird flavors, too, like mocha and pistachio together. And then sometimes, I think... Roquefort.... Why not?"

"Roquefort ice cream?" Aurora asked.

"Sometimes I'm weird that way."

Zane showed up in time to see Aurora's face contort into a look of exaggerated disgust. "Everything okay?" he asked.

I want to die, Aurora thought. Right this minute. "Yes," she managed to say, ironing out the wrinkles in her face.

He set the Coke in front of her and then left so quickly she barely had time to thank him. Dangit. She should have ordered something that would require him to stick around. Bananas flambé, prepared tableside.

"He's cute," Sarah said.

"Uh-huh."

"Are you friends with him?"

"As if. Zane's in ninth grade and I'm in seventh. I'm sort of friends with his brother, Ethan, who's in my grade." Ethan was neither cute nor cool, but he was just a heartbeat away from Zane.

Aurora sighed. "How do you get a boy to notice you?"

Sarah smiled and licked the back of her spoon. "You quit caring whether or not he does."

Aurora slipped the straw into the bottle. "All right. From now on, I don't care."

"Good for you."

"Speak of the devil." She pointed at a skinny kid in baggy jeans and black T-shirt, surfing toward them on a two-wheeled in-line skateboard. "That's Ethan." He was a skater who dressed in black, wore glasses and liked school way too much. Still, there was something about him, something serious and mature, that appealed to her. She hoped he'd still be that way when she hit sixteen and her dad let her date. In the meantime, Zane was at the center of all her dreams.

Ethan jumped off at the curb, popped the board up and caught it one-handed. “Hey,” he said to Aurora.

“Hey.”

Zane came out. “Did you get the stuff for tonight?”

Ethan opened the small paper sack he was holding to reveal a can of kerosene. “Bonfire at the beach tonight,” he said to Aurora. “Are you coming?”

She could feel Zane behind her, motioning for his brother to shut up.

“Nah,” she said, then deliberately turned away. She felt kind of bad for him, but it would be worse to show up where she wasn’t wanted.

Ethan tossed the sack to Zane, flipped his board to the ground and skated off. Aurora thought Sarah was looking a bit pale and distracted. Indicating the sketchbook on the table, she asked, “What are you working on today?”

“This and that.” She flipped the book open to a page of cartoon faces.

Aurora sensed that she and Sarah had more in common than their love of drawing. Sarah was a misfit, too, yet she’d clearly embraced her inner freak. Aurora wondered if that somehow made life easier for her. The sketches offered a glimpse into someone’s private thoughts, something Aurora found very cool. The swift renderings resembled the comic strip, but these were artistic. Mr. Chopin, her art teacher, might call the sketches impressionistic. They were bigger, bolder, drawn in a hurry with an assured hand.

“I was brainstorming some ideas,” Sarah said. “I usually draw and think until something comes to me.”

Aurora slowly turned the pages. She recognized caricatures of people around town—the caretaker at the yacht club, the day care crossing guard, the barista at the latte stand, a guy down at the fishing dock. There were a lot of studies of Franny, sleeping curled in a ball or looking through a screen door.

"These are awesome," she said, stopping at a page of studies for the comic strip, *Just Breathe.* The character called Shirl had a smart mouth and a smarter mother. Lulu always seemed to be spouting advice, like "If your brain was as smart as your mouth, we'd rename you Einstein." Lulu always had something optimistic to say. Looking at the drawings, Aurora felt a familiar flash of longing. "Is she based on your real-life mother?"

"She's based on my mother, plus my own fantasies." Sarah's smile was a little sad. "The thing about cartoon people is you get to plan everything they're going to do and say. You plan their mistakes and you plan the things that work out well for them. I don't think real mothers always have the right thing to say at the tip of their tongue, like Lulu does."

Aurora paused at a panel showing Lulu contemplating a Brazilian bikini wax, and a laugh escaped her.

"It'll never be published, not in a paper, anyway," Sarah said.

"Why not? It's funny."

"Mainstream papers have rules—no sex, religion, torture or death, to name several. No fifty-ish women getting waxed. You don't want to offend readers because they complain to the editor, who then has to unruffle their feathers. The prevailing wisdom is that there's enough sex and torture in other sections of the paper." Sarah sighed and flipped the book shut. "Next time you're wondering why so many comic strips are so bland, there's your answer."

Aurora studied her and frowned. "Are you, like, okay?" Sarah's face had turned pasty white, and there was a sheen of sweat on her forehead that hadn't been there a moment ago.

"I don't feel so hot," Sarah said faintly. She slipped the

box of Pantone markers and sketchbook into her tote bag. "Probably just a sugar rush from the ice cream," she said. "It'll wear off during the walk home. I live a short ways up the road at a place called May's Cottage."

Aurora jumped up. "I know exactly where that is. I'll walk with you. If that's, like, all right." She couldn't stand the thought of sitting here all by herself, with a Coke she didn't want and Zane Parker seeing what a loser she was. Fumbling, she dug in a pocket of her backpack for some money.

"I've got this." Sarah left some money on the table. "Thanks," she called to Zane, who was inside.

"See you around," Zane replied.

Aurora nearly choked. *See you around.* Oh my God, she thought. I'm in love.

"Come on, Franny," Sarah said, patting her hip. Franny forged ahead, tugging the leash to its limit. They left the main street behind, heading along the shady lane that traced the edge of the bay. Aurora had been past the cottage many times. It wasn't far. Maybe Sarah would invite her in, show her more drawings.

She stole a glance at Sarah and was alarmed to see that she was paler than ever. Her skin was so translucent that Aurora could see a delicate tracery of veins at her temple. She felt a clutch of apprehension in her gut. This was not good. And she didn't know what to do. She barely knew this woman.

What if she was having some kind of fit? What if she was an addict or something? Aurora looked wildly around, but they were completely alone on the empty, tree-lined stretch of road.

"You really don't look so good," she blurted out. "No offense, but you don't."

"Yeah, well, I think there might be a reason for that," Sarah said, lurching sideways.

"What's that?"

"I feel like death on a stale sesame seed bun." She was trembling now, and sweat ran down her temples. "I need to sit down."

"There's nowhere to—oh." Aurora watched as Sarah sank to the grassy berm at the side of the road. She wasn't sitting like a normal person would sit down, but was crumpled in a heap, crushing the wildflowers beneath her. "Oh my gosh," Aurora said, feeling an icy thrust of panic. The dog whined, as if Aurora had scolded her. She got down on her knees and gave Sarah a little shake. She nearly collapsed with relief when Sarah blinked at her. "What happened?"

"I think you passed out," Aurora said.

"I've never fainted before." She looked dazed, her face still ashen. Her hands were damp and cold.

"Maybe, um, put your head between your knees?" Aurora suggested, setting down her backpack. She grabbed her phone out of a side pocket.

"Oh, come on," Sarah said. "Don't go calling 911."

"I'm calling my dad."

Sarah frowned and wiped her sleeve across her forehead. "So who's your dad?"

Aurora selected his number from the menu of her phone. "He pretty much *is* 911."

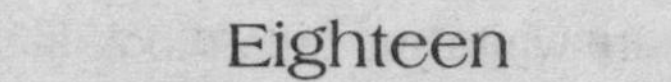

Eighteen

Aurora almost never called Will at work, so when his phone jingled with her unique ring tone, he picked up immediately.

"Aurora, is everything all right?"

"Yes. I mean, I'm fine, but I'm with someone who might need help."

He made eye contact with Gloria, who was doing some paperwork. By the time she nodded and waved him toward the door, he was already grabbing his jacket from a hook. "What's going on?"

"You know Sarah Moon?"

"Not exactly, but—"

"Doesn't matter," Aurora said. "We were just walking down the road together and she kind of collapsed."

Will heard someone in the background. He couldn't make out the words but there was definitely a sound of protest. He resisted the urge to yell at Aurora about talking to strangers. "Is she conscious? Bleeding?"

"She's kind of sick, I guess. All pale and sweaty."

The EMT rig was on call at the moment, responding to

a summons from a boatyard ten miles away. The substation in the next town could send one, but that meant adding twenty minutes to the response time.

"Where are you?" He signaled to Gloria that he was on this, and headed for the duty captain's truck.

Five minutes later, he found them—his daughter, Sarah Moon and a large mutt. At least, he supposed it was Sarah. Her short blond hair was tousled and matted with sweat, her face was pasty white and didn't look familiar to him in the least.

He got out of the truck and approached them, torn between worry and suspicion. What the hell was this stranger doing with his daughter?

She gazed up at him, expressionless and glassy-eyed. Drugs, he thought, and his suspicion deepened. He'd seen more than his share of people who couldn't keep away from the stuff. D, R, A, B, C, he thought, reminding himself of the rescue drill. Danger, Response. Airway, Breathing…what the hell was the C for? He couldn't remember. Though Will was trained in emergency medical techniques, this was not his area of expertise, so he simply asked, "What happened here? Are you okay?"

He could tell she wasn't expecting to recognize him. When she did, a small sound of confusion escaped her. "Will Bonner?" she asked.

"Aurora says you're not feeling well. Did you faint?"

"I'm not sure. I felt light-headed and had to sit down. Next thing I know, I'm down. Really, I probably need to sit still for a minute, and it'll pass." She frowned. "Are you a paramedic?"

"Fire captain. Are you on any medication?" Circulation. C was for circulation. He grabbed her hand and checked her pulse. "Are you a diabetic?"

She seemed dazed and disoriented. "No. I…no."

Putting two fingers under her chin, he tilted her face up to his to see if her pupils would respond to the light. Her skin felt clammy to the touch. Gently using the pad of his thumb, he held open one eye, then the other. Her pupils contracted with the light and her eyes were…extremely blue. He checked for the smell of alcohol or pot on her breath, in her hair and clothes. He felt surprised and perhaps a touch relieved to discover she didn't appear to be under the influence of anything. She smelled of bruised grass and wildflowers.

"Can you help her, Daddy?" asked Aurora.

"Aurora's your daughter?" Sarah looked even more confused than ever.

People were always surprised by that, and he was used to ignoring the question. He was no expert, but he didn't like the feel of her pulse. Too rapid and thready. Something wasn't right.

"Just as a precaution, I'm giving you a ride to Valley Regional. It's a fifteen-minute drive from here."

Aurora hopped to it, opening the passenger side door of the department's F-150.

"Take my hand," he said, offering it to Sarah.

She eyed his hand, and then Will. "Really, I just need to rest. If you could give me a lift home—"

"Nope. It's either Valley or your private physician."

"I don't have one."

"Valley, then." He bent down a little, moved his hand closer. "Let me help. It's my job."

Her eyes narrowed. The sharpness of her look nudged at a vague memory from the past. He didn't really remember much about her from high school, but in that moment he had a little flash of recognition. He thought maybe he recalled that narrow-eyed stare, emanating from the furtive, bitter misfit she'd been years ago—the oysterman's daughter who came to school with chapped hands and a bad attitude.

She grabbed his hand and let him help her up.

"I have your things," Aurora said. She was right there, at Sarah's other side. Together, they helped her into the backseat. The dog jumped in without hesitation. Will radioed Gloria to let her know what was up.

Once they were on the road, he checked the rearview mirror. "All right?"

She was pale and perspiring, her eyes closed. "This is a wild-goose chase."

"Think of it as a detour. And a chance to prove me wrong," he said.

"Priceless."

Aurora was quiet, next to him in the front seat, her school backpack at her feet. She held Sarah's bag in her lap. Their eyes met and Will gave a slight nod: *Good call.*

Every few seconds, he checked on Sarah in the mirror. The fact that she didn't resist being taken to the regional hospital was telling. If a person wasn't really sick, or if she had something to hide, she wouldn't agree to a trip to the doctor.

The dog sat alert in the rear of the vehicle. Will was grateful that someone had finally adopted the mutt. He'd seen it around and figured it wasn't long for this world. Too often, strays wound up dead at the side of the highway. Others disappeared late at night, victims of cougars, coyotes or wolves.

Pets were often a problem on a call. There was no prescribed protocol for dealing with them. More often than Will cared to think about, a fiercely protective dog tried to deter firefighting efforts or keep a rescue team from reaching a victim. And often, rescuers were too late to save an animal—or more than one—at the scene of an accident. The old image of the firefighter rescuing a kitten from a tree was a suburban legend.

He checked the rearview mirror. Sarah Moon was slumped against the door of the truck's club cab.

"Sarah," he said loudly. "Sarah, can you hear me?"

Aurora unbuckled her seat belt and twisted around. "Hey, Sarah. Sarah?" She whipped a glance at Will. "Dad!"

"Check her pulse and make sure she's breathing."

Aurora climbed into the backseat. "I'm pretty sure she has a pulse, and she's breathing."

"Keep shaking her and talking to her. We're almost there."

He was already punching in the code of the E.R. Valley Regional lacked a high-level trauma center but its E.R. was first-rate.

"This is Captain Will Bonner from Glenmuir," he told dispatch. "I'm headed your way with a female…in her twenties. Average height and build." This was not his specialty, and the information did not come automatically. Blond hair and blue eyes, he almost said, but figured that was irrelevant. To the E.R., anyway. "She experienced weakness, maybe a fainting spell."

"Is she altered?" asked the dispatcher.

"Negative. She claims she's not on any medication and is not diabetic. Now it appears she's lost consciousness, but she still has a pulse." Will probably shouldn't sound so certain of his own conviction. "We're about three more minutes out. Should I stop and reassess?"

"Just get here. We'll clear a bay for you."

The remaining few miles, winding through a thickly

wooded state park, felt endless. He had already flipped on the lights and siren. Now he buried the needle of the speedometer and it still took forever. It didn't help that he could hear Aurora calling Sarah's name over and over again or that the dog, sensing disaster, was whining.

At long last, he arrived at the emergency entrance of Valley. True to the dispatcher's word, a team waited with a well-equipped gurney.

Moments later, they were wheeling Sarah through the swinging double doors.

"Stay with the dog," Will instructed Aurora, pulling the truck into an ambulance slot. "I need to make sure she's all right, and call her father."

"What if she's not all right?"

"I have to call her father either way." He took off his shades. "What were you doing with her, Aurora? I didn't even realize you knew her."

"Shows what you know."

"Aurora—"

"We've talked a couple of times, that's all. We were at the Magic Bean and she was showing me her sketches."

"Did she seem sick to you?"

"Not at first, but then I noticed she got really pale. Then she became all sweaty, and she was swaying on her feet. I think she just wanted to go home and rest."

"She's lucky you came along." He wished he could hang around and enjoy the way Aurora beamed at him. Instead, he said, "I need to go inside. I'll be back as quick as I can."

A team of six had clustered around Sarah. She was conscious, lying back on an adjustable cot atop crinkled paper sheets.

She was still pale. A blood pressure cuff wrapped her

arm and an IV had already been started. An oxygen mask covered her nose and mouth. The fingers of her right hand were banded with white Velcro tape attached to a line leading to a monitor.

"Hey, how are you feeling?"

"All right." The clear mask made her sound as though she was calling down a well. "What about Franny?"

It took Will a moment to figure out who Franny was. "My daughter's with the dog in the truck. We'll take care of her until you get home."

A nurse stood beside the bed, hanging a bag of clear fluid.

"I'm going to call your father," Will said.

"He's probably at Mounger's garage, working on his car."

"Would he have a cell phone with him?"

"You can try." She dictated a local number.

Will took out his phone and moved away as he dialed. He grabbed a guy in a lab coat and pulled him aside.

"What do I tell her father?" Will asked.

"Probably dehydration," the doctor said. "We'll do some tests."

"So no cause for alarm."

"Not at the moment."

The call connected to voice mail, which was no surprise. Cell phone coverage in the area was all but nonexistent. Will was very clear in his message. "Your daughter is all right. I brought her to Valley Regional because she had a fainting spell. You should come as soon as you get this message." Then he rang off and stuck the phone in his pocket.

"You did that well," Sarah said in a thin voice that echoed within the oxygen mask. "I can see how you have to be careful of how you break news to people. At least now he won't freak out and have a heart attack."

"Hope not." Will tried to imagine getting a message that his daughter had been taken to the emergency room. He probably wouldn't wait around to hear the rest.

"Will you stay?" she asked suddenly, anxiously.

"What?" He was surprised she wanted him to stick around. Any port in a storm, he figured. "No problem." He hadn't planned to linger, but all she had to do was ask. He could see a lot more questions in her wan face and worried eyes, but he had to step back to let the house staff work, gathering samples and observations for the tests that had been ordered, bombarding her with questions about her medical history.

So here was Sarah Moon, all grown-up.

While the staff seemed to percolate all around her, speaking in medical code, Will hooked his thumbs in his back pockets, stood aside and held her distressed gaze with his. He wanted to tell her she was going to be fine, but he couldn't say so with certainty. Young, healthy people didn't collapse by the side of the road for no reason.

The E.R. looked just the same as it had the last time he'd had to bring Marisol here. He wished he didn't remember every detail, but he couldn't help it. He had memorized the conical shape of the overhead lights, and the greenish glare that fell over the exam table. He knew the hollow sound of a detached, faceless voice on the PA system, the clack of instruments on a tray.

The house staff melted away, at least momentarily. Stepping closer to the bed, he said, "Feeling better?"

"No." She lifted the oxygen mask. Her lips were still bluish. "Don't look so guilty. It's not your fault."

"You should put that back." He indicated the mask.

"I need to check on my dog. Franny doesn't like being separated from me."

"Aurora can take care of her. She's good with animals."

Sarah relaxed against the pillow. "I haven't had Franny for long, but once she made up her mind to trust me, she stuck to me like glue, just like that. It's a bit scary, how attached I am already. You'd think we'd been together forever." She put the mask back in place.

"Dogs can be like that."

For some reason, the statement struck her as funny. He saw a smile shine from her eyes, though the mask covered her nose and mouth. Then he realized she wasn't smiling at all. A tear slipped down her cheek and melted into the spongy gasket of the mask.

Oh, man, he thought. This was why he was a firefighter, not an EMT. He'd rather face a blazing forest than a hurting woman's tears.

"Do you want me to find the doctor?" he asked. "Are you in pain?"

She shook her head. "Sorry." She muttered something else he couldn't make out. Then she said distinctly, "You have a nice daughter."

"Thank you." It was something he heard often and never got tired of. He just wished it made Aurora happy. "I'm proud of her."

"I don't blame you." She shut her eyes and breathed into the mask.

Will felt awkward, which was unusual for him. Due to the nature of his job, he saw people in all kinds of circumstances, often during the most terrible moments of their lives. He saw families whose possessions had burned to ash, farmers whose crops or orchards had been destroyed, children who had just lost a pet. His job was no picnic, but it was who he was, what he was good at. Despite his preference for dealing directly with fires, he knew how to engage a person by looking deep into her eyes. He learned not to flinch at someone else's pain, and he understood that simply feeling their agony didn't help. You had to do something about it.

Agitated, he looked around the area. Why weren't they helping her? She seemed exhausted, lying limp against the pillow, her pale hair damply plastered to her brow. He stood quietly by, trying not to let his agitation show, because that might upset her. He wondered if he should pat her hand, try to comfort her somehow. He decided against it. Better to leave her alone, let her rest.

What an odd bird she used to be. As teenagers they could not have been more different. He had been full of the kind of dreams only a cocky young athlete could have. She had been, to him, a cipher. He had not known her, except as an annoyance in his life. Nor would he have bothered with her except that, for reasons he now understood all too clearly, she had singled him out for ridicule.

He recalled the first time someone had shown him Sarah's comic strip, which she'd titled "Hell on Earth." The publication had no school sponsorship. Yet it was the most popular thing going, passed around from student to student like a joint at a party.

Will hadn't thought about it in years, but he could easily recall Sarah's bold, somewhat crude drawings. She lampooned everything from the fall alumni parade to the food in the cafeteria to girls having cosmetic surgery—including Will's sister, Birdie. Most of all, though, Sarah Moon's sarcasm bit deep into people to whom life and all its pleasures came easily. People who didn't have to sweat for their grades or fight for their spot on a team, people who could sit anywhere at lunch, date anyone they wanted and charm any teacher on the faculty.

People like Will.

She had gone after him without mercy. Her bold, assured drawings reduced him to a vacant-eyed creature with a square jaw and shoulders so wide he couldn't fit through doorways. It had infuriated him to see himself as a cartoon character pumped up with his own importance, obsessed with his looks, using his talent and charm to manipulate every situation to his advantage.

He pretended to laugh at "Hell on Earth" along with everyone else, but deep down, the caricature of him made him squirm. Although he would never admit it, he knew the reason he hated her comic strip.

Because she was right about him. Her portrayal of him was bitingly accurate.

Maybe he hadn't been as stupid and clueless as the caricature, but he probably had been as self-absorbed and mean-spirited as she portrayed him. She held up a mirror and he didn't like what he saw.

"Sarah!" Nathaniel Moon strode into the emergency department and hurried to her side. "What's going on?"

"Hey, Dad." She lifted the mask and made a valiant effort to smile.

Her father seemed as ill at ease around her as Will felt. He felt an unexpected kinship with Nathaniel—they were both single fathers.

Nathaniel awkwardly patted her shoulder. "How are you? What happened?"

Will filled him in, trying to make everything seem routine. But he could see the concern on Nathaniel's face: there was nothing routine about a young woman collapsing.

When the doctor arrived a few minutes later, he wore a curious expression on his face. He wasn't exactly smiling, but there appeared to be a spring in his step. Will felt better, seeing the doc looking calm and confident. "I'm going to take off now," he said, stepping back to give them some privacy. "I'll watch your dog, bring it over after you're home."

"Thanks," Nathaniel murmured.

Sarah's gaze was fastened on the doctor. He had some forms on a clipboard. "Your labs are back," he said.

Part Four

JUST BREATHE

Nineteen

"Thanks for coming," Sarah said that night as she opened the door for Will Bonner.

He stepped inside the cottage, and she was instantly struck with the impression that he was too big for the place. Too tall, too broad, too present, too…everything.

Franny was ecstatic about her homecoming. She'd been with Will and Aurora all day. Will had offered to keep her for the night, since Sarah had not returned home until nine o'clock. That would have been the practical thing to do, rather than asking him to deliver the dog, but Sarah was not in a practical frame of mind.

"Will, I really appreciate this," she said, sounding remarkably calm.

"Not a problem." He stood with his baseball cap in his hand, watching her. Waiting and no doubt wondering.

Sarah held his gaze. The only way to say it was to say it. "I'm pregnant."

There. The words were out. The news delivered by the doctor now hung in the air, creating their invisible but inescapable reality. It was a moment that changed everything—her future, her dreams, the life she thought she would have. She had imagined it many times, but she'd never pictured herself sharing the news first with a relative stranger.

To his credit, he took the news well enough. "Are congratulations in order?"

"Yes and no. I mean, it's something I wanted. Just…not now." She could still hear the doctor's announcement.

She was pregnant.

Unexpectedly, impossibly, mind-blowingly pregnant.

It was a dream come true. It was her worst nightmare. She was still in a state of shock. Being pregnant was the last thing she'd expected. Sure, there had been symptoms over the past few weeks. She thought the missed period was the result of stopping the cyclical doses of Clomid, and she had dismissed the nausea and weird cravings as nerves. Today she'd learned there was a reason for all that, and it had nothing to do with ending her marriage and starting over. *A baby.*

"I can't thank you and Aurora enough for helping me today," she said. The moment felt entirely surreal. Here she was with a man she had once adored and hated with every fiber of her passionate adolescent being. "Please," she said, "have a seat. I mean, if you have time."

There was a world of meaning in his moment of hesitation. They were strangers, the way they had always been. No matter how much time had passed since high school, she was still the weird chick with a chip on her shoulder and he was still the godlike athlete.

"Thanks," he said, and took a seat on the chenille-covered sofa. "I just got off work."

"Can I get you something to drink?"

"I'm fine."

"I don't have any beer but there's a bottle of Pinot—"

"Sarah."

She took a deep breath. "I'm babbling."

"Sit down." He took her by the hand and pulled her down beside him. "Listen," he said, "just so you're clear on this—I want you to know I respect your privacy, a hundred percent."

"About me, uh…" Her mouth went dry. She could barely think it, let alone say it. "About me being pregnant."

"Totally your business."

Very diplomatic. He probably knew all kinds of scandalous things about citizens in his fire district. She figured that in his position, he sometimes had to burst in on people unexpectedly in order to rescue victims who got themselves into a jam. He would know who kept weird sex toys in their bedroom and who never cleaned the kitchen or returned their library books.

"I should tell your sister. As you probably know, I'm her client."

"Are you her friend?"

"No. I mean, she's great, but it's not a social thing."

"I'm thinking you need a friend more than a lawyer right now. Are you sure you're feeling all right?"

"Kind of overwhelmed, but otherwise all right." She eyed him with both curiosity and suspicion.

"What?" he asked.

"There was a time when Will Bonner would've spray painted the news on a train trestle."

"That was years ago." He didn't deny that the old Will would have done exactly that. "People change. I've changed. And whatever you choose to do about your situation is strictly your business."

The comment startled her. She caught his meaning, then vigorously shook her head. "Oh, I'm having this baby. And keeping it. No question about that."

There wasn't. She had wanted this for far too long and had worked too hard for it.

"Then I guess congratulations *are* in order." He sent her a smile so genuine that she blinked.

"Thanks. After the doctor, you're actually the first one to congratulate me." She paused. "My father neglected to do so."

"I'm sure he was preoccupied with the fact that his daughter had been brought to the E.R."

"I don't get it. You're making me feel better about things." She was not only charmed by him, but intrigued. "I wasn't expecting that from you."

He laughed. "I'm going to take that as a compliment, even though I'm not sure you meant it that way." He relaxed against the overstuffed sofa, looking as though he belonged there after all. "Anyway, if you feel like talking, or want to unload or something …"

She wondered if her lower jaw was really on the floor, or if it just felt that way. Will Bonner, holding out the hand of friendship? What was wrong with this picture?

Maybe it was in his job description to check on hysterical pregnant women and make sure they didn't go off the deep end.

She felt him watching her and realized she hadn't replied. When she did, it was with a question of her own. "Why?"

"Why what?"

"Why would you invite me to unload on you?" In spite of herself, she felt her gaze being drawn to him. His big shoulders looked as though they could support the weight of the world.

"You're by yourself. You just had some big news."

"You are an extremely kind person," she said, studying him. *Same great looks,* she thought in a TV announcer's voice. *New, improved insides!* "When did that happen? Where's the Will Bonner who used to call me Oyster Girl?"

He spread his hands, palms up.

Correction, she thought. He didn't look the same as he had in high school. He looked better. He'd filled out, and his smile was genuine and deep, growing from within. His eyes—hazel, she had no trouble remembering—crinkled at the sides, adding character to looks that had once been too perfect.

"Did I really call you Oyster Girl?" he asked.

"You and the entire basketball team."

"We had nicknames for all the girls. Believe me, you could've done worse. You're right, though. I wasn't nice in high school. I suppose I was the guy in your comic strip."

"For what it's worth, I feel bad about that."

"Don't. Maybe seeing myself in your comic strip made me determined to be a better person."

"Your parents get credit for that, not my drawings."

"How much did you listen to your parents when you were in high school?"

"I barely remember having a conversation with them."

"I rest my case."

Chitchat. She, Sarah Moon, was making chitchat with Will Bonner. In high school, he was the sort of person you looked at and thought, he's got a great life ahead of him. She used to fantasize about him. She and every other girl in school.

"I want you to know, it's okay to tell Aurora. She's probably wondering."

"Yeah, she wanted to come with me but I made her stay home. It's a school night. But your news isn't mine to tell."

She could feel her color come up, like mercury rising in a thermometer. "Aurora's great," she commented. "You must be incredibly proud of her." She wondered how many times she had stared at the photograph of Will and Aurora in Birdie's office. Sarah had never connected the tiny angel in the picture with Will's nearly grown daughter. People left pictures in their frames forever, she reflected. Out of laziness, or because they wanted to freeze a particular moment in time?

"I am."

Keep talking, she silently urged him. Don't make me pull the story out of you.

He didn't keep talking.

"So I'm guessing she's your stepdaughter," she ventured.

He nodded. "I married her mother the summer after high school. Legally adopted Aurora a couple of years after that. Sometimes I feel more like her older brother than her father."

He never said what happened to the mother.

You never asked, she thought.

"What's that look?" he asked.

"I'm not giving you a look."

"Sure, you were. I saw it. What are you thinking?"

"About what you just said about Aurora's mother. It's going to keep me busy for hours, speculating."

"Yeah?" He turned sideways on the sofa and held her gaze with his. "What are you going to speculate about?"

"Aurora told me you and your…wife are really close, but that she lives in Vegas now."

He stayed very still for a moment. Then he dropped his elbows to his knees and steepled his fingers together. "That's half-right. Marisol does live in Vegas."

"And the other half…?"

"Aurora's had a hard time accepting that we split up."

He was different when he talked about his daughter. There was a depth and gentleness in him that Sarah never would have thought him capable of. "I'm sorry," she said quietly. "And I apologize for bringing up a painful subject."

He kept staring down at his hands. "She left. It happens." A new kind of silence settled between them. This one was not awkward, but soft with a shared understanding.

Sarah felt oddly safe, talking to him. And she definitely needed to talk. He'd been absolutely right when he'd pointed out earlier that she needed a friend. She had this uncanny urge to tell him what it felt like to have her marriage end at the exact moment a life was beginning. With her father today, she'd been too stunned and her father too uncomfortable to analyze and speculate. With Will, she felt as though she'd explode if she didn't get the words out, and he seemed perfectly at ease with that. There was this thing he did, a way of listening with total absorption. She wondered if he felt the same instant bond she did, or if he was just being nice. It didn't matter. There were things she couldn't hold in any longer.

"Jack and I were desperate to have children," she said. "Jack's my soon-to-be ex."

Will didn't say anything. She didn't need him to.

"You want to hear something weird?" she offered.

"Do I have a choice?"

"Not if you stay on that sofa."

"I'm not going anywhere. Tell me something weird, Sarah Moon."

"It's so weird, it's practically cosmic." She was like a sinner with a confession that wouldn't stay inside.

He leaned back and laced his hands around one knee. "Try me."

"I didn't get this way by sleeping with my husband."

"I'm not here to judge you." He shifted on the sofa so that he was facing her. The slight flush on his cheeks was oddly endearing.

"Wait, it's not what you think. I didn't get this way by sleeping with anyone."

"I can't quite wrap my mind around that one." Now he was probably thinking she'd lost her mind.

"See, I'm ninety-nine percent sure this baby was conceived at the exact moment my marriage broke up. I wonder if that's a sign or something."

He stayed quiet. A crease appeared in his forehead.

"Sorry," she said. "I shouldn't dump this on you."

"I'm just trying to figure out the mechanics of…you know." His face turned even redder.

She was oddly charmed to see him blush. "We were going through fertility treatment. It was our twelfth try. The date of conception was the last day I had artificial insemination." She hesitated. "Is this too much information for you?"

"Probably. But don't let that stop you."

She wasn't about to. "So while I, uh, was undergoing the procedure, Jack was with someone else." Mimi Lightfoot, she thought. Mimi-effing-Lightfoot. "I can't believe I'm airing all this laundry."

"I don't shock easily," he assured her, and right or wrong, she believed him.

"So there I was, with a lifelong dream coming true at the same exact moment …" She shook her head. "This must sound crazy to you."

"What, a dream coming true? That doesn't exactly happen every day."

She let out a breath of relief. "Thank you. So if there's any decision to be made, it's when and how to tell Jack, and whether or not this changes things between us. I mean, I figure I should consider reconciling for the sake of the child. That was one of the first thoughts to cross my mind. Doesn't every child deserve the chance to grow up with both parents in the same house?"

"Are you asking me, or thinking aloud?"

She flushed, reminded of his circumstances. "The latter. And I don't have any answers. It's too soon for me to think straight." She grabbed a couch cushion and held it fast against her, because she needed to hold on to something. "This is the kind of thing you fantasize about, over and over in your mind—getting the news that you're pregnant, and telling your husband, picturing the expression on his face. It's always so cheesy, and so romantic." She was startled to feel a fresh stab of anger at Jack. He had robbed her of that, too.

"My advice?" Will said, and didn't wait to see whether or not she wanted it. "Don't rush into any decision. Meanwhile, be happy about the baby."

"It's such crazy timing," she said. "I can't imagine what my life is going to be like, no matter what I decide."

He offered a reassuring smile. "Sure, you can. You're young and healthy and you're going to have a baby. How can that be a bad thing?"

The words lifted her up and sent her soaring. She was amazed to discover she was still seated beside him on the sofa rather than floating in the clouds somewhere. "Thank you," she whispered. "I'm finally starting to feel like this really is the best news I've ever had."

"I have some more advice for you," he said. "I've never been in your situation before, but I know what a breakup is like. Be sure you let yourself be pissed. Get mad. Break dishes. Throw things."

"You're kidding."

"Do I look like I'm kidding? You'll be amazed at what throwing and breaking things does for your mood."

"I'm not angry. I'm happy about the baby. I mean, it's going to be a huge challenge, but it's truly a blessing and I'm…happy. Not angry."

"You will be, and that's okay. And when you really want to lose it and not cause any real damage, try taking it out on inanimate objects. You want me to bring you a box of old china from the thrift shop?"

"I'll manage. But thanks." She felt him watching her. "What?"

"You have a nice smile. I didn't remember that about you."

"I wasn't nice, and I rarely smiled."

He chuckled. "I doubt that." He studied her with an expression she couldn't read. "So are you going to be all right?" he asked.

"Boy, there's a loaded question. Tonight, I expect to be fine. This has been a truly strange day, and it's nice to have someone to talk to. I'm going to do my level best to be all right."

"That's good, Sarah. I'm here to help. Remember that."

She curled herself against the overstuffed arm of the sofa. "I'll remember." She felt comfortable with him, and grateful for the reminder that she wasn't alone. "I'm curious, too," she said. "You never left Glenmuir. I always thought you'd wind up somewhere far away."

"That was the plan," he said. "But plans change. Anyway, I should go." He planted his hands on his knees. Franny eyed him mournfully.

Don't go, thought Sarah. "Of course," she said.

He went to the drop leaf desk in the corner and wrote something on a piece of paper. "My numbers," he said. "At the station, at home and my cell." He handed the paper to her.

"Thanks," she said as she walked him to his truck. "And tell Aurora thanks, too. She did everything right today."

"Call anytime. You don't need a reason." He tilted his head and eyed her curiously. "Did I say something funny?"

"No." Sarah couldn't help herself. He made her smile. "It's just…you're the best public servant I've ever met."

Twenty

When she started her social studies project by interviewing Sarah Moon, Aurora had no idea the story would turn out to be so dramatic. She wondered if her teacher would give her bonus points for that. Or put it up on the school Web site, like Glynnis's interview of Aurora's dad. Of course, the teacher would want to know the outcome of the emergency, and Aurora didn't have an answer to that. Her dad told her it was Sarah's business, and it was up to her to explain what had happened. Or not.

Her dad was a secret-keeper. People thought because he was a fire captain, he spent all his time putting out fires. But also, he got calls to fish wedding rings out of drains or to pry kids out of places they should never have gone in the first place. One time Ethan Parker had climbed the town water tower and was too scared to come down, so her dad had to go up after him. Edie's mom once called him to get birds out of her chimney, and had answered the door wearing a silk peignoir; Gloria had let that slip.

"How about a game of one-on-one?" Her dad held the back door open and passed her the basketball.

"Beats doing homework." She went to the driveway and dribbled toward the goal. Thanks to her dad, she was good at sports. It was impossible to be his kid and not do well at basketball, baseball, soccer and lacrosse.

"We'll leave time for homework," he assured her, reaching for the ball.

She ducked away and twisted to block him. "It's going to take you all night to beat me."

When she was little, he used to cut her a lot of slack. Lately he pushed and challenged her. One good thing about being raised by a guy—it meant automatic acceptance by the jocks at school. And while she and her dad played, they talked. For some weird reason, they had better conversations while trying to beat the crap out of each other than they did while standing still.

"How come you never told me you knew Sarah Moon in high school?" She went for a layup and made it.

He snatched the rebound. "I wouldn't exactly say I knew her. I knew who she was. We were in the same grade."

"So let me guess," said Aurora, guarding him even though it was futile. "You were a jock and she was a dork."

Her dad dribbled thoughtfully. "What makes you think she was a dork?"

Aurora hid a smile. So he'd picked up on that. "Duh. People who grow up to be artists or computer geniuses were always dorks in high school. Or freaks. A lot of artists were freaks. Which was she?"

"Freak, I guess." He showed off a little, dribbling behind his back. "For someone who's never been to high school, you sure know a lot about it."

She reached for the ball. "You were reading her comic

strip on the Internet last night," she said. "You left the page open."

"After rushing her to the hospital, I was curious, so I looked her up."

Aurora lunged for the ball but he eluded her. There were times when she wasn't sure what was on his mind.

"Why?" she asked. "Why were you curious?"

He made an easy outside shot that went in. *Swoosh.* "Most kids who were freaks in high school turn into interesting people."

"So what was she like back then?"

"She used to draw comic strips," her dad said, letting her grab the rebound.

"Like for the school paper, you mean?" Sarah hadn't mentioned it in their interview.

He shook his head. "These were underground comics," he said. "You know what those are?"

"Were they pornographic?" She dribbled hand to hand, even though the move was technically illegal.

Her dad's cheeks turned red. "No. I can't believe that's the first place your mind went. The comics were satirical, I guess you'd say. They were controversial. She made fun of the school administration and the other students."

"Ha ha. You mean she made fun of you." She tried a bank shot but failed to score.

"She made me look like a goon with the IQ of a river rock. She tended to poke fun at people who seemed too satisfied or content."

Aurora recaptured the ball. Her worry about Sarah Moon eased. "Why didn't anyone make her stop?"

"She was entertaining, even then. People used to pass around copies of her drawings the minute they came out."

"So if you're entertaining, you can get away with anything."

"For a while."

"I'll have to remember that." She tried another shot and it went wild, bouncing off the asphalt of the driveway and into the rosebushes.

Her dad signaled "time" and grabbed two root beers from the fridge. They sat on the back steps in the cool of the evening air.

"I looked through the yearbooks at Grandma's house," Aurora confessed. "There wasn't much info about Sarah Moon, but plenty about you." Her father had been an actual golden boy, the kind who looked too good to be true. He'd been so handsome it embarrassed her.

"You must be really bored at Grandma's house if you're looking at old yearbooks," he said.

"Majorly bored," she agreed, and took a swig of root beer. She couldn't explain why she felt drawn to the old, oversize books in her grandparents' study, or why the photographs and scrawled messages from friends intrigued her. She supposed it might be because Dad didn't really like to talk about himself much.

"Did you learn anything?" he asked. "About Sarah, I mean."

"Nothing interesting. She dyed her hair black."

"I think I remember that."

"What'd you ever do to her?"

"Don't remember. I probably teased her. I teased everybody back then."

Aurora took another long drink of root beer and let the carbonation form a hard ball in her gut. When the moment felt just right, she let loose with a prolonged belch.

Her dad glanced over at her. "Not too shabby," he said,

then took a drink and answered in kind, with an even longer, louder belch.

Aurora wondered if her father was interested in Sarah Moon. Maybe he was thinking of asking her out, a possibility that made Aurora scowl. She hated it when he dated. Not that she thought he still felt any kind of loyalty to her mother. That, like Mama, was long gone. Aurora didn't want him dating because it stole him from her. She would never tell him so. It made her seem like a complete spoiled brat.

She wasn't spoiled. She simply didn't want to share her dad. There was too much of that going on already. Every few days, he left her. Even though she knew it was his job and that he would come back to her at the end of each shift, she hated it every single time he left.

She should want him to be happy. She *did* want him to be happy—but with her, not some woman. She'd been pleased when she saw him looking Sarah up on the Internet, but now that he and Sarah had met, Aurora was apprehensive. When her dad was off duty, she needed him with her. Fortunately for Aurora, the women he dated never lasted long. They almost all fell in love with her dad. Anyone with half a brain could see he was a hunk who was funny and nice. But he never fell for them.

He came close a couple of times. There was that organic tea grower from Gualala who wore natural fiber tank tops and no bra, and had zero sense of humor. He was into her, but Aurora seemed to make her nervous, so she didn't last. Oh, and that swimsuit model who lived in San Francisco. Some magazine was doing a photo shoot at Wildcat Beach, and all the models and crew had stayed at the Golden Eagle Inn. Her father had dated Mischa for several months, commuting back and forth to the city.

It started to get serious, and then one day, Aurora fell off the jungle gym at school and dislocated her collarbone. Her dad canceled a date with Mischa and she got all mad and broke up with him. Aurora had learned something that day. She had a lot of influence on her father.

She tried not to think of all the times she'd used that influence. Sometimes she got sick to her stomach when he was about to take a woman on a date. Others times, she needed her dad to help her with homework. It seemed that every time he started getting a little interested in a woman, Aurora had some kind of crisis that demanded his full attention.

Aunt Birdie saw straight through her and told her to cut it out. You couldn't get much past Aunt Birdie.

Fortunately, her dad hadn't met anybody in a long time. Not someone he clicked with, anyway.

Will glanced at his watch. He and Aurora were overdue at his parents' house for dinner. His mother invited the whole family—him and Aurora, his sister and her husband to dinner every Friday night. Will attended as his duty schedule permitted. Aurora was taking her usual sweet time getting ready. He had no idea what it was that she did in the bathroom for forty-five minutes every time they were supposed to go somewhere. In his heart of hearts, he didn't want to know.

"Let's go, Aurora," he yelled from the kitchen.

"Five minutes," she yelled back.

It was the same reply he'd had five minutes ago. "Now," he said. "We're already late."

Looking none too happy with his impatience, she came downstairs smelling of a slightly fruity perfume, every glossy black hair in place and makeup applied with a sure hand.

Makeup. On a thirteen-year-old.

"What's the matter?" she asked, grabbing her battered, oversize purse and holding it in front of her like a shield.

"Why do you ask?"

"Your jaw is all tight, like it gets when something is bothering you."

He forced his jaw to relax and held in a reply. Sometimes they bickered like a couple of kids, and once they got started it was hard to stop.

An unseasonable cold snap had gripped the area. He reached into the jump seat behind the cab and grabbed an ancient but clean letterman jacket—purple boiled wool with leather sleeves and trim and bright red varsity letters. He'd owned it since freshman year in high school, when he had earned letters in three sports, an honor that was practically unheard of. He'd strutted through the ensuing three years wearing the jacket like a mantle of ermine, and now it was a relic. It held no value for him except as a reminder: Don't get cocky. He kept it in his truck and occasionally dragged it out on foggy nights when the cold drilled into his bones.

They got in the truck, and he turned up the volume on the radio. The Libertines' "What Katie Did" drifted from the speakers. "Nothing is bothering me."

"Sure it is. Come on, Dad. You can tell me."

"Forget it."

"Why? Why won't you tell me?"

"You'll take it wrong, get all mad at me."

"I promise I won't."

He rested his wrist at the top of the steering wheel and reached over to turn up the radio. Sometimes it was best just to clam up.

She turned the volume down. "I said I promise."

"I forgot what we were talking about."

"You forget everything when it comes to me. You forget me."

"See? You're already getting mad."

"Because you never talk to me anymore."

"We talk all the time."

"About how much milk is left in the fridge and do I have enough punches left on my lunch card, and what homework I have. That's not talking, Dad. That's…taking inventory."

Damn. Where did she get this stuff? Was Birdie coaching her on the sly, or did the second X chromosome come equipped with pointless, searching questions?

The only stoplight in town was red. They idled at the intersection with the White Horse Café on the corner. Happy hour was in full swing, half-price pitchers and barbecued oysters. Guys like him, finished with work for the day, were inside shooting pool and joking around, in no hurry to be anywhere. Will couldn't help it. He felt a twinge of envy, because they weren't guys like him. They were guys his age, but he doubted any of them had a teenager to raise. Sometimes it was hard to keep from regretting the things he'd missed out on.

Will glanced over at the sullen girl beside him. The falling twilight outlined her delicate profile and he reminded himself that she hadn't asked to come into his life. And it wasn't her fault her mother had left, and she was stuck with Will, who was finding a teenage girl more mysterious and incomprehensible than the universe itself.

"Light's green," she said, gesturing.

He accelerated away from town.

Aurora leaned forward and turned down the volume of the radio. "You never told me what's the matter."

They were approximately one minute away from his parents' farm, where he'd grown up and lived his life until, at nineteen, he'd acquired a wife and child, a job and a house in town.

That was something, at least. The fight would only last one minute.

"You really want to know what's on my mind?"

"Yes. I really want to know."

"You are the prettiest girl in the whole world, and I'm not just saying that to be nice."

"You're my dad. Of course you'd think that." Her voice softened. "Thanks, though."

"It makes me wonder why you paint over yourself with makeup every day." Even without looking at her, he could feel her bristle and held up his hand. "Remember, you're the one who wanted to know what was on my mind."

"I don't paint over myself," she said. "It's called putting on makeup."

"You don't need it. You are prettier just the way you are."

"You always yell at me about makeup," she complained.

"Why not leave it off and I'll keep my mouth shut?"

"Dad—"

"We're here." Relieved, he pulled onto the gravel drive of his parents' place. He didn't want to argue with Aurora. He didn't want to hurt her feelings by saying that all that makeup made her look too grown-up, like someone he hoped she would never become.

"Saved by the bell, huh?" She swung her legs sideways and jumped down from the truck. As she slipped to the ground, he caught a flash of skin between her top and the waistband of her jeans.

"Aurora."

She clearly knew what he was talking about. She tugged at the bottom of her shirt but failed to close the gap. "Come on, Dad—"

"Cover up," he said. "We've been through this before."

"I didn't bring another shirt."

"Do as you're told, Aurora. I don't know why the hell everything has to be a fight with you." He started taking off his jacket to offer it to her.

"I just remembered," she said, rummaging in her bag. "I brought a sweater."

"Smart-ass," he said. "You already came prepared for my objections."

Ted and Nanny, his parents' border collies, barked as they ran to greet them. Leaning against the porch were the bikes belonging to Birdie and Ellison. His sister and her husband rode everywhere, always in training for some race or triathlon.

Will's aunt Lonnie, who ran a small air cargo service, came to say hello. For at least two decades, she had been in charge of transporting flowers from the farm and other local produce to wherever they were needed. "I'd like to stay and catch up," she said, "but I have my weekly delivery to that hotel in Vegas."

"Las Vegas?" Aurora perked up. "Hey, can I come?"

"Sure," Aunt Lonnie said with an easy smile. "I'd love the company."

Will tried not to let the exchange worry him. Aurora occasionally went flying with her great-aunt in the DeHavilland Beaver. When it came to her mother, the kid clung to hope, even though Marisol didn't even bother calling on her birthday anymore.

Shannon Bonner came out on the porch to greet them and to tell her sister goodbye.

"Grandma!" Aurora ran. In a split second, she changed from pretty baby to regular kid.

Will wished like hell she would stay that way. Kids were his favorite type of human being. As she spoke animatedly to her grandmother, he said goodbye to Lonnie, then stopped to pet the dogs. Nanny was way past her prime, fourteen years old now, and skinny. Ted was half her age and infused with a border collie's seemingly inexhaustible energy. He whirled in circles and leaped at Aurora until Will's mother commanded him to stay down.

His parents fit the profile of West Mariners to an almost embarrassing degree. They had met at Berkeley, graduated with honors and made their escape to Marin, wanting to live close to the land. Armed with advanced degrees in political science and sociology, they subscribed to the *Mother Earth News* and *Rolling Stone* and became farmers.

Not very successful ones, not at first. By refusing to use chemicals or artificial stimulants on their crops, they suffered numerous setbacks.

At last, facing foreclosure, they found a cash crop that was both legal and profitable—flowers. The climate and soil turned out to be perfect for Easter lilies, Stargazers, Amaryllis and a rainbow array of specialty blooms. With the crazed growth of the Bay Area, they found plenty of demand. Although the Bonners would never amass a fortune from their enterprise, they managed, most years, to make ends meet, which was all they ever asked for.

Birdie and Will grew up organic, enlightened and unconditionally loved. Each in their own way had a stellar high school career and a bright future.

When, instead of going to Stanford or Berkeley, Will chose to settle down in Glenmuir with a wife and child, people shook their heads in sympathy. Poor Angus and

Shannon Bonner, they said. Will had the whole world at his feet, and he'd blown it all in a single rash act. His parents must be devastated.

People who thought that way didn't know the Bonners. They didn't understand that having trophy children had never been on their agenda. Angus and Shannon did not go to cocktail parties to brag about their children's achievements, academic, athletic or social.

What they wanted for both Will and Birdie was so simple it was incomprehensible to most ambitious Marin parents: happiness.

Rather than seeing Aurora and Marisol as a burden, the Bonners saw them as a blessing. As far as Will could tell, his parents never thought wistfully of what could have been. They never reminded him pointedly about the future he could have had.

There were teachers, counselors and coaches at the high school who would never forgive him for turning his back on full scholarships, sports contracts, the chance to compete against the best. Fortunately, Will felt no obligation to anyone but his family.

He was so freaking lucky, he thought, watching his mother and Aurora. Holding hands as they went inside, they looked more like best friends than grandmother and granddaughter. His mother wore her hair long, and she was dressed in jeans and a hand-knit Cowichan sweater.

She was small, not much bigger than Aurora. People always wondered how a petite woman like Shannon could be the mother of strapping, six-foot-five Will Bonner… until they met Angus. Then they understood.

"Hey, big guy," boomed Angus when Will came into the house. "How have you been?"

They fell into a conversation about the usual topics—

weather and politics—over a dinner of lasagne and a salad of homegrown greens.

"Aurora's bored," Birdie said. "I can hear her rolling her eyes."

Aurora blushed, but she didn't deny being bored. "Current events and weather. Two things you can't do anything about."

"What would you like to discuss?" Shannon asked agreeably enough.

Aurora shrugged. "I hate being the only kid."

"You know you can always invite a friend to come with you," her grandmother said.

"That's not the same." She pointed her fork at Birdie and Ellison. "You guys should have a baby. My friend Edie's aunt had a baby, and it's the cutest thing ever, and she gets to babysit it all the time."

"Works for me," Birdie said.

Ellison spoke at the same time: "We're going to wait."

They exchanged a glance, and Will could tell it wasn't the first time the topic had come up.

"I think you should go for it," Aurora said.

Will wondered if she knew more about Sarah Moon's situation than she let on. Despite having Sarah's permission to tell Aurora, he had not mentioned the pregnancy to his daughter, but maybe she'd figured it out on her own.

"So you like babies," Shannon said.

"As cousins. Not all the time."

"Funny thing about babies," Ellison said. "Once you have one, it's around all the time."

After dinner, Aurora and Birdie rushed through the clearing of the table so they could watch *American Idol.* Will, his parents and brother-in-law steered clear of the TV room, not understanding the appeal of the show that held the others spellbound. They were card-carrying members of a club to which he could never belong—thank God.

Leaving his parents and Ellison with their coffee and conversation, he went to the study adjacent to the living room. The study, which doubled as the company office, housed a thousand books and was furnished with pieces reclaimed from the town library after it was remodeled.

The room breathed with memories; they were stored on the shelves alongside the *Compact Oxford English Dictionary* and the complete works of Ewell Gibbons.

Growing up the son of intellectuals and political activists had not seemed like anything out of the ordinary to Will. He had spent many an hour at the long, oaken table doing homework while his parents labored over the company books at the rolltop desk nearby. He still remembered the fall of light from the green shaded lamp, the scratching of his pencil on the coarse, recycled notebook paper.

Feeling unsettled, he went to a bookshelf and pulled out a volume of the high school yearbook—*Cosmos.* The book was from his senior year. He set the thick book on the table and flipped through it. Many of the pages were scrawled with greetings from people he barely remembered—Skye Cameron? Mike Rudolph?—and sprinkled with references that had long since faded: "Don't forget Lala land, dude!" He had indeed forgotten it. "FriendZ 2 the endZ" declared someone named JimiZ, whom Will could not recall seeing after graduation day.

There was one photo he remembered quite clearly—a shot of him with five other guys from the baseball team. The night of graduation, the six of them had made the journey that altered Will's life plans forever. Laughing and filled with cocky confidence, they had headed south of the border to celebrate the milestone of graduation.

Coming back from that road trip, Will's friends had told him he was insane. He was ruining his life for the sake of two strangers.

Will hadn't seen them as strangers. They were his wife and child.

He flipped the pages to the front of the book—the senior portraits. Will's was a shot of himself in silhouette, at the top of a craggy ridge with the sun behind him. He was holding up his arms as though supporting the sun itself. Show-off, he thought.

Turning the pages, he found the entry for Sarah Moon. It was weird, how his heart sped up in agitation when his gaze fell on her name. Then he frowned as he studied her photograph, a portrait of an unhappy girl with spiked hair, a fiery glare and her arms folded resolutely like a shield in front of her.

Beside her picture, instead of a list of accomplishments, she had drawn a partially opened oyster with nothing but two eyes peering from the darkness and a thought bubble that read, "I may not be much, but I'm all I think about." She had been the silent observer, lurking in the shadows, cataloging the nuances of human behavior she would later exaggerate in her art.

From his perspective now, Will clearly sensed she was probably the most interesting student in the book. Yet, sandwiched between cheerleaders and class clowns, she all but disappeared.

He wondered what it might have felt like, being the target of loud, sarcastic idiots like he had been. Now that Aurora was fast approaching that age, he found himself wondering how she would do when she reached ninth grade.

Ever since rushing Sarah to the hospital, he'd had her on his mind. For no reason he could name, he kept thinking about her. It was probably because of Gloria and all her talk. Those starry-eyed observations had lodged in his mind like an annoying kernel of corn in his teeth.

Find someone…

An arsonist, that was who he needed to find. Not a damned date with a pregnant woman.

Yet now that the idea had taken root, he had trouble escaping it. His mind kept wandering to that night at her house, the strangely honest conversation they'd had and the shock of desire he hadn't expected to feel. If he didn't know better, he'd say he was stalking Sarah Moon. When he was out driving patrol, he found himself going past May's Cottage, and he paid special attention to a certain blue-and-silver Mini when he saw it parked at the grocery store or post office.

More than once, he'd spotted her in town. She was always by herself. He came to recognize her light blue windbreaker and her quick, purposeful stride, the way the sea breeze tossed her short blond hair.

He'd asked—practically begged—her to call him. She hadn't, which was kind of ironic and quite a switch from high school. Back then, he had been oblivious to everything but the world according to Will Bonner.

His mother came into the library, carrying her ever-present stoneware tea mug. Almost reflexively, Will flipped the book shut.

"Everything all right?" she asked.

"Sure."

She glanced at the book on the table. "Were you looking someone up?"

"I was." He never told his mother anything but the truth.

There was no point. She was all but psychic in her ability to detect a lie or evasion. "Sarah Moon."

"Oh?" She leaned against the library table, crossed her legs at the ankles. "Aurora told me you drove her to the E.R. Everything all right?"

"She'll be fine."

"You were never friends with her in high school, were you?"

Will gave a dry laugh. "I made fun of her for being an oyster farmer. She hated my guts."

His mother raised one eyebrow. "Are you sure about that?"

"I was one of the main subjects of her cartoons, remember?"

"That means she had a crush on you."

"Not that chick. She was weird as all get-out."

"And now she's back."

Will took the book back to the shelf. "Do you ever think about it, Mom? About what I was supposed to do with my life compared to what I actually did?"

"All the time." She took a sip of tea. "People always question the paths they take in life. It's human nature."

The day Will had brought Marisol and Aurora home, he had been desperate for his parents to tell him what to do. They didn't, of course. Instead, his mother had asked him, "What does your heart tell you?"

"Anyway, is that what's got you so nostalgic?" asked his mother. "The fact that Sarah Moon is back?"

"Maybe. And…Aurora. Before we know it, she'll be in high school." He shook his head. "Crazy."

In the gap of silence, they heard a failed *American Idol* contestant warbling "Unchained Melody." Through the doorway, Will could see that his father and Ellison had been sucked in, and were now as enraptured as Aurora and Birdie.

"She's growing up so fast," his mother said with a fond smile.

"Too damn fast," Will muttered.

"Is everything all right?"

"We fight too much," he admitted. "I never see it coming. Everything's fine one minute, and the next, we're arguing about something."

"You're the adult. Don't be tempted to bicker with a child."

"Easier said than done. I don't get it, though. Aurora's my heart. I'd die for her, Mom. But lately, things sometimes get weird between us, which sucks, because I raised her. When she was younger, I understood what made her tick. When she was hurting, I made her feel better. When she was mad, I made her laugh. We were always on the same page."

"And now she's like a complete stranger with a mind of her own."

"She's changing so fast, and I'm all alone."

"Son, every man who has a daughter goes through this. You're doing fine. Just remember, girls her age need a father more than ever."

"She brought up her mother again the other day."

"Do you ever think about contacting Marisol and—"

"No." Will made a cutting motion in the air with his hand. "She knows exactly where we are. Our address and phone number haven't changed since she left." He ducked his head and wondered if evasion was the same as a lie. What he could never tell his mother—and Aurora—was that Marisol had been in touch. And God help him, he was keeping the contact a secret. There was no point in telling

Aurora that Marisol called on a regular basis, because she only ever called about needing money, never about her daughter.

Another *American Idol* voice raced up to a high vibrato note and hung there, wavering desperately.

"How's Gloria?" his mother asked.

"As bad as ever."

"Still nagging you to go on dates?"

"Always. She thinks it'd be good for both me *and* Aurora."

For the briefest of seconds, his mother's gaze flicked to the yearbook. Shannon Bonner never did anything by chance, and Will knew it.

"Come on, Mom. Not you, too."

"I didn't say a word."

"I heard you loud and clear."

"She's from a wonderful family," his mother pointed out.

"She's getting a divorce. Doesn't sound so wonderful to me." He thought about Sarah's predicament and added, "You have no idea how *not* for me she is."

Twenty-One

"You have an amazing brother," Sarah told Birdie Shafter at their next meeting.

"I've always thought so."

Sarah studied the photo of him and Aurora, which she now realized had been taken at least five years ago. He'd changed very little. Beside him, Aurora looked tiny and fragile, and the contrast brought out Will's air of gentle protectiveness.

Birdie cleared her throat, and Sarah flushed. "Did he tell you what's going on with me?"

"No." Birdie leaned forward, folding her arms on the desktop. "Something I should know about?"

Sarah nodded, even as she felt a wave of appreciation for Will. He'd kept his word about her condition being her business. She crossed her arms over her middle. So far, there was no visible evidence of the pregnancy, but she felt like a different person. Tender and vulnerable, full of wonder.

"I'm pregnant," she told Birdie.

Her attorney set down her notepad and leaned back in her chair. "And is this happy news?"

"Definitely," Sarah said. "I mean, it's scary and crazy, but this is something I've wanted and dreamed about for so long." She quickly explained the circumstances of the conception. "Of course, I didn't quite envision being in this position when it finally happened…"

"It's going to be wonderful. I'm sure of it." Birdie's smile lit her face. Sarah was struck by a strong impression of family resemblance.

"So now what?" she asked. "I'm guessing I need to tell Jack."

Birdie nodded. "The issue of child support comes into play."

Sarah took a nervous sip from her ever-present water bottle and voiced something she'd worried about all night. "Can he file for custody?"

"He'd never get it, but visitation is a possibility."

"I was afraid you'd say that."

"Do you expect trouble? Is he a threat to the child?"

"Not physically, of course, although I honestly don't know what to expect," Sarah admitted. "I was so wrong about so many things…" She looked down at her hands in her lap. Ink smudged the fingers of her left hand. She had been drawing all morning. "When should I tell him?"

"Soon. We'll file to have your health plan extended. Pregnancy is a covered event, so that shouldn't be a problem."

"I'll call him today."

"Are you feeling okay, Sarah?"

"Yes. I don't know what I would have done without your niece and your brother, taking me to the hospital." She glanced at the framed photo on the shelf. "I was so surprised to see Will. Why didn't you tell me he was in Glenmuir?"

"It didn't occur to me that you'd want to know."

"We were in the same grade in high school—"

"So was Vivian Pierce. She's still around," Birdie said. "And Marco Montegna. He enlisted in the marines and came back from the Middle East on permanent disability. I can go down the whole list if you like."

"I get your point. Will is different, though. He's your brother." Sarah wanted to ask about Aurora's mother but didn't want to put Birdie on the spot.

"Well." Birdie made a couple of notes. "I'm glad the two of you reconnected."

"We didn't have much of a connection in the first place. I wouldn't say we were exactly friends in high school."

Birdie didn't look up from her notes. "Maybe you'll be friends now."

Sarah headed toward the town marina, where benches along the dock faced the bay, the perfect spot to sit and stare at the horizon while dealing with difficult matters. It was also one of the few spots where she could get a cell phone signal. She knew she needed to get this call over with, but the small silver phone in her hand felt leaden and cold.

She passed a mother and daughter who were window shopping, chatting animatedly as they discussed a display of handmade bags. She could tell they were mother and daughter instantly, not because of some obvious family resemblance but because of an affinity between them. They had the same posture as they leaned in to study something in the window, the same timing as they turned to look at each other.

An unexpected wave of nostalgia hit Sarah. I'm pregnant, Mom, she thought. And I've never missed you more than I do right now.

Gran and Aunt May had embraced the news when she told them. They had beamed with happiness and said all the right things. But at the center of all the emotion, Sarah couldn't help feeling a huge, gaping hole. Being pregnant was the kind of miracle a woman shared with her husband, and then with her mother.

A dizzying sentiment washed over her. A baby. She was having a baby, and she'd give anything to share the news with her mother. She pictured the abandoned loom in her father's house, still strung with her cashmere yarn, the color of new roses in springtime. "Tonight, Mom," she whispered. "I'll tell you in my dreams tonight."

Jack could wait, she decided, putting the phone away. She went into the grocery store and bought some basics—eggs, lemons, oranges, potatoes, apples, broccoli, dog food. Though still prone to strange cravings, she was determined to take care of herself. "My refrigerator will be a virtual monument to the almighty food pyramid," she vowed.

On her way out, she passed three more women, hoping they hadn't noticed her talking to herself. Clearly they had not, as they were absorbed in each other. All the women were attractive and stylish enough to belong in the cast of *Sex and the City.* Three friends, laughing and chatting away. Girlfriends. Now, there was a concept. I'm pregnant, she wanted to tell them. Isn't it wonderful?

She thought about calling a couple of friends in Chicago to tell them her news. But most of these friends were people who had known Jack "forever." And they weren't kidding. In Jack's world, bonds were formed at a young age and endured through thick and thin.

Except the marriage bond, she thought. Clearly he considered that one expendable.

There, she thought, feeling a nauseating burn of anger in her stomach. Now I'm fired up. I can make this call.

She decided to drive somewhere more private. She knew of a spot where her cell phone would catch a strong signal from the towers by the Point Reyes lighthouse. As she drove, she imagined her child growing up here, surrounded by the stunning beauty of the seashore, the crash of waves against towering cliffs, the mysterious fog shrouding the shoreline and the green shadows of the coastal forests. It was the first time she'd let herself create a specific mental picture of an actual child, barefoot and lithe as a fairy, running through a field of wildflowers or playing in the sand on a sunlit beach. She smiled at the image, knowing it was idealized, yet wasn't that what daydreams were for?

She pulled off to a gravel parking area near a marshy place with a mirrorlike lagoon and thick reeds fringing the water. While waiting for her call to connect, she watched a blue heron on stick legs in the shallows. Statue-still, the bird was fishing, instinctively knowing the most effective means to accomplish that task was to do nothing. It didn't even seem to be breathing, but she imagined its heart racing as its beady eyes scanned the clear bay waters for prey. She wondered how long the heron was willing to wait.

"Daly Construction." Mrs. Brodski, Jack's executive secretary, was another of those loyalists who had known the family "forever."

"It's Sarah. I need to speak to Jack, please." She took out a Sharpie marker, one she always kept in her purse.

"I'll see if he's available, Sarah." Mrs. Brodski's voice was crisp with disapproval. No doubt she and everyone else believed Jack was the victim, abandoned by his weirdo wife from California.

Idly, Sarah took a lemon from the grocery sack on the seat beside her. She drew a round-faced, sour-mouthed Mrs. Brodski saying, "I'll see if he's available."

Then Sarah used the Sharpie to draw Jack's face on an egg. As the cartoon woman spoke, she was looking straight at Jack, asking him with her eyes if he was willing to speak with his wayward wife. They hadn't talked in a while. Most communication lately was done through their lawyers. Just a few months ago, such a development would have seemed impossible, but now—

"Sarah." Jack picked up abruptly.

Her marker bled onto the surface of the egg, creating an unexpected blob in the middle. Could an egg get egg on its face?

"I have news," she said, drawing a tail on the blob. Now it looked like a tadpole. Or a sperm cell. "It's kind of strange."

"So what else is new? Everything's been strange since you left."

Sarah clenched her teeth. He managed brilliantly to forget the circumstances of her leaving. He sounded wounded, bereft. The injured party.

She took out one of the oranges and drew another Jack, this one with a befuddled look on his face.

"I'm pregnant," she said. "I just found out."

Jack fell into a rare lapse of silence. "No shit," he said finally.

"Nope," she said, refusing to let her voice tremble. This was not how this conversation was supposed to go. Where was the tenderness, the wonder, the joy? "Kidding about this would be in extremely bad taste."

"Why? Your comic strip managed to make a joke out of my cancer."

A painful, shocked silence fell between them. This was why communicating through lawyers was preferable. Each time Sarah and Jack talked, they found new ways to hurt each other.

"Can this not be about you, for once?" She kept drawing methodically, without thinking. Within minutes, every egg and piece of fruit had his face on it, each with a different expression. All lined up in the carton, the eggs looked like spectators at a baseball game. She eyed the sack of potatoes. Mr. Potato Head, she thought.

"Fine. You having a baby has never been about me." His tone mocked her. "So is it mine?" he asked.

She held the phone away from her in disbelief. Very faintly, she could hear his voice, still talking. With every fiber of her being, she wanted to hurl the phone as far away as she could, into the water, but she'd already tried throwing a phone away while Jack was talking, and it hadn't changed anything. She'd still needed a phone, and Jack was still an asshole.

Instead she sat back and watched the shorebird. It darted like an arrow shot from a bow. The heron's head delved underwater and then emerged, a gleaming fish clasped in its beak. The bird scarfed down the still-squirming fish and then took off like a seaplane, gathering speed and then soaring, its great wings beating with smooth strength.

With studied gentleness, Sarah turned off the phone and put it in her purse. Then she got back in her car and drove until she could go no farther. Point Reyes was at the far edge of nowhere, standing sentinel above the vast Pacific. She stopped at a place where bitten-off cliffs towered over a raging sea and weathered signs warned against going too close to the edge. Approach With Caution, Particularly In Windy Conditions was spelled out in large letters.

She parked and got out of the car, feeling the wind sweep upward over her, lifting the hem of her jacket, ruffling her hair. She walked to the edge of the cliff and for a long time, stood frozen and stared as though mesmerized by the swirling, white-veined swells that gathered like great fists drawn back for a blow, then smashed themselves against the rocks below, exploding into a spray of diamonds. Some of the spray was so fine that a series of rainbows were thrown up, fleeting and blurred, one after another. The pounding of the sea made a strange and compelling music, driving her to surrender to the feelings inside her.

She watched a black crow pick up a clam and drop the shellfish on the rocks, repeating the process again and again until finally, the shell broke open and the bird took its reward. The small bite of food appeared to be worth the trouble, for the bird went after another clam right away.

Perched on the brink of infinity, she felt both heady power and intimidating vulnerability. The breeze rippled against her, and stirred the tufts of wildflowers around her feet.

Is it mine?

Jack's words seemed to ride the wind, starting in a whisper and crescendoing to a howl she couldn't escape. Dear God, he'd actually said that. Her rage ran bone deep, a poison that could pervade her whole system, destroy her and the new life inside her if she allowed it to consume her from the inside out. She took in a deep breath, filling her lungs with mist and sea air, sharp with salt spray from the crashing waves. She reached her arms toward the empty air in front of her, spread them like wings. She didn't feel fragile at all now, but supremely powerful.

Then she thought about the advice Will Bonner had given her. *Get mad. Throw things.*

She brought the sack of groceries to the overlook, took out an egg with Jack's face on it and let fly. The egg soared high in a perfect arc into the sky. Then it plummeted to the rocks below and the waves surged in to carry the mess out to sea.

She picked up another and threw it. *Take that. And that.* One after another, she hurled the eggs, and when she ran out, she moved on to the lemons and oranges and potatoes. With every throw, the poison ebbed as though sucked out to sea.

Minutes later, the sack was empty. Her shoulders ached, her arm muscles felt slack and fatigued and her mind was quiet.

Just as Will had promised.

Twenty-Two

"The first thing Jack did was ask if it was his," Sarah told the divorce support group. "And I finally understood what some of you told me about anger. Prior to that moment, I didn't realize how angry I really was. I'd buried it so well I didn't know how deep it ran until he said that."

The group absorbed this in silence, but the lull felt safe, like a cushion of air. She had come to count on this group, an unlikely community of damaged souls, helping each other survive. She pictured them all huddled together in a lifeboat on a dark, stormy sea.

"I thought I was furious with Jack before," she said. "Now I'm thinking that rage was the tip of the iceberg."

"Some of us have been coming here for years." The woman's name was Mary B., and she was softly middle-aged, carrying herself with a sort of weary dignity. "There's a reason for that. There's no way you can know the breadth and depth of your rage, let alone deal with it. There's no letting go. You just have to explore it. That's what this group is for."

Sarah nodded, acknowledging her confusion. "To be

honest, I don't even know how I feel about my future, but I'm trying my best to be happy."

"Good for you," said Mary. "Don't let what someone else says steal your happiness from you."

"Thanks. The timing is far from perfect but it's something I've dreamed of for a very long time," Sarah said, and then settled back into quiet reflection. She *did* feel the excitement, though it was tinged with uncertainty and sometimes even panic. Yet, since the day at the cliffs, she found it easier to surrender to her emotions, even to the anger. Maybe, she thought, the secret to a happy life was learning to get through the unhappy periods intact.

After that initial phone call, Jack had called her back several times, but she never answered, nor did she answer the calls from his mother, Helen, or his sister Megan. She erased all of his voice mail messages without listening to them and blocked his e-mail address from her in-box. According to Birdie, Jack's lawyer claimed his client regretted his reaction to the news and wished to retract his unfounded accusation. Jack had been caught off guard and wanted to discuss the matter with her.

She didn't want to discuss anything. She was beginning to see a pattern in his reversals, which seemed to take place when there was a price to pay. She told Birdie to request child-support payments.

Child support. The very idea was hard to grasp. As were the ideas of custody and visitation. Everything about the situation was hard to grasp. From the moment she'd been informed about the pregnancy, her world had gone through a paradigm shift. Now she had to make every decision with a child in mind. Prior to this, she was considering a move to San Francisco, maybe getting a bohemian walk-up in Bernal Heights. The pregnancy meant that was out of the question. For the foreseeable future, she was staying here, close to her family, knowing she and the baby would need them.

The baby. She could close her eyes and picture her unborn child at every stage of development. She felt oddly guilty that she hadn't realized she was pregnant sooner, despite the fact that after all the treatment she'd gone through, she considered herself an expert. She always thought she would know when it happened. A hundred times, she had visualized the ball of cells embedding itself in her womb, a secret smaller than the head of a pin. By the time she discovered what was happening, the child was a tiny curl of humanity with limb buds and its own beating heart. *I wish I'd known sooner,* she said to the baby. *I wish I hadn't missed a single second of your existence.*

She could imagine the baby's weight and warmth in her arms, its smell and the smoothness of its skin. Boy or girl, she had no preference. Either would be precious to her. Little Pongo or Perdita. Rhett or Scarlett. Zeus or Hera. Wonder Woman or Captain America. She lay awake at night, generating long lists of possible names, and she found the whole process dizzyingly delicious.

According to Birdie—and to the laws of common sense—she had to decide what Jack's role would be. It was easy to cling to righteous fury, but ultimately, there was another person involved here. A child who had two parents and deserved the best possible life Sarah could offer. No one had to tell her that nursing hate and anger for this child's father was a bad idea.

After the meeting, Gloria Martinez came over to give her a hug. "I'm really happy for you."

"Thanks. I'm still adjusting to the news."

"You've got plenty of time to plan for this."

She nodded. "When I was married, I wanted a baby so much sometimes I couldn't see straight. I was sure it was the one thing missing from my life, and that once I got pregnant, everything would fall into place."

"And now?"

Finally, Sarah smiled. "Now that I'm going to be single again, I don't need a baby to glue my marriage together." She brushed her hand down her abdomen, a gesture that was fast becoming habit. "But I still want this child more than I want the next breath of air."

"That's good," Gloria observed. "It's got to be hard on a baby, gluing a marriage together. Just a wild guess, but I think kids do better when they don't have to be anything but kids."

Sarah nodded, watching two of the newer people leaving, a man and a woman. He held the door for her, then followed her out to the parking lot. "What about dating?" Sarah asked.

"Some people meet someone in group, but it doesn't happen very often."

Sarah flushed. "I didn't mean this group. Just…in general."

"So you don't have anyone specific in mind?"

"No, God…no." Yet in spite of herself, Sarah's mind formed a very specific image. At the coffee service table, Gloria picked up a tote bag stenciled with a familiar logo and the initials GFD.

"You work for the fire department?" Sarah asked.

"That's right. I'm a firefighter. An engineer, actually."

"Maybe you work with Will Bonner."

"Yep." Gloria put on her jacket and lifted her hair over the collar.

"He was the one who took me to Valley Regional the day I found out I was pregnant. I don't know what I would've done without him."

Gloria slung the bag over her shoulder and offered Sarah a smile. "A lot of people feel that way about Will."

Aurora was avoiding Sarah. She started off doing it without thinking, but later realized she was seriously ticked. She wasn't happy about the fact that her dad and Sarah had finally met.

She's *my* friend, Aurora wanted to tell her dad. I met her first. She knew she couldn't say that, though. It would make her sound like a complete and total baby.

When she got a text message from Sarah asking to meet her after school, she was tempted to ignore the invitation. Trouble was, she liked Sarah and wanted to keep being friends with her.

Shouldering her backpack, she got off the bus first instead of waiting for Mandy and the others in hopes that for once, they'd invite her to hang out. So that was something, anyway. At least she'd quit moping about not being part of the group.

Sarah was right where she said she'd be, with Franny on her leash, sniffing around a clump of wild sage. Aurora found herself checking Sarah out with a worried eye. "You all right?"

She grinned. "I promise I won't pass out on you like I did last time we were together."

"Thanks. That was too much drama for me."

"So I guess your dad didn't say much about why I wasn't feeling well that day," Sarah said.

"He said that's between you and your doctor."

"I disagree," Sarah said. "You deserve to know and besides, it's no secret."

Aurora braced herself. What if there was some awful disease? Aurora knew vaguely that Sarah's own mother had died young, of something terrible. Had Sarah inherited the same condition?

"Okay. Shoot."

"Turns out I'm expecting a baby."

Like an idiot, Aurora couldn't think of anything to say. Part of her reaction was relief. Now she knew it was totally dumb and paranoid to worry about her dad and Sarah dating. What with getting a divorce and being pregnant at the same time, Sarah could not possibly have guys on her mind.

Could she?

Aurora told herself to quit being such a worrywart. She stared at the ground, her jaw tight, her emotions scrambled by confusion.

"It's good news," Sarah said quickly, probably rattled by Aurora's silence. "My doctor says everything is okay, so long as I take care of myself."

"That's cool, then. I guess." Aurora didn't know much about babies, had never really been around them.

"Why am I getting the idea that you don't think a baby is great news?"

Because you don't have a husband, for starters. Because probably the only thing that sucks worse than being a single parent is being the kid of a single parent. Glynnis's mom was always saying how hard it was. In health class, even the textbooks said it was a struggle. "Kids are a lot of trouble."

"Parents would say they're worth it."

"Not all parents," Aurora muttered. Then she thought, Shoot, why did I say that?

Sarah narrowed her eyes, tilted her head a little. "You wouldn't be talking about your own situation, would you?"

"It's the only situation I know." Aurora had an urge to talk about her mother, but squelched it. Instead, she said, "Once there's a kid in the picture, everything has to change, all your plans."

"Change can be good."

"Or not," Aurora insisted. Then, before her mind caught up with her mouth, she said, "I ruined my dad's future."

"What do you mean, ruined?" Sarah nearly choked.

"Before I came along, he had all these plans. He was supposed to go to college, maybe even go pro, play for the Athletics and become a celebrity. And make everybody proud. Instead, he got stuck with my mom and me and wound up right back here. So his plans flew out the window."

"A change of plans is not the same as a life being ruined. Where on earth did you get that idea? Is this something your father told you?"

"No way. My dad acts like I'm the best thing that ever came along. I had to hear the truth from a teacher at school. Mr. Kearns, who teaches health and coaches baseball, told me. He was really disappointed that my dad ended up staying here and taking care of me."

Sarah remembered Kearns, a mediocre teacher and aggressive coach. What a jerk, saying something like that to Aurora. "And you believe some teacher over your own father?"

"I believe my father would do anything to keep me from hearing stuff like that, but I hear it anyway."

"A child is the biggest thing that can happen to anyone. I'm just coming to realize this myself."

"Because you're pregnant."

"Because that's the way it is. You know, before I figured out that there was a baby, I was going to head into San

Francisco and find a great bachelorette apartment. I pictured myself living single, like a West Coast Bridget Jones, and I had all these plans for the Bohemian life of an artist. And then—*wham.* I find out I'm pregnant. This news has changed everything I thought my future would be. Is it ruined? Am I disappointed? Not even close. I feel the way I suspect your dad felt when you came along. Blessed and lucky and overwhelmed. And happier, I think, than I've ever been about anything."

"Does this mean you're getting back together with your husband?" Aurora asked.

Sarah choked some more. "Not going to happen." She paused and studied Aurora. "Do you ever think that might happen with your parents?"

Wham is right, she thought, staring at the ground. "No," she admitted, feeling regret pierce her in a tender place. She felt embarrassed, too, because she had once told Sarah she and her dad were going to move to Vegas to be with her mom. By now, Sarah must have realized that was just a story. "I used to wish for it, but now I know it's a stupid wish that will never come true. No offense," she added hurriedly, "but when kids are little, they always want their parents to get back together."

"You're awfully smart, for a kid," Sarah said.

"About some stuff, I guess."

She and her dad used to be happy, even when it was just the two of them. But lately, she sensed a change. Sure, she wasn't a little kid anymore. She didn't expect him to swoop her up in his arms or cuddle with her in bed anymore. He seemed so distracted these days, she practically had to yell *fire* in a crowded building just to get his attention.

Twenty-Three

Sarah stopped in the foyer of the Esperson Building, found a ladies' room and rushed to a stall just in time to vomit. This had become a common occurrence lately. Routine morning sickness. Dr. Faulk, her OB, was not concerned.

This morning, however, the nausea had persisted, her silent companion in the traffic surging across the Golden Gate Bridge, down into the parking garage beneath the blocky office building and up the elevator to the office of the Comic Relief Syndicate on the twenty-third floor.

She'd consumed nothing stronger than tea and oyster crackers for breakfast. Most days, she managed to keep her first meal down, but not today. This morning, everything was exacerbated by nerves.

Snap out of it, she told herself. She needed to focus on providing for her child. It was one thing to indulge her own misery, curled in the fetal position under an eiderdown comforter. It was quite another to realize that she didn't have the luxury to wallow. Not anymore. When you have a child, you have someone else to live for—and to make a living for.

One stroke of luck—she had the entire washroom to herself. It was bad enough being sick. Throwing up in the presence of a stranger would only stress her out even more.

Still a good fifteen minutes early for her appointment, she took her time putting herself back together. She washed her face, redid her hair and makeup, and popped in a Tic Tac. Even the best foundation money could buy didn't mask her pallor, but maybe people who had never met her would think it was natural. They would think she had the complexion of a Charlotte Bronte heroine.

"I'm Sarah Moon," she told the guy at the desk. "I have an appointment to see Fritz Prendergast."

Confidence, she thought. Show nothing but confidence that they're going to love the material. Forget about the fact that the syndication editor was a humorless, middle-aged male, and that this was one of the most competitive syndicates there was. Don't think about that.

She nearly crumbled when the receptionist escorted her into a conference room lit by a bank of tall windows with a view of the bustling wharf area. A series of easels had been set up at one end. The mahogany table, as long and gleaming as a bowling alley lane, was surrounded by cushy swivel chairs on wheels.

There was a setup for a PowerPoint presentation. Moments before Fritz and his three associates arrived, she had time to load the program. She met his assistant editor, a managing editor and a female intern who was a senior at San Francisco State.

"Thank you for seeing me," Sarah said. "I really appreciate the opportunity." This process was so fraught with tension. She was submitting herself to their judgment, asking them to deem her worthy, to place a specific value on something she had created. No wonder she hadn't pursued syndication until now.

"We are always interested in fresh talent," said Fritz, sounding halfway between bored and comatose.

The presentation went as though scripted. Everyone said what they were supposed to say and made all the appropriate noises. Because of this, Sarah understood perfectly well that the meeting was going badly. *Just Breathe* was dead on arrival.

Once she admitted this to herself, she relaxed. Since she was already a goner, there was no danger of shooting herself in the foot.

"I know what you're thinking," she blurted out.

Fritz sent his assistant a glance highlighted by raised eyebrows. "All right," he said. "I'll play. What am I thinking?"

"That the strip is not unique enough."

"Ah. You've done your homework, at least. According to the *Comics Marketing Guide,* that's the number one reason for rejection."

"So you've probably heard all the answers to that," she said.

He enumerated them one by one on his fingers. "You're not giving us uniqueness, but freshness of vision. Your strip features characters and situations readers can relate to. You want to foster a long-term bond between the audience and the material."

She couldn't suppress a rueful smile. "You've done your homework, too."

Fritz glanced at his watch. "You're a good artist. The strip has potential and it's been well received in a few markets. But I'm not sold, Sarah. You still haven't given me a reason to take a chance on you."

Good artist…potential…well received. And those aren't reasons? she wondered. What more did he want?

"My assessment?" he said, even though she hadn't solicited it. "The strip is well drawn, sharp and honest. However, as we've said before, it's also not unique and it isn't all that funny."

She took a deep breath, trying to fill her suddenly empty lungs. "I'm not funny," she said. "I agree with that."

"Then why should I put you in the funny pages?"

"Because *Just Breathe* is about pain and truth."

"So is the obituary page."

"So is comedy," she said, clicking on a shot of Shirl at the fertility clinic. "My readers don't laugh at her," she said. "But they don't look away, either."

Nancy, the intern, studied each image, growing more and more agitated. At least, that was how it seemed to Sarah.

Fritz took the remote and swiftly scanned the next few frames. "You're offering me pain and truth about a young woman who's trying to save her failing marriage by having a baby, is that it?"

"No." Sarah was shocked. "You've got it wrong. Up until the last possible moment, Shirl didn't believe there was a thing wrong with her marriage. And she was certainly not naive enough to believe having a baby would fix it. I can't imagine how the strip gave you that impression. She had a very good marriage."

He moved to a four-week series about Shirl and Richie remodeling their kitchen. "Doesn't look so hot here."

"Every couple fights when they're remodeling."

"But I thought the general rule of thumb is that the woman always wins," interjected Nancy. "Shirl doesn't get a single thing she wants here."

"She's fine with it," Sarah insisted, indicating the culmination of the story line. "Look at her. This story line was about a woman discovering what's really important, and it's not linear feet of counter space."

"It's about manipulation and subverting desire," the intern said. "Richie's a master at it."

"That's crazy," Sarah objected. "Richie doesn't manipulate Shirl. She's in charge in this relationship."

"Then how the hell did she wind up moving in with her loopy mother?" Nancy advanced to more recent story lines.

Sarah was not about to answer that. "Lulu is not loopy. She is the most self-actualized character in the strip."

"Hello? She's fifty years old and can't even decide on a hair color. She and Shirl are going to drive each other insane."

"Like a couple of Pomeranians," Sarah agreed. "Especially when Lulu finds out what's really going on with Shirl."

"What's that?"

Sarah had her hooked, and she knew it. With an almost-smug smile, she advanced to the most recent installment, one that had not yet been published. "Shirl is pregnant."

Nancy's jaw dropped. "Shut *up*."

Fritz and the others were watching like spectators at a Ping-Pong match. Finally someone mentioned that the meeting had run over.

Sarah fell silent and tried not to look too disheartened as she put away her things.

"I'll FedEx you a contract first thing in the morning." Fritz made a note on a pad of paper.

She blinked, thinking she had heard wrong. "I don't understand. I thought you hated the strip."

"You weren't listening. I said it wasn't unique and it wasn't funny. I also said it was honest and well drawn. But that's not what convinced me."

"Then why?"

"Truthfully, we've got three strips slated for cancellation, and there's room for something new. Besides—" he indicated Nancy, the intern "—when somebody starts arguing that passionately about a fictional character, I have to figure we're onto something."

Twenty-Four

It was too hot to think. Fortunately for Will, a firefighter could choose from any number of tasks that didn't require thinking. There was the mindless polishing of the engine's grills and chrome, for example. He opted for washing the truck. The water gushing from the hose was a welcome respite from the ferocious heat wave.

He wore only rubber boots and khaki turnout trousers with suspenders hanging down, his shirt peeled off and slung over a laurel bush. Within minutes, he was soaked and in a much better mood. He was scouring the running boards and whistling tunelessly between his teeth when he sensed someone watching him.

He killed the stream of water with a twist of the nozzle and glanced around. There stood Sarah Moon, eyeing him with an expression he couldn't read. She wore a blue sundress and straw hat, and carried a portfolio under her arm.

Will felt different around this woman. And for the life of him, he didn't know why. He ought to run the other way. This was a woman who had dumped her husband and was newly pregnant—not exactly the picture of stability. But…damn.

"Everything all right?" he asked her.

"Just fine," she said. "I stopped by to bring you something." She held out the portfolio.

"I'm dripping wet," he said.

"I know." She seemed distracted in a way he found flattering. Her face was flushed and she was trying not to look at his bare chest, yet he could feel her gaze pulled there and he couldn't deny the feeling that gave him.

"It's a little thank-you gift. I made a drawing of you and Aurora."

He grinned. "Uh-oh. Last time you drew a picture of me, it wasn't exactly flattering."

"Think of this as my way of making up for it." She slid a picture out of the portfolio and angled it toward him.

The drawing was matted, framed and signed. It showed him and Aurora sitting on the city dock, dangling their feet in the water. "I based it on a photo I borrowed from your sister," Sarah explained.

"Wow," he said. "It's fantastic. Thank you."

She beamed at him. "Do you really like it?"

The drawing showed his five o'clock shadow and the slightly rumpled condition of his jeans and plaid shirt, yet it was oddly flattering. Even better, Sarah had managed to capture Aurora's beauty and the way she was poised between being a little girl and a young woman. "Yeah," he said, "I really like it." It was on the tip of his tongue to ask her out to dinner when he got off duty. No, that was too…datelike.

He studied her, trying to see if there was any hint of her pregnancy yet. She wore a womanly, somewhat mysterious smile, yet her eyes were haunted by melancholy. Will suspected he knew why. Expecting a baby was something a couple in love was supposed to savor with happiness and trepidation and anticipation. He was no expert, though. He had never experienced it himself, since Aurora had been five years old when she came into his life. Right from the start, Marisol made it clear that she was completely uninterested in having any more children.

"You're staring," Sarah pointed out.

He blinked. "What? Oh, sorry."

"Why were you staring at me like that?" she persisted, clearly not about to let him off the hook.

Busted, he thought. "I guess because you look…real nice." Liar, he thought. Tell her what you really think. "You're beautiful."

"Whoa. I wasn't fishing for compliments."

His smile was unapologetic. "It wasn't a compliment. I do think you're beautiful." He put on his shirt, then fixed her tea and they sat together in a pair of folding wooden lawn chairs under the leafy arms of a huge California oak. He watched her throat work smoothly as she took a long drink. It was strange to think they'd known each other all their lives, yet he was only getting around to feeling attracted to her now.

She set down her glass. "Are you flirting with me?"

"I might be."

"Flirting with a bitter, pregnant woman. That's a bad idea."

"Probably."

"You were such a flirt in high school, it was disgusting."

"An opinion you made abundantly clear in your comic strip."

"Yes, well, I was resentful."

"About what?"

"About the fact that you flirted with everyone except me."

"No way was I going to flirt with you," he said, shaking his head. "You were scary."

She sniffed. "Flattery will get you nowhere."

"I thought I was making headway when I said you were beautiful."

"I can't believe we're having this conversation," she said.

"I don't get out much these days. My skills are rusty."

"You're doing all right," she said.

We're some pair, he thought, watching her hold the icy glass to her forehead to cool off. And of course they weren't any sort of pair at all. Just two people whose paths had unexpectedly crossed. Yet—and this was the insane part—he felt as if he had a crush on her.

Impossible, he thought. If he'd learned nothing else from Marisol, he'd learned it was insane to give his heart to a woman who had another man's child. Why would he risk that again?

Aurora went to the station house after school. Her dad always had plenty of cold drinks on hand, and in this heat wave, she was dying of thirst. She also needed to talk to him about the mysterious fires that were occurring in the area. Or maybe not. She hadn't decided yet.

The pavement was wet, the engine half-washed. Maybe he'd gone in to watch that crazy old show, *Peyton Place,* on cable. He and Gloria and the others were weirdly bonkers for it. She followed the sound of voices and spotted her dad and Sarah Moon seated together in the shade. The two of them seemed oblivious to everything but each other.

She's *my* friend, Aurora wanted to wail. I found her first.

If her dad and Sarah started liking each other, that would

ruin everything. There was an unwritten rule that Aurora had to dislike or at least disrespect every woman her dad dated. The trouble was, she liked and respected Sarah. It might not be so simple to turn those feelings off.

She watched them for a minute, noticing the way Sarah's eyes sparkled like stars when she looked up at Aurora's dad.

Correction, Aurora thought, hurrying away from the station house before they saw her. It wouldn't be hard at all.

"Hey, Dad." Aurora burst into the kitchen, startling him.

He had just gotten home and had cracked open a beer. That was as far as the celebration went, though. He sat at the desk paying bills. When Aurora came up behind him, he discreetly covered the checkbook with a stray piece of paper so she wouldn't see who he was writing a check to. "What's up?"

She studied the framed drawing propped up on the desk. "Is that from Sarah?"

"Uh-huh. You like it?"

She frowned, crossed her arms. "It's pretty good, I guess. Why'd she give you a drawing?"

"To thank us for helping her."

Aurora shook back her glossy dark hair. "So are you dating her?"

"No." His reply was swift and assured. "Why would you think that?"

"You guys were hanging out at the station house today."

"I hang out with Gloria at the station house. Sometimes Judy deWitt comes to see me there, too. That doesn't mean I'm dating them."

"Sarah's different."

No shit, he thought. Just because he wasn't dating her didn't mean he didn't want to. It was nuts, they were wrong for each other, the timing couldn't be worse.

And yet he couldn't stop thinking about her—not-yet-divorced, pregnant as hell, temperamental Sarah Moon.

He had figured out long ago that he couldn't control his own heart. His heart controlled him.

"We're friends," he told Aurora. "You got a problem with that?"

"No."

"If I did happen to date her, would you have a problem with that?"

"Probably, yes."

Great. All the child-rearing books in the world warned him that kids her age were prone to lie. In the matter of Sarah Moon, he knew his daughter was being scrupulously honest.

"Okay, why?"

"A zillion reasons. If you date her, where does that leave me? It'll be weird."

"So you're saying I should manage my dating according to whether it makes you feel weird or not."

She stared at the desk, studying the drawing Sarah had done. "Everything you do affects me."

"Yeah? Ditto," he said. "That's the way it works in a family. The things a person does affects the others in a family. It's not a bad system."

"Even if one person makes the other person feel weird?"

"I'm not making you feel weird."

"Right," she said.

He wadded up an empty envelope. *Damn.*

Twenty-Five

Due to the nature of his job, Will tended to fully awaken when a bell rang, even when he was off duty. He simultaneously sat straight up in bed and snatched the receiver off the phone cradle in the middle of its first and only ring.

In that smallest beat of delay, between the ring and hello, he had just one thought. Marisol. Then another—Aurora. She was having a sleepover at her friend Edie's house.

"Bonner," he said. His voice was terse and gravelly. He rubbed his eyes and checked the clock. 2:14 a.m.

"I'm so sorry to wake you. I didn't know who else to call."

"Who…?"

"It's, um, Sarah Moon."

The rhythm of his heart changed. So did his breathing. When a pregnant woman called in the middle of the night, it couldn't be good.

"Are you all right?" he asked. Her father and brother both lived nearby; why wouldn't she call one of them?

"Yes, completely fine. I feel terrible calling you like

this, but—" She broke off, and it sounded as though she dropped the phone. "Can you come over?"

He was already stuffing his legs into blue jeans, the receiver tucked under his chin. "What's this about?"

"It's Franny."

"Franny." He set down the phone momentarily to pull on an old Cal sweatshirt, then picked it up again.

"…babies are coming," Sarah was saying. "Please, Will, I'm sorry to bother you, but…I just can't do this alone."

Finally, his confusion cleared, a ray of clarity piercing through the fog. "Your dog's having the puppies."

"I already called the vet's emergency line. He didn't want to be contacted unless there's real trouble."

"And is there?" His hands made a decision before his head. He yanked on a pair of work boots, leaving them unbuckled as he headed downstairs.

"Only my own," she admitted.

"I'll be right there."

He wasted no time driving to her place. The night was as quiet and empty as only the heart of nowhere could be, the mist-shrouded roads filled with secret life. Toads, deer and raccoons were all invisible until the last moment, flashing past like hazards in a video game. *What the hell are you doing, Bonner?* His nagging inner voice refused to be stifled.

"She's in distress," he muttered, his body registering a sharp craving for coffee. "A damsel in distress."

He knew what his wiseass sister would say. "That's the way you like them, Will."

Did he? Birdie liked to psychoanalyze him, an armchair Dr. Phil. Was he inexplicably attracted to women in trouble? Based on the choices he'd made in the past, that would appear to be the case. And what, precisely, was the attraction? The woman, or the trouble?

He cruised straight through the town's only stoplight. If Franco was even in the vicinity, he was probably napping in his squad car with the radio on, hoping the dispatcher wouldn't call.

Will parked in Sarah's driveway and bounded up the front steps. She was waiting at the door, pale and disheveled in a strange outfit of sweatpants, a pajama top and a bib apron. Her hair was mussed and she looked strangely, unexpectedly appealing.

He dismissed the thought and stepped inside. "Where is she?"

"The hall closet. She won't come out."

They went to the short hallway between the living room and kitchen. The closet door was ajar. A flashlight lay on the floor nearby. Slowly, hoping he wouldn't scare the poor dog, Will eased himself down.

"Hey, Pooch," he said, "remember me?" He switched on the flashlight, aiming the beam away from the dog so he wouldn't startle her.

The dog made a sound, a combination whine and growl. Another damsel in distress, for sure. Panting like a bellows, she lay amid a nest of jackets, sweaters and windbreakers and at least one old towel. There was a peculiar smell, not just dog, but a rich scent of dampness. Did a dog's water break like a woman's?

"Since I've been on the job," he said, "I've never attended an emergency birth. I've read up on it, though. In most cases, you leave things up to Mother Nature."

"Does she look comfortable to you? I fixed her a nice basket a few weeks ago, and she seemed to like sleeping there. Then tonight she disappeared, and I found her here. She pulled some coats off the hangers." Sarah knelt down beside him. "She has good taste. The coat underneath her is cashmere."

"You want me to try pulling it out of there?"

"No," she said quickly. "That coat is…from Chicago."

She didn't say so but Will guessed it was something she associated with her ex.

"Poor Franny," Sarah said. "She looks as if she's in pain."

"When was the last time you had her at the vet?"

"A week ago. He said it was likely to be this weekend."

"So she's right on schedule."

"Appears to be. Is it normal for her to be panting like that?"

Will spread his hands. "I'm way out of my realm of expertise here."

They sat in silence for a while. The dog stirred and got up, then turned in circles before lying down again. Then she was possessed by an urge to lick herself slowly and methodically.

"How about we give her some space," Will said, faintly embarrassed by the odd intimacy of the moment.

"Good idea." They stood up together.

He felt clumsy, his leg tingling. "I could use a cup of coffee."

"I'll make you some."

They went into the kitchen and she loaded up an old basket percolator, the kind his grandmother used to use. "Is Peet's all right with you?"

"My favorite."

"Oh, my God," she said, suddenly wide-eyed.

"Something wrong?"

"Aurora. Did you leave her home alone to come here?"

"I wouldn't have done that, not even in a town like

this. I tend to be overprotective in that way. She's spending the night at her friend's house."

Sarah leaned back against the counter. "This whole parenting thing—I've got a lot to learn."

"You'll learn it," he said as she handed him a mug. "Kids have a way of giving you a crash course."

They checked on the dog again—still licking purposefully—and had a seat on the sofa.

"So," Will said, fully alert now and inordinately happy to see her despite the circumstances, "other than the fact that your dog is about to give birth, is everything all right?"

Sarah smelled of shampoo and vanilla flavoring. When she smiled at him, the truth struck him: The attraction here was definitely the damsel. Not the distress.

She pulled the apron taut to reveal the outline of her stomach. "I have my next doctor's appointment on Wednesday. I think everything's right on schedule."

Will choked on his coffee. Damn. She'd definitely grown a belly since the last time he'd seen her.

She misunderstood his startled reaction. "Sorry. That's probably more than you want to know. I can't lie. But I have to admit, except for the morning sickness, I seem to be pretty good at being pregnant. My OB says if there was an Olympics for gestating, I'd be a contender."

"Uh, that's great." He didn't know what else to say.

She laughed. "I guess you're sorry you came over. I'm giving you way too much information, I can tell."

"It's all right."

She regarded him speculatively. "Why are you being so nice to me?"

"I'm a nice guy. It's something I've been working on, you know. Since high school." He hoped his answer sounded neutral, noncommittal. Time for a change of subject. "So what else is new with you?"

"Well, I have a syndicate that's going to distribute my comic strip. They say they have big plans for me, so I'm happy about that."

"Congratulations." He touched his mug to hers.

"The downside is that I have a lot of work to do. I kind of let myself get behind, with all that's going on." She gestured at a drafting table set up in a corner of the living room.

"Can I have a look?"

"Sure."

He was surprised at how many sketches she'd done, varying the placement of a character or rewriting the words. Although it wasn't really evident in the printed comic strip, the artistry and attention to detail came through clearly in the originals. He was intrigued by her comic strip. He recognized that embedded in the humor were her hopes, fears, dreams and aspirations. And her disappointments. "Aurora read all the episodes of *Just Breathe* in the archives on the Internet. She's a fan. Her favorite character is Lulu."

"Lulu's got her own fan club." Sarah hesitated, looked away. "Sometimes I wonder if she's the person my mother would be if Mom was still alive."

He felt a beat of sympathy for her. Jeanie Moon had died some years ago, while Sarah was away at college. He studied a sketch of Lulu treading water, saying, "Hey, you! Get out of the gene pool!"

"I was close to Helen—my soon-to-be-ex-mother-in-law," Sarah confessed. "I've been putting off calling her about the baby, but I'll need to, soon."

"Why's that?"

"It just seems like the right thing to do. She would've been an outstanding grandmother. God, what a mess this is turning out to be."

"You'll sort it out," he said. "Don't worry." He shook his head. "That sounds lame as hell, but I know you're going to be okay." Sarah had been completely open with Will about her husband—his ambition, his illness, his infidelity. If she could survive all that, she sure as hell could raise a child without him. "You'll be a good mom. I can tell. I was worried about having a kid but there's really no secret. Usually the kid tells you everything you need to know."

She was quiet for so long, he thought she might have fallen asleep. Then she asked, "What's the story on Aurora's mother? You don't talk about her much."

Whoa. "True," said Will. "I don't."

"In general, or just to me?"

"She left a long time ago," he said. "What is it you need to know?"

"There's nothing I *need* to know."

Good, he thought. Then let's leave it at that.

There was another silence. Then she said, "Statistically, a divorced man will remarry within two years of splitting up with his first wife."

"I'm not a statistic."

"I know that." He hoped she'd abandon the topic. Instead, she remarked, "You're remarkably closemouthed about her."

He grinned. "And you're remarkably persistent."

"Just say the word, and I'll shut up."

"I don't want to shut you up."

"Then tell me about Aurora's mom. She doesn't stay in touch with Aurora?"

"That's…not her style. Aurora doesn't hear from her too regularly," he told Sarah.

"Are these questions too personal?"

"Not yet. They're headed that way, though."

"And that's a problem?"

"That depends."

"On what?"

He paused. "On whether or not my answers are going to end up in the funny pages."

"Everything is fair game for the funny pages."

It wasn't the answer he expected. "Does that mean there's something funny about everything?"

"If I didn't believe that, I doubt I could pull through my current situation. I may come to you for tips on single parenting."

He chuckled. "You'd be barking up the wrong tree. I'm no expert."

"You've done a wonderful job with Aurora."

"She made it a snap—until lately," he admitted.

"What's happened lately?"

"Puberty, I think it's called."

"Ah."

"I feel like…" He paused, gathered his thoughts. Sarah was incredibly easy to talk to. "We're pulling apart. We used to be best buds, but now we fight. One minute, she wants me to tuck her in and read her a bedtime story, and the next, she's slamming the door in my face."

"Sounds pretty typical to me."

"I have a hard time with the physical changes she's going through." There it was, out in the open at last. He was worried—freaking intimidated—by Aurora's blossoming maturity, and deeply uncomfortable with the new dynamic. "Most girls turn to their mothers when things start…"

Sarah waited, then supplied, "Sprouting?"

"Exactly."

"I have a feeling this age is hard for all fathers, and extra hard for a stepfather. But what was it my favorite public servant likes to say? 'You'll sort it out. Don't worry.'"

He resisted the urge to hug her. "Touché."

Franny made a sound, a whine that crescendoed into a howl. They hurried to check on her, and both were struck speechless. She had delivered the first puppy, a slick ball of dark tissue that was all but unrecognizable. With calm efficiency, the dog neatly severed the cord and licked the puppy through a small tear in the sack. The tiny, toothless mouth opened with an audible gasp, its first breath of air. Franny nudged it into the protective curve of her body, and it squirmed unerringly home. Then Franny whined again, ready for the next round.

"My Lord," Sarah whispered. "I've never…this is…" Her voice trailed off as she stared at the just-born puppy.

Will looked down at their hands, and discovered they were tightly joined in anticipation. He didn't remember grabbing her hand.

"Do you think she's all right?" Sarah asked. Self-consciously, she extracted her hand from his.

"Seems like she knows exactly what to do."

The dog didn't appear to need anything from them except a little peace and quiet. At some point between the fourth and fifth puppies, Will and Sarah dozed off, side by side on the sofa. He awoke to find his arm dead asleep from the shoulder down. He had slipped it around her, and her head rested heavily against him.

For about thirty seconds, he didn't move a muscle. He simply stayed where he was and felt everything. The weight of her and the warmth that kindled where their bodies met. The vanilla shampoo scent of her hair. The quiet rhythm of her breathing. There was no room for self-deception in this moment, so he didn't even bother. He liked being close to her while she slept. It was as simple—and as complicated—as that.

The sun was coming up. A faint gray light slipped through the bay window facing the water. Will thought about Aurora. She wouldn't be up yet, since today was Saturday.

"Hey," he said, giving Sarah a gentle nudge as he withdrew his leaden arm.

She gave a soft moan and stretched slowly and luxuriously in a motion that reminded him how long it had been since he'd held a woman. Then she gave a little gasp. "Oh, God. I can't believe I fell asleep."

"We both dozed off." He waited for his arm to fire back to life. She massaged the side of her neck. He wondered if the weight of his arm had hurt her. Best not to ask.

He went to check on the dog. The puppies lay all in a row, nursing contentedly or resting. Will counted them twice to be sure. "Six," he told Sarah.

She smiled sleepily. "Are they all right?"

"I think so. Franny's dozing."

Sarah drank the rest of the tea in her mug, made a face and then dropped to her knees beside the dog. "Good girl," she said, and put out her hand. The dog blinked drowsily and allowed Sarah to pat her head. "I've been lining up families to adopt the puppies," she said. "So far, four are spoken for." She turned to Will. "Thank you."

"No problem."

"Really? I didn't keep you from work?"

"Nope. And as far as I know, nobody needed rescuing last night." He held out his hand to help her to her feet.

She studied him briefly, then let go of his hand. "I did," she said.

Twenty-Six

As she sometimes did when nobody was around, Aurora tuned the kitchen radio to a Spanish-language station and let the familiar voices and rhythms drift through her mind. When she did this her head filled up with dreams and memories, and she couldn't tell the difference between the two.

She remembered the sensation of a woman's hand brushing across her forehead. Was that Mama or someone else, a nun at the clinic where they used to go for penicillin? Aurora couldn't recall.

The snare drum banter of the radio announcers sounded relentlessly joyous. Her native language had a naturally upbeat cadence, so that even the Lord's Prayer sounded like a jump rope rhyme. Before coming to Glenmuir, had she really had a yard full of cousins to play with, or was that something else she had dreamed?

Her past was like a distant, undiscovered country, glimmering on the horizon just out of her grasp. She suspected that if she tried very hard, she could go there and find out what it was really like. With the right amount of concentration, she could separate dreams from memories and wishful thinking, and figure out the life she had lived before Will came along.

The big question was, did she really want to know?

With a restless sigh of discontent, she shut the radio off.

It was all so pointless, Aurora thought, such a waste of time to wonder and worry about someone who had walked away and never looked back.

As everyone was always pointing out to her, she had a devoted family to provide a great support system. The trouble with that was, try as she might to deny it, she still wanted her mother. A part of her longed to ditch the "support system"—which sounded like something you got at an electronics store—for five minutes of her mother's imperfect love.

The sudden ring of the doorbell startled her. What she saw when she opened the door startled her even more—Zane Parker. For a few seconds, all she could do was stare. He was so good-looking it was almost freaky. He belonged on a TV series, playing the hot guy. Every girl Aurora knew liked him. If crushes could actually crush, he'd be flat as a pancake by now.

It was like something out of a fairy tale, Zane Parker coming to her house, as though she had wished him here. She was afraid to speak for fear of breaking the spell.

"We're selling bulbs for the Mount Vision Renewal Project," he said, blinding her with a perfect smile. It took her a moment to realize that in his shadow stood his younger brother, Ethan.

"You mean, like, lightbulbs?"

"Like flower bulbs, genius." He laughed, as though she'd made a joke. But no, she thought. She really was that dense. Being around a cute boy sucked all the brain cells out of her head.

Bringing flower bulbs to a Bonner was like bringing ice to Eskimos, but Aurora didn't care. "Um, sure. Come on in," she said, practically tripping over her feet as she held open the door. She heard music in her ears and realized it was the beating of her own heart. She was so excited she nearly forgot about Ethan. "Sorry," she said, stepping aside. "Hi, Ethan."

"Hey." Ethan was the exact opposite of Zane in every way. He wore low-slung black jeans and a black T-shirt. His too-long hair fell over his brow. The thing about Ethan was, he didn't really have the attitude to match his looks. There was too much kindness in his eyes, and his smile was too quick. Too sweet.

Lugging a heavy-looking box, he joined his brother. "Mind if I set this on the table?"

Observing them side by side, Aurora thought what a bummer it must be to have a brother like Zane. Yet Ethan didn't seem bummed in the least as he grinned at her a little shyly.

"Sure, no problem." She led the way to the kitchen. At the table, she hurriedly swept aside books and newspapers.

Zane tapped his pen on his clipboard. "So is your old man around?"

"He's out doing some errands." As usual, her dad had invited her to come along. When she was little, she used to love his off-duty days, when the two of them would tend to ordinary things, like going to the library or the grocery store. A part of her wished she could still tag along, but at her age, that was just babyish, so she was now in the habit of bailing every time her dad invited her to do something.

She saw the brothers exchange a glance and hurriedly added, "I'll buy some bulbs from you. I mean, it's for a good cause and all." She had her own money from babysitting, which she kept in her own bank account. She'd been saving up for some Pantone markers like Sarah's, but suddenly this seemed more important.

Zane dazzled her again with a smile. "Excellent." He gestured to his brother. "Show her what we've got."

She wished Zane would do the showing, but he seemed more interested in looking around the kitchen. Suddenly she had a brilliant idea. "Would you like something to drink?" She pulled open the fridge and showed them the selection.

"Thank you." Ethan helped himself to a root beer.

"Ah, Budweiser," Zane said, grabbing a can.

Aurora laughed. "Yeah, sure. You go right ahead."

"Don't mind if I do." He eased back the can tab, releasing a distinct hissing sound.

"Hey! I wasn't serious," Aurora said. "You can't have that."

"Too late." Zane took a big gulp.

Ethan rolled his eyes. "Idiot," he said under his breath.

Zane let out a prolonged belch. He took a brochure from his clipboard. "So do you want to hear my spiel or are you ready to buy?"

Aurora felt an icy thrill of apprehension in the pit of her stomach. "You owe me for that stolen beer," she said boldly. "Let's hear it."

"Fine," he said. "Whatever." He started reading from a prepared script, describing the disastrous fire that decimated two thousand acres of wilderness.

Ethan sipped his root beer while perusing the *Bay Beacon.* It lay open to the funny pages, which Aurora never missed since Sarah Moon's comic strip, *Just Breathe*, was now featured in it. Shirl and Lulu were driving each other batty, and Shirl had just dropped a bomb—she was pregnant. It was peculiar and cool, knowing the comic strip reflected what was happening in Sarah's life.

After a moment, Aurora realized she'd zoned out during Zane's sales pitch.

"'...founded in 1997 to aid in the renewal of the natural wilderness,'" Zane continued. "Hey, are you really interested in this?"

I'm interested in you, she thought, and the idea made her blush. "Sure." She went and scrounged some money from her wallet while Zane finished the beer, drinking it like he meant business.

Aurora chose a custom selection of bulbs on purpose, so they'd have to open packages, which would require them to stay longer. She pretended not to realize this, even though she knew tons about flowers, thanks to her grandparents. A huge part of her childhood had been spent in the Technicolor world of their farm amid lilies and sea thrift and dahlias, and she could identify entire families of blossoms by scent and sight.

As soon as she handed the money to Zane, he zipped it into his bankers' pouch, recorded the sale and headed for the door. "Sorry I can't stay," he said hurriedly. "I have to turn this in by six o'clock. Ethan will help you with the bulbs."

Aurora suppressed the impulse to insist that she wanted Zane to help her, not Ethan. She took a deep breath as she turned to Ethan. Unlike his brother, he seemed to be in no hurry at all. Maybe, Aurora thought, this kid might be useful. Maybe if she won him over, she could score points with Zane.

"It's great that you and your brother are doing this," she commented. "It's a really good cause."

"Zane is doing this to fulfill the high school community service requirement."

"Why are you helping?"

"Because…never mind." He sipped his drink.

She thought it was kind of cute, in a dorky way, that he pretended not to care about the environment. She could tell he really did.

"Listen, there's a group of us going out on Saturday to clear fireweed," he said. "You want to come?"

"Is Zane going?" She hoped the question didn't sound overeager.

He stuck his thumb in his back pocket. "Does it matter?"

"No," she said quickly. "I just wondered, is all."

Ethan turned to study the books on the shelves as though they held the key to the meaning of life.

"You sure have a bunch of books," he observed, checking out a floor-to-ceiling bookcase. "Is your dad going to night school or something?"

"Nope. He just studies a lot on his own."

Ethan flipped through a dog-eared volume about navigating the teen years. "These are all about raising kids. Maybe he finds you a big mystery."

"Maybe I *am* a big mystery."

"Ha. You wish. You aren't mysterious at all."

She sniffed. "I suppose you think you've got me all figured out."

"It's not that hard."

"Prove it. Tell me something you've figured out."

"You have the hots for my brother," he said. "That's something."

Aurora's cheeks caught fire. "That's bull. I don't know where you got that idea."

"It's right here in this book," he said, flipping to a random page. "'It is a known fact that the adolescent girl always gets a crush on an older boy who dresses fly and acts cool.'"

She tried to hold back laughter as she grabbed for the book. "Liar. Show me where it says that."

He held her off. "There's a footnote, too," he said. "What do you know? It says here that the girl's feelings for the older boy are totally bogus, and that deep down, she likes his younger brother."

"You dork," she said.

"'Insults are a sign of affection,'" he pretended to quote. "Good to know." He smacked the book shut.

She couldn't help laughing, even though she was annoyed. Ethan was easy to be around, and he made her smile. She liked him—as a friend, of course. "Put it back, smart aleck."

He reshelved the book. "Have you read any of these?"

She hesitated, then decided to share something with him. "You know what I do sometimes? I find stuff in these books, like bulimia or OCD, and see if I can fake the symptoms, you know, just to see if my dad will notice."

"Doesn't it bother you to worry him?"

"Well, that's the thing. So far, I've never managed to convince him that something is wrong."

"Why would you want to?"

"I swear, sometimes it's the only way to get him—Never mind." She shouldn't have said anything. Spoken aloud, it sounded totally lame. She decided to change the subject. "So what does a habitat restoration crew do?"

"We clear the nonnative plants so the native ones can grow back." He started sorting through the bulbs, picking out the variety she had checked off on her order form. "You ought to come along sometime. Sure beats reading parenting books and thinking up problems that don't exist."

He grinned as he said it, so she didn't take offense. And

she carefully considered his offer. Three hours of pulling weeds held no appeal to her, but the idea of working side by side with Zane Parker more than made up for that. "Where do we meet?"

The back door swished open and her father came in, carrying four grocery sacks across both arms.

Aurora and Ethan looked at one another; then, simultaneously, their gazes flew to the empty beer can on the table. Oh, crap, she thought.

"Hey, Dad." She hurried over to her father and blocked his path. "Let me help you with this stuff."

"I've got it," he said.

"But—"

He went around her and set the packages on the table. Aurora nearly freaked, but then she noticed the beer can was gone. Trying not to look too relieved, she said, "Dad, this is Ethan Parker. He's in my class at school."

"Ethan." Her dad held out his hand. He never tried to look intimidating in situations like this, but he couldn't help that he was ten times bigger than everyone else. To people who didn't know him, he seemed really scary and protective even when he was trying to be friendly.

"Ethan and his brother are raising money for the Mount Vision Renewal Project," Aurora said. "Selling flower bulbs." What was not to like about that?

"I see," her dad said. "So where's your brother?"

"He had to go turn in the money," Ethan said. "And I'd better be going, too. Thanks, Aurora."

"Sure."

He picked up the box of bulbs. "So you're coming on Saturday?"

She looked at her father. "If it's okay with my dad." She explained about the weed-pulling party.

"We'll talk about it," her dad said.

Great, she thought, rolling her eyes as she walked out the front door. He could never give her a simple yes until he grilled her about her request. "I'll let you know at school," she said.

"All right." He looked at her for a moment, and she felt a funny little skip of nervousness. Then he looked past her and said, "Bye, Mr. Bonner."

"Just what we need," Aurora said, returning to the kitchen. "More flowers."

"Sounds like it's for a good cause."

Yeah, she thought. Getting Zane Parker to talk to me.

"You look pretty happy about it," her dad observed. "Didn't know you cared about fire restoration."

She was blushing so much, she was afraid the roots of her hair were turning red. "Maybe I do," she said.

"Right," he said with a teasing grin. "How about giving me a hand with these groceries? I'll do something with these bulbs."

Aurora saw the instant he found the beer can. He glanced at the bookcase and his face changed. "What the hell is this doing here?"

She took refuge in defensive anger. "I have no idea. You probably left it there yourself. I bet it's been there for ages."

"It's still cold from the refrigerator," he snapped. "So was it you, or your friend who drank it?"

"I don't know what you're talking about."

He turned the can upside down and beer dripped out. "See these numbers? They're all the same on the bottom of the cans in a six-pack. Wonder what I'd find if I compared them to the six-pack in the fridge."

Crap. Who knew about the series numbers on the bottom?

He reached for the phone. "Do you know the Parkers' number by heart or should I call information?"

Oh, God, thought Aurora. I'm done for now. She had one tiny chance with Zane, and her dad was about to ruin it. "I drank the beer myself," she blurted out, hoping he wouldn't try to smell it on her breath. "I just wanted to see…what it was like."

"You're grounded without a chance for parole," he said as he carefully set down the phone. "You can see what that's like, too."

Twenty-Seven

When Sarah first moved back to Glenmuir, she had still felt like the misfit she'd been in high school. Self-conscious about being the spurned wife, she'd fallen into her old habit of keeping to herself. She tended to order supplies off the Internet, a virtual woman living a virtual life.

Getting pregnant was a huge wake-up call. This place was going to be her child's hometown. She didn't want her kid to grow up with a social misfit for a mother. She was going to do what she had neglected to do as an unhappy teenager and later as Jack's wife. She was going to quit being a loner and create a wider network of family and friends.

Breaking old habits wasn't easy, and now there was a new wrinkle. Being divorced was not so rare. However, being divorced and pregnant edged toward pitiful. She imagined the news fanning across the town like a Santa Ana wind.

Get over yourself, she thought in Lulu's voice. People have better things to do than gossip about you.

She started to have her doubts when she went into the paint and art supply store and everyone within earshot fell silent. Telling herself to quit feeling so paranoid, she approached the clerk behind the counter.

"Judy?" she said, recognizing the young woman. "It's me, Sarah Moon."

"Sarah! I'd heard you were back in town." Judy deWitt had worked here ever since they were both in high school. In addition to being one of the strangest girls in high school, Judy had been one of the most gifted, creating fantastical sculptures out of wire and driftwood, embellishing the works with seaglass, shells and found objects.

Like Sarah, she'd been artistic and quiet. Unlike Sarah, she'd always been utterly comfortable in her own skin. She was Judy the Goth, with so much hardware on her person and face that she set off the metal detectors at the school's entryway. Deep down, Sarah had envied Judy, because Judy loved who she was—unique, out-there and talented. She never seemed haunted by shame that her family didn't have money, and she'd never been the victim of a crush on a boy out of her reach.

Judy had lost several of her facial piercings, although she still sported an extremely distracting stud in the middle of her chin. Other than that, she had hardly changed at all.

"It's good to see you," Sarah said.

"You, too. We should get together sometime," Judy said.

"I'd like that." Sarah felt stiff and awkward, out of practice.

"Can I help you find something?" Judy asked.

"I'll have a look around." This wasn't so bad, she thought. Maybe she and Judy would reacquaint themselves. Maybe, like a latter-day Gran and Aunt May, they would hang out together, do art and talk. Sarah wished she'd stayed in closer touch with the people she used to know.

"Sarah Moon," someone else said. "I heard you were back."

Even without turning, Sarah could identify her by voice. It was the same voice she remembered from high school, chirpily leading cheers at pep rallies. "Hello, Vivian. How have you been?" Sarah arranged her mouth into a smile.

Vivian Pierce smiled back. If possible, she was even more gorgeous than she had been in high school. Same blond waterfall of hair pulled back in a ponytail. Same sparkling smile. Same flawless sense of fashion—with one subtle difference. A fabulous diamond wedding set flashed on her left ring finger. Sarah dutifully declared how good it was to see Vivian again, how great she looked. Then she asked a question Vivian had clearly been waiting for. "What have you been up to?"

"I'm so excited," she confided, gesturing at her cartload of cleaning supplies and brushes. "We just bought a house."

"Congratulations," Sarah said.

"It's a sweet place over in Point Reyes Station," she said. "Needs a lot of TLC, though."

"I don't suppose it needs a free puppy," Sarah suggested, gesturing at Franny, on her leash out on the sidewalk. "My dog's got a litter at home." She figured Vivian would reject the notion out of hand.

Instead, Vivian surprised her by handing her a card. "Call me when they're ready to be adopted."

"I'll put a flyer in the window for you," Judy suggested, "if you want."

They were both so…nice. Sarah hadn't expected that.

Vivian showed Judy some color sample cards. "I've made a decision. I'm going with celery for the walls and cadmium red for the trim."

Judy took the sample over to the paint mixer. "I was afraid you'd go for pink and white."

"You were not."

Sarah covered her surprise at their easy camaraderie. Judy and Viv had been miles apart in high school. The prom queen versus the Goth. Now they acted like best friends, especially when Judy promised to visit Vivian that evening and help her paint. What do you know? Sarah thought.

As she picked out supplies, she surreptitiously studied the women. Not only was Vivian more beautiful than ever, she looked prosperous in cashmere and designer jeans, cowboy boots and a flawless haircut.

"Remember to follow directions," Judy told Vivian as she boxed up the painting supplies. "This ingredient in particular is volatile. Keep the area ventilated, and don't use it near an open flame."

Vivian winked at her. "Maybe if I start a fire, Will Bonner will come rescue me."

At the sound of Will's name, Sarah came to attention.

"I thought you were a happily married woman," Judy said, mildly scolding.

"A happily married woman with an active imagination," Vivian said. "Face it, half the women in this town would set themselves on fire if they thought it would get Will's attention."

"And the other half?"

"They'd set their husbands on fire."

Sarah wondered about Vivian's husband and pictured a distinguished lawyer who worked in the city. Did they know what "happily married" was? Really know, or were they fooling themselves? In a perfect world, Will himself would be married to Vivian. They had even been prom king and queen together in high school, a perfect match. There had been some drama senior year, she recalled. Will's longtime girlfriend dumped him right before prom, and he and his friends went on a road trip south of the border.

Sarah added some archival markers to her basket.

"Viv, I'll help you take this stuff to your car," Judy offered.

"That's all right. I brought my hubby along for that."

Sarah was galvanized. She couldn't wait to see the hubby. She lingered over the Monolith Woodless pencils, stalling for time.

"He had to stop at the hardware store. He'll be right over." While they waited, Vivian and Judy chatted like old friends. Sarah felt an unexpected touch of yearning. Loneliness hit her like a slap in the face. Just to have someone to talk to, or to go to lunch with, or to discuss paint colors with…suddenly that seemed as important as food and air.

The bell over the door sounded and in walked yet another familiar person.

"Mr. Chopin!" Sarah burst out. "It's Sarah Moon. Remember me?"

Viktor Chopin offered her a dazzling smile. He had been her art teacher and mentor all through junior high and high school. He'd been the one teacher who had considered her a gifted student, giving her a feeling of worth. With his bold Eastern European good looks and the hint of an exotic accent flavoring his words, he had caused high school hearts to flutter. If anything, the passage of time had made him more dashing than ever.

"I certainly do, Miss Moon," he said, smiling as he picked up on her formality. "Are you home for a visit or are you back with us for good?"

His eyes were depthless pools of chocolate. A girl could drown in them and not gain a pound.

"I am…here to stay," she said.

"Still the artist, I see." He indicated her shopping basket, which had inexplicably sprouted a Durer grid, something she hadn't used since Drawing 101.

"I am so very glad to hear that," he said.

"Thank you, Mr. Chopin."

He treated her to another cordial smile, then went to the paint counter.

"We're all set, handsome." Vivian raised up on tiptoe to kiss his cheek. "Five gallons of Judy's finest."

Sarah watched with her jaw unhinged as her favorite teacher carted Vivian's paint outside. Mr. C. had married the prom queen.

"You look surprised," Judy said as she rang up Sarah's purchases.

"I shouldn't gawk," said Sarah, chagrined.

Judy smiled. "Funny how some things turn out, eh?"

As Sarah loaded her things into the car, she spotted Franny trotting along the driveway that separated the shop from the storage shed. The dog was still an escape artist and had managed to slip her collar. "Franny," she said, "dammit, get back here." Nose to the ground, the dog scurried to the rear of the shop, Sarah in hot pursuit and growing more frustrated by the moment.

"Don't take it personally."

Sarah turned to see Judy leaning against the back door of the art supply shop, smoking a cigarette.

"What, the fact that my own dog keeps running away from me?" Sarah asked.

Franny circled back. Sarah resisted the urge to chase her down and put the collar and leash back on her. That would only turn into a contest she had no hope of winning. Instead she made a big show of ignoring the dog.

"So how have you been?" she asked Judy, keeping one eye on Franny.

"All right." Judy expelled a plume of smoke.

"And Mr. Madsen?" Sarah asked, referring to the owner of the store.

Judy hesitated. "He died four years ago. I bought the store from his estate. I figured I'd better take over the place, or I'd go broke buying my supplies here."

Judy the Goth, a business owner. Sarah took a moment to process this. "I plan to be one of your regulars," she said.

Judy motioned Sarah through a set of tall doors into the warehouse of corrugated tin. Most of the space was taken up by supplies stacked on pallets, but one corner housed a metal sculpture studio. There were burners of all sizes and blowtorches at the ready, stacks of cut metal and jars of soldering material.

Sarah recognized the peculiar airy quality of the abstract sculptures. The beaten metal shapes seemed weightless, as though they were feathers in flight. "You did the installation at Waterfront Park," she said.

"That's right." Judy showed her a work-in-progress, commissioned by a winery in Hopland. She noticed Sarah studying her hands. "Burn marks," she said, holding them out in front of her. "Occupational hazard."

They walked outside together. Judy tossed her cigarette butt into a sand-filled bucket. "I'd better get back to minding my business."

Sarah nodded. "See you around." Then she paused. "Hey, would you like to meet for coffee sometime?"

"Sure, I guess. Vivian and I usually meet at the White Horse Café around nine in the morning on weekdays. Just to talk, you know?"

Sarah didn't know, yet the prospect had enormous appeal to her. "Thanks. I'd like that," she said.

Twenty-Eight

Sarah's earliest memories were bathed in the sea-scented atmosphere of the oyster farm. As a child, it had been her whole world. She used to stand at the water's edge with arms outstretched, embracing the very air around her. But as a teenager, she grew to view it as a trap and yearned for escape. Now she felt a sense of balance here. She liked taking Franny for walks along the shell-paved road leading out to the long, narrow buildings towering on stilts over the spartina grass that fringed Moon Bay. Every single oyster the company sold began life as a spat the size of a pinhead. On one of their frequent walks, she pointed these things out to Will, who, despite being a lifelong resident of Glenmuir, was unfamiliar with the workings of an oyster farm.

"When I was little," she told him, "I thought everyone's daddy took off each night at dark when the tide went out. As I got older, I learned it wasn't just unusual but downright bizarre."

"Maybe that's why you turned out so twisted."

She slugged his arm, and then they ambled along in

companionable silence. She and Will were not dating. That would be insanity and they both knew it. They called each other, though. They went for long walks on the beach at sunset. They had dinner together and sometimes there were candles involved. But they were definitely not dating.

"Did you miss him?" Will asked. "When he was out working?"

"No." She understood completely why he was asking. "He was supporting our family, and I knew he'd be back."

"I hope Aurora feels that way about me. With my crazy work schedule, I'm either all there or all gone."

"Why don't you ask her?" Sarah suggested.

"She's barely speaking to me. She's still mad at me for grounding her." He blew out a weary sigh. "She asked Birdie about suing me for false arrest."

"I wasn't much older than Aurora when I sneaked out and drank beer with the oyster workers. Got caught, of course. Punished, too. But you're doing more than punishing her. You're putting out a candle with a hose on full force. Why is that?"

"Drinking and lying are hot buttons for me."

"Why is that?"

He didn't respond, and Sarah knew she was treading a fine line between nosiness and caring. "Your daughter means a lot to me, Will. I want to understand."

"She looks just like her mother," he finally admitted. "When she starts acting like her, it scares the crap out of me."

They watched Franny sniffing furiously around the weathered dock that jutted out over the tidal flats. Sarah tried to picture Marisol, as beautiful as Aurora. What sort of woman ruined her marriage with drinking and lying?

"That's the thing about being a parent," Will said.

"There are as many ways to screw up as there are minutes in a day."

"Attitude, Bonner. She's a great kid. Why not think about all the ways it's great between the two of you?"

"That's sort of hard to do when she's giving me the silent treatment." He hooked his thumbs into the back pockets of his jeans. "I used to understand everything about her. At least, I thought I did. Somehow she turned from a perfectly good kid into a…I don't know. A troubled teen."

"She wants to talk," Sarah assured him. "Believe me, I know how a troubled teen thinks."

"Yeah? Were you one of those?"

"Duh." She couldn't believe he even had to ask.

"And is Aurora troubled?"

"The fact that you're asking means she could be headed in that direction." There was no sense in pulling punches with him. "So listen, I don't know the first thing about being a parent, especially to a thirteen-year-old. But the way I see it, she's taken her punishment. Now it's time for forgiveness."

"For your information, I'm about to take her off restriction, and I forgave her long ago."

"Does she know that?"

"I assume so."

Sarah thought about her own father. Had there been a moment in her childhood when he could have reached out, taken away her doubts and insecurities? "Don't assume. Tell her she's forgiven."

"She's still pissed at me."

"You're still pissed at her," Sarah said in a flash of understanding.

"What the hell do you mean by that?"

"Just a wild guess. What's really going on, Will?"

He braced his arm on the weathered dock railing and stared down at the water. "She lied, okay? She said she drank that beer, and I know damn well it was some other kid. Like you said, every kid sneaks a beer now and then. I'm angry because she lied to me."

"At the risk of sounding like a broken record," Sarah said, "does she know that?"

He grinned and shook his head. "I get it. I'll talk to her."

"Good plan." Sarah touched his arm. "I've been thinking."

"Uh-oh."

"Since her grounding is going to be over soon, I think you should give her one of the puppies."

"Right. Reward her with a puppy after the way she's acted."

"I'm not talking about a reward. A puppy is a long-term commitment. I think Aurora's ready for that." She watched Franny dart amid the dock pilings, grabbing a beard of seaweed, giving it a shake.

"No way. My work schedule's too crazy. There's no room for a dog in our lives."

"My grandmother says the things that matter come along in their own time, not necessarily when you're ready."

"We're talking about a dog here."

"We're talking about the things that matter."

"No dog, Sarah. And don't even think about mentioning it to Aurora."

"I'm still grounded," Aurora informed Ethan Parker as they got on their bikes at the parking lot at the summit above Bear Valley. "I can't go to the concert at Waterfront

Park tonight." While she was grounded, the community service work was the only thing her father allowed. She and a group of volunteers with the habitat restoration team met each Saturday to build erosion controls and weed out nonnative plants.

"That sucks. You shouldn't have been grounded in the first place," Ethan said, pushing off down the hill.

Aurora matched his speed, savoring the fresh wind in her face. The work was hard and not all that rewarding, especially on days when Zane decided to skip out, like today. Hacking away at the hillside had merely been tedious. "Why do you say that?" she asked Ethan. "What was I supposed to do? Tell my dad your brother took the beer?"

"At least it would have been the truth."

"And my dad would have called your parents, and one way or another, all of us would have wound up in trouble. The way I see it, I'd be grounded either way. Might as well leave you and Zane out of it."

"Or here's a concept," Ethan said. "Zane could have owned up to everything and taken the heat himself." He shifted into high gear and sped off down the hill.

The worst part of being grounded, Aurora thought, was not the loss of freedom, of TV and Internet time. The worst part was the hard work of staying mad at her father. She wanted to, though. Keeping a wall up took more time and energy than she had imagined. She carried around a lump of hurt in her chest and it grew heavier, day by day. It took all her strength to keep from begging for liberation, just so she could quit being mad.

Sometimes she thought about running away to find her mother. It wouldn't be that hard. Aurora knew she could convince Aunt Lonnie to take her along on a delivery run of fresh flowers or oysters to Las Vegas. She could even stow away on the cargo plane, maybe. But once she found her mother—then what?

All the way home, she envisioned different scenarios in her head—a tearful reunion, bitter recriminations, familial bliss. None of them seemed to fit, and she knew why. She simply didn't know enough about her mother to understand the situation. Her memories were mostly hazy fragments, although she believed she had a sharp recollection of the day Mama had left. At seven years old, Aurora hadn't realized right away that Mama was gone for good. Her father found her home alone after school one day, eating a bowl of cereal and watching Nickelodeon with the sound turned up high. She remembered that she was sitting on a moss-green floor pillow in the middle of the room, pretending to be a shipwreck survivor on the smallest of rafts.

"Where's your mother?" Daddy had asked, bending to kiss the top of her head.

She shrugged, then beamed up at him, showing off the beginnings of a new front tooth. "I'm glad you're home, Dad." She knew he loved being called Dad, because it made him grin and hold his shoulders really straight.

Aurora always paid close attention to the way she spoke, too. She had been determined from the start to talk just like the Anglo kids in her class.

Her dad kept smiling that day as he put the milk back in the refrigerator, but she could tell he wasn't happy about something. His shoulders went from straight to stiff, and his movements were sharp as he grabbed the cordless phone and stepped out back. Even though Aurora was pretty sure he wasn't mad at her, she felt a little worried, so she listened in on the conversation.

"...the hell was Marisol thinking, leaving a seven-year-old alone in the house?" Dad said to the phone.

Aurora could tell from the tone of his voice that he was talking to Granny Shannon. There were lots more conversations that night, a lot more worry. That night, her dad took her in his lap and said Mama had moved to a place called Las Vegas and wouldn't be living with them anymore.

"Then let's go with her," Aurora had suggested.

"We can't do that, baby girl." Her dad had looked as sorry as can be.

"Why not? I'll be good," Aurora had insisted. "I promise I will."

"Sure you will, baby girl, but your mama…she's got other plans. She can't have us with her. It's better for all of us if you and I stay right here."

To this day, Aurora didn't know much more than that, and her dad never talked about it.

When she arrived home, she saw that her father's truck was in the driveway. Great. Now she'd have to muster up a crummy attitude again.

She slammed into the kitchen. On the counter were some very large sacks from Bay Hay and Feed. "Hey," she said noncommittally.

"Hey, yourself." At the counter, he started unloading the bags, and she was startled to see a pair of metal bowls and a fat sack of all-natural dog food.

She frowned at him. "What's going on?"

He took out a red collar and leash. "Are you busy tonight?"

"Depends." Her heart was pounding now. *Please, oh, please.* "What do you have in mind?"

"I thought you might want to help pick out our new puppy."

"Dad!" Forgetting her vow to stay mad, Aurora ran to

him and leaped up, hugging him tight. "Really? We're getting one of Sarah's dogs?"

"They're eight weeks old now." He gently set her away from him. "Ready for adoption."

"Are we going right this minute?"

"As soon as you're ready."

She was already speeding to the door.

"Just a minute, young lady," her dad said.

A catch, thought Aurora. There was always a catch. With a sinking heart, she turned to face him. "Yeah?"

"A puppy's a lot of work."

"I know that, Dad. Geez."

"So if we bring one home, you're going to need to walk it and take care of its every need. I just don't see how you can do that if you're on restriction."

She didn't even bother to fight the smile on her face. *Finally.* "Me, neither, Dad."

Twenty-Nine

When Sarah opened the door to her house and greeted them with a smile, Will knew he was in trouble. No matter how much he tried to deny it, he was nuts for her and had been ever since the day he'd rushed her to the hospital with an undiagnosed pregnancy.

A pregnancy, Bonner, he told himself again and again. Fresh from a failed marriage. You might as well get a crush on Angelina Jolie. It would make about as much sense.

But when Sarah smiled at him the way she was now, he forgot all that. Taking off his baseball cap, he stood aside and let Aurora go first.

"We're getting a puppy," Aurora said. "I can't believe you didn't tell me."

Watching them together, Will felt a surge of affection. Sarah treated the kid like an equal, a friend. From the start, they had shared a connection that made it all the more obvious to him that Aurora longed for a mother figure.

"Let's go out back. You get the pick of the litter," Sarah said.

Aurora rushed for the door. Will followed more slowly. The puppies were on the screened-in porch in a large cedar box Sarah's father had built for her. Franny's bed lay nearby.

She thumped her tail in greeting, and Sarah bent to scratch her ears. "Hey, girl. You seem tired." She stood and rubbed the small of her back. "Does she seem tired to you?"

"She's been nursing the pups for eight weeks. I figure that would make anyone tired."

Aurora got in the box with them and they swarmed her, clambering into her lap and straining to lick her face. The puppies' father was an unknown quantity, but Will suspected strains of golden retriever, judging by the pups' coloring and the wandering habits of George Dundee's dog, Buster.

Aurora threw back her head and laughed with joy as the puppies vied for her attention.

"You should have brought a camera," Sarah said.

"You're right. I wish I had."

"Maybe I'll draw you a sketch."

"I'd like that." He knew no photograph or sketch could capture Aurora's laughter or the joy on her face. He'd have to remember that on his own.

"Dad, how am I ever going to choose?" Aurora asked. "They're all perfect."

"I know what you mean."

"Maybe one of them will choose you," Sarah suggested.

"What do you mean?"

"I'm not sure. Let them out into the yard, and take your time."

Will and Sarah went and sat on the porch swing facing the small fenced yard and the expansive sea beyond. The air was redolent of honeysuckle, and Aurora's voice carried lightly across the yard. She set down the first puppy and it made a beeline for the roses.

"I hope she figures out a way to make up her mind," Will said. "I can't take the whole litter."

Sarah was quiet as she regarded him with an expression he couldn't read. When she smiled at him, he always felt as if he'd won something or passed some test. The trouble was that Sarah had different smiles for different things, and it was a challenge to read her.

"Well," he said, "I swear I can't."

"Could you handle two of them if you had to?" she asked.

"That's not what I signed up for."

"Sometimes you get a bonus."

"A bonus puppy. I don't think so." The chains of the porch swing clicked as he shifted in agitation. "I thought you said all six were spoken for. Did someone change their mind?"

"No, you can relax. You only get one. I was just trying to scare you."

"It'll take more than that to scare me off." A little chagrined, he turned to watch Aurora with puppy number three. The dog seemed to want nothing more than to dig a trench in the dirt and take a nap.

"I like that answer." She turned quiet again, reflective.

Will sensed a different air about her today. The tension between them felt more intense, too. There was always tension, but neither had acknowledged it.

"Are you doing okay?" he asked.

"Yes," she said. "Yes, I am."

In the yard, Aurora made a kissing sound with her mouth to get the attention of puppy number four.

"Speaking of bonuses…I have news," Sarah said.

"Yeah?"

Her hand curved around the swell in her belly. "Twins," she said simply.

Will found himself staring at her breasts until her meaning sank in. "No kidding," he said. "Wow."

"That's what I keep telling myself." She gave him a smile filled with desperation and fear and a pervasive joy she couldn't suppress.

"That's great, Sarah," he said. "Really."

"Thanks." She rocked the swing with her foot. "My last visit to the doctor confirmed it. I was getting big, fast, and I knew that sometimes expecting twins makes you twice as nauseous—no lie. On top of that, my family background has an incidence of fraternal twins, and the fertility drug I was taking raised the likelihood as well. The sonogram blew my mind, Will. I wish you could have seen—" She stopped herself, shut her eyes briefly.

He pictured her alone at the doctor's, marveling at her babies. *I wish I could have seen it, too.*

"It was amazing," she said. "I could see them both, like two little ghosts… Two against one," she added. "That's the part that scares me."

He didn't argue with that. "It's going to be good, you'll see. I sometimes wish Aurora had a brother or sister," he said.

"Siblings are overrated."

"You didn't get along with your brother?"

"When we were growing up, I used to think he was put on this earth to show up my inadequacies."

Will didn't know Kyle Moon very well. Unlike Sarah, he embraced the family enterprise. His method was simple but ingenious. He raised the same oysters the family had for generations. What changed was the perception of the oysters. He hired a media firm and, with some clever public relations, advanced the perception that Moon Bay oysters were the most rare and prized on the Pacific Coast. He made exclusive arrangements with the best restaurants in the Bay Area and turned the annual oyster festival each October into a major cultural event. Will had no idea how all this translated into being a good brother, though.

"Everybody's family is different," he said. "I bet your kids will drive each other nuts sometimes and other times, they'll be best friends."

The smile that lit her face was incredible. "I love how you just called us a family, and referred to them as my kids."

He glanced at her stomach, which was draped in a flowery dress that looked as if it belonged to her grandmother. "I don't think there's any question that they're yours," he said.

She laughed, tipping back her head. Down in the yard, Aurora stopped what she was doing and looked at them. Her eyes narrowed a little and she frowned. Aurora had made friends with Sarah first and didn't want to compete with Will. Seeing them laughing and talking together on the porch swing might give her the impression that he was interested in Sarah romantically.

And she would be absolutely right, he thought. He intended to keep that little tidbit to himself, though.

Sarah's laughter subsided. "I have no idea why that struck me as funny. When I first found out, I flat-out denied it, even though I could clearly see two of them on the screen. I kept telling the doctor there was a mistake, I couldn't possibly be having two babies."

"I'm happy for you, Sarah. Honest." He felt himself

working too hard to convince her of that. The truth was, he was struggling with the complexities of falling for a woman who was pregnant with another man's child. The fact that there were two babies seemed to compound everything. If by some miracle, things worked out for him and Sarah, he'd find himself the father of three, none of whom were his. Sometimes he lay awake at night, wondering if he'd ever have kids of his own. He couldn't say for sure he wanted that; it was the sort of thing to talk about with the woman you were falling for. Of course, he and Sarah couldn't talk about it, since they had barely acknowledged their attraction. He wasn't even sure she was interested. When she looked at him, what did she see?

"I suppose people in town will have a field day with this. Being single and pregnant is pathetic enough. Being single and pregnant with twins—now *that's* something to talk about."

"You don't have a very high opinion of small-town life," he said.

"Maybe you're right. I used to hate being the girl from the oyster farm. Since I've been back, I've discovered there's a sweet side to life here. I made some friends—Vivian Pierce and Judy deWitt."

"That's good, Sarah." He thought it was a promising sign. He liked the idea that she was settling in.

She turned her attention to Aurora, who had gone back to the puppies. "Why'd you change your mind about letting her get a puppy?"

He wanted to tell her in a rush of honesty that it was because Aurora had lost her best friend—him—and needed a new one. And that she'd lost him because he was too chickenshit to stay close, now that she'd grown older, difficult and secretive. He was still haunted by the memory of the day Aurora got her first period. He'd thought he was prepared. Birdie and his mother had long since given her the talk and plenty of reading material. They had provisioned her with all kinds of supplies and paraphernalia. And each night, he prayed—coward that he was—that it would not happen on his watch.

It did, of course, and Aurora was great. She was happy, even. Worse than that, she was…chatty. She wanted to talk about it.

Will had cut her off. Changed the subject and pretended he had something to do. Something that couldn't wait. He gave her twenty bucks and told her to go to the movies.

All of which flew in the face of the parenting books he had read. The last thing a father was supposed to do was reject, dismiss or deny his daughter's sexuality and the milestone that signaled her leap into maturity. He was supposed to accept, even embrace, her coming of age.

There was something missing from all those parenting books. He hadn't found the instruction manual for how a man should raise his stepdaughter alone. There were moments where the narrow difference in their ages separated them like an unbreachable gulf. Will knew he was a member of a small group—single stepfathers raising a teenage girl—and that some of the other members of the club were guys like Lucas Cross from *Peyton Place.* Was there no such thing as a good-guy stepfather in fiction?

"I figured she was ready for a dog," he said to Sarah, setting the swing in motion again. "She's been a lonely-only long enough."

"There's another solution," she said in a teasing voice. "Marry a woman with kids and you'll have an instant family."

He chuckled. "It's the American way."

"Don't be so cynical. People make it work every day."

"Miss Moon. Is that an overture?"

"As if. I was speaking hypothetically."

Will put up his hands in surrender. "Just checking."

"Half the town thinks we should be a couple," she said. "Have you noticed that?"

"Kind of hard to miss."

"Don't you think it's possible for us to be friends?"

The question haunted him, but he answered with a light-hearted grin. "It'd be a sad state of affairs if we couldn't. I understand you're not in the market for a relationship."

She patted his arm. "That's why we're so good together."

Aurora took a break from her scientific puppy search and let them all out of the box at once. She lay back in the grass and giggled while they climbed all over her.

"I bet you wish you had ten Auroras," Sarah said.

"Maybe not ten. We have our ups and downs."

"She seems great to me. How do you do it? How do you raise great kids?"

He laughed. "You're asking me?"

"I ask everyone I meet. I need all the help I can get."

"Stop by the house sometime. I've got some books I can lend you."

"Aurora told me about the books. More than a hundred at last count."

"I can spare a few. I don't have anything on twins, though."

She tucked both hands around her stomach. He had an insane urge to touch her there. He felt a fascination with her body. Not just the rounded belly but the swelling breasts and that ineffable air of mystery about her. He found her incredibly sexy. He wondered if that made him a pervert.

"I had Birdie tell my ex," Sarah said. "Jack and I do all our communication through lawyers now. I was terrified about what his reaction would be. I kept envisioning a custody battle that ends up like *The Parent Trap,* you know?"

"Birdie will protect you and the babies," Will said.

They sat quietly together as the shadows deepened in the folds of the hillocks sloping down to the sea. Aurora was in no hurry to make up her mind about a puppy.

"Good," Sarah said. "Feeling safe is the most important priority of a single mother. That's something I heard in this divorce group I joined in Fairfax."

"Is it helping?"

"Everything I've done since I left Chicago is helping." She stretched her feet out in front of her and sighed. "I'm glad I came back here. I feel as if I can breathe again."

"That's good, Sarah."

"When I was a kid, I couldn't wait to leave. I wanted to live in the big city, see the world. Did I tell you I spent my junior year of college studying in Prague?"

"No. How was that?"

"A lot like Chicago, but with older buildings and a more polluted river."

He smiled and turned to her on the porch swing. The hell with being just friends. She was no longer communicating with her ex. "I'm glad you came back, too."

Her gaze dropped, even as her smile widened. "Yeah?"

"Sarah—"

"Dad!" Aurora called from the yard. "I figured it out."

He hesitated just a moment longer, then got up from the swing and offered his hand to Sarah, palm up. She looked at him. "Helping the poor, pregnant lady to her feet?"

"Get used to it."

"Dad, come *on.*" Aurora's voice was edged with impatience.

"So what have you figured out?" As he and Sarah crossed the yard, he took care not to trip over the puppies underfoot.

"The right dog."

"That's great, honey."

Aurora wore a smile he'd never seen before. He thought he knew all the ways she had of smiling, but this one was new, tinged with a peculiar depth.

"See, this one wants me the most," she said, indicating a pup that kept straining to lick her face. She pointed out two others. "Those are the prettiest, don't you think? And the two over there, playing with each other, are the friskiest." She went and scooped up the last puppy, which was trying to get to the porch, back to its mother. "And this one," she said, cuddling it against her chest until its whimpers subsided, "needs me the most. So I choose this one."

Thirty

Jack started calling Sarah again. He was completely taken by the idea of twins, even though it doubled his child support liability. He clearly regretted joking about who had fathered them. Sarah knew this because not only did he resume calling her—calls she refused—but both his mother, Helen, and sister, Megan, got in on the act.

Sarah didn't hate Helen and Megan. Having lost her own mother, Sarah had liked having Helen in her life. And now that Sarah was carrying the heir apparent, her stock with the Daly women had risen. Even so, they were not the ones who had carried on an affair with Mimi Lightfoot and God knew who else. They had never done a thing to her except give their loyalty to Jack. Out of courtesy, she took their calls. Once Jack was informed about the twins, their calls doubled in number. Which, when Sarah thought about it, made sense.

"He's miserable," Megan confessed.

Sarah used her speakerphone while she worked at a lap desk in bed. Her perinatal specialist urged her to spend plenty of time on bed rest as the pregnancy progressed.

"Not my fault," she said calmly and refused to let herself feel guilty. Back when he was sick, it had been her mission to make him feel better. The reflex was still surprisingly strong, even now, but she resisted it.

"I'm not saying it is, just stating a fact."

"It's also not my problem."

"You were married to him," Megan said. "You were with him when he nearly died of cancer."

"I don't exactly need a reminder of that." Since being on her own, she'd had plenty of time to think and analyze what had gone wrong, to ponder the reasons two people who had once loved each other had ended up apart, and hurting. It was easy enough to point the finger at Jack, and she had done plenty of that. However, Sarah had learned that in order to find her own peace and inner healing, she would need to ask hard questions of herself, too, and acknowledge her role when all she really wanted to do was blame Jack.

"He's still with Mimi Lightfoot, last I heard," she pointed out.

"He'd break that off in a minute if you said you want to try again," Megan confided. "For the sake of the vows you took, shouldn't you try to overcome this?"

Vows, thought Sarah. She had sworn to be his wife in sickness and in health. She had managed the sickness part—so had Jack. It was sticking together in health that had been impossible. Something had broken down between them, and like it or not, she'd had a hand in that process.

"...forgive him and try to pull together?" Megan was saying.

"No," Sarah said. She was surprised and a bit relieved when the conviction resonated inside her. She wasn't kidding herself. She didn't want him back. Not for herself, and not even for the babies. She knew him too well, knew the novelty of being a dad would wear off and they'd drift apart again.

"That's all you have to say—no?" Megan sounded incredulous.

"No, thank you?"

"This is not a joke, Sarah. It's not funny at all."

At last, something they agreed on. "He broke my trust in a way that can't be mended," she explained. "I won't raise my children in a home like that."

She ended the unsettling phone call and headed for the White Horse Café to meet Judy and Vivian for coffee. This had become part of her morning routine and she found herself cherishing the time they spent together. They genuinely cared about her, and seemed to have an endless capacity to listen.

"I brought too many expectations to my marriage with Jack," she confessed over a decaf latte and a coconut scone. "He was supposed to be the knight in shining armor, rescuing me from my unbearable life on an oyster farm. What I refused to see was that he wasn't that guy, and my life wasn't unbearable."

"That doesn't excuse what he did," Vivian pointed out. "There's no excuse for infidelity."

"He's the father of these babies." Sarah touched the hard swell of her belly. "We'll always have this connection. I can't escape it."

"You're going to have to forgive him so you're not angry all the time," Judy said.

"That's psychobabble," Viv pointed out. "She deserves to be angry."

"I'm supposed to avoid stress," Sarah confessed. "And

you know what's funny? When I was with Jack, and had this so-called perfect life, I was more stressed out than I am now, alone and pregnant with twins."

"That's just it," Viv told her. "You're not alone. Not here. Not anymore."

"And not," Judy added, "with Will Bonner at your beck and call."

Sarah's face heated. "He's not at my beck and call. What *is* one's beck and call, anyway?"

"It's from Old English," Viv explained, exaggerating a professorial expression, "a shortened form of beckon—a mute gesture." She demonstrated a come-hither movement with her hand. "I think Sarah's got it down pat."

"Look at that blush," Judy observed. "You like him. You totally do."

"What is this, high school all over again? We're friends, all right?" Sarah said. "That's all. Nothing more."

"Liar," said Viv. "In fact, I'm going to call our local fire captain right now. Someone's pants are on fire."

While Megan was the youngest and most volatile of the Daly family, Sarah's former mother-in-law, Helen, was an icon of feminine accomplishment. A graduate of Northwestern, she had been superwoman before the concept was invented. She managed to juggle a successful career in finance, four children, a husband and a busy household all at once.

"You make it look so easy," Sarah had told her soon after she and Jack had married. "What's your secret?"

"It comes in a small, brown plastic bottle," Helen had said with a laugh, and Sarah could never figure out if she was kidding or not.

The only thing that had ever fazed her mother-in-law

had been Jack's illness. Helen had conquered the Chicago Board of Trade, but her son's battle with cancer undid her. Sarah had once found Helen in the hospital chapel, screaming at God. Not begging for her son to recover but demanding it. Ordering it and refusing to take no for an answer.

Sarah knew she was no match for Jack's mother. She never had been. When Helen dictated the menu at Thanksgiving or handed out Christmas gift lists, Sarah simply obeyed, because resistance was futile. The twins would be her first grandchildren. Sarah knew Helen would fight to be in their lives.

When she called, she didn't mince words. "I was disappointed when you left Jack," she said, "but I held my tongue. However, the babies change everything, as I'm sure you know. You and Jack have had plenty of time to cool off, and now I think it's time for a reconciliation."

Sarah doodled a cartoon woman hanging on to her tongue. "I've always admired you, Helen, and I suspect that will never change. When Jack and I were married, I did as I was told but things are different now. I'm going to do what's best for these babies."

"Well, thank goodness," Helen said. "No child deserves to be cut off from his father."

"My attorney is open to discussing limited visitation rights."

There was a pause as her meaning sank in. "Court-ordered visitation is no substitute for a family," Helen said. "Sarah, men stray. It's what they do."

Sarah heard a hardness in Helen's voice that made her shiver. And Sarah knew—John Henry cheated. It seemed so obvious now. Her silver-haired father-in-law, whose son was so like him.

"The good ones are smart enough to come back," Helen continued, "where they belong. I know Jack is a good man."

Like his father, Sarah thought.

"Don't you believe every child deserves to grow up with both parents together, in a decent home?"

Sarah bit her lip, resisting the urge to spill the fact that Jack was doing his best to minimize his child support contribution. "There is nothing decent about a home built on lies and betrayal. Jack cheated on me. And you know what? I believe I have it in me to understand why he did it. I even have it in me to forgive him."

"Oh, Sarah. Dear, it's such a relief to hear this."

"I'm not finished. I'm trying to tell you that I can understand why he cheated. I can forgive him. But the one thing I cannot do is love him again."

"Sarah, you can't mean that."

"And I won't raise my children in a house without love."

"Children have a basic need to know their father. You're letting your bitterness toward Jack cloud your judgment. He has a right to be a part of their lives."

"He gave up his rights when he broke a vow he made in the church where he was raised."

"Now you're being dramatic."

"Must be the hormones, Helen," she said. Instantly she felt contrite. None of this was Helen's fault. "I don't blame you for sticking up for Jack's interests. Any mother would. If we didn't, what kind of mothers would we be?"

It seemed strange to Sarah that, although she'd grown close to Aurora and Will over the past months, she had never visited them at their house. When they invited her over to eat something called "Truesdale Specials," she eagerly accepted.

Aurora greeted her at the front door along with a gangly puppy, whom Aurora had christened Zooey. The house was a Craftsman typical of the area, originally built in the 1940s as a retreat from San Francisco. She was gratified to see that her drawing of Aurora occupied a prominent place on the wall. Aurora eagerly showed Sarah around the house.

"Is that your mother?" Sarah asked, indicating a framed photo on the dresser. It showed a smiling woman looking directly into the camera. She bore an eerie resemblance to Aurora, yet there was a barely discernible difference, a hardness in the eyes and in the set of the jaw. Or maybe it was sadness.

"That's Mama."

"I bet you miss her." Sarah's hand strayed to the swell of her stomach. She had yet to hold her babies in her arms, yet she felt such a fierce and elemental connection with them that it was hard to imagine doing what Marisol had done, walking away from them.

Aurora shrugged. Sarah sensed a world of suppressed emotion in that shrug.

"I miss my mom," Sarah said, "every day." She refused to turn maudlin, though. "How about you show me around some more."

"Through here," Aurora said, heading down the hall. Clearly, she did not want to pursue the conversation. The tour concluded with a visit to a long, cluttered room upstairs that connected to Aurora's bedroom through the bathroom. There was a counter with built-in drawers, two tall windows letting in the light, odds and ends of abandoned furniture and stacks of unlabeled storage boxes.

"This was going to be a sewing room," Aurora said. "Mama wanted to be a dressmaker, so my dad fixed this room up for her. She never made anything, though. Do you know how to sew?"

"Not a stitch," Sarah admitted. She tried to imagine the beautiful, sad-eyed Marisol seated at the window, sewing a dress. She paused at another photo in the doorway and thought, *What were you thinking, Marisol? You broke their hearts.*

Right then and there, Sarah vowed to always remember that being a mother meant protecting your loved ones from hurt, not inflicting it.

"Dad's out back," Aurora said, clomping down the stairs. "He just lit the grill."

When Sarah saw Will, she knew she was deceiving herself about the way she felt about him. The sight of him on the patio, in a white T-shirt and faded jeans, drew a flush of warmth over her. She hesitated for a moment, in her mind drawing a comparison between Jack and Will. Jack was always on the go, with no time for flipping burgers. Will knew how to be in the moment.

I'm a goner. The sight of him grilling burgers was a turn-on. She had been telling him and Aurora and herself she wasn't in the market for a relationship.

All lies. She looked at him and wanted to frame his broad shoulders with her hands. She wanted to feel the texture of his hair and the taste of his lips, and every time she saw him, she wanted him more. She fought the attraction with everything she had, because it could only lead to heartbreak. There was no way she could be falling for someone now.

She clung to that resolution as she waved at him through the kitchen window while she and Aurora fixed a salad. She repeated it like a mantra in her head when he served dinner with a flourish and a heart-tugging grin.

"It's okay if you don't like the burgers," Aurora said. "Not very many people do."

"You'd be amazed at what I like these days," Sarah said, inspecting the meal on her plate. It looked a bit strange and sounded even stranger—a patty made of SPAM, Velveeta and onions.

"It's best when you dip it in the tomato soup," Aurora advised, demonstrating.

Sarah gave it a try and took a bite. She felt Aurora and Will watching her intently. This was some sort of test. "Delicious," she said.

"Really?" Aurora asked.

"Totally." She touched her belly. "We all like it."

After dinner, thc phone rang and Aurora disappeared into her room.

"She and her friends talk for hours," Will said. "No idea what they talk about."

"Boys and clothes. You want some help with the dishes?"

"Nope, you're company."

She leaned back and put her feet up on the chair next to her. "Oh, but I insist."

"Sure thing." He grinned and went to work.

She watched while he cleared the table and cleaned the kitchen, admiring his assured movements as he performed mundane chores. Every once in a while he'd glance at her, a sideways look of almost palpable intimacy. At odd moments, his presence nearly unraveled her. This wasn't supposed to be happening. Not here. Not now. And not with him.

But it had been so long, she thought, since she'd been close to someone. There was a kind of loneliness, she discovered, that settled in the bones and turned to ice, and when that cold numbness began to thaw, every nerve ending came to painful life. Worse, she wasn't just lonely in general. She was lonely for him.

It had been a pleasant evening. She could ruin it with her next question. Don't, she told herself. She took a deep breath and asked anyway. "I think it's time you told me the full story about Aurora's mother."

"I told you the night of the puppies."

"You gave me a few facts, but not the reasons behind them." She watched him closely. His shoulders stiffened and his jaw tightened. She took another breath. "What happened, Will?"

Will's heart was racing even before he turned to face Sarah. He stood with his hands on the edge of the counter, the sharp angle pressing into his palms as he braced himself. There were things about Marisol he'd never told anyone, and yet here was this woman, urging him to open up. "Why do you want to know?" he asked, feeling a mixture of suspicion and relief.

"Because I care. About Aurora and…about you."

They'd been working up to this moment for a while now. He realized that if he wanted to be closer to her—and he definitely wanted that—he was going to have to level with her. In a way, it was a relief to share the old, old burden. "Outside," he said.

She glanced toward the stairs. He could hear Aurora giggling, still on the phone.

Zooey, the puppy, followed them into the twilit yard and immediately started sniffing the perimeter. Will motioned Sarah to a lawn chair and waited while she lowered herself awkwardly. Then he sat down next to her and stared off into the distance, trying to frame an explanation. Sarah deserved one. She really did care about Aurora. He had to be cautious, though. There were things about the past he didn't ever want Aurora to know, things he'd never told a soul.

At the end of his high school career, everyone had expected Will Bonner to take off like a rocket. Certainly Will himself had expected it. All through his senior year, he weighed offers from a host of Division I schools. The bush league team for the Athletics was putting together an offer for him, should he choose to postpone college or even try to juggle the two.

And he'd wanted it all. Nearly had it, too, except that fate threw him for a loop.

He was a typical impulsive teenager in every sense of the word. When he and his friends decided to celebrate high school graduation by driving to San Diego and from there, taking a tour company bus to Tijuana and getting blazing drunk, it was nothing out of the ordinary. Stupid kids had been doing this since the beginning of time. The young man's pilgrimage to a Mexican border town was a rite of passage. Their fathers had made the journey, returning with bags of Acapulco Gold stuffed in their Levi's. Their grandfathers had, too, and their fathers before them, bringing back cheap tequila and souvenirs. Some said these border town weekends had started in the days of Prohibition, when it was the least risky way to find something stronger to drink than lemonade. Others traced the custom even further back to Victorian times, when the lure of easy women tempted young men from their chaste lives. California boys grew up hearing about Avenida de las Mujeres, the legendary street festooned with bougainvillea spilling from window boxes, adobe walls painted with bright swirls of color, and willing women framed by every doorway.

"The summer after high school, I went down to Mexico with a group of guys," he told Sarah. "We took turns driving to San Diego. Somebody—I think it was Trent Lowery—got tickets on a party bus from there to Tijuana. You park on the U.S. side and the bus takes you across the border."

"I think I get the picture."

He steepled his fingers together and relived the occasion, which had begun as such a lark. He had headed south of the border for a night of drunken revelry. The journey ended up changing his life. He hadn't seen it coming, not any of it. The only things on his mind had been drinking tequila and getting laid.

Through a fluke—or, according to his friends, an error in judgment—Will had made it through high school with his virginity intact. This was not a testament to his virtue but to his habit of going steady with a girl who was adamant about saving herself for marriage. Although he endured locker-room teasing and worse, the situation never changed.

Until graduation weekend. His girlfriend of two years broke up with him. Will was determined to revel in his freedom. It was high time to end his celibacy.

The old part of the border town had reached out to embrace the boys from the Bay Area—rowdy kids who had too much money and too little sense—with arms draped in temptation. The women themselves were intoxicating with their soft, musky flesh, oiled hair and ripe lips. At first Will was dazzled, but no amount of tequila could completely blind him from seeing beneath the painted lips and cheap, colorful dresses. These women—some of them excruciatingly young—were virtual slaves to sleazy pimps and hard-eyed madams who moved like wraiths through the streets, addressing tourists with hissing voices.

"So that's what we did," he told Sarah. "In Tijuana, we started at the horse races, and almost immediately, I won a huge purse. A run of dumb luck netted me $11,000."

"My Lord. You had the Midas touch."

Up to that point, his whole life had gone along in that fashion. Nothing but pure luck was on his side. He had no idea that within hours, his luck was about to change.

"I probably would have lost it on the next race, except it was time to party," he said. "We found open-air bars, bands playing on every street corner, people selling souvenirs and trinkets from blankets spread out on the sidewalk." Absently, he ran his hand over the dragon tattoo on his arm—another souvenir of that crazy trip.

Will and his friends, already lit with tequila, were invited to Casa Luna, located at the end of the avenue. "We were in a *baila*—a dancing club," he said, using the euphemism. The house's colorful, flower-decked façades concealed tiny rooms that reeked of harsh cleaning fluid, sweat and urine, the backyard crammed with manure, goats and garbage, a miserable lean-to where assorted children were left on their own to play. Business was conducted in semiprivate berths separated by moth-eaten drapes. By the door of each room was a stoneware holy water font. Patrons were invited to anoint themselves upon entering and leaving.

"I was pretty wasted on tequila," he said. The telling got tricky here. He lost his virginity to a girl whose lazy-lidded eyes concealed a look of boredom and despair. He hadn't yet learned her name was Marisol. The experience had been exhilarating, sordid and distasteful all at once. The girl invited him to linger afterward—for an extra price. And through a pink tequila haze, he'd been tempted, because by that time, he'd convinced himself he was half in love with the girl, but she laughed and sent him on his way.

It was said that a young man came of age with his first sexual experience. Will knew that wasn't true. Getting some girl to give you a blow job or even to go all the way with you didn't mean a damn thing. In his case, the transformation from boy to man had happened overnight, that was true. But it had nothing to do with sex. He had turned into a man thanks to the desperate need of a child.

Just before midnight, he decided to head home. His plan had been to make his way back to the bus, sleep off the tequila while dreaming of the girl with the lazy-lidded eyes and waiting for his friends to show up.

"I was about to leave when I noticed the smell of something burning. It turned out to be a fire, and everybody had to evacuate into the street." He had never told anyone what sort of house it was, how the fire had started or how he had come to be in the middle of it all. "A crowd gathered in the street but nobody seemed that concerned. There were goats and dogs in the backyard, going crazy. It took forever for the firefighters to arrive and once they did, the building was a goner."

Sarah's face was pale by now. "Aurora was in the house, wasn't she?"

He nodded. "On the roof. Four years old and scared to death."

"And her mother…?"

"It was chaotic," he said. "They got separated."

"By the fire?"

He didn't answer that and hoped she didn't notice. "The ladder truck couldn't get into position. The street was too narrow. The firefighters couldn't access the roof through the inside, and there was no outside fire escape."

"How did you get her off the roof?" Sarah asked.

He hesitated. "How did you know it was me?"

She smiled briefly. "Will. Give me a little credit."

In that moment, shocked sober, Will had discovered something new about himself. He was born to save people. "I went to the roof of the building next door."

He could hear the screaming and praying as though it were yesterday. With no training, working only from instinct and adrenaline, he had no time to hesitate or weigh his chances as he crossed a rickety pipe that connected the roofs. The roofing material had felt soft and yielding under his feet, and the soles of his shoes seemed to stick in it.

The tiny child he did not yet know as Aurora shrieked with terrified sobs while her fists pummeled at the billows of smoke. He must've looked scary as hell, a big guy running at her, scooping her up and grabbing her in a football carry. He remembered how light she felt to him, like a small wooden toy. The fire crew used the ladder to form a bridge between the two buildings. The crossing was more stable than the corroding drainpipe.

He didn't look down, and he didn't let go.

"That's when the situation got complicated," he told Sarah. He was staggering down a twisted iron staircase in a rain of water from the fire hoses when he heard a sound as if someone had dropped a whole raw turkey onto concrete. In the alleyway behind the unkempt backyard, he spied the young prostitute he'd been with, spectacularly pretty despite being drenched with water, being beaten by her *encargado.*

"Mama!" the child had cried out.

Will set her down and charged like a freight train. The pimp probably never knew what hit him. The woman was hysterical. Not because of the beating or even because of the danger to her child, who was now clinging to her skirt. But because, she shrieked, when Uncle Felix came to, she would be punished. Worse than another beating, she told Will in a tortured mixture of border-town Spanish and broken English, she would be banished. Shoved out into the street to whore for table scraps, like a stray dog. She'd have to sell her child just to survive. She'd end up selling her to a man like Felix, so what good had it done to attack him?

In fumbling Spanish, Will told her that surely there had to be other options. Then he had looked at the terrified young prostitute and the wide-eyed child with scabs and sores everywhere, and realized she spoke the truth. They had no future, these two. None at all. Unless he could think of something to do.

He had hesitated, sensing that this had the potential to be a career decision. Then he took them both by the hand. The woman stumbled and cried out in pain from her injuries, protesting that she couldn't walk. He swept her up into his arms and carried her while the child clung to the hem of her mother's skirts.

"*Como se llama?*" he asked the woman.

"*Marisol Molina, y mi hija se llama Aurora,*" she said.

Aurora, like the dawn. Marisol told him her "uncle" had put her to work at age thirteen and she'd given birth at fourteen, naming the baby after her favorite Disney character.

Will looked for shelter half the night, it seemed. Churches were supposed to provide sanctuary, but their doors were locked and barred against intruders. Finally, he discovered a health clinic staffed by an elderly doctor and nurse whose air of weary compassion had mingled with a resigned sense of futility. They treated Marisol's wounds, the worst of which was a dislocated shoulder, and gave Aurora medicine for her cough and ointment for her sores. The nurse had a lengthy, private conversation with Marisol that caused her cheeks to flush with shame, and the three of them left together.

Out on the street in the hazy light of morning, Will felt more confident. He shouldn't have. The police stopped him. Felix Garcia—the pimp—was looking for his "niece." He was worried sick about her. He feared she might have been kidnapped. Will gave the police the reassurance they were looking for—an enormous bribe from his winnings at the racetrack. With their pockets lined, the police lost interest in detaining Will. But they still intended to deliver Marisol back to Felix.

Marisol had given the police a long and desperate explanation. Will had trouble following the conversation but he thought he understood.

"Did you just tell him we're getting married?" he asked her.

"Today," she said. "Right now. It is the only way to keep from being sent back to Casa Luna. You will need to give them more bribe money, of course."

It was then that Will discovered he would do anything to rescue people.

Sleepy with fever and the medicine from the clinic, Aurora had napped through the hasty wedding, which had to be expedited by still further bribes at the *pasillo,* the city hall. They emerged with all the proper documentation.

"Just like that?" Sarah asked, her eyes round with wonder. "Wasn't there some kind of blood test or, I don't know, a waiting period?"

The border guards on the U.S. side had also been incredulous. They took Will aside, told him a dozen ways to get out of his predicament. They'd seen it before—upstanding American boys trapped by wily Mexican *putas*. They could fix it, they assured Will. Within a few hours, he would be free to walk away from the woman and child, leaving them behind in Mexico like so much unclaimed baggage.

"Thank you," he said. "But this wasn't a mistake." He didn't want his freedom back if it meant throwing the woman to the wolves. Besides, he truly believed his feelings for Marisol would turn into love. "I meant to marry her. We're staying together."

It wasn't that simple. The actual process took weeks and the intervention of a compassionate immigration lawyer, one of Birdie's professors at San Diego State.

He shook his head. "If you know the right people to ask, and if you meet their price—which I was able to do, thanks to the racetrack winnings—anything is possible. Back then, $11,000 was a small fortune in Mexico."

Sarah stared at him as though he'd turned into a stranger. "I don't know what to say."

He shrugged. "It'd be nice to say we all lived happily ever after, but it got complicated."

The first order of business was to have both Marisol and Aurora seen by doctors in the U.S. Aurora was found to be remarkably healthy for a child who had suffered such neglect. Marisol—to the surprise of no one but Will—had a sexually transmitted disease.

Fortunately, it was treatable, and Will hadn't caught it from her. Finally, after they had been married for several weeks, they had their wedding night. Introduced at last to pleasure by a beautiful, experienced woman, Will Bonner fell in love as only a nineteen-year-old of limited experience could.

Some in Glenmuir were aghast. What about the future he'd planned for himself?

Will never answered that question. Something had changed deep inside him, that night in Mexico as he stood on the soft, tarry roof of a burning building. For the first time in his life he'd felt a tangible sense of purpose. He had been put on this earth for a reason, and that reason was not to score runs or win awards or sign contracts. "I would not have picked this life," he concluded. "This is the life that picked me."

In the flower-scented yard, darkness had fallen and the peepers came out. Will felt shaken and hollowed out, as though he'd just run a marathon. It wasn't easy, baring his soul. He'd never done it before, never taken this risk with his heart, but this was Sarah. He trusted her. He wondered how it was possible that he could have such an intimate relationship with a woman he'd never even held in his arms. He had no idea what she tasted like, or if her lips were as soft as they looked, or if she would fit into his embrace as though she belonged there. Maybe he ought to—

"How much of this does Aurora know?" she asked, getting awkwardly to her feet.

"Almost nothing," he said, the moment gone, even though the desire still lingered. "Her mother never had much to say about it."

"Why would Marisol turn her back on someone like you?" Sarah asked.

"Why would Jack turn his back on someone like you?" he countered. "Love's funny that way, eh?"

They went inside, and Sarah asked for a cup of tea. He went to find a tea bag. In the short hallway between the back door and the pantry, there were photographs and artwork, a gallery of Aurora's childhood since the day he'd brought her and Marisol to Glenmuir. His mother, who had taken classes in art therapy at Berkeley, had urged him to encourage Aurora to draw. The early stick figures were like ancient cave drawings, scratches of someone who no longer existed, their meaning unclear. Even Aurora herself couldn't explain the significance of the dark scribbles, the crudely drawn figures. They were locked somewhere deep inside her memory along with her recollection of the fiery night in Mexico when she'd come into his life.

One of the gifts of childhood was the resilience of the human spirit. The thready scribbles of Aurora at age five quickly gave way to sunny, sophisticated drawings she'd brought home from kindergarten with pride—pictures of him and her mother flanking her smiling self. The riotous color of her stepgrandparents' flower farm. The natural beauty all around, from Alamere Falls to the deeply shadowed forests of bishop pine to the majestic lighthouse station at Point Reyes.

"She never asked?" Sarah looked mystified.

"Plenty of times," he admitted, waiting for the water to boil. "But I never had the answers."

The most recent drawing came from her seventh grade art class. It was a nearly photographic rendering of an abandoned stone cabin burned out by the Mount Vision fire, its broken walls hunched against the lush renewal of the landscape.

"I bet she knows more than you think she knows," Sarah said.

He nodded. Sometimes, that was what scared him the most.

Part Five

JUST BREATHE

Thirty-One

With each passing week, Sarah came to depend on Will more and more. His friendship had grown to mean that much to her. And that friendship was at risk, because she kept wanting it to turn into something else.

While getting dressed for her baby shower, she heard a dull boom. She dismissed it as a rumble of thunder or a jet overhead, but the crescendo of a siren touched her spine with ice. Instantly, she thought of Will. What had happened? Was he hurt?

Moving as fast as her ungainly body would allow, she finished dressing, then scooped up her handbag and keys and headed to town. Black smoke was pouring from a structure at the shoreline. She didn't think she'd ever get used to this, to the idea that every time disaster occurred, a firefighter was put in danger. She used to take these men and women for granted until now. Until Will Bonner.

It was his job, she reminded herself. His routine. The calling he'd discovered one eventful night in Mexico. Still, the idea of Will in harm's way made her skin tingle with fear for him.

When she arrived at the site of the fire, he was nowhere to be found, and she felt awkward asking about him. She did anyway, though.

"Captain Bonner's off today," said a volunteer firefighter. "Took his daughter up to Mount Vision."

Sarah felt an intense flood of relief. She cared about him so much. It was hard work, trying to keep her heart closed like a bud resisting the warmth of the sun. But she knew it would be even harder to let Will and Aurora into her life while she was still raw from the pain and devastation of her ruined marriage.

"Is everything all right here?" she asked.

"No one was hurt. It was an abandoned boat shed, hasn't been used in years," the volunteer said. "The arson investigators will have to come and check things out." He gestured. "His partner's over there, if you want to talk to her. She's doing an extra shift, subbing for someone."

Sarah scarcely recognized Gloria Martinez in her gear. She was leaning halfway into the cab of the engine, yelling something on the radio. "Maybe later," Sarah said.

As she drove along the head of the bay, she glanced at the clock in the car's console. There was enough time to drive up to Mount Vision and still get to the shower on time. She didn't question the sudden, bright, foolish urge to see Will. She just acted on it.

She took the twisting upward route to the scenic overlook parking lot. There, she spotted Will's truck and a group of people clustered around, putting on sunscreen and filling water bottles. She pulled off and rolled down the window.

Aurora hurried over. "Hey, Sarah."

"Hey, yourself." She turned off the car and opened the door. Getting out of the Mini with thirty extra pounds of pregnancy was a challenge these days. To her embarrassment, she couldn't quite manage.

"Let me give you a hand," Will offered, joining them.

She placed her hand in his. With a gentle pull, he helped her out. "Thanks," she said, flustered as she always seemed to get around him. As time went on, the attraction intensified, though she kept telling herself she was being ridiculous. "Pretty soon I'm going to need a block and tackle to get myself around."

Aurora's gaze traveled from Sarah's untreated hair, over her protruding breasts and abdomen and down to her swollen ankles. "Whoa."

"Thanks," Sarah said.

"You look good," she said quickly.

"I look like a human Winnebago," Sarah said. "It's all right. Not much I can do now but wait and satisfy my weird cravings for Roquefort ice cream and fried pierogies. I figure if my career as a cartoonist fails, I can always moonlight as a fertility goddess."

"On the National Geographic Channel, they always show them nude," Aurora pointed out.

"Which explains why I never watch the National Geographic Channel." Each day, the babies were becoming more and more real to her. She was getting to know their little quirks, like the way they stretched or got a case of the hiccups. Thanks to the team of specialists monitoring her pregnancy, she was a walking medical encyclopedia. Yet rather than demystifying the gestation process, her knowledge only deepened the magic of what was happening to her.

"You're all dressed up," Aurora observed.

"April Cornell meets the tent maker," Sarah said, eyeing the fabric draped over her mound. "My grandmother and great-aunt are giving me a baby shower at their house." The very idea of a shower, with a group of friends coming to celebrate her pregnancy, was incredibly gratifying.

"That's cool," Aurora said.

Will excused himself to look over a topographical chart with the leaders of the work crew.

Something in Sarah's eyes must have betrayed her as she watched him walk away, because Aurora said, "So did you come all the way out here to tell us you're having a baby shower?"

"You're welcome to come, if you like, but you'd probably be bored." Sarah flexed one swollen ankle, then the other. "There was a fire down at the head of the bay. It's under control, though, and no one was hurt."

Aurora ducked her head. "That's good. If they'd needed Dad, they would have radioed for him. We're fine, you know," she added sharply. "Why wouldn't we be? My dad's off duty. And even if he wasn't, he'd still be fine. He's a professional firefighter."

Sarah bit her lip, knowing Aurora understood the risks involved in his job and knowing, too, that she sensed the undercurrents between Sarah and Will. Aurora glanced over her shoulder at the kids putting on Day-Glo smocks. "I have to go."

"Off to restore the wilderness?"

"That's right."

"I'll pick you up right here at four," Will said, rejoining them. "Wear your sunscreen and watch out for poison oak and sumac."

"Got it, Dad. Bye, Sarah. Have fun at your baby shower."

Sarah watched Aurora run off to join the work party. "Good for her. Her friends are probably home gaming on their computers while she's out saving the forest."

"I'm not sure her motives are that pure."

Sarah saw Aurora talking to two boys as they headed for the trail. She recognized the older one from the ice-cream shop in town. "Zane Parker. The one she has a massive crush on."

"She told you that?"

"She actually used the word *massive.* Who's the other boy?"

"Zane's younger brother, Ethan."

Even from a distance, she recognized Ethan's unrequited yearning as he followed along behind Sarah and Zane. Welcome to the club, kid, she thought.

"She's growing up too fast," Will said. "She's not ready to be hanging around with boys."

"You mean *you're* not ready."

"I mean she's not. She's still just a kid."

Sarah touched his arm. "It's a supervised crew."

He leaned back against the car, watching the members of the work crew fan out across the mountain meadow. Within minutes, Sarah and Will were the only ones left in the parking lot.

She looked up at him, and her pulse sped up.

"What are you staring at?" he asked.

"You." She could hear thc hum of bees through the wildflowers, the rustle of the wind through the reeds and birds twittering in the meadow grasses.

"Why?"

"I'm trying to make up my mind about something."

"About what?"

What the hell. When your stomach was the size of a

third-world country, you could get away with saying anything.

"About whether I have a massive crush on you or if it's just hormones."

He laughed. "You can't tell the difference?"

"I found my alarm clock in the refrigerator the other day and have no memory of putting it there. Lately I'm questioning my own judgment."

"I'm not. *My* judgment is sound. I have a massive crush on you, too."

"Oh, shit."

"Oh, shit is right." He smiled amiably enough.

"What are we going to do?"

"I don't know, Sarah. I honestly don't."

"The timing couldn't be worse," she said.

"Sure, it could. At least now, we're both single."

"Almost," she said, wishing her impending divorce were final. "What will Aurora think?"

"She'll hate this…if we do anything about it."

"She doesn't like you dating. And people might think it's strange."

He grazed his knuckles alongside her cheek. Sarah took in a breath, her skin burning beneath his touch.

He lowered his hand. "I've never made choices according to what people think, Sarah."

I have. She didn't know how to trust herself at all anymore, or what she had to offer. She was still sorting through the aftermath of her marriage, trying to figure out who she was all by herself again. According to the experts, which included the people in her support group and all the self-help books she'd consulted on surviving divorce, this was her crazy time. Maybe *he* was part of her crazy time.

"Not even your daughter?" she asked Will.

"Not even her." He braced his hand on the side of the car.

She had an urge to lean against him, to know what he felt like. She wondered what the dark curls of his hair would feel like between her fingers. Then she noticed him looking down at her with an expression she had never seen on his face before. His stare lingered on her mouth, and she found herself measuring the distance between them in heartbeats. One...two...fewer than three.

She became unmoored from who she was and her place in life. She shifted, or maybe she was pushed by the salt-scented wind, and she leaned into him, whispering his name. The moment shone with a peculiar clarity, as though reflecting the sea light in the late afternoon.

Things were about to change between them, permanently and irrevocably, assuming he felt the same way she did. So there it was. A choice to be made. A decision. A part of her desperately wanted to avoid making it at all. Will was the best friend she had. They shared everything. Could she risk losing that?

"Will..." She said his name again, louder this time. The cool air seemed to press against her skin.

Then, just as it appeared that he was as caught up as she, the twins stretched and kicked, reminding her she had someplace to be. The mooring line went taut. "I have to go," she said, and retreated from the moment.

He hesitated, and she found herself half wishing he'd carry her off like a caveman and satisfy every yearning in her hormone-drenched body. Instead, he held open the car door for her. "Drive carefully."

She didn't leave right away. Something was happening between them, and they'd both be lying if they denied it. "Do you think it's possible for us to simply be friends?"

He stared at her intently and was quiet for so long that she grew uncomfortable.

"Will?" she prompted.

"No," he said at length. "No, Sarah, I don't believe that's possible."

Her pulse sped up. It was the answer she dreaded. And the one she craved. "Then what are we supposed to do?"

"I guess we're doing it." Once again, he offered his hand and this time, she took hold and lowered herself into the driver's seat.

All during the drive to her grandmother's, she felt out of sorts. She needed to learn to stand on her own for once in her life. She had no business falling for Will Bonner or anyone else. She was going to have to let him go, before she ever really had him.

Gran and Aunt May went all-out for the baby shower, which was held on the wraparound porch of their house at the edge of the bay. The tables were festooned with flowers, and the eaves had been strung with twinkling lights of colored baby shoes. There was a cake decorated with two cradles and a spread of food that made Sarah wish she had more room inside her.

For Sarah, the greatest surprise and deepest pleasure was the group of women who had gathered—Birdie, Vivian, Judy, LaNelle, Gran, May, their garden club friends. Gloria and her partner, Ruby, arrived late, after Gloria's shift was over. Everyone's gifts were so thoughtful, but what affected Sarah the most was the outpouring of goodwill she sensed from the women. When Gran proposed a toast with sparkling apple juice, Sarah took the opportunity to speak.

"I came back home with my tail between my legs. I

thought I had this perfect life and I felt like a failure when it ended. Now I've got a home, thanks to Aunt May, mornings at the White Horse, evenings with the Fairfax group, an almost-final divorce, thanks to Birdie, my lawyer…" She rubbed the small of her back. "This is starting to sound like an Academy Awards speech."

"And the thirty-second light's blinking," Aunt May said with a wink.

"I just want to make sure everyone knows how grateful I am. I don't think I'll ever again jinx my life by saying it's perfect, but I know I'm going to be all right." She touched her stomach. "We're going to be fine."

"Hear, hear," declared Gran, and everyone clinked glasses and settled into the cushioned white wicker furniture while Sarah ripped into the gifts. Her doctor had offered to tell her the sex of the babies but she didn't want to know, which drove her friends crazy. She received everything from the practical—a three-month supply of diapers—to the whimsical—two pairs of tiny Keds, hand-painted by her grandmother.

Sarah was touched by how special everything felt to her. The day itself seemed to glow with possibility. The women talked about everything—the commission for a sculpture Judy hoped to get from a Napa winery, Birdie's upcoming bicycle race, Viv's latest home improvement project. As usual, Gran and May were busy with a community project—a knit-a-thon to raise money for the senior center. Gloria and Ruby announced that they were going to have a commitment ceremony, and everyone raised their glasses of sparkling apple juice.

"So soon?" asked Vivian. She had been friends with Dean who, only the year before, was married to Gloria. "Are you sure?"

"I've waited for her all my life," Gloria stated.

"Good for you," Aunt May declared.

Sarah looked around at the women and listened in amazement to their chatter and laughter. These were her friends. Their good wishes surrounded her like a comforting embrace. At the end of the afternoon, she found Gran and May in the kitchen, hand-washing the heirloom china.

"I owe you an apology," she told them. "I used to think all your gatherings and meetings were pointless. I was wrong. I get it now."

"It's lovely of you to say so, dear," said Gran, polishing a lemon platter. "We're terribly lucky that you've decided to come back," Gran explained. "Your babies are such a blessing in our lives."

"I'm counting on you to give them lessons in being twins."

"We'll start the moment we meet them."

Sarah touched her belly, where the skin itched. "Dr. Murray says every day I go over thirty-six weeks is a day closer to a plain, uneventful birth in labor and delivery. Which is the goal, even with twins." She heard the sound of a car door slamming.

Gran and Aunt May shared a look. "Why don't you go and see who that is?" Gran suggested.

Sarah went out to the front porch. Her gifts had already been boxed and loaded into the back of the Mini, and she had been looking forward to going home and putting her feet up. "Hey, Dad," she said. "You missed the party." She grinned at the sheepish expression on his face. "You planned it that way, didn't you?"

"Guilty as charged."

"You want some cake?"

"Maybe later. There's one more gift." He held out a large, flat box.

"You bought me a shower gift?"

"I'm not saying I *bought* it."

Mystified, Sarah took a seat on the wicker chaise. She untied the ribbon, lifted the lid of the box and gasped. There was nothing she could say. For a moment, she couldn't move. There in the box lay a luxurious folded shawl, handwoven from yarn spun by her mother. She knew it was her mother's work. It had that signature blend of softness and strength she spun into every strand of yarn, the deep color of a just-opened peony.

"I figured you'd get plenty of baby blankets," her father said. "This is for you. From me…and your mother."

"Oh, Dad." Sarah's hands shook as she plunged them into the box and filled them with her mother's softest tropical cashmere. She brought the blanket to her face and inhaled, fancying she could sense her mother's subtle essence embedded in the strands of wool.

"The piece was on her loom, wasn't it?" she asked her father, her voice breaking.

"That's right. Couldn't bring myself to touch it for years. Maybe it was just waiting for the right purpose. I had Florence from the yarn shop help me finish the thing. It's pretty obvious where the weaving changes."

"I like it this way. It shows where she stopped and you took up in her place." She slung the shawl around her shoulders and gave a soft gasp of wonder. *It's a hug from Mom.*

Sarah would forever carry the ache of missing her. That would never change. But she knew now that her mother's love burned inside her, a flame that would never go out. "Thank you," she told her father. She studied his craggy face, etched by years of working in the sun and wind. She knew then that this man, this dear, caring man had been there all along for her, loving her from his remote distance and not knowing how to be closer. And yet he did know. And now, so did she.

"Dad, I wish I hadn't been such a lousy teenager, because I didn't appreciate it here enough, or—"

He turned and tucked the shawl more securely around her shoulders. "You look just like her. You sound like her. It hurt to look at you," he said, a rasp of emotion in his voice. "Every time I saw you, it broke my heart all over again."

She took this in, feeling a dart of pain for him. Yet at the same time, a deeper understanding took hold. As terrible as it was to lose her marriage, her father's loss was infinitely worse. He'd lost his wife, his best friend, his life mate. "I'm sorry, Dad. I wish you'd told me."

"I'm telling you now. Anyway, I was mistaken. You are your own person, not her, and I need you in my life and I hope to God you'll stay."

Her father sat on the end of the chaise and she leaned her cheek against his arm. "You're okay, Dad," she whispered.

He stroked her hair. "Runs in the family."

They sat together looking out over the water, where the sea and sky met over the oyster beds in the distance. The wherries bobbed quietly in a light wind. "I need to ask you something," she said.

"Sure."

"How would you feel about being my birth coach?"

He froze for a moment, and then he let out a long breath. "Scared."

Her heart sank. "I mean, I need somebody to go through the classes with me. You don't have to come into the delivery room if you don't want, but I'd love to study with you, and practice—"

"You didn't let me finish. I said I'd be scared. And proud. I'd do anything for you, honey. You know that."

Thirty-Two

Sarah couldn't sleep. This was nothing new; she couldn't sleep most nights. At her last weekly appointment, the babies weighed in at six pounds each and they were still growing, leaving little room for anything else. She lay in a tangle of covers, bathed in sweat, the skin of her stomach itching horribly. Her bladder was about to burst, too. She felt cranky and restless, ready to be done with this whole ordeal. On the heels of that thought came the inevitable fears, and if it wasn't so hard on her feet and legs, she'd get up and pace the floor.

Even though her perinatologist, Becky Murray, assured her that everything was progressing beautifully, all the haunting statistics and lists of complications plagued Sarah. Her increased bed rest only gave her more time to worry. She pondered the perils of premature labor, preeclampsia and prolapsed cords. She fretted about every sort of fetal distress they'd gone over in childbirth class. She even dreamed about vanishing twin syndrome, in which a lost twin was re-absorbed into the mother's body, leaving no trace behind. Dr. Murray promised her that at this stage of the pregnancy, the syndrome was a physical impossibility, but that didn't stop Sarah from worrying. She worried about everything—the health of the babies. Complications. A difficult birth. A C-section. Whether or not she'd wake up when they cried. She worried about where they would live. Health insurance coverage.

Thanks to Birdie, the settlement from Jack and the child support were generous but ultimately she would have to provide for them. Drawing a comic strip suddenly seemed as ludicrous as Jack had always considered it.

The fourth time she got up to go to the bathroom, she noticed a thread of light on the horizon and decided to stay awake. Franny was only too happy to get an early start on her yard patrol. Sarah opened the door and followed the dog outside to the still air. Fog obscured the view, creating a world of shadows. The plume of the dog's tail marked her progress through the mist.

Sarah realized it wasn't morning at all. The light came from the moon, and it was 2:00 a.m. The moon was not full but getting there, a white ghost face staring down at her with those blank, empty depths for eyes.

"I wish you were here," she said to her mother, gathering the peony-pink shawl around her. Its soft weight settled around her shoulders like an embrace, and she was grateful all over again for her father's gesture, finishing her mother's final project and giving it to her. Her mother was just as gone, but finally, years after her death, she'd managed to bring Sarah and her father closer. Still... "I do, Mom. I wish you were here."

As she called the dog back in, she felt a wave of terrifying melancholy. Awaiting a birth was supposed to be the most thrilling and fulfilling time of a woman's life. Most days, Sarah managed to convince herself she was thrilled and fulfilled, but at times like this, in the middle of the night when even the peepers were silent, reality set in. She was in this alone. Despite the support of friends and family, she had no true companion on this journey.

Throughout the pregnancy, everyone did their best to mitigate that fact. She and her father diligently attended preparation classes. Tomorrow, her isolation would end. To avoid the risk of traffic on the Golden Gate Bridge, they were moving to a furnished efficiency across the street from Mercy Heights, where the babies would be born.

Sarah told herself to snap out of it. She was damned lucky to be where she was. Before going back to bed, she made a pot of jasmine tea and brought everything to the bedroom on her lap desk, which was her constant companion these days. This past week, she had been in a creative white heat. She'd done dozens of episodes of Lulu and Shirl. Sketches littered the bedside table. Some were quite good—but she was still struggling with the key event she'd been building to for months—Shirl's baby.

The story line was working better than anything she'd imagined. Certainly it was working better than her own pregnancy, she conceded, studying her elephantine ankles. Shirl's story was getting a great response from readers. Although the syndication editors were nervous, they stuck with it. Several of her papers had moved her above the fold.

The trouble was, she didn't know how or when Shirl would give birth. Often if she simply kept still and didn't try to force anything, the right idea would come to her. She closed her eyes and breathed deeply, hoping to clear the way for the answer.

Unfortunately, her mind was not cooperating. She didn't feel like keeping still. Maybe it was the dinner she'd eaten last night. Her father had brought her takeout from the

Dolphin Inn, which included dessert. As big as she was, it was a miracle she had room for anything, but she managed to pack away the Alaska halibut and Duchess potatoes, no problem.

The refrigerator needed cleaning, she decided, ignoring the fact that it was three o'clock in the morning. What the hell. She'd been diligent about bed rest for eighteen hours a day or more. She could stand to be up and about for a little bit. She might as well get the fridge knocked out.

With the radio playing eighties rock tunes, she methodically removed each shelf, then scrubbed every surface. This was one of the benefits of living alone. You could act any way you wanted and no one was around to tell you it was weird to clean the refrigerator in the middle of the night, when you were pregnant with twins.

During Jack's illness, she would sometimes find herself wakeful, but back then, all she could do was put on her headphones and crank up the music, leaving the lights off because one of the medications made him painfully sensitive to light. Now she had only to worry about her own needs and comfort, and if she felt like being up all night with the lights blazing, then she would.

The divorce would be final within a few weeks. She wanted it to be over before the babies came, but Birdie warned her it was unlikely. Each time Sarah thought everything was settled, Jack's lawyer found something new to fret about, insisting on obsessively detailed minutiae and manipulating the numbers regarding his assets. His latest parlor trick was claiming that Sarah had threatened to abandon Jack during the darkest stage of his illness.

The surprises just keep on coming, she thought, throwing away a questionable-looking jar of pickles. The biggest surprise of all, of course, was Will. What were the chances that she'd connect with someone like him, at a time like this? He couldn't be more different from Jack. Her husband covered all his bases, his way of taking responsibility. But Will—he was a rescuer. He protected the people he cared about with every bit of his great heart. Now that, she realized, was responsibility.

She reached for a jug of grapefruit juice, but as she lifted her hand, an intense pain ripped through her, stealing her breath. She found herself clinging to the door of the refrigerator, bathed in a sudden surge of sweat.

The Braxton Hicks contractions she'd experienced up to this point were nothing compared to the iron-fisted agony she felt now. Even so, she denied that anything was amiss. She had drilled herself thoroughly on procedural matters. The perinatologist's goal was, of course, a vaginal delivery, but Sarah understood that with twins, a C-section was twice as likely. They even had a target date for the birth, based on the rapid growth rate of the babies and ultimately, their presentation. If Twin A was breech, there would be no question—she would have them both by Cesarean. She was okay with that. Working with her father, she had written out a detailed birth plan, covering every eventuality. Franny would stay with Gran, and her father would drive her to the city. Everything was set for tomorrow.

Unfortunately, the twins hadn't gotten the memo.

She managed to slam the refrigerator shut before a second pain sent her to her knees. Franny must've sensed something was going on. She roused herself and hurried over to Sarah, nails clicking on the floor. The dog nuzzled Sarah, who now lay on her side on the kitchen floor, legs drawn up as high as her enormous belly would allow.

The dog sat back on her haunches and whined inquisitively. Sarah felt a wave of nausea and remembered a key piece of information she'd gleaned in childbirth preparation class: when a woman went into labor, all other body functions slowed down or stopped altogether. Including digestion.

Using the handle of the refrigerator door to pull herself up, she staggered to the bathroom where her five-course dinner made a reappearance.

She used a towel to clean herself up, and caught a glimpse of herself in the bathroom mirror. Wasn't this supposed to be a magical, memorable moment in a woman's life? Wasn't she supposed to tap her slumbering husband on the shoulder and whisper sweetly, "Darling, it's time"? Wasn't her face supposed to be aglow in dewy-eyed wonder and mystery? Surely she wasn't supposed to look like this—sweaty and pasty-faced, puke stains on her nightgown, her eyes wild with uncertainty.

She made it to the bedroom, grabbed the cordless phone and collapsed sideways on the bed. Left side, she remembered. Gets more blood to the uterus. Scared, I'm so scared. Sip water and apple juice.

She couldn't quite reach the water glass on the bedside table. It was a mile away. A sense of utter isolation closed over her. She lay gripping the phone, her vision blurred by pain, her thumb fumbling over the buttons. If she dialed 911, would Will come?

Of all the things she could be thinking at a time like this, why would she think of Will Bonner?

She wasn't ready to answer her own question. Focus, she reminded herself.

With firm resolve, she pressed the numbers. A lifetime elapsed between each of the four rings. Pick up, she thought. Pick up, pick up, pick up. Maybe she would have to call 911 after all.

"Hello?" The voice, raspy with sleep, kept her from hanging up.

"I'm in labor," she said. "Can you come?"

"I'm halfway there," said her father. "Relax, honey. Just breathe."

Thirty-Three

"So now you're the overachiever in the family," Kyle said, bending to kiss Sarah's forehead. "Congratulations."

Floating in a pastel fog of exhaustion and wonder, she smiled up at him from the hospital bed. "Did you see them?"

"We did," said LaNelle. "They're perfect. We can't wait for you all to come home."

Sarah had thought she was ready to love her children. What she discovered, while giving birth and later holding the babies against her heart, was an emotion so intense that it burned a hole clean through her. Could the word *love* even begin to describe the feeling that swept over her? Could any word? She had expected a strong, intense bond, but nothing of this magnitude, this incredible protectiveness and tenderness that closed her completely in a grip of iron. Maternal love wasn't all gentle sweetness. Instead, it was fierce and consuming, more a force of nature than a feeling.

She shut her eyes briefly, fighting a sudden and inexplicable burn of tears. The ordeal was over. The twins were stable and would be rooming in with her as soon as their bilirubin counts were within range and they'd each had a successful feeding. The pediatricians—both of them—had promised.

"Home sounds good," she said in a thick whisper.

"Then why the tears?" LaNelle asked, patting her on the shoulder.

In her wildest imaginings, Sarah could never have pictured her sister-in-law like this. Then again, she had never bothered to get to know LaNelle. Now she opened her eyes and saw a woman who was her friend.

"Aunt LaNelle," she said. "Or are you an 'auntie'?"

"We don't need to decide that just yet. You've got more important decisions to make."

"Yeah, like naming your kids," said Kyle. "Speaking of overachieving, this list of names is as long as my arm." He held up several pages covered with Sarah's handwriting.

"I want to make sure I get the names exactly right," she said.

"I'm with Sarah," LaNelle said. "There's no need to rush. She has to choose two first names and two middle names, and everything has to coordinate with the last name."

Sarah closed her eyes again, remembering a recent conversation with Jack. They had talked last week while she was on bed rest.

"The babies should have my last name," he insisted.

She thought he was kidding. "You weren't even there at the time of conception," she said. "It would make more sense to name them after the nurse-practitioner."

"You're making a big mistake," Jack had warned her. "They deserve their father's name, like any other kid in America."

"They deserve a father who takes responsibility for

them." She couldn't help making a reference to his battle to minimize child support payments.

"So their naming rights are for sale?" he'd taunted. "You want me to pay for the privilege, like they're a baseball field?"

She pushed aside the memory and opened her eyes just as her father came into the room. "Hey, Dad."

"Hey, yourself. What's that frown? I just came from the nursery and the kids are doing fine." His face shone with pride.

"It just occurred to me that Jack needs to be told."

"I'll call him, if you want."

God, she loved that. Loved handing the task over to him. Not for the first time, she felt a wave of gratitude for her father. Against all expectations, he'd really come through for her. Now, despite the gentle pride radiating from him, he looked almost as exhausted as she felt, with grayish skin and red eyes. His salt-and-pepper beard stubble was a reminder of the overwhelming process that had begun with a jar of spoiled pickles.

The drive to the hospital had seemed endless, the amber highway lights passing in long glowing streaks as she'd practiced her breathing techniques. "Breathe, honey," her father had said, his voice shaking. "Just breathe, okay? We're almost there…"

The haze of pain had draped everything in gauzy softness. There was something dreamlike about the agony. It was overwhelming, muffling everything, making her feel completely alone, floating in the universe. She had only the vaguest recollection of their arrival and check-in at the hospital, though there was never a moment when her father left her side, leaving the car to be parked by a stranger.

She had the twins in the operating room, the surgeon's 10-blade poised over her like a guillotine about to drop. She'd fought it, though, allied with Dr. Murray, knowing vaginal delivery was still an option. Both babies were in the headfirst position, connected to the outside world via the internal fetal monitor wires that snaked through her. At times, the room felt like rush hour on Chicago's El, with a crush of people surrounding her. IV drips and monitor wires tethered her to the bed like Gulliver in the land of the Lilliputians. Each baby had a pediatric team, Sarah had her perinatologist and since Mercy Heights was a teaching hospital, there were medical students, too. She lost count of the number of different people who did pelvics and checked her dilation.

Finally, after the second student in a row educated himself about what seven centimeters felt like, she'd gritted her teeth and said, "I'm starting to feel like an ATM machine."

Her father stepped forward. She hadn't even realized he'd been standing back against the wall behind her head. "No more," he'd said, and the exams had stopped. By that time, Sarah was in a haze of pain and exhaustion, her hands raw from gripping the draping. She could hear a terrible barking noise from a woman in a nearby room, and another woman yelling prayers in Spanish. Sarah's own pain had a sound, a wail that came from a place inside her she didn't know existed. And then, only minutes before she was going to surrender to a Cesarean, she was fully dilated and instructed to push. A convex mirror high in the corner of the room showed Baby A crowning, then emerging like a small wild animal before being engulfed by a five-person pediatric team. She remembered wishing she hadn't checked the mirror again, because the second view showed a resident with his arm buried seemingly to the elbow in her to deliver Baby B. Apgar scores—an impressive nine for the first twin and a more iffy six for the second—were noted; then the babies were swaddled and given to her to hold briefly before being whisked away.

Those minutes with her newborns were precious. The ordeal of the birth, primal and violent and full of agony, subsided like an ebb tide. Sarah's pain went away somewhere, unremembered, as though it had been a bad dream that dissolved upon waking. Feeling the soft press of the babies' weight on her chest, she sensed every cell in her body glowing with pure joy. She was transformed, a mother now, with a soul as deep and infinite as time.

"Thanks for everything you did," she said to her father.

"It wasn't anything at all."

"It was exactly what we needed."

Thirty-Four

Will figured Sarah probably had enough flowers, so he didn't bring any to the hospital when he went to see her. Instead, he stopped at a shop near the hospital and picked out a simple digital camera, one that could be operated in light or dark with one hand, and a battery that lasted forever. He'd checked with her grandmother, who'd told him it was just what Sarah needed.

A good camera was something he remembered wanting when he brought Aurora home. It was like falling in love again, not the way he'd fallen in love with Marisol, but in a way that was completely uncluttered and crystal clear. Here was this wide-eyed, new little person in his life. He would wake up each morning, eager to see her, to hear her speak, to watch her apprehension warm into curiosity and, before long, genuine happiness. He always wished he had known Aurora as a baby. At birth, at the moment she'd drawn her first breath. If he had, would their bond be stronger? Would he understand her better?

Marisol had no photographs of her newborn, but he

imagined Aurora as a fairy child, with skin of pale perfection, jet-black hair, her mouth a red bow. At that point, the godmothers were supposed to step in and give her all the gifts she needed to make it through life. Instead, Aurora had been thrust into a life of poverty and corruption so bad it made Will cringe even now, when he thought about it.

He wondered what Sarah's babies looked like. Did they have her light hair and eyes? Or did they look like her ex? What did her ex look like, anyway? Will tried never to think about the guy, but now, confronted with the reality of his DNA, he caught himself wondering.

The salesgirl put the camera in a big glossy bag with some tissue paper, and he all but sprinted across the hospital parking lot in his haste.

Throughout Sarah's pregnancy, the unlikely friendship had deepened between them, along with an even less likely but undeniable attraction. They kept their distance, though. She had so much on her plate, ending her marriage while becoming the mother of two. And Will had his own concerns, not the least of which was Aurora. All the child-rearing books seemed to agree that seeing a single parent live a rich emotional life was considered a good thing for a young girl. Unfortunately, those books had never seen Aurora's smoldering resentment, nor had they been charged with safeguarding her fragile heart from further pain.

Still, he couldn't keep himself from caring about Sarah Moon. When he heard she had gone to the city to have the babies, he'd been restless with worry and torn by indecision. His position with Sarah was unclear, and he hated that. Hated that he couldn't just drop everything and go be with her. Hated that he had to wait until his sister called to report that everyone was fine.

He was done with all that, starting now. His heart was on fire for her, and like the movement of a fire, in a V-shaped spread of flame, it followed the path of least resistance.

He knocked softly at the door to her private room in the birthing center. A woman in pink scrubs let him in. The badge dangling from her shirt identified her as a member of La Leche League. "Sarah, are you up to having a visitor?" she asked.

"Absolutely," said a quiet voice from the bed, and the woman stepped aside and left. He stood uncertainly just inside the door, taking in the dimly lit, sleekly furnished room and then shifting his gaze to her. Bars of light through the slats of the Venetian blinds fell over her. The air smelled of flowers, disinfectant and…something indefinable. It was a rich, fecund aroma, a birth smell, perhaps. He wasn't sure how he knew such a thing existed.

Standing there, with his gift bag and the gleam of unfamiliar objects in the room, he wasn't prepared for how happy he was to see her, or for the curious reality of the two brand-new strangers lying swaddled in clear bassinets on wheels. A rolling table was cluttered with various drink holders and a cafeteria tray with a plate that looked as though it had been licked clean. The counter and windowsill were crammed with flowers and balloons, and a stack of books lay on the bedside table.

At the center of all the bright chaos was Sarah, raised to a sitting position in the hospital bed, serene and glowing like the sun through the mist. Will knew he looked like an idiot, grinning at her, but he couldn't help himself.

"Hey, Sarah," he said. "Congratulations."

"Hey, yourself. Come check out the twins."

"They look great." Too late, he realized he was staring

at her chest. He cleared his throat, feeling too many things at once—tentative, intimidated, out of his element and inappropriately turned-on. "And you look great, too," he added.

"I do?" She touched her hair.

"I was just thinking, Madonna-like." Surely she'd be reassured by that, he thought.

"Liar. You were thinking about my boobs."

He didn't answer. Caught in the act. They were like the elephant in the room—so enormous, you couldn't *not* see them. Don't look down again, he told himself. Don't look down.

"I admit, they surprised the heck out of me, too," she said.

He made himself turn away and moved toward the bassinets. "So we meet at last," he said, studying the two swaddled forms. They weren't beautiful. They didn't look like the babies on the Gerber jar. They were dark red in the face, their fists no bigger than a man's thumb. Though closed, their eyes were puffy, their lips bowed and swollen. They looked exactly alike—indistinguishable. The sight of them lit him on fire. He hadn't been expecting this flood of emotion—a singular mixture of tenderness, relief and protectiveness.

"You're awfully quiet," Sarah said.

"I don't know what to say." He felt a peculiar tightness in his chest. "Two boys. Two little boys. Damn, Sarah."

"I can't get over it," she agreed. "While I was pregnant, I didn't want to know the sex. They did so many tests, I wanted at least one thing to be a surprise."

"Were you surprised?"

"Everything about them surprises me." Her voice shook, and her face shone with all the love in the world.

One of the babies grimaced and made a soft whimpering sound. The feeling in Will's chest intensified. This is not happening, he thought. It can't be happening. And yet it was. He felt himself going crazy—for Sarah and these tiny babies.

"What are their names?" he asked, his gaze still riveted on the babies.

"I still haven't decided," she said, "and please don't nag me."

"I wasn't planning on it."

"My brother is out of patience with me. He calls them Thing One and Thing Two, like in the Dr. Seuss book. If I'm not careful, those names will stick."

"No rush. They don't look like it matters too much yet." He held out the glossy gift bag. "This is for you. It's from Aurora and me, both."

She beamed up at him as she took out the shiny camera box. Watching her, he suddenly felt stupid. Maybe he'd bought the wrong thing. Maybe he should have—

"Will. It's perfect. It's exactly what I'll need in my arsenal for doting mothers." She smiled up at him. "Thank you so much."

"Sure," he said.

"I'd give you a great big hug," she said, "but…"

But it would be too much of a turn-on, he thought.

She made a helpless gesture with her hand. "I'm kind of stuck here for another day or two. They want me to take it easy, and they want to make sure the babies know how to eat."

"Good advice." On impulse, he slipped his hand under her chin and then touched his mouth to hers. He intended only a quick brush of the lips, but it ignited into something else entirely.

She felt it, too; he could tell by the surprised intake of her breath and the sudden desperation with which her fist clutched at his sleeve.

Will supposed he could have been more calculating about the time and place of their first kiss, but he'd never been so good at timing. She was as soft and sweet as a toasted marshmallow. He didn't want to stop kissing her, but forced himself to step back. He had a hard-on that could drive nails. He hoped like hell she wouldn't notice.

Her lips were moist and full now, and he wanted nothing more than to kiss her again.

"So," she said, her cheeks turning red, "is this your way of saying you're welcome?"

"It's my way of saying I'm falling for you, Sarah. I have been for a long time."

The color dropped from her face. Not exactly the reaction he was looking for. Damn. But what had he expected, that she'd be up for giving birth to twins and falling in love the same week?

Her gaze darted like a trapped animal's. "You've got a lot of damn nerve, Will Bonner," she said.

"Yeah, it's not the best moment in the world, I get that. But I've given this a lot of thought, and I needed to tell you."

"Why?" Her voice broke with pain. "We were fine before."

He understood that she was on the rebound, her divorce still a fresh wound, her babies only days old, and that she couldn't possibly be ready for a relationship. Yet his heart told him Sarah was worth the risk.

"We weren't 'fine,'" he said. "We were friends."

"Exactly. Will, you turned out to be my best friend. But when you start saying these things…everything changes."

"I'm not going to hurt you, Sarah." But he could tell from the expression on her face that she didn't believe him.

Her eyes filled. "You already are."

"Come on," he said, "that's not—"

"Sounds to me like this visit is over," said a voice from the doorway.

Will turned and saw a guy standing there. He was wearing creased slacks, expensive-looking loafers and a dress shirt but no tie. The sleeves were rolled back, and he held a finger hooked into a sport jacket, slung over one shoulder. In his other hand he held a Tiffany-blue box. Will instantly knew who this was, but he turned to Sarah, just for confirmation.

All the color that had drained from her face a few moments ago now returned, and her eyes lit up with blinding brightness.

"Jack," she said.

Sarah held the crumpled wrapping paper from Will's gift against her chest as he left the room. He didn't hurry, but simply said, "I'll call you." Then he walked past Jack with purposeful strides and disappeared out into the corridor.

She was still reeling from the things Will had said, but now she had to shift her focus to Jack. Dear God, Jack was here. A fierce protective instinct rose up in her. She didn't want to share her babies with this man, even though on paper, she had committed to limited visitation. "Jack," she said again, "I wasn't expecting you."

"I know." He stood aside, and in walked his mother, Helen Daly. "We caught a flight as soon as we heard."

"Hello, Helen," Sarah said. She touched her hair, feeling suddenly self-conscious. It struck her that she always felt this way around Jack and his family—unkempt, out of fashion. Even though, at the moment, she had the mother of all excuses, she found herself wishing she'd put on lipstick or something.

"Sarah, we're so happy for you," Helen said. "How are you feeling?"

Completely freaked out, thought Sarah. She realized she didn't need to answer, though.

Helen locked eyes on the clear bassinets. "Jack, come see." She spoke in a reverential whisper. "Oh, my stars," she said. "Look at them. Just look at them."

The babies were still sound asleep, neatly and expertly wrapped by the nurses. Sarah hoped they'd stay that way, because her newly bounteous breasts tended to go off like geysers when the babies cried.

Jack approached the bassinets, craning his neck and leaning over to see. Sarah tried to read the expression on his face, but she couldn't. How strange, that she couldn't read him anymore. She hadn't been expecting that. He was as handsome as ever, she observed, in his high-fashion, well-maintained way. And he looked good. Healthy, thank heavens.

His reaction to the babies was so different from Will's. Whereas Jack was proprietary and proud, Will had turned visibly emotional. She could still picture him, his face suffused with tenderness, his stance unconsciously protective.

"What are their names?" Jack asked.

"I haven't decided."

He frowned. "You didn't think about this all those months you were pregnant?"

"I wanted to see them first." Sarah warned herself not to get defensive.

"They're wonderful," Helen said. "I'm sure you'll find the perfect names for them." Unexpectedly, it was Helen's presence that moved Sarah the most. She would be a world-class grandma, Sarah knew. There was something in her face, in the deep lines around her mouth as she smiled, that made Sarah think of her own mother. It was unbearably sad that her mom was missing out on this. And here was Helen Daly, desperate to be a grandmother. Sarah knew she couldn't deny her. It was all so new, though. They were all like actors whose roles hadn't been written yet. They were waiting to figure out what to say.

"We brought you this." Jack handed her the box from Tiffany. It contained a pair of sterling silver picture frames. "The date of birth is engraved on each one, but I guess you'll have to fill in the names later."

"Jack, thank you," Sarah said. "I'll do that."

Their gazes held for a few moments, and Sarah felt a strange shift of disorientation. Despite her urgency to finalize the divorce, things were proceeding at a leaden pace. She knew the door was still open—maybe just a crack—to a reconciliation. She imagined remaking her life with him and their sons. It could be done. It could work. In some ways it could work rather well. Financially for sure—but then she considered the other costs and knew the idea was insane.

She could give him something, though. She had two perfect babies. Jack had nothing but a monthly payment. "Their middle names will be Daly," she said. "I hope that's all right."

He offered a sharp, bitter laugh. "It's far from all right," he said, "but why let that stop you? Ever since you took off, you've done exactly as you pleased."

Sarah sent Helen a look: *Are you hearing this?* But

Jack's mother seemed totally preoccupied by the babies. She had picked one of them up and carried him to a chair by the window and then gazed down at the tiny, sleeping face with total absorption. Sarah was on her own.

She looked from Helen to Jack, then felt a light-headed rush of relief. The anger was gone. She didn't know when she'd let go of it, or how it had happened, but she no longer carried that hard ball of fury around inside her chest the way she had since the day she'd walked in on him and Mimi. In its place was a sadness, though, and it tinged her voice when she said, "Jack, there was a time when all I ever wanted was to have your children, and it went without saying that they would carry your name. You changed all that—on the day of their conception, in fact."

"That's a low blow, Sarah."

She still didn't feel angry, though the sadness deepened. "Yeah, I know how that feels."

Thirty-Five

For the past week and a half, Aurora had watched visitors come and go, to and from Sarah's house. The old aunt and grandmother were regulars, arriving in the morning and staying practically all day. Judy deWitt from the art store and Mrs. Chopin brought covered dishes and could be seen taking out bags of crumpled gift wrap and drooping bouquets of flowers whose stems had grown rank and mushy in their vases. Gloria and Ruby, Glynnis's mom, paid a visit, and Aurora just bet that still drove Glynnis crazy. It was bad enough when your single mom dated. When she dated another woman, well, that was completely unacceptable. And when they went out in public together? As Granny Shannon would put it, Katie, bar the door.

Aunt Birdie had already gone to see the babies, giving Sarah a pair of cream-colored cotton receiving blankets. Aurora didn't really understand why they were called receiving blankets. As far as she knew, they would be used for wrapping up the kids.

Birdie said Sarah had asked about Aurora and indicated

that she would welcome a visit. Aurora wanted to see her, bad, and she even had a special gift for the babies—a drawing of the Point Reyes lighthouse she had made to hang in their room. The babies wouldn't give a hoot about that, but Sarah would. Plus, Aurora had used two months' worth of babysitting money to get it professionally framed. The lighthouse was her favorite place in the world. She hadn't been to a lot of places, but she was pretty sure it was one of the most beautiful. She'd gone flying with Aunt Lonnie, had seen the Golden Gate Bridge and San Luis Obispo, Bryce Canyon and Yosemite. None of them matched the dramatic, edge-of-the-world splendor of Point Reyes.

She felt bashful about showing up at Sarah's, though. She was torn between wanting to be her friend and worrying that Sarah might hook up with Aurora's dad.

She finally spotted a window of opportunity one misty afternoon. It was one of those days when the fog hung around long into the day. It was disorienting and difficult to tell what time it was. Sarah's house sat in a thick cloud of white, the front fence and flower bed seeming to float on a river of mist. The elderly sisters left and no new visitors had arrived.

Aurora went to the door and knocked. Inside the house, Franny barked once and then sneezed in friendly fashion when she recognized Aurora. She waited, feeling inexplicably tense. She and Sarah were friends, she reminded herself. She wanted to be here, wanted to see the new babies.

When she answered the door, Sarah chased all the tension away with her smile. She looked really good, even though she wore baggy pajama bottoms and a hooded, zip-up sweatshirt. Without the gigantic stomach, she seemed younger and quicker.

"Hey, stranger," she said, giving Aurora a hug. "I missed you."

Aurora flashed her an uncertain smile. "How are you?"

"A lot different than I was the last time you saw me. Want to meet the babies?"

"Are you kidding?"

The house looked the same, but the air itself felt different. There was a hush, as if someone was holding her breath, and a peculiar soft smell. The babies lay swaddled in their cribs, their tiny heads covered in soft hair, white as dandelion fluff.

"They're asleep," Sarah said. "They sleep a lot."

Aurora cocked her head to the side. "Their faces are so cute," she said, feeling an unexpected burst of emotion in her chest. "I can't believe how tiny and cute they are."

"Me neither." Sarah's face softened with love and pride.

It was amazing to Aurora that every human being started out like this, brand-new and helpless. Seeing two of them, exactly alike, underscored the impression that everyone started out the same. Don't ever leave them, she wanted to say to Sarah. Instead, she asked, "So, what are their names?"

"Still undecided. When I left the hospital, their records said Baby A and Baby B. Picking the right names is turning out to be harder than I thought it would be."

"It's been a week and a half. What are you waiting for?" She hoped Sarah was not doing something crazy, like waiting for her ex to help pick out names.

"I don't want to rush this decision."

"They look totally identical."

"Pretty much. They're fraternal twins, though, like my grandmother and great-aunt."

"How can you tell them apart?"

"I figure as their mother, I should simply know one from the other," Sarah said. "I'm not taking any chances, though." She untucked a corner of one of the blankets to reveal a doll-size foot with a hospital bracelet around the ankle. Printed on the plastic band was Baby A Moon.

"You really ought to give them their names," Aurora whispered. "How about—"

Baby A started crying. The tiny, mewling sound startled Aurora and woke up the other twin. Within a few seconds, the sound wasn't tiny and mewling anymore. They sounded like a couple of bleating goats, and the noise had a funny effect on her, as if it was rattling her back teeth or something.

Sarah glanced at a clock on the wall. "Feeding time. They eat every two hours."

"All day?" The rhythmic insistence of the crying scraped over her nerves.

"And all night." Sarah looked weary as she bent over one crib and checked the baby's diaper, which appeared to be dry. The other baby accepted a pacifier, which decreased the volume a little, but only for a second. The baby spat out the pacifier and started up again.

"Can I do something?" Aurora asked.

"They like being held," Sarah said, and sure enough, Baby A quieted down as soon as she scooped him up.

Aurora ducked into the adjacent bathroom and washed her hands with soap, which her grandmother had told her you should always do around newborns.

"Support the head," Sarah coached her as Aurora picked up the crying baby. It was harder than it looked, because he kept squirming and quivering, but once she got him in the crook of her arm, he settled down a little. He kept turning his head toward her and opening his mouth, which embarrassed her a little. She gave him the pacifier and he quieted down a bit, though he still made an angry-sounding buzzing noise.

Sarah had a seat in an armchair. "I need to nurse them. You don't mind, do you?"

"No. Geez, of course not." Aurora discovered that the buzzing sound stopped if she swayed back and forth gently with the baby.

Sarah unzipped her sweatshirt and the shirt beneath. She was wearing an ugly bra with enormous cups and snaps at the top. Aurora watched in shock and fascination as Sarah held the baby to her and he latched on. Sarah let out a sigh, then caught Aurora staring. "It's okay to check it out," Sarah said. "When I was your age, I would have been really curious."

Aurora blushed and ducked her head. She felt like an intruder and now she was trapped, holding this baby.

"It's called the let-down reflex, a reaction to the babies crying. I swear, I will never take a glass of milk for granted again." She gave a tired smile. "I'm glad you came. This is always easier with help."

"What do you do when you're by yourself?"

"They have to take turns, and sometimes I just cry right along with them. I'm all right, though," she added quickly. "My family's taking good care of me. Franny, too." She indicated the dog, who sat quietly and obediently nearby, eyes alert to every movement. "I wasn't sure how she'd deal with the babies, but she seems totally accepting of them."

"I'm not surprised," Aurora said. "She was a good mom, herself."

"I'm just glad we found homes for all the puppies before the babies came."

The room grew so quiet that the baby's swallows could

be heard. Within a few minutes, the eager nursing slowed and the infant emitted a soft burp, and then dozed. Sarah laid him in his crib and covered him up. "Next," she said, switching sides.

None too soon, because Baby B had caught on that the pacifier wasn't the real thing and was starting to snuffle and fuss. Aurora placed him in Sarah's arms. By now she felt less self-conscious. Sure it was strange—the big full breast like a flesh-colored balloon, the hungry, searching mouth, but it was beautiful, too, in a way. She watched how Sarah's face seemed to relax, and the protective way her whole body seemed to curve around the child. Aurora wondered if her own mother had ever held her like that, with her entire being glimmering with love. Probably not, Aurora decided. Once when she was little, she'd said, "Mama, tell me about when I was a baby." All Mama would say was, "You cried all the time. You kept getting sick."

"What do you think of Adam Moon for Baby A?" Sarah asked. "And Bradley for Baby B."

"I think they're fine." Aurora liked names like Cody and Travis. And Zane. Zane was a great name.

"Just fine? I want their names to be better than fine. Adam is my father's middle name, and Bradley's my mother's maiden name. Is it too cute that I kept the A and the B?"

Aurora looked at the tiny round head, the star-shaped hand. Bradley? Did he look like a Bradley? He just looked like a baby to her, but as she watched, she imagined him growing up, walking and laughing, and one day going out into the world. "I like Bradley," she said. "And Adam. I like them both."

"Really?" Sarah put the now-sleeping infant in his crib. She smiled down at him. "Two more hours and then we'll do this all over again."

"When they get older," Aurora said, "don't tell them about the crying."

Sarah was still smiling. "I'm not complaining, really. I don't hate this. In fact, I love it. Strange, huh?"

"Naw." Aurora went and got the gift she'd brought. "I made this for you," she said, feeling a little bashful. "For you and your family."

Sarah's eyes shone as she ripped off the paper. Then she gasped. "Aurora, it's beautiful. You're a fantastic artist." She studied it as only another artist would, exclaiming over the paper Aurora had used, the precision of the drawing and the quality of the light, even, and the framing job. Then she propped the picture on the mantel over the fireplace. "It's a treasure," Sarah declared. "I'll think of you every time I look at it."

"So what's up with you and my dad?" Aurora blurted out. She couldn't help it. The question had been in the back of her mind the whole time she'd been here.

And now that she'd asked it, she watched its effect on Sarah. Her skin turned blotchy and maybe she was sweating a little. "What do you think is up?" she asked Aurora.

"I don't know. You guys act like you like each other."

"We're friends. I can't explain it." Sarah touched her fingertips to her lips in a gesture that was probably unconscious. When she saw Aurora watching her, she folded her hands in her lap.

"Just friends?" Aurora persisted.

"Have you asked your dad this question?"

"He gave me the same answer."

"He said we're friends?"

"He's not much for talking about stuff like this. That's why I asked you. And you're not telling me anything, either."

"That's because I don't have any answers. Honey, I don't even know what time it is or whether I've got my shoes on the right feet. Analyzing my relationship with your father is not the best idea, not right now. Okay?"

No, it was not okay, Aurora thought, but she knew she wouldn't get any answers from Sarah, not today.

Part Six

JUST BREATHE

Thirty-Six

The twins passed their three-month checkup with flying colors. It seemed a peculiar cruelty to reward their amazing growth and development with a hot dart of pain to the thigh, but that was exactly what they got for their troubles.

"Here we go with the shock and awe," said the pediatrician. He had already given each baby a drop of Tylenol, just as a precaution. "You ready, Mom?"

Sarah cupped her hand over Adam's head, bit her lip and nodded. All ignorance, the baby chortled and cooed, a perfect poster child for pediatric health. Then came the quick, chilly swipe of the sterile cotton ball and the prick of the needle.

For a moment, all was silence. Adam's gorgeous blue eyes opened wide and his mouth formed a perfect O of flabbergasted agony. Then came the prolonged intake of breath—the wind-up to a howl of pain so heartfelt that his little tongue quivered. His pain nearly sent Sarah to her knees. "I'm sorry," she said. "I'm sorry, I'm sorry, I'm sorry."

Bradley joined the chorus because this was how they were. When one cried, the other did the same. However, when it was his turn for the inoculation, he broke his brother's record for bloodcurdling noise. By the time it was over, Sarah was on the verge of asking for a Valium. Then, as quickly as it started, the noise stopped. The boys lay in their carriers, tears drying on their flushed cheeks, pacifiers working busily up and down.

"That's how it is with infants," the doctor said. "The minute the pain's gone, so are the tears. If more people would do that, the world would be a happier place."

The pediatrician's assistant reminded Sarah to bring the boys back for a booster shot, and she wrote it down at least three times, so that when she got home, she would post reminders in three places—on the calendar, on a sticky note by the front door and on a note stuck to the refrigerator door. She was still pretty sure she'd forget.

She was all about forgetting these days, she reflected as she put the boys in their car seats and headed home. She could never remember what day it was, or the ingredients in a Denver omelet or her social security number. So why then, she wondered, was she unable to forget that day in the hospital when Will had come to see her? She was able to play that like a movie in her head, frame by frame, pausing to examine each moment. The kiss that made her every nerve ending fire to life. And then the words, fresh as a moment ago—*I'm falling for you.*

It was crazy. He had to know that. Had to know she wasn't going to let herself love him back. You didn't just fall out of love with one person and into love with another in the middle of a divorce. She shouldn't have spoken up, shouldn't have admitted to the crush. That was just her fear and loneliness coming out, wasn't it?

The course of true love didn't follow a predictable pattern. It wasn't like gestation, when the next step happened exactly according to some predetermined biological plan. And even then, even when the plan was followed to the letter, there were still surprises.

She flexed her fingers on the steering wheel. When she'd first taken off her wedding band and the platinum-and-yellow-diamond engagement ring Jack had given her, its ghost had lingered for months. Her finger was pale and shrunken where Jack's rings had been. It took the whole pregnancy, complete with edema, to erase the imprint. She wondered how long it would take for the mark on her heart to heal, and if she'd ever be able to give herself so fully again.

She kept encountering Will—at the farmers' market, the coffee shop, at Children's Beach, a small strip of sand by the bay, edged by the tall arching trees of the town park. In a place this size, it couldn't be helped and besides, even though she ached, being around him, his friendship meant everything to her. They talked about Aurora, about work and the babies, about life and laughter and pain and everything in their hearts.

But they had never again spoken of love, or of the future. The time for falling in love was when you were emotionally available and free of cares, when it didn't matter what time you came home or how late you were getting up the next day. When you had hours and hours to spend gazing into each other's eyes and even longer hours making love, uninterrupted.

If you wait for the perfect time to fall in love, said a little inner voice that sounded suspiciously like Lulu, *it'll never happen.*

Sometimes, when Sarah thought about her life, she wished Jack had never happened. In the end, it was just too painful. But if she hadn't married him, she would never have had her babies. Jack had given her a miracle, and she would always be grateful to him for that gift. They were so much a part of her that she could scarcely remember life without them. Although people swore it was impossible to tell them apart, Sarah could do so with her eyes closed. Bradley was sweetly emotional; he had a way of melting into her arms and draping himself over her like a warm, fragrant garment. Adam loved to watch the world, his round eyes sparkling and his jaw working as he sucked his thumb; even at a young age, he seemed alert to nuance.

She got home and sat in the car for a moment, loath to risk waking her sleeping sons. She was feeling low, probably because of the trauma of the booster shots and because when she checked her bank balance today, she saw that Jack's monthly payment for spousal maintenance and child support had arrived as it always did, like clockwork. This should not be depressing, but it was. Her kids had a bank deposit instead of a dad.

She'd snap out of it in a minute, she told herself. Everyone admired her, said how well she was doing, transforming her life. She'd escaped a bad marriage, survived a tough pregnancy and tougher birth and was now raising twins on her own while juggling self-employment. She was like those women you used to read about in books and articles who managed to do it all. The thing the books didn't explain was that there was a huge personal cost to doing it all. Sleep, sanity, a sense of self. The first few weeks, Gran and Aunt May had taken turns spending the day with her. LaNelle, Viv and Judy showered her with casseroles and produce from their gardens. Her father had ordered a milk delivery service from one of the local dairies. She was surrounded by friends, pampered and mothered to the best of their ability.

Ultimately, though, she had to figure out how to do everything on her own. One thing she knew was that you couldn't be in a hurry with infant twins. Even going from the car to the house was a prolonged journey. The days of dashing off with her purse, keys and shopping bag in hand were no preparation for this reality. By now, she was used to making several trips in order to get babies, diaper bag full of gear, grocery sacks, handbag and herself into the house. She had it down to a routine. Leave the kids in the car and unlock the door, dragging along whatever bags and gear you could handle. Prop the door open. Yell at Franny to stay inside so she didn't dash outside and get underfoot. Carefully unbuckle one son at a time and oh-so-gently set down his carrier, where he might sleep for an extra half hour. If she was very, very lucky, they would slumber through the time it took to put everything away and maybe even go through the mail. Lately, she almost felt cocky about her ability to juggle everything. She was like a performer in Cirque du Soleil.

Except that it only took one unexpected occurrence to disrupt the flow. When the occurrences happened in multiples, she was screwed. On this particular day, the phone started ringing in the house as she was unbuckling Adam. She had trained herself long ago never to hurry to the phone. If it was important, the caller would leave a message or call back. Still, the insistent sound drifting through the window screen rattled her enough to make her hasty in the process of unbuckling and pulling the carrier out of the Mini. Somehow, she managed to jostle the baby. He awoke with a scream.

She noticed then that the injection site, covered with a SpongeBob Band-Aid, was livid and swollen. Oh, God, she thought. He's having a reaction. Every terrible thing she'd read about immunizations came swirling back to haunt her. She had to get in the house, had to call the doctor right away.

Clutching the carrier, she whirled and shut the car door. She was about to make a dash for the house when the realization hit her.

Igni-second, she thought. Like a nanosecond, only it referred to the time lapse between slamming the car door and realizing the keys were still in the ignition. And that the doors were on autolock, an antitheft feature she kept forgetting to disable.

Ha, she thought. I'm prepared for this. She had a second car key stashed inside the kitchen cupboard, just for this purpose. She rushed inside, set down Adam's carrier, grabbed the key and headed for the door, pausing to make a soothing sound at Adam—a sound that only infuriated him further. In the car outside, Bradley, perhaps alerted to disaster, had set up a wailing of his own. She managed to drop the key through a gap in the porch steps.

Her children, she knew, were going to grow up knowing more cusswords than the proverbial sailor. She dropped to her knees to retrieve the key, only to discover that there was no way to reach beneath the steps. She ran to the car and tried the doors and the hatchback again, just in case. Bradley's face was a red ball of fury. She had an impulse to do something—anything. Throw a brick through the window? No. She didn't trust that the glass was shatterproof enough.

Panic happened in the heartbeat of time it took to realize she had no safe way to get to her baby. Before she even made up her mind about what to do, she called 911.

Twelve endless, agonizing minutes later, Will Bonner, looking like Captain America, opened the door with what appeared to be a blood pressure cuff. A few puffs of inflation created a gap wide enough for him to trip the latch. When he turned to her with her unharmed son safe in his arms, Sarah's knees wobbled.

"Let's go inside and sit down," Will suggested.

Sarah nodded and followed him into the house, where Adam now slumbered peacefully in his carrier. "It's not abnormally inflamed," Will said, checking the injection site. "Doesn't look that way to me, anyway."

"I think it's my imagination that's inflamed." She took several deep breaths, trying to regain her composure.

Bradley seemed perfectly content in Will's arms. Will seemed perfectly content, holding the baby.

The sight of them together made her cry. It was a little shocking, how quickly the emotion took hold. Humiliated, she grabbed a tissue and pressed it to her face. "Sorry," she said.

"Don't be. Anyone would find that stressful." He put Bradley in his crib, his movements awkward but careful.

Standing in the doorway, Sarah waited for a squawk of protest, but the baby settled down, blinking slowly and then letting his eyes drift shut. "You're good with babies."

"Am I?" Will grinned. "I don't have much experience, but they're not that complicated. The complications come later, around seventh grade." He took Sarah's hand and led her to the sofa. They sat for a few minutes in silence, then he said, "Sarah. What are we doing?"

"I'm not sure what you're asking." Oh, but she was. She knew exactly what he was asking. And he deserved an explanation. She took another deep breath. "I'm learning to stand on my own for the first time in my life. Until now, I was taken care of, first by my family, and then by Jack and his family. It's not like I was ever the little woman, but I never really learned to go it alone and it's about time I did that."

"What are you trying to prove?"

"I need to know I can do this. It's hard, but maybe that's why I need to prove it to myself. Life isn't easy. It's not supposed to be. That's not such a bad thing. When it was easy, I was sleepwalking through the day, pretending everything was fine. I woke up to a harsh reality, but ultimately that's what saved me."

He absorbed her words with a prolonged silence. Then, finally, he looked at her. "I love you, Sarah." There was no joy in his voice as he said it. "I don't know when it happened, but I think it started the night of Franny's puppies."

She stared at him, afraid to breathe and completely at a loss for words.

"So I've known it for a while," Will said, "but I backed off, gave you space so you could deal with all this." He encompassed the room with a gesture.

She reeled from his declaration. She almost returned it. *I love you, too.* An ache of longing thrummed in her chest. "Oh, Will. I never meant to mislead you, or make you think..." She stopped, tried to regroup, but there was still too much pain and confusion knotting her insides. This was exactly as she'd feared. She couldn't have him both ways. "I need you as a friend, Will—"

"Sorry to disappoint you, but we can't stop there. We're already past the point of no return."

She heard his honesty, and the passion behind his words. "I'm not disappointed," she said.

"Sarah," he said, "I've been waiting a long time for you to call me. Don't wait for there to be a problem. Just call."

"I don't think I should do that," she said. In her head,

Shirl's voice scolded, Hello? This is Will Bonner you're turning down. Are you out of your gourd? "Listen," she rushed on, "if this was just about you and me, things would be different. We're old enough to know what we're doing. Old enough to survive a broken heart. But think about the kids, Aurora and the boys. If we're wrong, or if we screw this up, you and I won't be the only casualties."

"Why are you so convinced we're going to screw this up?" he asked.

"I'm just saying, it's not fair to the kids to take that risk. Not now, anyway." There, she cracked open the door.

"When?" he persisted. "Next week? In a month? You can find an excuse that'll work anytime."

"These are not excuses," she objected.

"Right. Give me a call when you run out of them."

"Will," she said, "I'm…I think you're amazing, and I'm flattered, but my life is crazy right now."

"And when is life not crazy? Tell me that."

Touché, she thought.

Thirty-Seven

Sarah wasn't sure why she had agreed to attend the Oyster Festival on Sunday. Lately, she barely made it to 8:00 p.m. before exhaustion claimed her. The babies no longer woke up for night feedings, a small miracle that came in the nick of time, just before she lost her mind. Still, the routine was taking its toll.

However, her brother Kyle seemed to want her involvement, explaining that the annual festival was a key event for his buyers and restaurateurs. He and their father stopped by Sarah's house. As always, Dad hunkered down on the floor with the babies. He had given every inch of his heart to being a grandfather, and even at their young age, the twins seemed to recognize that here was someone special in their lives. They favored him with cooing and a great pedaling of legs and extra-wide smiles.

Sarah didn't kid herself about the challenges of raising two boys without a father. Knowing her dad and Kyle would be there for the twins was a precious gift to her.

Kyle showed her a folder of glossy brochures. "Everybody loves the idea of a homegrown family operation. The whole town is involved. The event even has a name—the Moon Bay Oyster Festival."

"If the whole town is involved," Sarah said, "then you don't need me."

"Sure, we do. Just be gorgeous and charming," Kyle said. "You could be the Oyster Queen."

Sarah gave an exaggerated shudder. "I thought they came for the oysters."

"They're coming for the whole experience," her father explained.

"Give them Moon Bay key chains and T-shirts and shucking aprons. I'd just be in the way."

"Still worried about what people might think?" Kyle asked.

She sent a quick look at their father. He stayed focused on the boys, and his face betrayed nothing.

"I beg your pardon," Sarah said.

"Come on," Kyle said. "When we were young, you always hated working for the family business, but you're an adult now."

"I didn't hate it." A sick feeling churned inside her. They had never talked about this before, yet both her brother and father seemed to know.

"Kyle, that's enough," their father said.

Sarah looked from her father to her brother. They were so alike, these two, both honest and hardworking—and also much more aware of her troubles than she'd ever given them credit for. "He's right. I was just a stupid kid."

"You were a very smart kid," her father said, "and I wish I hadn't made you work at the oyster farm." He took hold of Adam's feet and played with them. "No oyster farming for you and your brother, little man, and that's a promise."

He grinned at Sarah. "Being a parent is so much easier for a grandparent."

"I could say the same about being a daughter, now that I'm a mother. Seriously, I wish I'd done more. The family business gave me the best education money can buy. I never appreciated that." She swallowed past the ache in her throat. "Dad, I'm so sorry."

He levered himself up from the play area on the floor to enfold her in a hug. Bit by bit, the tension inside her eased and slipped away. Forgiveness was such a simple thing, she thought, once you surrendered to it. Smiling through tears, she reached for her brother. "I don't have cooties anymore," she said, and he let her hug him.

"So does this mean you're in?" Kyle asked.

"Just don't make me be the Oyster Queen."

The morning of the oyster festival, Sarah's father asked her to meet him at Glenn Mounger's garage. "I have a surprise for you," was all he said.

On the way to the garage, Sarah took the babies to Gran and Aunt May. They insisted on keeping the babies all day and overnight. It was time, they said. Sarah couldn't argue with that, and she couldn't dispute the sturdy competence with which the old girls took charge. Ultimately, she surrendered the boys with a feeling of relief and gratitude.

Being a mother encompassed every moment of her life. She was sucked into it, and often forgot to come up for air. Her doctor, concerned about exhaustion, insisted she wean them onto bottles, and they were now eating cereal, too. As she left her grandmother's house, she steeled herself not to look back. They're fine, she told herself.

And they were, of course. There was even a certain symmetry in the twin old ladies looking after the twin boys.

On her own for the first time since the babies' arrival, Sarah felt strange and light, unencumbered. She kept worrying that she'd forgotten something. When she parked at Mounger's garage and got out, she stood beside the Mini for a moment, feeling naked without her usual drape of baby gear and the babies themselves. Then she took a deep breath and went in search of her father.

The auto body and repair garage had been a fixture in Glenmuir for as long as Sarah could remember. It was the kind of place that appealed to guys far more than women, which was probably why her father spent so much time there. The barnlike garage had repair bays for lease, along with a bewildering array of tools and equipment. An old-fashioned Wurlitzer jukebox played surfer music. The long walls were hung with enameled signs for motor oil and radial tires, vintage neon clocks and calendars, and lighted glass cases displaying the prizes Glenn had won in car shows all over the country.

In search of her father, she passed cars in various states of repair, some with their engines dismantled, others with missing body parts or denuded upholstery. At the far end, bathed in sunlight through an open bay door, stood her father, next to the Mustang. Dad's face shone with love and pride. "Surprise," he said.

"You finished your car." Sarah couldn't believe her eyes. The last time she'd seen the Mustang, it had been little more than a corroded exoskeleton and a collection of unconnected parts. "Dad, it's beautiful."

The car gleamed with multiple coats of poppy red paint. Every bit of chrome shone like a mirror and the top was down. Seeing the car, and the expression on her father's face, reminded Sarah of so many moments from her childhood—drives to the city, with her mother looking glamorous in a silk scarf and dark glasses, her dad singing along with the radio and Kyle in the backseat beside her.

"I'm so glad I came back here," she said to her father.

"Wouldn't have it any other way," he replied, holding open the door for her. "Let's go pick up your brother and LaNelle."

Rolling along at the dignified pace of visiting royalty, they drove through the main street of town in the Mustang. With their shoes off to keep from damaging the upholstery, Sarah and LaNelle sat in the backseat of the convertible, waving like homecoming queens as they passed the crowd that came out for the festival. Sarah tilted her head back, feeling a glow of warmth from the Indian summer sun. *See, Mama?* she thought. There's nothing to worry about, not anymore. We're all right.

Although initially organized to generate goodwill between vendor and buyer, the festival had expanded to encompass the whole town. In a pavilion set up by a catering firm, the Moon Bay Oyster Company showcased the oysters of autumn. Guests sampled raw kumamotos with sauces of lemon or horseradish, pan-grilled Tomales Bay oysters and barbecued, baked and broiled Mad River oysters. A local microbrewery supplied a coffee-colored porter beer to go with the creamy oysters and dark, rich bread. A winery from Napa served a dry Muscadet, another perfect pairing with oysters. The Bonner Flower Farm supplied floral arrangements.

There was a picnic in Town Park, races on Children's Beach and a sailing regatta across the bay. The fishing fleet strung twinkling lights through the rigging of every boat, and live bands took turns performing all day and into the night.

The festival was as fun and exhausting as her brother and father had promised. The hours passed in a blur, and the girl Sarah had been, the one who had resented being an oysterman's daughter, who had hidden her chapped hands but not her attitude, slipped away finally and completely, her disappearance unnoticed and unlamented. In her place was a better person, a daughter and sister filled with pride and excitement for her family.

It wasn't a perfect day. Will never showed up. It wasn't as if he were obligated, she told herself. Their relationship—such as it was—had been progressing at a snail's pace and actually, she wasn't even sure it was progressing at all. Someone told her he had been watching Aurora in the regatta, cheering her on as she crossed the finish, but Sarah didn't see him.

It was better this way. Whenever she was near Will Bonner, she felt the tension of unbearable yearning, so strong that it hurt. He made her want to do foolish things, but she was a mother now. With her two boys depending on her, she couldn't afford to make mistakes.

At sunset, the middle of the pavilion was transformed into a dance floor. A new band arrived, and the musicians began tuning up their instruments. Sarah felt inexplicably nervous but at least, she conceded, she'd bought a great outfit for the evening. It was a pale blue chiffon dress, with a halter top clasped behind her neck and a floaty skirt that whirled like flower petals. The matching pumps made her feel like Cinderella.

Back in Chicago, she used to feel trapped in her fine clothes but she realized now it wasn't the clothes at all. The problem had been with her old self, a woman who thought she knew what her life was supposed to be. In a way, losing Jack had been the best thing that could have happened, because if it hadn't, she never would have made a change on her own.

Her father claimed her for the first dance. Despite the dress, she felt clumsy and awkward, but when she looked over at Kyle and LaNelle, who were lost in each other's arms, she realized that style and grace didn't matter. "What's so funny?" her father asked, catching her smiling.

"People don't care what other people look like when they dance," she said.

"And that's funny?"

"What's funny is I never realized it before."

"How's the whiplash?" her father asked.

"What?"

"You know, the whiplash. From looking around and trying to see if Will Bonner has showed up."

"That's crazy, Dad."

"Uh-huh. Try telling that to this guy." Her father turned her in his arms, and there was Will. He looked incredible in faded Levi's and a crisply pressed shirt, his hair still slightly damp from the shower and his face lit with a smile.

"Oh," she said, feeling her cheeks fill up with color.

"Hello to you, too," he said. "Dance with me."

Her father handed her off and faded away, and she found herself whirling amid the dancers with him. "You look beautiful," he murmured in her ear. His hand splayed across her bare back.

She nearly melted; it had been so long since someone had told her she was pretty and held her in his arms. "Thanks," she said. "This is quite a change for me. I was getting used to T-shirts with spit-up on them."

"You clean up real well."

"Why are you so nice?" she asked him.

"You wouldn't ask that if you knew what I was

thinking." He lowered his mouth to her ear and whispered a suggestion that made her blush to the roots of her hair.

Helpless, she leaned her forehead on his shoulder as the music slowed to an old favorite, "Dock of the Bay." There was something both leisurely and erotic about the way he moved against her, and she forgot the whole world as she gave herself up to sensation, closing her eyes and tipping back her head. Their first dance. He leaned down and nuzzled her throat, and it felt exquisite. "You're a good dancer," she said.

"Everyone seems to think so," he agreed with a chuckle in his voice.

The comment brought her back to earth and her eyes flew open. Feeling slightly frantic, she looked around and saw furtive glances darting in her direction. "Let's go get something to drink," she said, pulling away from him.

He kept hold of her hand. "I've got a better idea. Let me take you home."

Oh, God. She thought about the things he'd whispered in her ear. Her heart started pounding. Their last conversation hovered between them, the old dispute still open because there was no way to resolve it. She tried to dredge up as many excuses as she could find. "What about Aurora?"

"She's out watching the fireworks, and then she's having a sleepover at a friend's. And I already know your grandmother's watching your boys overnight."

She took a deep breath. Felt the firmness of his muscular arm beneath her hand. "I'll be right back," she said, and slipped away. As she crossed the pavilion, she grabbed Vivian and pulled her along to the ladies' room. "He wants to take me home," she said, practically hyperventilating. "What am I going to do?"

"Well, you could take two cars, or leave one here and pick it up in the morning—"

"That's not what I'm asking, and you know it." Her eyes burned with tears, and she grabbed a paper towel to blot them away.

"Sweetie, a lot of girls have shed tears over Will Bonner, but never because he wanted to take them home."

"Ah, Viv. You know why I'm scared. I can't just do this as a lark. It matters too much. I failed so miserably with Jack. How can I be sure—"

"You can't," Vivian told her, shoving her toward the door. "No one can, but why on earth would you let that stand in your way?"

They could see the fireworks from her front porch, the starbursts reflected in the still waters of the bay. Muted jazz was playing on the radio, and Will opened a bottle of champagne. He'd come prepared with the bottle in an ice chest—just in case, he'd told her.

In case of fire, she thought, break glass. A comic strip popped into her mind.

They clinked their champagne flutes together.

"So," he said, gently trapping her between himself and the porch railing. "Here we are." Framed by twining roses and the white scroll-work of the porch trim, he looked like something she'd dreamed.

"I'm afraid," she blurted out, thoroughly taken aback by the sensation of his thighs pressing against hers.

"So am I. Finish your champagne."

They emptied their glasses and with the tips of his fingers, he cupped his hands over the flutes, clinking them together as he set them aside. Then he kissed her long and deeply. It was the kiss she had been waiting for and dreading and hoping for ever since that day in the hospital, and it seemed to go on forever. At the end of it she felt drunk, not with the champagne but with emotion. He took her by the hand and they went inside, heading straight for the bedroom.

Do not pass Go, do not collect two hundred dollars, she thought in Shirl's voice.

Shadows and moonlight fell across the floor, creating shifting bluish patterns. The lace curtains whispered against the sill of the open window, and in the distance she could see the last of the fireworks reflected on the surface of the water. Will stopped and kissed her again, and she barely noticed when he unhooked the back of her dress and let it whisper to the floor.

She had carried twins—high birth-weight twins—and had nursed them for almost six months, and her body bore the evidence of that. For a moment, apprehension flared to sheer terror. Yet the way Will looked at her, the things he whispered in her ear and the tender glide of his hands over her breasts and hips made her feel light and beautiful and desirable. She paused, trying to calm the churning apprehension. Unless she stopped this—right here, right now—their relationship was going to change forever, and there would be no undoing it. Was she ready for that? Were they really doing this? Here? Now?

His wordless answer to her wordless questions came in the form of a long, leisurely, open-mouthed kiss. He didn't hurry or push as he laid her down on the lavender-scented bed, and took her with a slow eroticism that bound her up in its spell.

She had forgotten, or perhaps she'd never known, what it was to make love to a man who loved her, who didn't regard sex as a marital duty, who wasn't keeping secrets from her. Need and passion outweighed caution, and she explored his body, hungry to know every inch of it. It was almost embarrassing, how much she wanted him. "You must think I'm a maniac," she whispered.

"I was counting on it."

She rested her cheek on his bare chest, absorbing the gentle rhythm of his heartbeat and soaring with joy and an overwhelming tenderness. And relief. There was that, too. After so much time, she hadn't been certain that she was still this kind of woman. In his arms she felt reborn, as though he'd rekindled an inner flame. Still, old demons haunted her, and she spoke with uncertainty. "It's just… that it's been so long for me, Will. And I've never been all that good at sex."

"Where the hell did you get that idea?" He pressed a finger to her lips. "Never mind. Don't answer that. And don't say that about yourself, ever again. It's not a matter of skill or experience."

"Yes, but—"

He stopped her again, gently tracing his thumb across her lips. "End of discussion. You're good at it. You have no idea how good."

The birds woke Sarah up early. Last night might have been a dream, except that her whole body sang with memories, and there was a sleeping man beside her. She had an urge to wake him up, to breathe in the scent of his skin and run her hands over him but if she did that, they might not ever leave the bed.

Which didn't seem like such a bad idea, when she thought about it. Except that the world awaited—families and complications just outside trying to get in, like moths batting themselves against a window screen, seeking the light. She slipped from the bed and let Franny out. Then, in the quiet early morning, still wearing a soft smile, she made a pot of coffee.

The smell roused Will, and he appeared in the kitchen in nothing but his Levi's, the top button undone. "Let's sleep in," he said, coming up behind her and nuzzling her neck.

She caught her breath, then turned and handed him a mug of coffee. "I need to go get the boys."

He let out a long-suffering sigh and sipped his coffee while looking around the kitchen. He browsed through the guest book with all the notes left behind in the cottage by grateful guests. When Sarah had first moved in, she had resented the cheerful, romantic entries in the book. All those happy couples and families, so delighted with their seaside vacation. Now that she'd been here awhile with the boys, she was more understanding. There was a desperation of denial in some of the entries—" See? We *are too* a happy family" was the unspoken message.

Watching Will, she held her breath, not sure she wanted him to spot the entries she'd added at the end. With her, making smart-alecky drawings was almost a reflex; she'd never been able to resist a blank page. There was a cartoon self-portrait of her holding the twins like the Scales of Justice and the caption "Now we are three." She drew other little milestones—the boys' first smiles, first teeth, first success at crawling and pulling themselves up. And sure enough, Will paused at her rendition of Lulu saying "Getting married is like having your teeth straightened. If you do it right the first time, you won't have to go through it again."

He chuckled, then took his coffee out on the porch, looking as though he belonged here. That was the thing about Will Bonner, she thought, watching him from the doorway. He was so at home in the world, in his life, in his own skin. Yes, he had forfeited much to stay in Glenmuir, but she sensed no resentment in him. He embraced this place, with its small-town quirkiness and old seaside traditions. Instead of brooding about missed chances from the past, he delved into the life of this community, providing a vital service and taking joy from small things. She had felt that from him last night, from his unhurried lovemaking and unabashed delight.

"If you keep staring at me like that," he said to her, "those boys are going to be in kindergarten by the time you pick them up."

She blushed, but the heat of her skin was a pleasure in itself. "I'd better get going," she said, forcing herself to move away from him.

"I'll give you a ride."

"No, thanks. The car seats take too long to switch out. And before we start that, we need to talk about whether or not we're going to start acting like a couple."

"Babe, I think we settled that question last night." He came back inside and put his mug in the sink.

"Then you'd better go home and have a talk with Aurora before she hears it through the grapevine. And no, I won't be there for the talk."

"Chicken."

"Freely admitted." She kissed him one last time. "Now, go."

He groaned, but agreed that he'd better leave. Watching him drive away, she leaned against the front door and sighed with the sort of happiness she hadn't felt in a long, long time. The walking-on-air, grinning-at-nothing happiness that made life a beautiful thing. She pressed her fingertips to her lips and remembered the taste of him, and the way he felt inside her, and soon she was regretting that she'd let him go.

Thirty-Eight

Aurora was putting together her stuff to go stay at her grandparents' house. The routine, repeated every duty cycle throughout the year, was as familiar as brushing her teeth. Duffel bag with four changes of clothes and something to sleep in. School backpack. And lately, dog food and Zooey's inflatable bed. When she was little, Aurora used to cry every time her dad went on duty, because she knew it would be days before she'd see him again. Now, she didn't feel sad at all. Her grandparents were awesome, and from their house, it was walking distance to Edie and Glynnis's houses, and a little farther on was the Parker place.

Okay, walking distance was a bit of a stretch. In reality, it was a giant hike. If she just "happened" to walk past Zane Parker's house, he'd know it was deliberate.

Unless...*brainstorm.* She had the perfect excuse. "I have a dog now, don't I, Zooey? Don't I, boy?"

The dog pranced in response.

"We'll go on a nice, long walk, and we might even need to stop at the Parkers' to...let's see. Yeah! To borrow a book from Ethan." She added the dog's leash to her bag and went to get her cell phone. It was charging in its usual spot on her dad's bureau, in the surge-protector strip she'd given him last Father's Day.

Zooey followed her up the stairs. Ordinarily, Aurora would stop and play with him, but her granddad would be picking her up in a few minutes. "Chill," she muttered to the dog, who grabbed a stray sock and shook it wildly. The top of the bureau was his repository for phones, keys, stuff from his pockets, a book of matches, little clippings and business cards and his Rolodex. A business card for somebody with the arson squad. She paused when she came to this, picked it up, put it down again. The top drawer was partially open. She inched it open, recoiling when she came across a box of condoms.

With a shudder, she shoved the drawer shut, muttering, "That ought to teach me to snoop."

Zooey whined, then stretched into a playful bow. He trotted off and returned a few seconds later with a tennis ball, and dropped it eagerly at Aurora's feet. Grateful for the distraction, she bounced the ball high, laughing when the dog popped up and snatched it in midair. She had him jumping practically to the ceiling. He never missed, until she made a bad throw. The ball went under the bed and Zooey dived after it. The ball must have gotten caught or wedged somewhere, because she could hear him scrabbling around and whining. Soon it became clear he was having no success, so Aurora had to belly crawl halfway under the bed, feeling around among the dust bunnies. The dust made her sneeze, and the sneeze made her bump her head. Then her hand hit something hard and hollow. A box?

She dragged it out from under the bed, which freed the ball for Zooey to pounce on. She was about to slide the box back under the bed when something made her hesitate. It was a fireproof safe, locked with one of those four-digit codes. Put it back, she told herself. It's a bad idea to snoop. Put it back.

But she didn't. She fiddled with the rollers a few times. Her dad used the same four-digit PIN code for everything: 9344, which spelled "WILL" on a telephone keypad. She gave it a try, and felt a guilty start when the box opened.

The dog was skittering around, trying to get her to play, but she waved him away. The box contained papers and documents, which didn't look too interesting. At first. Then something caught her attention—a receipt from the Gilded Lily Jewelers. She stared at the item description: "1 ct. diamond solitaire 18k gold."

Her hand shook and she let the paper drift to the floor. She glared down at the receipt. Ever since the Oyster Festival, her dad had been dating Sarah Moon. Really dating, like with dinners out and long, whispered phone calls. If this receipt meant what Aurora thought it meant, she'd end up with a stepmom. That meant the death of all hope that Aurora's real mother would ever return. Not that she'd admit it to anyone, but after such a long time, she still dreamed of that. Now with Sarah in the picture, Aurora wouldn't even have the dream.

She rifled around some more and what she saw shocked her even worse. Money order receipts, all made out to her mother. The dates proved they'd been sent regularly for the past five years. Why had he kept sending money after her mother took off? Was he paying her to stay away?

Aurora dug deeper through the papers, some of them yellowing with age. There was a file containing forms and documents related to her mother's immigration and naturalization hearing. There was an old statement her dad had given, describing the circumstances under which he found Marisol Molina and her daughter.

She read it, riveted. Here was the real story, at last. The mystery unveiled. The truth. She started to tremble deep inside, and then the trembling radiated outward, causing her hands to shake and her chin to quiver. She felt kind of sick, too, because it was nothing like she had imagined her past to be. She never knew about the squalor, the cruelty, the fact that her father had rescued Mama and her from a nightmare. As Aurora read the words, tiny flashes went off in her mind. She didn't know if they were memories or her imagination, filling in the blanks. Fire and yelling, running feet, screams. A flight of stairs leading up and up, a hallway filled with smoke that made her gag and stung her eyes.

As she knelt on the floor in the bedroom, her eyes smarted with new tears. She never knew her mother had worked in a house of prostitution or that Aurora had played in a muddy yard soiled with goat dung, or that her mother had been the victim of frequent beatings. It was all there, starkly reported in an official report to the U.S. Citizen and Immigrations Services.

Her dad had let her believe he'd brought her and her mother into his life because he loved them. Now Aurora realized he'd merely rescued them like he would anyone else, like he would a stray cat.

In the company journal, Will made his customary entry—the date and time along with, "Capt Bonner relieves Capt McCabe on house watch dept., personal quarters in good order." He leaned back in the desk chair, a stupid grin on his face. He and Sarah were together, finally. He felt as though he'd won the lottery. No, more than that. He'd won the kind of future he hadn't let himself imagine—until now. He was done with waiting. Sure, she had a lot on her plate. Yet he saw no point in holding back. He loved her. He was only going to love her more as time went on. Waiting served no purpose other than to drive him nuts.

He'd even bought a ring. Was he jumping the gun? Probably. Did he give a shit about timing? Not anymore. He grabbed his wallet and took his patrol vehicle to the grocery store to pick up a few things for the next shift. He still had the stupid grin on his face as he swung through town. There had been a time when he'd thought Glenmuir would kill him, this tiny seaside hamlet where nothing ever happened. Now he knew this was where everything happened, where his future lay.

His daydream about Sarah was shattered when his radio sounded. The quick-call had gone off back at the station—a fire at the Moon Bay Oyster Company. "Structure fire, barn or outbuilding, *fully involved.*" The Moons' place.

"I'm almost there," he said, speeding past the grocery store. He was several minutes ahead of the engine and crew. A jolt of urgency tightened his gut. He was close by and hoped like hell the building had been empty.

He was the first to arrive and backed the patrol vehicle into place near a hydrant. Grabbing his radio, he raced to assess the situation. The building was isolated and no human life appeared to be involved. The bad news was, the building was an inferno, and the location was precarious, at the base of an upward-sloping ridge covered with dry grass and resinous pine trees parched by a recent drought.

Kyle Moon was there by himself. He filled Will in while Will pulled a hose line off the back of the truck. "…used to be housing for seasonal workers," he shouted over the noise of the fire. "Now it's used to store all kinds of things. We had some workmen here this week. They left a stack of pallets by the building. I know it's a code violation—"

No shit, thought Will. "Any solvents? Paint? Marine resins, varnishes, substances under pressure?"

A series of explosions blasted inside. "All of the above," Kyle said. "And…there's a propane tank. It's old, though. I can't remember the last time we had it filled."

A propane tank. *Great.* Will got down to business, planning the attack, although the engine crew was still several minutes out. Even from a distance, the heat nearly boiled his eyeballs.

There were more explosive bursts. Another flare-up briefly illuminated the area like a lingering flash of lightning, picking out ominous details. A stack of wooden pallets, burning brightly, lay nearby. There, surrounded on three sides by flame, was the hundred-gallon propane tank. He could hear the ominous whistle of a venting sound coming from the tank. "Fuck me," he whispered.

The season had been dry and tonight the wind was howling steadily. The adjacent ridge could go up, each pine tree flaring like a resin torch. It would be the Mount Vision Fire all over again—except that now the area was even more populated.

"I need to get a hose to that tank," he told Kyle. "It'll barely reach. You need to get the hell away from here—twenty-five hundred feet away, minimum." The risk of a BLEVE—boiling liquid expanding vapor explosion—was getting higher by the minute. If the tank blew, it would be like a bomb, spreading fire in every direction.

Kyle balked. "I can stay and help."

"The hell you can," Will barked. "Go."

Kyle must have heard something in his voice. He jogged

down the road, following orders. In the absence of the crew, Will radioed the battalion chief that he was going to put an unmanned nozzle on the propane tank to prevent a BLEVE. He prayed he'd have enough pressure to make the stream reach. A fount of water erupted from the nozzle…and a moment later, the hose went limp in his hands.

"Son of a bitch," he said. He grabbed his radio to check on the crew, but the tac channel appeared to be jammed. He keyed up several times, never getting a response. Damn.

He tried the hose again and felt a telltale surge of pressure. Yes. He leaned forward with the hose tucked under him, hauling it closer to the tank. Smoke and flame and flying debris all but blinded him. For a few seconds, he couldn't do anything but mutter his now-favorite word between coughs: "Fuck, fuck, fuck."

In between spasms of coughing, he expected to be hit by flying objects at any moment. All around, he heard the sucking *whoosh* of resin igniting. He felt more pressure coming through the hose. "Come on, come on," he urged it. He was rewarded with a small but well-aimed burst, scoring a direct hit on the flames licking at the propane tank. Then he had to close down the bale and wait for the pressure to build back up. The whistling sound intensified, screaming along his nerves. He had only seconds to plant the monitor nozzle.

He was racing for safety, putting a few hundred yards between himself and the tank, when an ominous vibration thrummed and pulsed around him. A second later, a sound like nothing he'd ever heard before crashed over him. Every bit of heat and light and air was sucked away, and then the dragon roared.

* * *

Aurora sent her friend Edie a text message: What R U doing 2nite?

Edie texted back: Busy. Sorry.

Then Aurora texted her other best friend, Glynnis, but got no reply. That was a little strange, because Glynnis lived for text messages. And really, Aurora wasn't heart-broken that her two friends were busy. She was just stalling for time as she tried to work up the nerve to do what she really wanted to do—run into Zane Parker.

She took a deep breath, then went and got the dog's leash. "I'm taking the dog for a walk," she called to her grandmother.

"Take a flashlight," her grandmother called, "and your phone."

"You bet." She stuck her head in the family room, where her grandmother was sitting, reading a book. With her legs tucked under her and her long hair falling over her face, Granny Shannon looked more like a girl than a grand-mother. Aurora wondered how much Granny knew about the situation in Mexico. Probably everything. Aunt Birdie, too, since she had worked on the case. Aurora wondered if they felt guilty for keeping her in the dark, or if they thought they were protecting her from something.

Granny looked up from her book. "Everything all right?"

"Sure." Aurora could lie just like everybody else around here. "I'll be back in a while." She felt like such a misfit in her family. In her whole life, come to think about it. She was a bad fit at school, too. Not belonging was the worst feeling in the world.

As she walked up the front walk to the Parkers' house, she rehearsed what she'd say. "Hey, Ethan. I forgot my geometry book. Do you mind if I borrow yours? And while you're at it, would you mind if I borrowed your brother?"

"Only if you promise to give him back when you're through with him," called a voice from the shadows beside the house.

Zooey gave a woof of greeting, straining at the leash. Aurora was speechless with humiliation. Good Lord, could this day get any worse?

Ethan Parker approached her, skateboard tucked under his arm. "You are so busted," he said, with laughter in his voice.

"Shut up." Her face was on fire. "So what if I think he's cute?"

"So you're wasting your time. And trust me, he's not that great."

"Of course you wouldn't think so." She sniffed and plunked herself down on the porch steps. "You're a guy."

"And I'm pretty great, not that you asked."

One thing about Ethan. Whenever she was down, he had a way of making her smile. Just a little. Sometimes.

"So is he here?" she asked.

"Nope. Said he had something to do. So you're stuck with me."

Zane was sixteen and drove his old Duster around everywhere. Aurora imagined driving around with him, on a date. Her dad said she wasn't allowed to date yet, and she was totally forbidden to drive in a car with a guy. Now, in light of what she'd found out about her mother, she wondered if that was the reason her dad was so cautious. Did he think she was going to turn out like her mother?

"Hey, Ethan?" she said. "What if you found something out that you're not supposed to know? What would you do with the information?"

"Put it on Facebook."

"Seriously."

"Seriously, I'd probably quit with the cloak-and-dagger stuff, and tell someone. Simple."

"Simple for you, maybe," she muttered. The urge to confess to him was strong, but he wasn't the one who could help her make sense of this. Only her dad could do that, so she dropped the subject. She and Ethan sat together on the porch steps, throwing a ball for the dog. One thing about Ethan, she didn't have to be any particular way with him. She just had to be, period.

After a while, Zane came home, driving his old Duster with the stereo turned up loud. The headlights swung across the yard and then went dark. "Hey," he said, getting out.

"Hey, Zane." Aurora could feel all the thoughts draining out of her brain. Yeah, he was so cute he gave her brain damage.

Zooey danced and skittered around him, inviting him to play. "Cute dog," he said.

"That's Zooey," she said. "I raised him from a pup."

Zane looked at his brother. "Mom and Dad home?"

"Nope."

Their parents owned a restaurant in Point Reyes Station, and most nights, they both worked.

"Cool." Zane took out a pack of cigarettes and, cool as anything, lit one up. "Want one?" he asked Aurora.

"Of course she doesn't want one, moron," Ethan groused at his brother.

Aurora shot him a grateful look.

"Jeez, I can't believe you're smoking," Ethan continued. "That's so lame."

Zane shrugged. "I'll quit one of these days." He took a

plastic lighter out of his pocket and flicked it off and on, off and on.

A car swung over to the curb in front of the Parkers' house. To Aurora's surprise, it was her grandparents' car. The window slid down and her Granny said, "Get in the car, Aurora."

"But—" Dangit. Zane had just arrived, and he was actually talking to her for once.

"Now, Aurora. There's been a fire."

"Earth to Sarah," Judy said, waving her hand in front of Sarah's face. "Your move."

The two of them were spending the evening at Sarah's house, playing Scrabble. Judy had just scored big with JUNKIE. Sarah had been staring at her letter tiles, her mind a million miles away. For the past hour, sirens had sounded in the distance, and hearing them always made her jumpy.

"Sorry," she said, frowning.

Judy sat back in her chair. "For someone who just got her sex life back, you're looking a little glum."

"It's complicated." She hooked RISK onto Judy's word.

Judy laughed. "Complicated is better than boring. See, my sex life is uncomplicated. Once-a-week-Wayne, that's what I call him. He shows up, spends the night, then hits the road again. To be honest, it's a little boring." Her boyfriend, Wayne, was a security systems salesman who spent most of his time on the road. She helped herself to one of the brownies Viv had brought over earlier. "These brownies are better than my sex life."

Sarah grabbed one off the plate. "Viv's brownies are better than everyone's sex life." Since high school, Vivian had turned herself into a world-class cook.

When a fresh set of sirens sounded, though, Sarah instantly lost her appetite. "I don't think I'll ever get used to that," she confessed.

Judy tallied up the score, then looked down at her hands. As always, there were tiny burns on her fingers, from her metal sculpture work. "Did I ever tell you about the time I caught my studio on fire? Will Bonner was fit to be tied, because I'd left some packing foam too close to my work area. He was in training back then, working long hours—"

"What was his wife like?" Sarah asked, blurting out the question. "I mean, he's told me about her, but what did you think of her?"

Judy finished her brownie. "I didn't really know Marisol, except to say hi. She worked for Mrs. Dundee as a housekeeper."

"Will took it hard when she left," Sarah said. "See, that's what's so crazy about us, about Will and me getting involved. We've both been so burned by our marriages."

"And you're both a lot smarter now. Quit being afraid of screwing up."

She stared at the Scrabble board, trying to see layers of meaning in the words there. Risk, junkie, rhyme, mayhem, all hooked together.

The phone rang, startling them both. Sarah got up to answer, seeing Kyle's number on the caller ID. It was her sister-in-law, LaNelle. "You'd better come," she said in a tight voice. "A storage shed at the oyster farm caught fire."

"Is anyone hurt?"

There was a hesitation. Just a beat, as brief as a single indrawn breath. "I haven't heard. There were some explosions."

"I'm on my way." Sarah's knees wobbled as she swung around to Judy. "Can you stay with the boys?"

* * *

The stars were beautiful, spinning gently overhead as though Will was lost at sea, lying faceup on the deck of a moving ship. It was said you could navigate by the stars, using their arrangement as a map into the unknown. In ancient times, mapmakers designated the places they didn't know with the ominous warning "Here Be Dragons."

A long time had passed since he'd gone where the dragons dwelled, into the vast unknown of dangerous wonders. Fire held no peril for him because he understood it so completely. For him, true risk was a matter of the heart. He had grown accustomed to the safety of the known world populated by friends and family. Now, he reflected as he studied the glimmering stars, a dangerous wonder had come into his life—Sarah Moon. For a long time he'd held off, keeping himself from discovering what life with her could be, forbidding himself to want it. All in vain. He wanted to be with her like he wanted the next breath of air. But damn. He could plunge into a burning building without hesitation. Yet with Sarah, he'd made himself wait, and for what? Because Aurora had a problem with him dating? Was he supposed to wait until his daughter grew up and left home? No way. Putting things off was not an option when you had a job like this.

He wasn't sure how long he lay in darkness, sounds muffled by a deafness he prayed was temporary. The wind had been knocked out of him, and maybe he lost consciousness or was dreaming or something. His chest was on fire, but he was alive. All his limbs seemed to work, nothing broken. Maybe a couple of ribs. He didn't sense that he was burned.

Gloria, he thought. The crew. Why hadn't anyone found

him? He struggled to get up, willed his arms to work. He managed to brace his hands behind him, pushing himself to a sitting position.

At some point, he saw the swing of a Q-beam through the woods. Good, they were searching. Pike poles reached through the night, plucking engulfed branches down to earth. Burning things showered from the sky—embers, pieces of the building and its contents, bits of the surrounding trees and bushes. Water, too. Not rain, but spray from hoses putting out hot spots.

He staggered up, feeling a host of bruises. He felt a stab of pain as his lungs, emptied out by the fall, reinflated. The explosion had thrown him far from his original location. Putting one foot in front of the other, he started walking, lifting his legs high over vegetation and debris. Burning pieces landed all around him, but he ignored them and walked doggedly on.

He'd gone maybe twenty paces before stepping back into himself, into the Will Bonner he knew. "Ah, God," he said, "my crew." Then he ran, his lungs feeling torn but working hard.

The engine crew had the blaze under control. Through a haze of smoke, he spotted Gloria. He tried to call out, but his voice was gone.

Aurora leaped out of her grandparents' car and raced toward the ambulance parked on the gravel road. She barely remembered the ride to Moon Bay. She'd left her dog with Ethan, who said he'd keep Zooey for as long as she needed. Dad was okay, he'd called while they were driving to the fire. Even though he'd assured everyone he only had scratches and bruises, Aurora was terrified that he'd hurt something in the fire that couldn't be fixed.

She spotted him leaning on the tailgate of the boxy ambulance. He was smudged with charcoal black everywhere. He held an oxygen mask over his nose and mouth. But his eyes, surrounded by goggle-shaped pale skin, were smiling.

Sarah was already there, Aurora saw, clinging to him as though she'd saved him herself. Aurora didn't like it that Sarah had arrived already.

This was the Moon family's place, Aurora reminded herself. Sarah didn't seem too concerned about the property, though. She was all over Dad.

Aurora called his name. At least Sarah had the decency to back off.

Aurora couldn't help herself. She flung her arms around him, knowing she was getting covered in soot. He winced and she jumped back. "You're hurt!"

"I might've bruised some ribs," he said, and hugged her gingerly.

Although he smelled of heat and smoke, he felt so strong and good she nearly cried, which was stupid, because he was obviously all right. He said her name in her ear, he said "Aurora-Dora" the way he always had, and she breathed hard and fast to keep in the tears.

"You're all dirty," she said. "You've got cuts all over."

"Once I get cleaned up, I'll be good as new," he assured her.

This time, she thought. What about next time? Did he know, did anyone comprehend what it was like to have only one parent, and to know that one parent could be blown away every time he went to work? Did he even care how that made her feel?

It was then that Aurora realized how completely ticked off she was about this whole situation. And now that she knew he was fine, she was dying to talk to him about the box of secrets under the bed. And the ring. Geez. Had he already given it to her? She glanced at Sarah's hand. No ring, phew.

"Listen, I need to go take care of some things," Dad was saying. "You wait here with Sarah, all right?"

No, it wasn't all right, but Aurora knew it would make her seem like a baby if she put up a fuss. She nodded and let go of him. She hadn't realized she was still holding his hand as hard as she could.

Dad had to go dictate his incident report into a digital tape recorder. Aurora stood behind the yellow-and-black Caution tape and watched a plume of smoke climb into the sky, blue-gray against the black. It was beautiful, in a weird way, and she couldn't take her eyes off it. Her fascination shifted to memory, or maybe something she thought was a memory. Staccato shouts in Spanish. Swearing and praying. Heat and smoke. A furtive figure in a red dress, darting in the opposite direction and moving too fast for Aurora to follow.

Mama.

"Hey, girlie." Gloria handed her a bottle of water. "Thirsty?"

Startled, Aurora took the water and thanked her. "Are you all right, too?"

"Yep, no thanks to whoever started this fire. Gotta go." Gloria touched her shoulder and headed over to the cluster of guys in their turnout gear. The fire had consumed a storage building, and the process of extinguishing it had left a wreckage of broken jars, an old-fashioned white produce scale, moldering rope and cultivation tubes. On the ground was a blackened enameled sign which had hung above the doorway: Moon Bay Oyster Company. Est. 1924.

She moved it with her foot. Underneath lay a half-melted piece of yellow plastic. She jabbed at it with her toe, then bent and picked it up.

A chill rippled through her as awareness teased at her mind. This felt like her memories of Mexico, something she knew but didn't know, a place her mind didn't want to go. What had Ethan said earlier? Something about ending the cloak-and-dagger stuff and just being honest. What a concept. "The truth will set you free" was something people liked to say, but that was garbage. The truth could get her so deep in trouble there would be no way out. And look at her dad, hiding so much from her. He obviously believed telling the truth was a bad idea sometimes.

"I'm so relieved your father's all right," Sarah said, coming to stand beside her. She wore rubber rain boots and a pink woven shawl over jeans and a hoodie. Wrapped up against the autumn chill, she looked pale and scared, even though the danger was over. Well, of course she was scared. She'd been planning a future with a guy who almost died tonight.

Aurora stuffed the yellow plastic bracelet away and didn't let herself respond, even though she wanted to confess how much she worried about her dad every single time he went to the station. She worked hard to keep from being cozy with Sarah. That sucked. She couldn't let herself fraternize with the enemy. And that was what Sarah was now—the enemy. Aurora kept her yearning closed tight in her fist.

Sarah stared at the smoldering wreckage. "I wish they could figure out who did this. It has to stop. These fires. So far, no one's been hurt, but that's just luck. And we can't count on luck."

To change the subject, Aurora asked, "Where are your babies?"

"I left them with my friend Judy. I hope they're sound asleep." She watched a crew of volunteers raking through the remains of the structure. "My grandfather built that shed," she said. "When Kyle and I were little, we used to play around it. Sometimes he'd put a raw oyster on a stick and chase me around with it. Brothers can be a pain."

Was she putting a special emphasis on the word *brothers?* Aurora wondered. Like, maybe Aurora would wind up with the twins as her stepbrothers? She refused to contemplate that.

"I guess your brother must be pretty bummed," Aurora remarked.

"Kyle needed more space for parking, anyway."

Thunder growled in the hills over the bay, like a wake-up call she had known was coming. Fat droplets of rain came down, a few at a time, but promising to thicken.

The thump of a slamming car door startled Aurora. She was back at home because he'd cut his duty cycle short, but had kept her waiting while he finished up his reports.

That was Dad. He was all about responsibility and duty, even after he'd narrowly escaped an explosion. Yeah, that was him all right. It was his duty to take responsibility for Aurora. He'd never been her dad because he loved her, because he wanted her, but because he had a freaking *duty.*

Years ago, she used to rush out to greet him, even if it was raining, like today, because she couldn't stand waiting another minute. Today she was still so mad at him she couldn't see straight. The minute he saw her, he'd guess that she was upset, and he'd ask what was the matter. Fine. She'd tell him today. Right now.

She marched upstairs and grabbed the papers and receipts she'd found. The rain that had started after the fire drummed relentlessly on the roof, and the wind rattled the windowpanes.

Defiantly, she clutched the receipts she'd found and marched downstairs.

"Hey, Aurora-Dora," her father said, oblivious to her mood. He had some scratches on his face and the outline of a bruise around one eye. He looked as if he'd been in a fight—and lost. But he was grinning as if he hadn't been blasted to kingdom come. Was that what made her so mad, that she'd almost lost him?

"Hey." Her tone of voice got his attention.

"What's the matter?"

She set the receipts on a table. "For one thing, you've been paying my mother to stay away."

He didn't act surprised or even sorry he'd been hiding this from her. Or mad that she'd snooped in his hidden box. "I sent her money when she said she needed it. Staying away was her choice."

"She's my mother." The word came out twisted by pain. "You knew I missed her every single day of my life. You told me she never called or got in touch."

"I didn't want you to keep hoping she'd come back. I didn't want you to be disappointed."

Aurora wanted to scream with frustration. Instead, she went to her room and started methodically stuffing things into her backpack. Her father stood in the doorway. "I'm sorry," he said.

"Sure." Inches from tears, she threw in a couple of schoolbooks, zipped her backpack and put on her raincoat. Rudely, she shoved past him.

Her dad followed. "Aurora, let's talk about this."

The cold rain slapped her in the face as she whipped around toward him. "There's nothing to talk about. You lied about my mother. You lied about *everything*. Why didn't you ever tell me the truth about Mexico?"

Now he looked pale, as though he really *had* been in a fight.

"I read your statement," she reminded him. "I'm not stupid."

"I just didn't see how it would do you any good to know how rough things were in Tijuana," he said, his voice raw with regret.

"It didn't do me any good for you to *hide* the truth." Thunder punctuated her words, loud as a stranger, pounding at the door. "I have to go to the library," she said, heading out into the pouring rain. It was miserably cold, but she barely felt it.

Her dad followed her out. He didn't flinch as the rain flayed at him. "Ah, honey, come back inside and let's talk about this."

She stopped at the end of the driveway and turned. "Why? You never wanted to talk about it before."

Without a raincoat, he was getting soaked to the skin, his shirt sticking to him, but he didn't move toward the house. "If I could, I'd rewrite your whole life for you, but I can't. All I can do is give you the best life I can right now."

"What, by hooking up with Sarah Moon? I know you're in love with Sarah," she yelled, the rain dripping off her nose and cheeks.

"I can't help it," he replied, holding out his arms, palms up, as if to catch the raindrops. "And I won't stop."

She turned to walk away, but he called out, "Listen, Aurora. I love Sarah—and I love her boys, too. But you…you're my heart. My life changed when you came into it. You made me into a father."

She turned back. "Bull. You rescued me because you had no choice."

He didn't deny it, but insisted, "We're a team, you and I. And if you think that's going to change just because I met someone, you're wrong."

"Everything has already changed." She backed farther away from him.

"How is that a bad thing?"

"Everything was fine before." She knew, though, that it wasn't. Her dad was always okay, but not *fine,* and now he seemed determined to do something about it. And there was nothing Aurora could do to change his mind. She wasn't important enough.

"There's something I need to tell you." He cleared his throat, looked her in the eye. "I'm going to ask Sarah to marry me."

She tossed her head, flinging raindrops from the hood of her jacket. "I know. I saw the receipt for the ring."

"I was going to tell you, but you beat me to the punch by snooping around." He had an expression on his face she'd never seen before. A glow. "Anyway, I hope like hell she says yes, and I hope like hell you'll be happy for us."

"Happy. Let's see. To have a pair of twin babies move into my house. A woman who's not my mom married to my dad. All this is supposed to make me happy?"

"Sarah loves you, Aurora. You know she does. And you can love her and the boys, if you let yourself. It's not possible to have too many people in your life to love."

Aurora couldn't believe what she was hearing. Then she couldn't believe what she was thinking. What if Dad had died in that fire? She could wind up with Sarah and the two kids until she was eighteen. "Maybe I'm not like you, Dad. I can't just start calling a group of strangers my family. I don't work that way."

"News flash, Aurora," he said, showing his temper. "The world doesn't revolve around you."

"You're right. It revolves around you and Sarah and those babies." Suddenly, Aurora felt sick. Her dad deserved Sarah, who was kind and good, who came from a nice family. Her dad and Sarah belonged together, two good people making a life together, not one rescuing the other. That was probably why it had never worked for Aurora's real mom. She and Dad had never been equals, and Mama's running away was proof of that.

"Where the hell are you going?" Dad yelled.

"I'll be at the library, doing homework," she said, shouldering her backpack and adjusting her hood.

There was a pause. Aurora knew he was trying to decide whether or not to make her stay and get yelled at some more. "We've got dinner at Granny's tonight, and we need to pick up the dog at your friend's house," he said.

"I know. I'll go straight to Granny's afterward." Under her breath, she added, "As if you'd care." Walking down the road, she fingered the wadded-up receipt in her raincoat pocket. She'd held on to it, because the receipt told her another thing her dad had kept a secret—her mother's physical address.

Thirty-Nine

After he took a shower and dried off, Will phoned his parents to warn them that Aurora was likely to be in a temper when she arrived. He got their voice mail and told his mother to call him.

He dressed in jeans and a flannel shirt, and did some things around the house, the fight with Aurora stinging far worse than the myriad nicks and cuts from the fire. When Aurora was little, she used to be so sunny and uncomplicated. Each time he had to head off to work, she had a little ritual. She'd hold his face between her tiny hands and say, "Bye, Daddy. I'll see you again when you come back around."

Hearing her call him Daddy—something she had taken to all on her own—filled him with a fierce, protective pride so strong that it drove away every regret he might have had about chances missed and paths not taken.

Today, she hadn't even bothered with goodbye.

"Knock, knock." Sarah stood in the doorway, smiling at him. Without waiting for an invitation, she let herself in. "Do you have time for a little company?"

The light seemed to change and the wind to shift whenever she was near. He looked at her and saw magic; she was all bright flares and mysterious shadows. "Sure," he said, taking her in his arms. She felt and smelled like heaven, and even though he was still troubled by Aurora, a deep contentment settled in his heart as he held her close. Whatever was going on with Aurora was something to be sorted out, and maybe Sarah would even help him with that. The concept of having help raising a child was a new one on Will. Thank God, he thought, remembering the sensation of being hurled through the night by the explosion. Thank God he'd survived. He needed this, needed Sarah, needed to love her. This was what love was supposed to be—calm, not chaotic.

With Marisol, everything had been chaotic. And one of the things he found most unsettling about Aurora was that sometimes, she reminded him sharply of her mother. Today as she'd hurled her angry accusations at him, what he saw in her eyes frightened him—dark flickers of Marisol.

"I'm so glad you're all right," Sarah whispered against his chest.

"Don't ever worry about me. I'm a professional."

"Yeah, tell that to the propane tank."

"I'm fine, Sarah. I swear I am." He tightened his hold on her and they swayed a little, in a rhythmless dance of intimacy. His throat felt thick and his eyes burned. Damn, he thought. Damn. Loving her was moving him to tears. That was a first, for sure.

"What?" she whispered, and he realized she must have felt him shudder.

"I love you, that's what." His kiss was long and filled with things for which there were no words. That sense of peace settled over him, and, lifting his head, he wondered if she felt it, too. The soft expression in her eyes indicated that she did. "Sarah—"

"Notice anything different about me?" she asked, pulling away from him and turning slowly, hands out.

All right, so she still wasn't ready. "This is a trick question," he said. "So many ways for a guy to screw up the answer. I need a hint. Does it have to do with a new outfit or a haircut or losing weight?"

"Are you saying I'm fat?"

"Aha. It *is* a trick question."

"What I thought you'd notice is that I'm by myself. The boys are with my grandmother and Aunt May again."

"If I didn't have to go to my folks' for dinner, I'd be a lot happier about that," he admitted. He was on fire for her, all the time, and didn't get nearly enough of her alone.

"I just wanted to see you." She smiled at the expression on his face. "Don't look at me like that. Remember, before I started sleeping with you, we were the best of friends."

"And then we had to go and ruin it." He kissed her, though he forced himself to go no further.

"I saw Aurora after the fire," Sarah said. "I thought maybe she wanted to talk, but she didn't have much to say. She's pretty angry about us, Will."

He didn't disagree or try to deny it. "I doubt she's as mad at you as she is at me," he said. Then, taking a deep breath, he told her about Aurora discovering that he'd been sending money to Marisol.

"I thought spousal maintenance was fairly standard," Sarah said.

"It's not official or even mandatory. I just do it because…hell, I don't know."

"Because it's what you do. You rescue people. Bail them out."

"She gave me Aurora. And I know there's no price on that, but Marisol… She still needs me." The words sounded hollow, spoken aloud. "That's not true. She never needed me. She needs what I have to offer. There's a difference."

Sarah looked at him for a long time. "I wish I could understand about her, Will."

"I've told you. I—"

"No, really tell me. Everything."

He started to evade the issue again, but then he nodded, feeling a curious sort of relief in his chest. He loved Sarah. He trusted her. She already knew about the journey to Mexico, the hasty marriage, the dramatic change in his life plans. She even knew that he fell crazy in love with Marisol and stayed that way like a fool for far too long. What he hadn't told her was how it had all unraveled.

"I guess Marisol was never happy, not with this town and not with me," he said. He had taken charge of securing Marisol's green card and initiated the process of applying for U.S. citizenship. In the meantime, he was working every crappy minimum-wage job he could find, training as a firefighter and waiting for a position to open up.

Marisol grew restless within the insular confines of Glenmuir. Inadvertently, Will himself set in motion the demise of their marriage. Thinking it would cheer her up, he left Aurora in the care of his parents and drove Marisol to Las Vegas for a vacation. She had been enchanted, like a fairy-tale princess who finally found her kingdom. The lights, the noise, the smoky casinos and even the glamorous call girls in the hotels all captivated her. After that trip, Will heard nothing but Vegas, Vegas, Vegas. Ultimately for Marisol, the lure proved a stronger force than her ties to Glenmuir. Will's steadfast devotion could not hold her. Nor could the quiet need of her small daughter.

"Actually," he explained to Sarah, "Birdie was still in law school when I realized things weren't good between Marisol and me. But my sister was already thinking like a lawyer. She was the one who came up with the suggestion that I should legally adopt Aurora. If not for that, I might not have custody of her now."

Looking back on events, he had to admire his sister's foresight—and her cynicism. It was as if Birdie had seen something he couldn't. If he'd had a little of his sister's caution and attention to detail, he might've sensed something—a warning, a premonition—to indicate trouble brewing. He'd been blind, though, maybe willfully so. He wanted to believe he was making the American dream come true for two who needed it most, and he'd stubbornly clung to that notion for far too long.

"When Aurora and Marisol became U.S. citizens, my folks threw a big party to celebrate." He shook his head, steepled his fingers. His chest hurt; he wasn't used to baring his soul about a painful episode. "Even then, I kept thinking everything would work out. Then a few days later, with her documents stashed in her pocketbook, Marisol took off." She'd absconded with as much cash as she could find in the house, as well as what she could get the ATM to cough up before I closed the account.

"By herself?" Sarah asked, looking mystified. "She didn't try taking Aurora with her?"

He shook his head. He probably should have guessed at her impending defection for months beforehand. She'd even taken a couple of trial runs, although he hadn't seen them as such at the time. Every once in a while, he'd discover that she'd left Aurora by herself, never seeing her actions as a warning of things to come.

"I had to drive over to Petaluma on some errands," she'd

explain, usually in simple Spanish, which he understood perfectly well. "Aurora is happier staying home for a couple of hours."

"She's too little to be left alone." Will had struggled to keep his temper.

"In a town like this, nothing ever happens, good or bad, so where is the harm?" Marisol had been willfully clueless.

"Everywhere," he'd told her, hot with irritation. "In a box of matches you left out on the patio, or a jug of antifreeze in the garage. Or what about her bike? If you're not here to supervise, she might take it into her head to go riding without a helmet, and she could crash or get lost."

Marisol was genuinely baffled. For someone raised the way she had been, leaving a child alone to fend for herself was common practice.

Even after incidents like that, he'd refused to see her desperation for what it was. When he woke up and found her crying at night, he thought she was simply tired from work. Sometimes he saw her staring out at the horizon with a look of yearning so stark in her eyes that it haunted him. Sometimes, it reminded him of the life he'd given up in order to be a family man. The difference between them was, Marisol followed her yearning while Will fought his.

He had just made captain—the youngest in county history—the day he finally had to face facts. He looked at Sarah, grateful for the compassion he saw in her face. "I came off duty one day and found Aurora home alone. It wasn't the first time. But I told myself it was the last, even if I had to walk away from work and look after her myself. That day, she didn't come back. I was going to mobilize a search, and then the phone rang. Marisol was at a rest stop on I-15. She said she was going to live and work in Las Vegas. She wouldn't be coming back. Ever."

"Oh, Will." Sarah's eyes shone with tears. "I'm sorry."

Marisol told him she knew this was unforgivable, but she also knew if she stayed in Glenmuir, she would suffocate. She would be like Mrs. Dundee's pet pigeons with their clipped wings, miserable and caged.

"What about Aurora?" Will had demanded, feeling the hurt but not the anger, not yet.

"She is your daughter now," Marisol said. It was true. Thanks to Birdie, he had adopted the child and was her legal parent.

There was a date on the divorce decree that had come through—along with the electric bill—in final form months later, but Will paid no attention to it. He knew the marriage had broken apart long before that.

He told Sarah how hard it was to explain to Aurora that her mother was away, that she planned to stay away, maybe forever. He could still see the look on his daughter's face—wide-eyed and hurt, a look of abandonment.

"She never came back?" Sarah asked softly.

"Not once. She'd call at Christmas and sometimes on Aurora's birthday, but that was it. Eventually, those calls stopped, too, and I only heard from her when she was broke."

There was a long silence, filled with the cries of seabirds.

"You deserved better," Sarah said.

"Who the hell knows what I deserve? I ended up with Aurora, which is like winning the lottery."

"Oh, Will. I love you so much—"

A pickup truck swung into the driveway. Gloria jumped out and ran up to the house. "Sorry to interrupt, but I just got a real interesting call. There's been an anonymous tip about the arson."

Will could tell from the expression on Gloria's face that she believed the tip was genuine. When the phone rang, he was tempted to ignore it. Another call about the arson? He snatched it up with a distracted, "Bonner here."

It was his mother. "I'm worried about Aurora. She's not here yet."

Will glanced at the clock. Hours.

As he listened to his mother, he felt all the air rush out of him. The panic must have screamed from his face, because when he hung up, Sarah demanded, "What happened?"

In a flash, he remembered Aurora confronting him: *You've been paying my mother to stay away.* She'd found the receipts. No doubt she'd figured out where Marisol lived, too.

"Aurora went to find her mother."

Forty

In Las Vegas, Aurora felt the slap of desert heat in her face. It made her think of what Hansel from "Hansel and Gretel" must have felt, being shoved into the witch's oven. Or maybe what her dad felt when he fought a fire.

Don't think about Dad, she reminded herself. She'd come too far and there was no turning back, so thinking about him wasn't going to help a thing.

Stowing away with Aunt Lonnie's cargo had been fairly easy, the flight wedged between shipping containers uncomfortable but short. Aurora had slipped away from the cargo hangar while Lonnie was dealing with the delivery. Aurora didn't want to get Aunt Lonnie in trouble, but she had to do this, and she intended to do it on her own. Although unsure of what would happen when she finally came face-to-face with her mother, she just had to see her.

It was a quick walk to the main terminal. She felt a little intimidated by all the people rushing around, dragging luggage, and the shrieks and bells from thousands of slot machines, but fear only made her more determined to see this through. At the ATM, she helped herself to some Quick Cash using her card and the usual PIN code that spelled her dad's name. The taxi line moved fast, and within a few minutes, she was giving the address to the driver and praying her life savings—a wad of bills amounting to about a hundred dollars—would cover the fare.

In just a few blocks, boom. She was smack in the middle of Las Vegas. In the late afternoon, the city was hot and dry, the huge highway interchange crammed with traffic, the sidewalks crowded with tourists and booths where you could buy just about anything. All the buildings had glittering false fronts. There were man-made water features and palm trees that didn't belong, but were kept alive by workers irrigating them in the sweltering heat.

She felt sick to her stomach, but it wasn't from the flying or even from the hot, smelly cab. She tried to feel right about this but instead, she felt terrible. She was a bad daughter. Her dad deserved to be with people like his parents and Sarah—people who loved him and would never leave him. He had given up his dreams to rescue Aurora and her mom. Well, she was older now. She didn't need rescuing.

It was a little shocking to see the apartment complex where her mother lived. The place was made of fake adobe and surrounded by desert plants with thorny-edged leaves like giant fans. Aurora paid the driver, squared her shoulders, and went to find apartment 121-B. The front door faced a courtyard that contained a landscaped play area and a swimming pool that sparkled in the sun.

Well, she was here now. She'd ask her mother. She curled her hand into a fist and knocked firmly at the door.

The wait was endless. She was almost relieved when no one answered. Maybe her mother had moved away, left no forwarding address. Aurora decided to count to sixty. Then she'd turn on her cell phone, call Aunt Lonnie and beg her forgiveness. Aurora scuffed her foot against the bristly doormat, disturbing a colony of pill bugs, running for cover. When she reached forty-eight, she knocked one last time. And the door opened a crack, pulling a brass security chain taut. It stayed open only a moment, but she recognized her mother's face. A Spanish game show played on a TV somewhere.

"Mama?" she said, automatically switching to Spanish. "It's me. Aurora."

The door slammed in her face. Again, Aurora felt a welling of relief, but it was short-lived. There was a click as the chain was unhooked, and then the door opened wide. At the same time, a phone rang somewhere. They both ignored it.

"I can't believe you're here," her mother said, stepping back and motioning her inside. Then she hugged Aurora.

Awkward. That was the only thing Aurora felt. She had always pictured her mother as a large, powerful figure, but now she realized that was the impression of a little kid. Now she was taller and heavier than her mother. Mama still had that air of glamour, though. She wore lots of makeup, beautifully applied, and her hair was glossy and stylish. She wore a great outfit, too, a microsuede skirt, lacy camisole, tall wedge sandals.

"What are you doing here?" her mother asked, her large brown eyes seeming to drink in the sight of Aurora.

"I found your address on some papers and decided to come and see you. I didn't tell Dad. I just came. I need to call him later and let him know I'm all right."

"Come in," her mother said, seeming nervous and eager. "Come and sit. Look at you, all grown-up and so beautiful."

The apartment smelled of perfume and a slight dampness weighted the air, as though someone was using the shower. Then she realized someone was; she could hear the steady hiss of running water.

Mama noticed her glance flickering at the door, slightly ajar, which led to a bedroom. "Eduardo," she explained, fluttering her hand. "We were on our way out to dinner."

"Oh!" Aurora's nerves jangled. This was hard enough, seeing her mom. She wasn't quite ready to meet the boyfriend, too. Why did parents do this? she wondered. Why did they have a kid and then split up and expect the kid to deal with all these other people? "I guess I should have called."

"I'm glad you're here," Mama assured her. "Please, please, sit down."

Aurora lowered herself cautiously to the sofa. It was cushy, its tall sides seeming to close around her. The place was decorated with lots of pink and white. Aurora was beginning to think her dad was totally wrong about her mom. He seemed to think she had this sketchy lifestyle Aurora shouldn't know about. In reality, Mama was perfectly normal. Younger and prettier than other mothers, and the boyfriend in the bathroom was a bit of an issue, but still… The host on the TV talk show was annoying, rolling his *R*s and cheering when a contestant got the name of a song correct. She found the remote control and hit the mute button.

"Are you hungry?" her mother asked. "Thirsty? What can I get you?"

"Some water, I guess."

"Water. Of course. With ice?" Mama darted toward the kitchen, which was adjacent to the main room. She brought Aurora a big tumbler filled with ice and tap water, and had a seat on the sofa, tugging her skirt down. "So. Here you are. I still can't get over it." She reached out and touched Aurora's cheek. Her hand was damp and chilly from the ice water. "How old are you now? Remind me."

Remind her? Was she kidding? How could somebody not know the exact age of her own child? She laughed a little and ignored the question. "I found out some things Dad never told me, and I decided to come and see you," she said, getting right to the point. She explained about the statement describing their life in Mexico—the squalor, the danger, the building with no fire escape. "Is it true?" she asked.

Her mother wore an odd smile, not like she was happy, but maybe a little amused. The phone rang again and she grabbed the handset, checking the caller ID before she set it down and let it ring until it stopped. "Not everybody grows up like you did in America," she said. "I learned to survive on my own when I was younger than you."

Aurora wondered what she herself would do in order to survive. Become a prostitute? Take off her clothes for strange men and have sex with them? The thought made her dizzy with nausea, but at the same time, she realized she wouldn't be here if not for one of those strange men. She studied her mother, the face she didn't know anymore, the hands that flitted and fidgeted in her lap.

"Dad took you away from that," she said to her mother. "We had a good life—"

"*You* had a good life. I had a job cleaning for an old lady and no one to talk to, because your dad was working and training all the time. Every single day was the same, except that my back hurt more each night, and I was more and more bored." She scratched her hands up and down her bare arms, as if the recollection made her skin itch.

"If you didn't want that kind of life, why did you leave Mexico in the first place?"

Mama kept scratching her arms, not seeming to notice the long red welts she was creating. The memories must be painful, and Aurora felt bad for asking, but she really wanted to know.

"The statement William gave left that part out," Mama said. "I was arguing with Uncle Felix—the owner of the house." She hesitated, then took a breath and said, "I was the one who set it on fire."

Aurora watched her mother's hands, scratching up and down, up and down, on her arms. There were things about that night that haunted her, memories locked deep, but she felt them rising slowly to the surface. She saw her mother's hands, heard her voice, telling her to stay in the house. She heard her own shrill, baby voice, begging Mama to let her come.

"You set the fire with people in the house?" Aurora said. "With *me* in it?"

She waved her hand. "It was an accident. I was fighting with Felix. Everything happened so fast, and I couldn't get to you. But I knew you were safe, thank God."

Aurora's heart was beating fast with fury and betrayal. "How did you know, Mama? How did you know I was safe?"

"Because of William. He saved you. This is something else you were never told. When the house was burning, William climbed up on the roof and rescued you."

Even then, thought Aurora. Even before Dad knew her name or anything about her, he'd risked his life to save her. Oh, God, she thought. What have I done?

"William never wanted you to know these things about our last night in Mexico," Mama was saying. "He did not think you could handle it."

"And what do you think, Mama?"

"I think you are like me," she said, her hands coming to rest in her lap as she fixed Aurora with a keen stare. "I think you can handle anything."

"You don't even know me," Aurora said. "Why didn't you ever come back? Why did you stop calling?"

The phone rang yet again. This time, her mother darted into the next room and picked up. Aurora could hear the murmur of her voice, could smell the waft of steam from the shower. She sat perfectly still on the sofa, not wanting to disturb anything. The bald facts about the past stared her in the face, but it was as though they were written in code, incomprehensible.

At least she understood her father better now, though. He had lied and lied and lied. All to protect her. The day they met, he'd saved her, and through the years, he'd done so again and again. And this was how she repaid him. By running away to a woman who didn't know her, didn't understand her, didn't want her. Aurora felt tired, as though she'd reached the end of a long journey, much longer than the flight to Vegas. Her childhood lay behind her, like the wreckage after a storm.

When Mama exited the room, she looked different. Brighter and more animated and relieved, maybe. It was so hard for Aurora to tell what her mother was thinking and feeling. But it wasn't hard to figure out, finally, the real reason for her mother's behavior. She was on drugs. Maybe she was even an addict. Back when Mama lived in Glenmuir, she had to be taken to the hospital a lot, and Aurora's dad always said something vague, like she wasn't feeling well. Now Aurora knew it had to do with drugs. It hurt so bad to realize drugs had turned her mother into a stranger. The minutes seemed to crawl by. Aurora took out her cell phone.

"This is Eduardo," Mama said.

With a guilty start, Aurora stuffed the phone into her backpack and jumped up. "Hello," she said. "I'm Aurora."

He was older and nice-looking, with comb furrows in his hair and a neat mustache. "It is a privilege to meet you," he said. "Marisol has told me about you."

"She has?"

"Indeed." He held out his hand, and Aurora felt obliged to take it. Otherwise, he'd think she was rude. But instead of shaking hands, he did this really corny thing, bowing over her hand and lightly kissing it. The gesture was quick, but not quick enough. Maybe it was Aurora's own nervousness, but she swore he did this creepy, fluttery thing with his fingers. It made her want to wash her hand.

"So we will all go to dinner, yes?" her mother said brightly. "You must be hungry."

"Actually, I—"

"The restaurant is called La Paloma," Eduardo said, holding open the door. "It is a favorite of mine."

Though she tried to stammer that she needed to get back to the airport, Aurora felt swept along by his smooth manners and her mother's blithe chatter. At least the restaurant was in the main part of the city, right on the Strip. She could see planes landing and taking off. At the restaurant, people seemed to know Eduardo. There was some bowing and scraping, a sense that he was in command. Aurora could feel speculative stares poking at her.

"I need to go to the restroom," she said.

"We'll go together." Mama popped up.

Great, thought Aurora. Her mom might seem distracted, but she probably knew exactly what Aurora intended to do—call her dad, right away. "Never mind," she said, sitting back down. "I can wait."

Dinner was excruciating, with lots of different courses and these dumb little sorbets in between. Aurora wasn't hungry at all. She barely looked up, because the people who kept hovering around the table seemed way too interested in her. Finally, after a dessert of hot pastries dripping with honey, she said, "I have to go to the airport. I'm sure Lonnie's wondering where I am."

"We will take you," Eduardo stated, signing the check with a flourish.

"It's really close. I'll take a taxi, or walk."

"Nonsense. Let us take you."

As she stood waiting for the valet to bring the car around, Aurora felt as if she was on the way to her own execution. She knew she was being totally paranoid, but she had the feeling they weren't going to take her to the airport, that they had other plans for her. It didn't help matters that Mama and Eduardo were hissing and murmuring to one another, obviously caught up in a disagreement.

In the car—a fancy Cadillac—Aurora eyed the door handle next to her. If they didn't head straight for the airport, she'd jump out, even if the car was still moving. They seemed to move at a crawl. The lights of Las Vegas colored the sky. She fixed her attention on the airport and willed the car to go faster. After an eternity, they turned in and she pointed out the air cargo center.

Aurora couldn't get out of the car fast enough. "Thanks," she said, yanking on the door handle.

Nothing. The lock was down and she couldn't find the button to unlock it.

"Hey, what—"

"Aurora." Mama turned in her seat. "Now that you're here, I wish you would stay. Eduardo wishes this, too. We could have fun together, go shopping, go to restaurants. Movies and shows."

"I need to get out of this car." Aurora manually unlocked the door and, thank God, it worked. She jumped out, hearing her mother call her name. Maybe she'd only imagined the creepy looks, maybe she was being totally paranoid. It didn't matter now.

Because there, looking as though he had run all the way from Glenmuir, was her dad, striding toward her. Aurora almost cried with relief as she broke into a run. This was her dad, and he had chosen her, even when her mother abandoned her. It was time to quit pretending she had this cool mom in Vegas when the truth was, she had the best dad in the world, even if it meant she was grounded for life.

He stood there, sweaty and exhausted, his smile kind of sad but his arms wide-open, waiting for her.

Forty-One

The late-autumn fog carried a heavy chill that settled in the bones, and there was no defense against it. Sarah stoked the fire in the wood-burning stove and layered on extra socks and a sweater. She could only hope the boys didn't feel the chill as she put them down for their morning nap. They didn't complain or fuss; they seemed content enough zipped into their red one-piece pajamas and snuggled beneath lambs' wool blankets. She no longer felt clumsy and inept with her babies. She was getting the hang of this.

She went into the kitchen to brew a cup of tea to warm herself up. While she waited for the water to boil, she studied a photo of her and Will, taken at the Oyster Festival. It was a romantic shot with the shadowy bay as a backdrop; the two of them were dancing and they looked completely lost in each other. Defiantly, she had stuck the picture on the refrigerator. She was finished hiding her feelings for him. She wanted to learn to trust those feelings instead of constantly questioning them. But given all that had happened, she couldn't help it.

The explosion at the oyster farm still haunted her, sneaking up on her at odd moments, a reminder that in his profession, Will was one step away from death at any moment. With Jack, she'd lived with the fear of impending loss, and she was only now discovering how deeply that had affected her. The thought of going there again with Will was unexpectedly terrifying.

She reached down and scratched Franny behind the ears. You can't tell love to come when you're ready, Gran had said to her. Love comes when love is ready.

The teakettle rattled, and she took it off the flame before the whistle blew. While she waited for the tea to steep, she took out the cottage guest book and paged through it. Like a schoolgirl, she was tempted to record the first time Will had made love to her and spent the night, but she restrained herself. She didn't need to commit it to paper, anyway. All she had to do was close her eyes and think about him, and she could bring back every single detail, every touch and kiss and whisper, every pulse of ecstasy she'd felt that night. She and Will acknowledged that being in love was going to be hard work, given their situations. Yet there was something else she knew—the only thing harder than loving him was *not* loving him.

He had promised to call the minute he found Aurora. Sarah had slept fitfully last night, and just before dawn, the phone had rung. "She went to Vegas with my aunt," Will reported. "She's fine now. Tired. We'll call you later."

So all was well, though Sarah worried about what would happen now. Will still had to deal with the anger and hurt that had driven his daughter to pull this stunt in the first place. Sarah's role was unclear; the one thing she knew for certain was that loving a man with a half-grown daughter was no simple matter.

As she stirred honey into her tea, the thump of a car door sounded. She hurried to the door, finger-combing her hair.

"Hello, Sarah."

She froze in disbelief, dropping her hand, which suddenly felt numb. "Jack," she said.

He studied her, his assessing gaze taking in her short, tousled hair, the haphazard layers of clothes she'd put on to ward off the chill of the fog. Against her will, she felt herself flush as that gaze took her measure. At least, when he'd seen her in the hospital, she'd had an excuse. After the ordeal of birth, no one expected good grooming from a woman. She used to primp for Jack, to dress in smart slacks and sweaters because that was the image he wanted her to project. And now, even after all this time, she felt self-conscious.

Cut it out, she told herself. You're not his wife anymore.

"Come in," she said, her tone completely neutral. "You should have called first."

"I kept meaning to, but even after I landed in San Francisco, I still thought I might change my mind." He came inside, bringing the dampness of the mist with him on his Burberry coat and in his light, reddish hair. His eyes were bright, searching. Perhaps troubled.

Oh, God, she thought, her pulse kicking up to panic mode. He's sick again. "Are you all right?" she asked. "Please tell me you're all right."

"Clean as a whistle," he said. "I'm down to yearly checkups now."

She was glad about that, at least. He looked disgustingly good—fit and groomed, miraculously unwrinkled in spite of the trip. He offered a small smile. "Sweet of you to ask. Sometimes I think that was when you loved me best. When I was sick."

Bastard, she thought, shoring up her heart. "What do you want, Jack?" Then it struck her. *Of course.* "Oh, my God," she said. "Mimi dumped you, didn't she? That's why you're here. My friend Viv said this would happen. She said you'd turn up as soon as you got dumped."

"Yeah, your friend's a real wise guy."

She noticed he didn't deny anything she said. Yet she felt no vindication. She felt nothing at all, and she found this strangely liberating.

He slipped off his coat and laid it over the back of a chair. "Please, Sarah," he said in the kindest voice she had heard him use since everything fell apart. "How are the boys doing?"

"They're just waking up from a nap," she said, motioning for him to follow her. Adam was grasping the rail of his crib and shoving it back and forth with all his might. When he saw Sarah, he crowed and put up his hands. Bradley pushed himself up and clapped. Even after a short nap, her babies always greeted her as though they hadn't seen her in ages. She wished she could be half as wonderful as they thought she was.

"This is Adam," she said, lifting him out of the crib, "and that's Bradley. They're both going to need clean diapers and then lunch. You want to help?"

"Sure," Jack said, though he sounded anything but. "My God, they've grown so much. Sarah, I don't know what to say. They're just so…"

"Yes," she said. "I know." She changed Adam, who then clung to her knee while she attended to his brother. This was not going to harm them, she told herself. They were so little, there was no way it could affect them. Through a miracle of biology and technology, Jack was their father. It was a reality they would live with forever.

"Want to hold him?" she offered, picking Bradley up.

"Um, okay."

"If you just act friendly, they'll be fine with you." She did him a small kindness by starting with Bradley. He was the more easygoing of the two, and tended to be relaxed around people. It was such a miracle, the way their personalities emerged, more and more, every day.

Jack seemed stiff and uncertain, but the baby didn't appear to mind. He latched his chubby hands into the fine cotton of Jack's dress shirt and stared with solemn eyes into his face. Jack smiled, the baby smiled back, and suddenly she saw it—a family resemblance. It was uncanny, the way Jack's smile was mirrored in his sons' faces. She scooped up Adam and they went to the kitchen, where she showed him how to get the baby into a high chair. To his credit, he did things smoothly enough. "Lock and load," he said, grinning at the hungry looks on their faces.

Jack looked different, she noticed as she handed each baby a teething biscuit. Not better, not worse. Just different. She could still see the Jack who had knocked her off her feet—handsome, commanding, confident. She even felt a twinge of nostalgia about the things they'd shared and the way she used to feel about him.

"This doesn't have to be happening to us," he said quietly.

"This…meaning the divorce." She couldn't quite believe her ears. The divorce had been finalized at last, the decree arriving without ceremony in the mail, the Express Mail envelope sandwiched between her cell phone bill and a gardening catalog.

"We could start over, all four of us, a family."

The four of us. *A family.* The nostalgia tugged at her, hard.

He must have seen the softening in her face, because he pressed harder. "I mean it, Sarah. It's killing my mom, not to be part of this."

"Your mother is welcome to visit," she said.

"I'm not talking about visiting. I'm talking about fixing this, working things out. Maybe this time, we could try harder to make it work."

At that, she burst out laughing. Bradley clapped his chubby hands. "Try harder?" she asked, too amused to be angry. "You think I wasn't trying the first time around?" Studying him, she finally understood what Gran was trying to tell her. "Every day we were together, I was the best wife I knew how to be. But that wasn't enough for you. And that's your problem, not mine."

"All right," he said, "have it your way. I was the one who screwed up. I'm sorry I wasn't perfect like you," he said. "I'm sorry I got cancer and you didn't get pregnant. I'm sorry about the way I dealt with my frustration."

"Aw, Jack. I wasn't perfect. And I didn't expect that from you, either. I did expect fidelity, though. That's kind of a deal-breaker with me."

"In my heart, I never left you." He said it with a straight face.

"Oh, boy," she said, "I need to remember that line for my comic strip."

"Jesus, Sarah."

"Watch your mouth in front of my children, please." She leaned back, a feeling of enormous relief wrapping around her. Since leaving him, she'd been wondering where all the love had gone. Now she looked at her boys, that pair of beautiful miracles, and she knew. Being a mother had taught her so much in such a short time. She'd never known all the colors and shapes that love could take, had never known her heart could be so full yet still have the capacity to expand. Maybe if her mother had still been around, this all would have been explained to her long ago. Yet discovering it on her own was a special kind of triumph. Not that it was easy.

Taking a deep breath, she said, "I'm not the martyr here. I played a part in our troubles. I was focused on having a family, on making everything look normal. If we'd worked as hard on our marriage as we did on getting pregnant, we might have had a chance."

He nodded, but his attention was caught by Adam, who was reaching out for the big yellow box of Cheerios on the counter, his chubby hands opening and closing in a mute gesture. Jack picked up the box and shook a few onto each baby's high chair tray. The boys dug in with both hands, cramming Cheerios into their mouths and regarding Jack with nothing short of hero worship.

There was no resisting those wide, clear eyes, those adorable faces. A quiet rapture seemed to settle over Jack, and a beautiful smile—one she hadn't seen in a very long time—curved his mouth. "They're incredible," he told her quietly, his voice rough with emotion. "My sons."

The sweetness of his unguarded joy tugged at Sarah's heart. She shut her eyes, swaying a little. This was her sons' father. He was going to be a part of their lives forever.

When she opened her eyes, Jack was watching her with a curious expression on his face. "You look good," he said. "Really good." He touched her the way he used to, long ago, his knuckles gently grazing a line from her cheekbone to her jaw.

She was so startled by the poignant memories his touch evoked that she couldn't move, or speak. Not even when she heard the front door open and shut.

"I can't stay, babe," Will called as he made his way to the kitchen, "but I wanted to tell you—oh."

Both Adam and Bradley babbled greetings to him, little hands opening and closing in welcome.

Sarah's chair scraped as she stood up. Guilt stained her face; she could feel it. Flustered, she said, "Will! Is Aurora all right?"

"Yes. We were late getting back, but she's okay." His voice was tight and hard. So were his eyes as they darted to Jack.

"This is Jack Daly," she said. They'd brushed past each other at the hospital but had never been introduced. "Jack, this is Will Bonner. Jack, um, came to visit the boys," she added for Will's benefit.

"Uh-huh." Will's gaze flicked to Jack's hand, the one that had just been touching her.

Sarah wanted to die, just die.

"Is everything all right?" Will asked her.

"She's fine," Jack broke in.

Will didn't really change his expression or his stance, but he seemed suddenly protective, maybe even dangerous. "I was asking Sarah," he said.

"I'm fine," she blurted, echoing Jack, falling effortlessly into their old pattern. "Truly," she added, "and thanks for calling me this morning, and for coming to tell me about Aurora." She pleaded with her eyes, then gestured at her visitor. "I want to hear everything, but…"

"Later," Will said, his gaze licking Jack with contempt one last time.

Sarah's throat was dry. "All right," she said quietly, hating this moment, hating the way she still felt Jack's influence, even now. She walked out to the porch with him. "Will, I didn't know he was coming. I had no idea."

"It's all right. Look, he's their father. That's never going to change."

She had never seen him so down. Yes, there was the exhaustion and stress from the ordeal with Aurora, but there was something else, too. He seemed torn. Maybe even tormented. And the worst part about it was, she didn't know how to fix it.

"I need to go," he said. "Aurora and I have a lot of work to do."

"Of course," she said, her throat aching with tears.

"I have to focus on her, Sarah. She needs me even more than I realized."

She got it, then. He wanted her to back off, give him space and time to deal with what Aurora had done. In taking off, Aurora had demonstrated the truth they all knew. She was her father's priority. She had planted herself emotionally between him and Sarah.

"Anyway," he said, heading for his truck, "I'll see you around."

Trying to hold herself together, Sarah went back inside. Jack was watching the boys in the kitchen. The room was awkwardly quiet, and she reached over and turned the radio on, low. Her timing was exquisite—the song that drifted out was a nostalgic oldie, "Come See About Me."

"That the guy you're seeing?" Jack asked, his voice casual, as though her seeing someone was a nonevent.

"None of your business," she said, then winced because she sounded juvenile.

He studied her face, and she could feel the heat creeping into her cheeks. "Shit. You're in love with him."

She didn't deny it. How could she?

"And it sure as hell is my business, since I'm sending you a check the size of Milwaukee every month. That makes everything you do my business. The fertility treatments alone cost me a damn fortune. You're giving me a shitty return on my investment."

Just for a moment, a fantasy rose up in Sarah. She felt a blaze of violence toward Jack and she pictured her own drawn-back hand, the fierce set of her mouth, the wind on her arm as she swung out, the sting of connection as she hit him, then dropped her hand, loose with relief. But the fantasy vanished on a bitter laugh. "I suppose you think you can make me mad enough to tell you to keep your damn checks. Nice try, but I've got two kids to raise, Jack. Nothing can make me mad enough to throw away their future."

He snatched the picture of Sarah and Will from the fridge, and the magnets went pinging across the floor. "You think you love this clown? Don't be stupid, Sarah. You might think you're in love with him, but you're not. Nothing you feel is real. You're still on the rebound from us."

"You don't even know me anymore, Jack."

"That's why I'm here. I thought I was going to reconnect with you on some level, you know, for the sake of the kids. Instead, I fly all the way here, and find the mother of my children fucking around with some local yokel."

That did it. Sarah strode to the door and held it open. "You just said the magic word. Nobody talks that way in front of my kids. It's time for you to leave."

Jack hesitated, and there was something in his face, something she remembered from the time when she used to love him. He said nothing else, but turned and walked out the door. She stood watching him, hearing her babies in the background while Jack seemed to fade into the thick mist and then disappear.

Jack's unexpected visit had clarified some things for Sarah. The notion that you "got over" a failed marriage did not apply to her, and never would. There was no getting over what had happened with Jack. This wasn't a bad thing. It was one fewer item on her list of things to do.

She knew now that love was not just one thing; it changed in shape and intensity. Her feelings for Jack had been very real, but there was an end to them, and she considered herself one of the lucky ones. Staying in a marriage when the love was gone was like being half-alive. It was an existence, but it was flat and colorless, like one of the panels in her comic strip.

With Will, she had found new depths of love and new heights of passion, but shadows of doubt hung over her. There was a time when she thought Jack was the perfect man, and she'd been wrong. What if she was wrong about Will? What if time changed them, too?

She told herself to quit worrying about the answer to that. Her heart opened up like a flower, though she had become a realist. A person couldn't endure what she had and escape with some pink romantic vision intact. It hurt to love so hard, Sarah found out, and it was so impossible not to. And it wasn't just a state of being, but something alive and vital that was going to take everything she had. She had work to do.

Getting close to Aurora might be a fool's errand. Knowing that didn't stop her.

When you wanted to tear down a wall, you didn't start with what was behind the wall but with the one who'd built it.

Aurora's honors art class had gone to the Point Reyes Lighthouse to work on a project. Viktor Chopin had told

Sarah she was welcome to visit the class anytime, and the field trip would give her the perfect opportunity to talk to Aurora. She left the twins with her grandmother and headed up the winding asphalt road.

Parking the Mini behind the yellow school bus, Sarah surveyed the students, who had fanned out across the hills and promontories in search of the ideal spot to sketch. Every vantage point revealed a different vista. This was one of the most dramatic spots to watch the migration of the gray whales, who passed the point on their journey between Alaska and Mexico, and Sarah knew the beacon was one of Aurora's favorite subjects to draw.

In contrast to the placid bay, the extreme western edge of the region was a place of drama and danger. The sea hurled itself at rockbound cliffs, which soared like the buttresses of a Gothic cathedral over the vast, empty beaches strung with sea palms that had washed up on shore. The dull boom of the waves reverberated in Sarah's stomach, which churned with nervousness.

The Vegas incident had clarified something for Sarah. It was time—past time—for her to define her relationship with Aurora. It wasn't that Sarah needed the girl's permission to love Will. It was that she wanted the girl to understand that Sarah's love took nothing away from Aurora's bond with her father.

It was a chilly day and the three hundred concrete steps leading down to the lighthouse seemed like a descent to nowhere. The lower portion of the steps disappeared into thick fog. Sounds were muted—the muffled explosion of waves on the rocks far below, the regular bleat of the foghorn. There were few tourists around, and the art students were stationed at various points around the area, sketching egrets and rock formations and wind-sculpted cypress trees. She found Aurora perched on the upper level of the old lighthouse, a sketchbook across her knees and a box of oil pastels at her side. She didn't seem surprised to see Sarah.

"Hey," she said.

"Hey." Aurora glanced up, but quickly went back to sketching.

"Got a minute?"

Her drawing hand fell still. "I'm sorry, okay? I know I owe you an apology, like I owe everybody else. I shouldn't have taken off, and I'm sorry."

It had the quality of a rehearsed speech. Sarah studied her, the glossy blue-black hair falling across a creamy olive-toned cheek, the girl's beautiful mouth set in an unhappy line. "I didn't come here looking for an apology from you," she explained. "In fact, I don't blame you for going looking for your mother."

Aurora determinedly kept drawing. A seagull swooped near, hovered with the wind filling its wings and then glided off.

"I can totally understand that," Sarah said. "Believe me, if I could figure out a way to see my mother, I'd do anything to make that happen. But I have to know. Did you leave because of me?"

"It's not about you. It never was." She scowled down at the page. "Anyway, I don't need a lecture from you, so before you start yelling or blaming or—"

"I'm not going to yell at you or blame you. I'm just telling you to stop torturing your dad."

"I'm not torturing him."

"Forcing him to choose between you and me—you think that's not torture?"

"I'm not forcing him to do anything."

"Acting like the perfect daughter when it's just the two of you together, and turning into Sybil when I show up."

"Who's Sybil?"

"Character in a cool movie. We'll watch it together sometime."

"You're not making sense." Hugging her knees to her chest, she stared at a line of wind-sculpted evergreen trees, all leaning the same direction.

"You're not listening. I'm trying to explain that you never have to worry that if your dad falls in love, you'll lose him."

"We were doing fine, the two of us, before you came along," Aurora said.

The girl had Will's fiercely protective instinct, Sarah realized. But she didn't yet have his judgment. "Your father is always going to be there, looking out for you, Aurora. You don't have to do things to get his attention or worry about being slighted. Just because he's preoccupied or busy doesn't mean he's disregarding you. And just because he and I fell in love doesn't mean the end of the world. Like it or not, you're going to gain three more people in your life who love you."

Aurora stayed silent, concentrating on her drawing as the wind howled down the rocky cliffs. Sarah could feel her slipping away. This was an advantage, actually. Because now Sarah realized she could speak her heart with nothing more to lose.

"I had this whole speech planned out," Sarah said. "I was going to tell you that I hope, for your dad's sake, that we can be friends and move forward from there. That I'm not going to try to be your mother because I respect the fact that you have a mother. I was going to discuss the whole step-family thing. But you know what? That's crap. Maybe I wasn't around for your birth and your first day of kindergarten, or your first school dance, but I'm here now. I want to take care of you and worry about you and fight with you and embarrass you at school functions and take you shopping. I want to love you all your life, every bit as much as I love Adam and Bradley. And if you can't handle that—"

"Stop," Aurora snapped, slapping the sketchbook shut. "Will you just shut the hell up for a second?" She pressed her hands to her face, looking very small and afraid. Then she tilted up her chin in pride and defiance.

"Honey, I wanted to clarify this before you decide—"

"I've already decided," she broke in. "If you'll listen for a minute, I'll try to explain. Maybe you think I was an idiot for going to find my mother but at least I found out for myself that she's not going to be a part of my life, not anytime soon. I didn't understand her when I was younger, didn't know why she was back and forth to the E.R., which is why my dad was so freaky about going there, even that day he took you. My mother has a problem with drugs, even though she says she doesn't. She steals and lies. Maybe she'll wake up and get better one day. I wish she would, but I can't make her do that. Nobody can."

Sarah touched her shoulder, and when she didn't resist, brushed a wave of black hair back from her cheek, now damp with tears. "I'm sorry, Aurora."

Aurora shuddered with broken sobs. "I'm just so mad at her. So pissed. It doesn't matter if I act like the perfect daughter or if Dad is the perfect husband. None of that ever made her stop."

Sarah offered her a Kleenex and she wiped her face, though the tears kept coming.

"My dad never did one single thing for his own happiness. Every choice he made was to help someone or protect someone. Now he finally wants something for him, to make him happy. He's the best person I know, and he deserves the best." Her eyes cleared and she swallowed hard. "I guess I'm saying, if you're not too pissed at me, then maybe we could, like, try again?"

"Well, then," Sarah said, the world seeming to expand with each beat of her heart, "I guess there's just one last detail to take care of."

"What's that?" The girl's eyes widened with apprehension, and Sarah realized how afraid Aurora was of change.

"I'm going to have to sell the Mini."

Forty-Two

Gloria came into the office at the station and dropped a thick manila file on Will's desk. She looked calm, but haggard. "Six months in juvey. Tell me it gets no harder than this."

Will knew she had struggled with the reality that Ruby's daughter had been setting the fires. "I wish I could."

"But you can't." She sighed and leaned against the edge of the desk. "At least she didn't hurt anyone."

"How about you and Ruby?"

Gloria—his partner, his engineer, his rock—blinked back tears. "We're this close to calling it quits." She measured an inch with her fingers.

"That's nuts. You guys are great together."

She nodded, offered a wobbly smile. "That's why we're not calling it quits. The judge ordered Glynnis to attend counseling classes on alternate lifestyles. After that, we'll hope for the best."

"Smart girl." He stood up and gave her a hug. "I'm proud of you."

"It's common sense. You live your life letting a kid call

the shots, that's no kind of life at all. Once the kid grows up and moves away, then you find out you forgot how to call the shots yourself."

"How'd you get so smart about kids?" he asked, stepping back.

"Maybe I'm just smart. Maybe I'm smart enough to know that you're one to talk, Will Bonner." She slugged him on the shoulder. "You with your heart full of love."

After Gloria left, Will shut the file cabinet drawer with a ring of finality. He felt no sense of justice. For him, the situation was not as simple as Gloria seemed to want it to be. It had taken a near disaster for Aurora to finally come forward with the truth. He could only hope she'd trust him more now. Time would tell, and he didn't want to push right now. She was still reeling from the realization that her friend had put people at risk. And Aurora still hadn't fully dealt with the visit to her mother. Maybe he'd been wrong to try to protect Aurora from who Marisol really was. His daughter would need to grieve for the woman who had walked away from her, and then, he prayed, she'd let go and move on.

And Sarah? His heart and his dreams were full of her, yet nothing was simple between them.

When you were a single parent, Will knew, your first loyalty was to your child, every time. Even when the child was wrong.

Or so he used to think. The Glynnis thing was a wake-up call. Sometimes blind loyalty to your kid could lead to disaster. Regardless, he was going to quit worrying about things that hadn't happened, things that might never happen. He had kept his distance from Sarah because he used to worry that Aurora would see her as a mother figure, and if things didn't work out, then his daughter would have her heart broken again.

Well, hell. A broken heart was a survivable event, and she was old enough to know that now. He prepared to head home, spend the next few days with Aurora and finally have the talk with her. He would remind her there was going to be more in his life than just work and raising her. Sarah and her boys were a part of his heart, and he wasn't going to hold back anymore. After Marisol, he never thought he'd fall in love again, because it was too damn messy when it ended. He'd been wrong, and this time was different. This time, he wasn't a kid. And Sarah wasn't Marisol. That didn't mean it was going to be easier, he knew that. But this time, he knew what it was going to take to make it last.

He went down to his truck, tossing his duffel bag in the back.

"Looks like you have a hot date with a load of laundry," someone said.

He turned, a smile already lighting his face. It was as if his thoughts had conjured her. This had to be a sign. "Sarah."

She stood in the station driveway, a light breeze blowing her hair. The rare autumn sunlight had taken its time burning away the mist, but at last, the air sparkled with dazzling clarity. "Hey, yourself."

"I was just thinking about you," he said, suddenly wishing he had the ring with him. The way she looked right this minute, the way he felt in his heart, he wanted to give it to her.

"Yeah?" She walked toward him, slipped her arms around his neck. "What were you thinking?"

He bent down and kissed her, long and intimately, tasting memories of every moment they'd spent together, promising more. She went sweetly limp against him, her body soft and welcoming as she said, "That's pretty much what I was thinking, too."

"Where are the boys?"

"I get a little time off for good behavior," she told him. The smile faded. He could see the weight of something in her eyes.

Oh, no, he thought. Oh, shit.

"Do you have a minute?" she asked.

"What's up?"

"I never explained to you what happened with my ex-husband."

Will's heart skipped a beat as he thought about the cozy scene at her house, with her ex and their sons—a family. "Look, you don't have to—"

"I want to."

Will tried to interpret the expression on her face. She'd lived with the guy for five years, nursed him through cancer, had not one but two of his babies. Was she going to decide that ultimately, that was too much of a commitment to walk away from?

"I'm glad he came. Seeing him again was…" Her eyes looked damp. "…confusing," she concluded.

"Listen, if you're going to say you're still not over him, you're telling the wrong guy, honey." Will's defenses locked into place. "I love you, but I won't be your shoulder to cry on about your ex."

She nodded sadly. "I'd never ask that of you, Will."

Thank God for small favors. "Then why the confusion?" he asked.

"I kept thinking I had something to prove to Jack. That I needed to show him I could make it as a single mother, self-employed, raising twins on my own. He—Jack—said some things…about us—about you and me—even though it's none of his business. He swears I'm on the rebound. I know it's nuts to put any stock in anything he says, but he's always had this weird way of undermining me, even now."

"Only if you let him, Sarah. Are you going to do that?"

"No, but the reality is, he's part of the boys' life."

"And he always will be, but so what?" He cleared his throat, wishing he was better with words, wishing for a way to explain his feelings so she would understand. The human heart was such a complex organ, fragile and sturdy all at once. "I know you got your heart broken, Sarah," he said. "But I know the heart can heal, too. And I know what it feels like to love again. I love you so much, I can't sleep at night. Sometimes I forget to breathe. And in a hundred years, that's never going to change."

She stared at him, looking…what? Horrified? "Will, do you mean that?" she whispered.

"I said it, didn't I?" He didn't intend to sound angry. "Listen, I'm done waiting. There's never going to be a perfect time to ask you this. So I'm asking you now, Sarah. Will you marry me?"

She shut her eyes for a moment, looking for all the world like a high diver about to take the plunge.

Her hesitation made him nervous. "I'm not withdrawing the question, Sarah," he persisted. "And I'll wait as long as you need to get an answer. Where you're concerned, I have all the patience in the world."

Opening her eyes, she smiled up at him. "Will, I love you, and I don't want to wait, either. I want to spend the rest of my life loving you, too. Can we do that, Will? Can we blend our families together, figure out a way to make this work? Because, you know, *that's* what I have to prove. Which, by the way, is a *yes*."

Finally, he thought. Finally. He picked her up and held her against the length of his body. He shut his eyes, closing this moment into his heart forever. His purpose was so clear now. This woman didn't need rescuing. He just needed to love her. He set her down, kissed her. "I just kissed my fiancée for the first time."

"You're the one who did the asking, but if you hadn't, I would have done it myself."

"Really?"

"Really."

"So when do we tell Aurora the good news?" He even felt positive about Aurora now.

Sarah blushed. He would never get tired of the sight of her blushing. "I think she already knows," she said softly.

"Knows what?" He had to hear her say it.

"About the fact that I love you so much I can't see any way to live my life without you. And her. I had a big talk with her about it. She's a mess, Will, and I adore her."

He nearly lost it, then, undone by happiness. "Ah, babe. I wish I could say it'll be easy going with her—"

"It doesn't have to be easy, Will, but you're underestimating her. Your daughter's got a heart as big as yours. She takes after you in that way."

No one had ever said that to him before. It was the one thing he wanted to be true, and finally, here was someone, telling him so. He wrapped his arms around Sarah and kissed her again, holding her so close he felt her feet leave the ground. "So how much time off do you have, for good behavior?" he asked, setting her down to nuzzle her neck.

"Not enough for that. I told Aurora to meet us here…right about now."

"She's watching the twins?"

"She took them down to Children's Beach." Sarah

smiled at Will's startled expression. She reached up and touched his cheek. "We're going to be all right, all of us," she said. "Maybe not perfect, but perfectly fine." And then she gave him the kind of kiss he had been dreaming about since the first time he'd kissed her, the kind that felt so right his chest ached with emotion.

A moment later he heard voices—his daughter saying something in Spanish, and babyish laughter. He pulled Sarah close. A moment after that, there they were, gilded by the day's last sunlight, the boys with Aurora pushing their stroller—the whole world, coming toward him.

Epilogue

JUST BREATHE